THE BOOK
SELLER

CYNTHIA
SWANSON

TWO
ROADS

www.tworoadsbooks.com

First published in the United States of America in 2015 by HarperCollins Publishers.

First published in Great Britain in 2017 by Two Roads
An imprint of John Murray Press
An Hachette UK company

1

A CIP catalogue record for this title is available from the British Library

Paperback ISBN 978 1 473 674103
Ebook ISBN 978 1 473 674110
Audio Digital Download ISBN 978 1 473 674127

Printed and bound by Clays Ltd, St Ives plc

Hodder & Stoughton policy is to use papers that are natural, renewable
and recyclable products and made from wood grown in sustainable
forests. The logging and manufacturing processes are expected to
conform to the environmental regulations of the country of origin.

'Leavin' on Your Mind'
Words and Music by Wayne P. Walker and Webb Pierce
Copyright © 1962 Universal-Cedarwood Publishing
All rights reserved. Used by permission.
Reprinted by permission of Music Sales Ltd.

Hodder & Stoughton Ltd
Carmelite House
50 Victoria Embankment
London EC4Y 0DZ

www.hodder.co.uk

For my parents, Dennis and Audrey Fisher, with love and gratitude.

Trust your happiness and the richness of your life at this moment. It is as true and as much yours as anything else that ever happened to you.

—Katherine Anne Porter, *Letters of Katherine Anne Porter*

Chapter 1

This is not my bedroom.

Where am I? Gasping and pulling unfamiliar bedcovers up to my chin, I strain to collect my senses. But no explanation for my whereabouts comes to mind.

The last thing I remember, it was Wednesday evening and I was painting my bedroom a bright, saturated yellow. Frieda, who had offered to help, was appraising my color choice. "Too much sunniness for a bedroom," she pronounced, in that Miss Know-It-All tone of hers. "How will you ever sleep in on gloomy days with a room like this?"

I dipped my brush into the paint can, carefully wiped off the excess, and climbed the stepladder. "That's entirely the point," I told Frieda. Leaning over, I began cutting along a tall, narrow window frame.

Oughtn't I to remember what happened next? Oddly, I do not. I cannot recall spending the evening painting, then standing back to admire our work before we cleaned up. I have no memory of thanking Frieda for her help and bidding her good-bye. I don't remember going to sleep in the sun-colored room, the sharp smell of fresh paint filling my nostrils. But I must have done those things, because here I lie. And given that *here* is not my home, evidently I am still asleep.

Nonetheless, this is not my typical sort of dream. My night-time forays tend toward the fantastical, toward dreams that place one outside of conventional time and space. This, I have concluded, is because I read so much. Have you read *Something Wicked This Way Comes*? It just hit the stands this past June, but is anticipated to be one of the best-selling books of 1962. Ray Bradbury is splendidly readable; I press the novel on everyone who steps into Frieda's and my bookstore looking for something "really gripping."

"It will haunt your dreams," I assure such customers. A self-fulfilling prophecy: the night before last, I dreamed I was stumbling behind Will Halloway and Jim Nightshade, the two young protagonists of Bradbury's book, as they were enticed by the middle-of-the-night arrival of the carnival in Green Town. I was trying to persuade them to proceed with caution—but they, being thirteen-year-old boys, simply ignored me. I remember how difficult it was to keep up with them, how I could not get my feet to operate correctly. Will and Jim moved farther away in the shadows, their shapes turning into dark dots and then finally to nothing, and all I could do was blubber in frustration.

So you see, I am not the type of woman who dreams about something as straightforward as waking up in another person's bedroom.

This dream bedroom is quite a bit larger and swankier than my actual bedroom. The walls are sage green, nothing like the deep yellow I chose for home. The furniture is a matched set, sleek and modern. The bedspread is neatly folded at the foot of the bed; soft, coordinating linens encase my body. It's delightful, in a too-put-together sort of way.

I slide under the covers and shut my eyes. Surely, if I keep my eyes closed, soon I will find myself hunting whales in the South Pacific, dressed rather grubbily and swilling whiskey with the mateys on my ship. Or I'll be flying high over Las Vegas, the wind blowing my hair back against my face, my arms transformed into enormous wings.

But nothing of the sort happens. Instead, I hear a man's voice. "Wake up. Katharyn, love, wake up."

I open my eyes and look into the deepest, bluest eyes I have ever seen.

And then I close my own again.

I feel a hand on my shoulder, which is nude, save for the thin strap of my satin nightgown. It's been a good long while since any man has touched me intimately. But some feelings are unmistakable, no matter how infrequently one experiences them.

I know I should be terrified. That would be the appropriate response, would it not? Even if one is asleep, one should be horrified to sense an unfamiliar man's hand placed on one's bare flesh.

Yet, curiously, I find this imaginary fellow's touch utterly enjoyable. The clasp is gentle but firm, the fingers curled around my upper arm, the thumb gently caressing my skin. I keep my eyes closed, enjoying the sensation.

"Katharyn. Please, love. I'm sorry to wake you, but Missy's forehead feels warm . . . she wants you. Please, you need to get up."

Eyes shut, I consider this information. I wonder who Missy is, and why her warm forehead should be any concern of mine.

In that rambling way in which events occur in dreams, my thoughts are replaced with the lyrics to a song that was popular on the radio a few years ago. I can hear the melody, though I'm sure I don't have the words right—Rosemary Clooney sang the tune, and it was something about having stars in one's eyes. Something about not letting love turn one into a fool. The idea makes me smile; clearly, I am being about as foolish here as one could possibly be.

I open my eyes and sit up in bed, instantly remorseful that this position shift causes the blue-eyed man to remove his warm hand from my shoulder.

"Who are you?" I ask him. "Where am I?"

He returns my quizzical look. "Katharyn, are you okay?"

For the record, my name is not Katharyn. It's Kitty.

All right—it really is Katharyn. But I've never cared for my given name. It's always felt too formal. *Kath-a-ryn* doesn't roll off the tongue, the way *Kitty* does. And since my parents bestowed on me an unusual spelling of an otherwise ordinary name, I find it tiresome having to clarify whenever I am asked to spell it.

"I *think* I'm okay," I tell Blue Eyes. "But really, I have no idea who you are or where I am. I'm sorry."

He smiles, and those handsome peepers twinkle. Other than the eyes, he is fairly ordinary-looking. Medium height, medium build, a slight love handle around the middle. Thinning russet hair that is starting to go a bit gray. I'd put his age at around forty, a few years older than me. I inhale, noticing a woodsy, soapy scent about him, as if he recently finished shaving and showering. He smells delectable, and I feel my heart skip a beat. Good heavens, could this dream get any *more* absurd?

"You must have been in some deep sleep, love," he says. "You know who I am. I'm your husband. You're in our bedroom, at our house." He sweeps his arm around the room, as if to prove his case. "And right now, our daughter—whose name is Missy, by the way, in case you've forgotten—is likely running a fever, and she needs her mother."

He holds out a hand to me. As if on instinct, I slip mine into his.

"Okay?" he begs. "Please, Katharyn."

I furrow my brow. "I'm sorry, you said you are . . ."

He sighs. "Your husband, Katharyn. I'm your husband, Lars."

Lars? What a peculiar name. I cannot think of a single person I've ever met called Lars. I half smile, thinking about my oh-so-imaginative brain. It couldn't just invoke a Harry or an Ed or a Bill. No, ma'am, my mind has fabricated a husband named *Lars*.

"All right," I say. "Just give me a moment."

He squeezes my hand and releases it, then leans over to kiss my cheek. "I'll take her temp while we're waiting for you." He rises and leaves the room.

Once again, I close my eyes. *Now* the dream will shift, surely. But when I open my eyes, I'm still there. Still in the green bedroom.

I see no alternative, so I get up and cross the room. With its clerestory windows above the bed, its sliding glass door that looks as though it leads to some sort of patio, and its large, adjacent bathroom, I deduce that this room, were it real, would be part of a rather modern residence. More modern—and presumably bigger—than the one-bedroom, 1920s-era duplex that I rent in the Platt Park neighborhood of Denver.

I peek into the bathroom. The fixtures are light green, shiny and chrome-accessorized. The long vanity has two sinks and a gold-flecked white Formica counter. The vanity is composed of blond wood cabinets that gently taper downward and inward toward the wall, such that the vanity is deeper at the countertop level than it is near the floor. The tiled floor is a fresh mosaic of mint green, pink, and white. I have no idea if I'm in Denver anymore, but if so, this certainly is not old-time Platt Park, where nothing new has been built since before the war.

Examining myself in the mirror over the dresser, I half expect to see some entirely different person—who knows who this Katharyn is? But I look exactly like myself. Short, buxom, with exasperating strawberry-blond hair that cowlicks itself over my forehead and frizzes everywhere else, no matter how often I go in for a wash-and-set. I put my fingers through it, noting that on the ring finger of my left hand are a sparkling diamond and a wide gold wedding band. Well, naturally, I think. And how optimistic of my brain to have invented a husband who can afford a nice-size rock.

Foraging in the closet, I find a navy-blue quilted bathrobe that fits me perfectly. Belting it around my waist, I enter the hallway, on my way to find the oddly named Lars and his unwell child Missy.

On the wall directly in front of me, clearly positioned so that it can be seen from inside the bedroom, is a large color photograph. It shows a mountain scene: the sun sunk over the horizon, the peaks backlit with pink and gold tones. Ponderosa pines rise the length of the photograph on the left-hand side. I've lived in Colorado my entire life, but I have no idea where this is, or even if it's the Rocky Mountains.

I'm trying to decode this mystery when I am tackled around the waist on my right side. I struggle to regain my balance and keep from falling over backward.

"Ouch!" I say as I turn around. "Don't do that. Remember to support yourself entirely. You are too big now to lean on other people and expect them to hold you up."

What in the world? Who is this woman saying these things? It can't be me. These words don't sound like anything I'd ever say, or even think.

Looking up at me is a small boy. He's got Lars's piercing blue eyes and a neat, short haircut that nevertheless can't hide a reddish-blond cowlick over his brow. His peaches-and-cream face is scrubbed clean. He looks like he could be in an advertisement for milk or Popsicles. Yes, he's that cute, and I find that my heart melts a bit, looking at him.

He releases me and says he's sorry. "I just missed you, Mama," he says. "I haven't seen you since yesterday."

I am speechless. Then, reminding myself that I am, after all, asleep, I smile at the boy. I lean down and give his shoulder a squeeze. I'm just going along with this dream now. Why not? So far, this is a pleasant enough place to be.

"Take me to your father and Missy," I say, grabbing the child's soft, plump hand.

We walk down the hall and go up a half flight of stairs. At the top is a girl's bedroom, with carnation-pink walls, a little white wooden bed, and a low bookcase filled with picture books and stuffed animals. Sitting upright in the bed is an equally angelic child, a female version of the boy who holds my hand. Her expression is forlorn and her cheeks are flushed. She is about the same size as the boy. I am terrible at deciphering children's ages, but I'd guess they are around five or six. Twins?

"Mama's here!" Cherub Boy says, climbing onto the bed. "Missy, Mama's here and you're going to be fine."

Missy whimpers. I sit next to her and touch her forehead, which feels distressingly warm under my hand. "What hurts?" I ask her gently.

She leans toward me. "Everything, Mama," she says. "My head especially."

"Did Daddy take your temp?" I can't believe how easily these words, these motherly actions, are coming to me. I feel like an old pro.

"Yeah, he's washing the ther-mon-eter."

"Thermometer," Cherub Boy corrects her. "It's a ther-*MOM*-eter. Not a ther-*MON*-eter."

She rolls her eyes at him. "Mind your own beeswax, Mitch."

Lars appears in the doorway. "One hundred one-point-six," he reports.

I am unsure what that means. Oh, I know it means her temperature is 101.6 degrees Fahrenheit. But I do not know what it means in terms of medication, bed rest, staying home from school.

Because I do not have children. I am not a mother.

I don't mean to imply that I never wanted children. Quite the contrary. I was one of those little girls who loved baby dolls, who fed them pretend bottles and changed their pretend diapers and pushed them around in a tiny doll-size pram. An only child, I begged my parents for a sibling—not because I wanted to be a big sister, but because I wanted to be a little mother to somebody.

For a long time I thought I'd marry Kevin, my steady during college. He left for the Pacific theater in '43, along with just about every other young man who hadn't already gone. I remained faithful to him—girls in those days did that, remained faithful. Kevin and I exchanged letter after letter. I sent him care packages of cookies, socks, shaving soap. In my sorority house, we stuck thumbtacks on a map of the South Pacific, marking our soldier boys' progress. "It's hard to wait, but it will be worth it when they're home," we girls told each other. We sobbed into our hankies when we got word that someone's fellow wasn't coming back. But we also sent a little silent prayer of gratitude to heaven that it wasn't *our* fellow, not this time.

Much to my relief, Kevin returned from the war intact and seemingly unchanged, eager to resume his studies as a premed student and attain his goal of becoming a doctor. We continued dating, but he never did pop the question. We were invited to wedding after wedding, where everyone asked when it would be our turn. "Oh, you know, someday!" I'd say, my tone overly gay and nonchalant. Kevin simply changed the subject whenever it came up.

Year after year passed. Kevin finished medical school and began his residency; I worked as a fifth-grade teacher. But as far as our relationship went, one year was as static as the next. Finally I knew I could no longer put off an ultimatum. I told Kevin that unless he wanted to make our relationship permanent, I was through.

He sighed heavily. "That's probably for the best," he said. His good-bye kiss was brief, perfunctory. Not a year later, I heard he'd married a nurse from the hospital where he worked.

Well, clearly, in this dream world, none of that—those wasted years, Kevin's callous rejection—matters at all. In this world, I landed myself a winner somewhere along the line. *Good for you, Kitty*, I can hear my Delta Zeta sisters congratulating me. *Good for you.*

The thought strikes me as absurd, and I stifle a laugh. Then I put my hand to my mouth, mortified. This is a dream; nonetheless, there is a sick child here. I ought to behave appropriately. I ought to be suitably, maternally troubled.

I look up from Missy's bed, and my eyes meet Lars's. He's staring at me with admiration and—could I be reading this correctly?—*desire* in his eyes. Do married people truly look at each other this way? Even in the middle of a kid-has-a-fever crisis?

"What do you say?" Lars asks me. "You always know what to do when these things happen, Katharyn."

Do I? How interesting this dream is. I glance out the window at what appears to be a winter morning, the windowpane frosty and snow falling lightly.

And then, suddenly, though I cannot explain it, I *do* know exactly what to do. I rise and walk across the hall to the bathroom. I know precisely where on the medicine cabinet shelf I will find the tiny plastic bottle of St. Joseph's Aspirin for Children. I pull a paper cup from the dispenser attached to the wall and run a bit of cool water into it. Opening the bathroom's linen closet, I remove a facecloth, hold it under cold water, and squeeze it out.

Walking purposefully, I carry the medicine bottle, facecloth, and cup to Missy's room. I apply the cloth to her forehead, gently pressing it against her warm skin. I hand her two aspirin tablets; these she swallows dutifully, using the water to chase them down. She smiles gratefully at me and leans back against her pillow.

"Let's let her rest now." I settle Missy under the covers and fetch several picture books from her shelf. She begins paging through *Madeline's Rescue*—a volume in that delightful children's series by Ludwig Bemelmans about a Parisian boarding school student named Madeline and her eleven classmates—the house covered in vines, the girls in two straight lines. Missy's fingers trace the words on each page as she sounds them out in a whispery, throaty voice.

Lars comes forward and takes my hand. We smile together at our daughter, and with our adorable son beside us, we quietly leave the room.

But then, as suddenly as it happened, the dream is over.

My bedside alarm clock is ringing sharply. I reach over, eyes shut, and press down hard on the button that stops the alarm. I open my eyes, and the room is yellow. I am home.

Chapter 2

Goodness," I say to myself. "That was quite the dream." Stiffly, I sit up in bed. Aslan, my yellow-hued tabby, is curled up next to me, purring softly with his eyes half closed. I named him after the lion in C. S. Lewis's novel *The Lion, the Witch, and the Wardrobe*—an extraordinary book, especially if one adores children's fantasy stories. I read each Narnia novel as it came out, and I've read the entire series at least half a dozen times since.

I look around my bedroom. The windows are bare, stripped of their curtains and shades. Masking tape still frames the woodwork. My bed and nightstand are the only pieces of furniture in the room; before I began painting yesterday, Frieda and I moved the bureau and hope chest to the living room, to make space and keep splatters off the furniture. The room smells of paint, but the color is extraordinary—it's the exact color of the sun on a bright day. It's just what I'd hoped for. With a satisfied smile, I rise and don my robe, padding across the newspaper-covered floor.

Heading to the kitchen to make coffee, I stop to switch on the radio that sits on one of several scratched, tag-sale bookshelves that line my living room, overflowing with books and journals. I twist the knob to turn up the volume and tune the dial to KIMN. They're playing "Sherry" by the Four Seasons, which I've been hearing constantly on the radio this week—I'd put money on it topping the Billboard chart this weekend.

I place my percolator under the kitchen faucet and fill it with water, then pull a can of Eight O'Clock Coffee from an upper cabinet and begin measuring it into the stainless-steel top chamber of the percolator.

". . . *Out tonight* . . ." I sing along under my breath as the song on the radio fades away.

"And now here's an oldie but a goodie," the disc jockey says. "Does anyone out there remember this one?"

As the next song begins, my hand freezes, my fingertips holding the coffee scoop and hovering midair over the percolator. Rosemary Clooney's voice fills my small duplex.

"Now that's just plain eerie," I say to Aslan, who has wandered in to check whether his morning dish of milk has been set on the floor yet. I finish pouring the coffee and switch the percolator to On.

The song—I remember now that it's titled "Hey There"— dates back at least seven or eight years. I don't remember the exact year it was so popular, but I do remember humming it often in those days. I haven't thought about that song in ages. Not until I heard it playing in my head, in my dream last night.

I recall my dream man's eyes, piercing and blue, like the water in a postcard from some exotic locale. I remember thinking that I *ought* to have been frightened, but I was not. Did I look at him with stars in my eyes? I suspect one could say I did.

Well, but how could I help it? The way his eyes gazed into mine. He looked at me as if I were everything to him. As if I were his whole world.

That, to me, was without a doubt exotic. No one, not even Kevin, has ever looked at me like that.

And the way Lars spoke! *Katharyn, love, wake up. You must*

have been in some deep sleep, love. You always know what to do, Katharyn.

No one, here in the real world, says such things to me. And certainly no one addresses me as Katharyn.

There was a brief period, some years ago, when I toyed with calling myself Katharyn. This was right around the time when Frieda and I opened our bookstore. With a new career and a new decade of life—I'd turned thirty a few months prior—I felt it was time for a sea change. Despite my general dislike of the unwieldy *Katharyn*, I could think of no better way to bring about a grand change of character than to alter my name. Perhaps, I mused, I needed only to get used to it.

And so I charged forward. I had personal stationery printed with the name "Katharyn Miller" on it. I asked Frieda and my other friends to call me Katharyn. I said my name was Katharyn when introducing myself to customers, to the other shopkeepers who we were just getting to know on our little block of stores on Pearl Street. I even asked my parents to use my given name— which they, albeit reluctantly, did. They have always been over-indulgent with me.

Frieda was not so easy to push over. "Kitty suits you," she said. "Why change?"

I shrugged and said that perhaps it was simply time to grow up.

I even used that name when introducing myself to potential suitors. It felt good, a fresh start. A chance to be someone new. Someone a bit more sophisticated, a bit more experienced.

Nothing happened with any of those fellows—a random first date here and there, but no second ones. Apparently, changing my name was not going to automatically change my persona, the way I'd hoped it might.

A few months later I placed the remaining "Katharyn Miller"

stationery in the dustbin and quietly went back to calling myself Kitty. No one commented.

I take my coffee to my desk, which faces my two living room windows. I open the curtains. Seated here, I can look out onto Washington Street. It's a sunny, warm September day. The postman is coming down the street; I wave as he fills my mailbox and that of the Hansens, who own this duplex and live in the other half of it. After the postman leaves, I go outside to get my mail and my *Rocky Mountain News* morning paper.

Lars, Lars . . . I am still running the name over in my mind. Lars who?

And where have I heard that name before?

I go back inside, glancing at the newspaper headlines. President Kennedy gave a speech at Rice University yesterday, promising a man on the moon by the end of the decade. I'll believe it when I see it. I cast the paper on my dining table, planning to read it over breakfast.

My mail contains only a few items. Besides several bills, there is an advertisement with a coupon for a free car wash—not that that would do me any good; I don't even own a car—and a postcard from my mother.

Good morning, sweetheart,

I hope you have nice weather. It's 85 degrees here and humid, but lovely, of course. There is nowhere lovelier on Earth, I assure you!

I want to remind you of our return date. We'll take the overnight flight on October 31st. We'll make a connection in Los Angeles and arrive in Denver on Thursday, November 1st.

We are having a wonderful time, but we can't wait to be home and see the fall colors! And you, of course.

Love,
Mother

P.S. I am also eager to get back to the hospital; I miss the babies terribly. Wonder how many have been born since we left????

I smile at her note. My parents have been in Honolulu for the past three weeks and will be there for about five weeks more. It is a huge trip for them, the biggest they have ever taken away from Denver. Their fortieth wedding anniversary was this past June, and the trip is a celebration. My uncle Stanley is a chief petty officer at the Pearl Harbor naval base. My parents have been staying with Uncle Stanley and Aunt May in their apartment off-base, in Honolulu.

This trip is a wonderful event for them, the experience of a lifetime, but I could see why they—especially my mother—wouldn't want to be away from home any longer than two months. My mother is committed to her work in the Unwell Infants Ward at Denver General; she has been volunteering there for almost as long as I can remember. ("The oldest candy-striper on the planet," she cheerfully calls herself.) My dad worked for the Colorado Public Service Company for years, assembling electrical meters for homes; he took early retirement last year, at age sixty. Dad spends his time puttering around the house, reading, and going golfing with his cronies twice a week, even in the winter, as long as there is no snow on the ground.

I think back to the dream, and how it was snowing when I looked out the window in the girl's bedroom. Missy? Is that the name? Yes, snow was falling outside the window in Missy's room. I wonder that I can remember such a detail from a dream, that my mind can create entire snowscapes for my viewing pleasure while I am asleep.

I smile at the memory of the view inside the room, as well: those two darling children, and the man with the beautiful eyes.

Finishing my coffee, I file Mother's latest postcard in a manila folder, nestling it with the others I have received—at least three or four a week. I keep the folder on my desk beside a framed photograph of my parents.

I rise and go draw myself a bath. Nice as that dream life was, I need to get on with my own, very real day now.

I walk to our bookshop on Pearl Street. It's only a few blocks. Frieda walks from her home, too, and sometimes we meet on the way. Today, however, I am alone as I turn the corner onto Pearl. For a moment I stand still, taking in the quiet, the desolation. There is not another soul about. No automobiles pass my way. The drugstore is open; I can see their neon sign lit up in the left-hand window. The sandwich shop, too. I know from experience that throughout the course of the morning, perhaps a handful of passersby will stop in there for coffee or a salami on rye to go. But only a handful.

It was not always this way.

When Frieda and I first opened Sisters' Bookshop in the fall of 1954, we thought this the perfect location. Back then, we got the streetcar traffic from the Broadway line, which veered onto Pearl. We're just down the block from the Vogue Theater, and we made sure to stay open in the evenings when a feature was playing, to cater to the before-and-after movie crowd. We saw a lot of evening customers in those days; people loved to browse our bookstore at night, no doubt hoping to meet a mysterious beauty or handsome stranger among the stacks.

Things are much more iffy now. The Broadway line has been shut down—all of the streetcar lines have been shut down, replaced with buses. The new bus line does not run down Pearl Street, so we don't get that traffic anymore. The Vogue still shows films, but they don't draw the crowds that they did years ago. People simply don't shop and amuse themselves on our block and in other small commercial areas like ours, not the way they used to in bygone years. They get in their cars and drive to the new shopping centers on the outskirts of town.

We've been talking about that, Frieda and I. What to do about it. Ought we to close down, get out of this business entirely? Ought we to—as Frieda suggested years ago, and I held back—close down this location and open in one of the shopping centers? Or ought we to just maintain the status quo, believing that if we stick with it, why then, things will surely turn around? I don't know, and neither does Frieda. It's a daily topic of conversation.

What I've learned, what we've both learned over the years, is that nothing is as permanent as it appears at the start.

Before we opened our store, I'd worked as a fifth-grade teacher, a job that I told myself I was crazy for. *I love my job, I love my job, I love my job*, I would silently chant to myself each morning as I bicycled from my parents' home, where I still lived, to my school a few miles away.

How could I *not* love it? I'd ask myself. After all, I adored children, and I adored books and learning. What sort of person would I be, then, if I did not, logically, also love to teach?

But standing at the chalkboard in front of a large class of ten-year-olds made me as nervous as a novice musician who had somehow faked her way into performing in an overflowing concert hall. Small and alone, seated at the grand piano under the spotlight, that phony musician would realize too late that the moment she struck a key, she wasn't going to hoodwink anybody.

That is how I felt, standing there in my classroom. My palms would sweat, and my voice would become too quick and high-pitched; often a student would ask me to repeat something. "Miss Miller, I didn't catch that," one would say, and then they all would take it up: *Me, neither. Nor did I, Miss Miller. What did you say, Miss Miller?* I felt that I was a joke to them. But not a good joke, not one that I was in on, too.

Every year I had a few standouts—thank goodness for the standouts—those students who could learn in any environment, students who were smart and adaptable and quick to grasp concepts all on their own, without much help from me. But such pupils were few and far between.

And then there were the parents. Oh, the parents.

I remember one particularly awful morning toward the end of my teaching career. Mrs. Vincent, whose daughter Sheila had just received a D in history on her midterm report card, stormed into my classroom before the first bell. She waved Sheila's report card angrily. Sheila trailed behind her mother.

"What is the meaning of this grade, Miss Miller?" Mrs. Vincent demanded. "Sheila tells me that you don't even study history in your class!"

"Of course we do," I replied, trying to keep my voice steady. Crossly, I bit my lip; why should I have to defend something so obvious? "We've been learning about the Civil War all term."

"The Civil War? The Civil *War*? What possible use does a young girl have for something as prehistoric as the Civil War?"

The question was so absurd, I could not even come up with an answer. Sheila stood smugly next to her mother, dark eyes challenging mine. I wanted to slap her. I knew I never would, but the impulse was so strong, I had to put my hands firmly at my sides to control myself.

"That is the curriculum," I said. "That is what I am asked to cover, ma'am." I walked to the classroom doorway as the bell rang, ready to greet my other students. "I am just following the curriculum."

Mrs. Vincent smirked. "Well, *that's* creative, isn't it?" she asked. Without waiting for an answer, she whirled around and left the room.

I was a wreck; honestly, it took me weeks to get over that one. Over time, I began to blame myself. Yes, I was just doing my job. But if my students couldn't, or wouldn't, learn—why then, I was at fault. Learning had come so easily to me over the years; I assumed therefore that it would be easy to teach others. I didn't know how to fix things when that turned out to be untrue.

During those same years Frieda, who had been my best friend since high school, worked in an advertising firm. It was demanding but glamorous work, and she was good at it. Her firm's accounts were mostly local businesses, but many of them were sizable companies— the Gates Corporation, Russell Stover Candies, Joslins Department Store. She went to parties and grand opening events. She wore gorgeous evening gowns, which she would model for me beforehand, to see what I thought. I always thought they were fabulous.

On the surface, Frieda seemed to be having a fine time. But when she and I were alone, comfortable on the weekend in dungarees, low-heeled shoes, and sweaters, she'd confess that it was all too much, it was all a sham. It made her feel, she said, as if she were acting in a play. "Acting is fun once in a while," she said. "But it's tiresome to do it all day, every day."

Frieda and I talked a lot about our situations. How much she hated the phoniness of her work. My fear that I was failing at the one thing I had thought I'd be good at.

"What would a different life be like?" she asked me one Sunday afternoon toward the end of March 1954, as we took a walk in my new neighborhood. I had moved out of my parents' house the month before—approaching my thirties, I'd felt that it was time for me to be out on my own, so I had leased an apartment in Platt Park. My new place was not far from the school where I taught; it was also less than a ten-minute walk to the small house that Frieda had purchased two years earlier. It was a typical Denver spring—as usual, we'd had more snowstorms in March than in any other month. That year, as in most years, the storms were generally followed by several warm, sunny days, during which the snow melted into puddles and new grass poked up in muddy yards. The day before, we'd had one of these characteristic late-season snowfalls—but that Sunday, as Frieda and I took our stroll, it was clear and bright, with temperatures in the fifties.

Frieda watched heavy droplets of melting snow fall from a nearby house's eaves. She turned back to me and asked, "What if the work we did was gratifying?"

"What if I didn't end most days in tears?" My mind felt open, alive, as I considered the possibilities.

Frieda nodded slowly. "Indeed, sister," she replied. "Indeed."

Finally we decided that it was time to stop dreaming and start living our dreams. We raided our savings accounts, borrowed from our parents, and got a business loan. As single women, we had to have a man cosign our loan; fortunately, Frieda's father was agreeable. Thus Sisters' was born.

I remember our elation when we opened the store. At last, we were doing what we wanted to do with our lives. We would have a thriving business that we co-owned; we would make our own choices and determine our own fates. From here on out, no one—parents, bosses, not to mention a horde of contrary ten-year-olds and their mothers—would have a hand in determining who Frieda and I were going to be. Nobody would decide that for us, nobody save for each other.

We'd both come through our twenties without marrying, something that no other girl we'd known in high school or college had done. Neither of us is perturbed by singlehood. The goal I once had to marry Kevin—that seems irrelevant now. It was the desire of a young woman—a girl, really. A girl I no longer am.

Over the years, I've come to realize that being unmarried gives me—and Frieda, too—an element of freedom and quirkiness that other women our age do not have. It's like being a singular necklace that might catch one's eye in the jewelry section of a department store, the one strung with colorful, random beads, rather than the monotonous, expected strand of pearls.

Who needs men? Frieda and I ask each other. Who needs children? We smirk at our station-wagon-driving counterparts, feeling relief that we never fell into *that* trap.

It is not a life that either of us has wanted for a long, long time.

O̶ur day is challenging, Frieda's and mine. We have only two customers in the morning, each of whom purchases a copy of that new Bradbury novel—a rising star in our humble little line-up, that book. In the afternoon a few folks come in to browse, and several people ask if we have Rachel Carson's *Silent Spring*—the book, about the hazards of pesticides, was presented as a series of essays in the *New Yorker* earlier this year and will be published as an anthology later this month. *Silent Spring* is much anticipated in local literary circles, but unfortunately, we won't receive copies from our distributor until the last week of September.

All day long, Frieda is edgy, irritable. Her mood rubs off on me, and I notice that my hands shake a lot, even though I've only had two cups of coffee today. Perhaps it is just the memory of the dream, which lingers in my mind.

"I need to get out of here," Frieda tells me at four thirty. "I've had enough for one day. Will you close up?"

I nod and watch her leave. Outside the shop, she furiously lights a cigarette and stomps down the street.

"Sister, I'm so sorry," I whisper, although she is long gone and cannot hear me. "I'm so sorry for the way things are going for us."

And then, after I close the front shades, as I am gathering the meager amount of cash in our register so I can store it in the safe out back, it comes to me.

I know where I've heard that name before. Lars.

The recollection dates back some eight years. It was just before Frieda and I launched Sisters', during the phase when I began calling myself Katharyn. Back then I read with great interest the personal ads section in the *Denver Post*. And finally I ran an ad myself. It was something to do, I suppose, another brave something that went along with my new job, my new name, my desire to make myself over into someone different.

Lars was one of the fellows who responded to my ad. In fact, now that I think of it, Lars was *the* fellow.

What I mean is that, out of the twenty or so men who wrote, the eight or ten that made the first cut and to whom I talked on the telephone, and the few that I went on a date with (none of them to be repeated, generally not to my disappointment)— out of all those men, Lars was the only one with whom I truly thought there might be potential.

Like all of the men, Lars wrote me a letter to introduce himself. But unlike many of the notes I received, Lars's letter was more than a few lines scribbled on a piece of paper and stuffed in an envelope, with little thought of the outcome. I could tell, just by what he'd written, that Lars had put a great deal of time and consideration into his letter.

I am a saver. I have an enormous file cabinet at home, and I save every piece of paper that ever had meaning to me. I have letters, recipes, travel itineraries, magazine articles—you name it, and it's in that cabinet

So it is no surprise, when I rush home from work and go through my files, to find a manila folder marked, simply, "Ad Respondents." And in this folder are a smattering of letters and pieces of paper with first names and telephone numbers scribbled on them. There is also a yellowing copy, cut from the newspaper, of my personal advertisement:

> Single Female, age 30, Denver. Optimist
> with faith in self, family, friends,
> abilities. Honest, forthright, loyal.
> Seeks gentleman who is playful but not
> silly. A man with interests (outdoors,
> music, books). Man should desire a family
> and secure home life, yet also enjoy
> adventures, travel, and fun. If this is
> you, please write.

I think about that, what I wrote in that ad. How I presented myself to the world. Looking back, I see how the years have changed me. In those days, marriage still was on my mind. Kevin had disappeared from my life a few years prior, but the idea of finding someone just right with whom I could settle down and start a family—plainly, that idea still held appeal for me back in '54.

What I have now—running the store, my independence, the life of a single working woman . . . well. I may have wanted to start a business with Frieda. After the disaster my teaching career turned out to be, I may have wanted to surround myself with books all day, to spend my days on *my* terms.

Evidently, however, I did not expect the years to pass in the manner in which they have.

I ruffle through the rest of the papers in the file, until I find Lars's letter:

Dear Miss,

I know you don't know me, and I know that most people say that this is a foolish way to go about meeting someone. I have heard that it never works. For the most part, I have believed that, because I have not seen too many people succeed at it. But I read your advertisement (actually, I have read it about a dozen times now), and from your description, I think that I might be someone you would be compatible with.

You said you were looking for someone who is playful, but not silly. Here are some things I like to do. One is to visit my nephew and niece and have football games in the street. Don't worry, we use a soft ball and have yet to break an automobile windshield—and the kids are 12 and 8, so they are pretty good about watching out for oncoming traffic. I also like to build things for other people. When my niece and nephew were little, I built a swing set for my sister's backyard. I built a doghouse for a friend's dog that was spending its nights in the cold. Perhaps those are not playful things, but they are things that make others happy, and that makes me smile.

You mentioned travel. I have not had the opportunity to

do as much traveling as I'd like. I immigrated to the United States from Sweden with my family when I was a teenager. I've had to work hard to make my way in this country, but things are better now and I have the means to live a more comfortable life. I am hoping that will include more travel in the future, both within the country and internationally. Have you been to Europe? I have not been back, but I would like to go someday, especially if I were accompanied by a travel companion who might appreciate the Old World for all its beauty and history.

Another of my interests, which you did not mention, is American sports, particularly baseball. Perhaps you are not a fan. I hope that if we were to meet and get to know one another, you would forgive me this indulgence. They say baseball is America's pastime, and as an American myself now, I find that it has become mine as well.

I'm glad you were not afraid to say you are looking for a man who wants a family. A lot of ladies seem afraid to admit that, as if they think it makes men desire them less. I guess they might be justified, because a lot of fellows (especially past a certain age) are either on the fence or adamantly say no to the idea of children. I don't feel that way. I've always wanted a family and I hope it's not too late! (I'm only 34, so I suppose there is time.)

So you see, miss, why your advertisement appealed to me. I hope you'll respond. I would love to get to know you.

Sincerely,
Lars

I sit there, rereading the letter. I stare at the telephone number he wrote in a postscript. And then I read the letter through a few more times. True, he is not Shakespeare. But it's clear why I wanted to contact him. There is something there; I can't deny a connection, just through those few pages of written words.

Later, while cutting up vegetables for my dinner, I telephone Frieda. Although I am worried that she'll still be in a mood, I need to talk to her. Perhaps, I think as I dial, her brisk walk will have cleared her head.

She answers on the third ring; her voice, when she hears mine, is friendly. "Miss me?" she asks. "I know it's been almost two hours since you saw me."

I laugh. "Of course," I say. "But that's not the only reason I'm calling." I plunge in and ask her, "Do you remember a fellow named Lars? From the personals?" There is no response, so I ask again.

"Thinking," she says. "Yours or mine?"

When I ran my personal advertisement, I realized—after skimming a few of the initial replies—that not all of the respondents would turn out to be likely suitors for me. "I am wunderfull. Pleeze call me" was the entire content of one rather revealing letter. Sadly, it was not an anomaly.

There were others, too, in whom—while they were capable of stringing basic sentences together—I did not feel a spark of interest. My reasons varied: too tall, too talkative, too slick sounding.

One evening Frieda came over to my apartment, and we went through the letters one by one. We made three piles: "Kitty," "Frieda," and "Discard." Into the Kitty pile went letters from those who intrigued me. "It's *my* ad, after all," I told her, laughing. "I get first dibs." Into the Frieda pile went letters from the fellows for whom my initial reaction was lackluster. Frieda selected several of these to contact. "Why not?" she reasoned.

"They're just going here otherwise." And she waved her hand at the Discard pile.

Ironically, she had better luck than me with the letters. She went on quite a few dates, and actually went steady for several months with a man she met through my personal ad. I thought they were going to get serious, but it was not meant to be. When she told me their relationship had ended, Frieda shrugged flippantly. "He simply wasn't good enough for me," she'd said. "He didn't think as highly of me as you do, Kitty."

You might think that with a name like Frieda, my best friend would have wiry red hair and be a little self-centered, like the Frieda in the *Peanuts* comic strip. And while Frieda has her vain moments—don't we all?—she certainly looks nothing like that little girl. Tall, with long, straight dark hair, she is nearly the opposite of me. She is athletic and strong; she played softball and was on the swim team in high school, and to this day she still swims a few times a week in the field house pool at DU. She strikes up conversations with everyone she meets, from the teenage girls who sell movie tickets at the Vogue to the occasional confused passerby who stumbles into our shop looking for directions to an entirely different part of town. Other shopkeepers on our block call Frieda "the sales-y one." I am "the bookworm."

"Lars was one of mine," I tell her now. "I know you don't remember mine that well."

She laughs. "I can barely remember last week. You want me to remember who you went out with—what was it—eight years ago?"

I select a carrot from the refrigerator and start to peel it. "I was just hoping."

"Why? Did you run into him again?"

"In a manner of speaking." But I don't speak it, because even telling Frieda seems ridiculous.

"Did you run another ad?"

"No, nothing like that." I cut the carrot into small disks. "Look, I have to go. I'm about to start cooking dinner. I'll see you tomorrow."

After we hang up, I reread Lars's letter and my advertisement. I've read them over and over since I got home.

And then I remember something else. We talked. We talked on the telephone.

It was just once. I called him, because that's the smart thing to do in these circumstances—that's what Frieda told me. "That way," she said, "if they sound like they just escaped the loony bin, no harm is done. They can't call you back."

So after reading Lars's letter several times that evening, I took a deep breath, picked up the telephone, and rang the number he'd given me. He answered right away.

"This is . . . Katharyn," I said, testing the name on my tongue. It felt fresh and tingly, like a breath mint. "From the . . . the ad."

"Katharyn." In his voice, the name sounded magical, unique, special. "I knew it would be you."

This scared me a bit. "How did you know?" I asked nervously.

He laughed. He had a nice laugh. "I just knew."

I turned down the radio, so I could hear him better over the line. Oh, good heavens—now I remember when that Rosemary Clooney song was number one on the charts.

It was playing on the radio that night. The night when we talked on the telephone.

Stars in one's eyes, indeed.

Lars asked how my day had gone, what I did for work. "I'm actually between jobs at the moment," I said. Then I told him about the bookstore, which was scheduled to open a few weeks later.

"What an exciting prospect," he said. "You're very impressive, Katharyn."

Impressive. I can honestly say that never before in my life had anyone described me using that word. Smart, yes. Friendly, yes. Impressive? That was a tall order, one I'd never considered myself having the shoes to fill.

"I'm actually thinking of opening a business myself," Lars told me. "But not nearly as thrilling as yours. Just an architectural firm."

I laughed. "That sounds plenty thrilling to me," I said. "How did you get into that line of work?"

"Oh, I've been at it for years," he replied. "I've always loved building things. Back home in Sweden, my father was a carpenter, and I used to help him on his jobs. In a small town like ours, when you built someone's house, you designed it, too. Over here, after my parents passed, I took odd jobs. Finally I saved enough dough to attend UC-Denver. I knew by then that I wanted an architectural degree. I graduated college late for my age—in 'forty-four, when I was an old man of twenty-four. I was hired by a small firm here in town, and the rest just came naturally."

" 'Forty-four." I thought for a moment. "Didn't you serve?" Everyone I knew, Kevin and every other boy I went to DU with, or knew from high school or church or my neighborhood, was serving in '44.

He didn't say anything for a few moments. I asked softly, "Lars? Are you still there?"

"I couldn't serve," he said quietly. "I was Four-F."

"Why?"

I could hear him take a deep breath and let it out slowly. "I have a heart condition . . . arrhythmia," he said, and then quickly added, "That's not as terrible as it sounds. But it does mean . . . it means . . . my heartbeat is irregular." He was silent for a moment, and then he said, "It means I have a bad heart."

I didn't reply. I thought of my father, easily the most patriotic man I've ever met. During the war his plant went on strike, and he was the only worker who broke the picket lines and went to work side by side with the scabs. The plant had ceased making home electric meters, and the workers at that time were assembling electronics for the war effort instead. My father said that anything he could do to help our soldiers was worth more than a few extra pennies in his pocket. I wondered what he would think of me going out with a man who'd been 4-F during the war.

"Katharyn?"

"Yes?"

"Is that all right? That I didn't serve?"

I didn't say anything for a few seconds. And then I replied, "Well, it hardly sounds like you could have done anything about it." I laughed lightly. "Tell me more about being an architect."

"I tend toward commercial projects," he said. "Office buildings and the like. Not as glamorous as residential work, but there is more demand for it. So many houses are prefabricated these days, the same layout over and over. I'd love to design and build my own house someday, make it one of a kind." He sighed, and I could hear the longing in his voice. He went on to tell me about the architectural firm he was thinking of starting on his own. "I know as much as the bosses at my current firm," he explained. "The only difference between what they do and what I do is the name on the doorplate and the amount on the pay stub."

"Well, good for you," I replied, and I meant it. I admired him for wanting to branch out on his own. I knew from my own experience, mine and Frieda's, that even thinking about going out on a limb like that is not the easiest thing to do.

The conversation went on for over an hour. Finally, I said it was getting late. "This has been truly wonderful," Lars said. "I'd love to speak with you again, Katharyn."

I hesitated a moment, and then I said, "Oughtn't we just to meet? It seems silly to keep talking on the telephone. We ought to just meet in person and see how things go."

"Really?" He seemed surprised.

"Of course."

"Well, then, Katharyn, let's make a date." We made a date to have coffee two evenings hence.

"All right, then," he said after our plans were finalized. "I guess this is good-bye for now."

"I guess it is."

"Katharyn . . ."

I paused, and then said, "Yes?"

His voice was soft. "Nothing . . . I just . . . I'm really looking forward to meeting you."

"I'm looking forward to it, too."

He didn't answer. I could hear his breathing; it sounded a bit rapid. "Is there anything else?" I asked.

Slowly, he said, "No, I . . . no, I suppose not. Good night."

"Good night," I replied. And we both hung up.

I hold the letters, the papers, the file folder. I sit in my desk chair, staring out the window. My lips are pressed together. A little hot burst of anger forms under my skin.

Because that was it.

He never showed up for our date.

Chapter 3

Of course, it's all just silly. I imagine things like that happen all the time. Dating through the personal ads was a bumpy business. I learned the hard way that there are a lot of strange birds out there—men who might sound perfectly normal in letters, even on the telephone, but get in the same room with them, and you realize that something is off. Maybe they have no notion of what it means to be a gentleman. Maybe they have a girl already. Maybe they *think* they want to be attached, but what they really want is to be able to tell their mother or sister or whoever that they are trying. But deep down, they just want to be left alone. The last thing they want is a steady gal—or, heaven forbid, a wife.

So I was disappointed, but not all that surprised, when I sat alone in that coffee shop eight years ago, dutifully drinking my coffee, waiting it out for fifteen minutes, twenty, thirty-five. Through the plate-glass window, I people-watched. Couples strolled by, old ladies with little dogs on rhinestone-studded leashes, mothers with chunky infants in prams. I wondered if Lars was sitting in his car across the street, hunched down, watching me. I guessed that he could be deciding based solely on my looks—which weren't all *that* bad, I told myself rather contritely; just that afternoon I had gotten my hair done, and I'd spent extra time on my lipstick—that it wasn't worth squandering an hour of his time to have coffee with me.

Finally, two refills later and my coffee cup again empty, I stood. I pulled on my coat and walked out the door with my head held high. I put a bright, brave smile on my face. If he *was* watching, I wanted to be sure he knew that I didn't care.

After dinner, I spend an hour stripping the masking tape from my bedroom's windows and baseboards. I pull up the newspapers from the floor, rehang the curtains and shades, and consider moving the furniture by myself, ultimately deciding that it's not worth the effort. Instead, I climb into bed and fall instantly into a dark, initially dreamless sleep.

And then I am there. In the green-wallpapered bedroom. Grayish morning light filters in, and through the patio doors I can see that again small flakes of snow are falling. Does it always snow in this place?

Lars and I are spooning, his right arm around me. I can feel the solid weight of his forearm on my waist, his warm breath on my neck.

I turn slightly to look at him. *Who are you?* I ask him in my head, afraid to speak aloud and wake him. *What am I doing here with you?*

As if I have spoken, he opens his dazzling blue eyes. "Good morning, love," he says, turning my face toward him so we can kiss. His kiss is warm and instantly familiar. I feel as if I have been kissing him daily for years.

"Good morning," I murmur. It feels so good; I want to enjoy this for as long as I can.

I turn and press against him, feel his hardness against my thigh. I hesitate. And then, remembering that I'm only dreaming, and therefore nothing I say or do actually matters, I ask him, "What time is it? Do we . . . can we . . ." I stammer, not sure exactly how to find the words, even in this not-at-all-real world.

"If we're quick." He smiles. "I love Saturdays."

And so we begin to make love fiercely, furtively, the way I imagine married couples do when they find themselves with a few moments to spare in the early morning. They must do it quickly, before the children awake.

He caresses the length of me, tenderly, with experienced, gifted hands. Unbuttoning the top two buttons of my night-gown, he presses his lips to my nipples. I arch my back to meet him, moaning softly. I had forgotten how miraculous this feels.

He places himself fully inside me, and I move my hips— slowly at first, and then gaining momentum as I become at ease with the feeling of his length inside me. My climax comes hard and fast, more powerful than any other sexual moment in my memory. I am astounded at how strongly I feel the sensations of it, all the way through my body. I cry out, and then I bite my lip, afraid I might be making too much noise.

He goes on, his breath quickening, and I can feel his heart pounding against my chest. And then, abruptly, he slows his pace until he is almost, but not quite, still.

"What's wrong?" I ask, alarmed. "Are you all right?"

He speeds up slightly, his strokes quicker but not nearly as rapid as before my climax. "I'm okay," he says. "I just needed to . . . slow down . . ."

I am silent, moving with him, altering my rhythm to the change in his.

After he comes, he slides off me, adjusts the fabric tie of his pajama trousers around his waist, and lies quietly by my side. I pull my nightgown down over my legs, curl up next to him, and put my hand on his chest.

His heart is pounding. "Are you all right?" I ask him again.

"I'm fine." He smiles, turning to face me. "You know how I have to slow down sometimes . . . it's easier if I do . . ."

"Easier . . . how?" I ask carefully.

He taps his chest, his fingers warm against mine. "Easier here," he says. "It's easier on my heart." He draws me close and whispers, "You know this, love."

Neither of us says anything for a moment. I watch him carefully as his breath slows to a regular pace.

"It was wonderful." I tell him. "It felt so . . . satisfying." I grimace. He must think I'm nuts.

"You were intense," he said. "As if it had been a while. But it hasn't been." He looks thoughtful. "Only a few days, right?"

If only he knew. "Well, I suppose it just feels that way for me sometimes."

There is a hesitant tap on the door, which is ajar. A small voice says, "I knocked. Just like you want me to. I remembered, and I knocked."

Lars smiles. "Come on in, buddy," he calls.

The door opens fully, and towheaded Mitch sidles in, coming directly to my side of the bed and standing next to it. "It's after seven," he reports.

"So it is." Lars glances at the alarm clock on his nightstand.

"I waited, just like you asked me to."

"Good job," I say.

I am not sure if this is allowed—who am I to know the rules of this house?—but nonetheless I am overtaken by the urge to snuggle with this child. I throw back the covers and invite Mitch in. He eagerly climbs onto the bed, wraps the coverlet around his legs, and puts his arms around my neck.

"Did you go potty?" I ask him, at the same time wondering

what gave me the presence of mind to even think of something like that. Mitch nods.

"You're the only one up?" Lars asks, and the boy nods again. Lars rises from the bed. "Go get a book, buddy," he says. "Mama will read to you in bed. Won't you, love?"

"Of course I will." I lift myself up and get comfy against the pillows.

Lars leans over to kiss me. "I'll get breakfast started."

And so it is that I find myself in a charming, stylish bedroom, with a soft snowfall outside, snuggled with what has to be the most delightful little boy on the planet, reading a book about transportation.

Vehicles, it seems, are Mitch's thing. All kinds of them. Airplanes. Trains. Antique autos. Ocean liners. "I'm going to be an ocean liner captain someday," he tells me proudly. "I'll sail around the world, and my family will come along and you'll have first-class cabins." I smile and hug him a bit tighter.

We are deep in the evolution of train travel—did you know that the first steam engine was built in 1804 by Englishman Richard Trevithick? I didn't, before today—when the door opens again and Missy enters the room. "Daddy says it's almost time for breakfast," she tells us. She twirls for me in a pink nightgown with a princess in a yellow dress appliquéd on the front.

She leans over for a kiss. After obliging, I ask her, "How was your first night in your new princess gown?" *How did I know that?*

Her grin is enormous. "It was swell. It's so comfy, and when I woke up in the middle of the night and the princess was right there on my tummy, it made it so easy to go right back to sleep." Missy gives me a quick squeeze. "Thanks again, Mama," she says. "You're the best sew-er-er!"

"Seamstress," I correct her.

Except that I am not. Not since the days of Home Ec class, more than twenty years ago, have I sewn anything more complicated than a loose button on a blouse. Yet in this life, I have made (or at the very least attached an appliquéd princess to) a child's nightgown. Where did I acquire such a skill?

"You two skedaddle," I say to them both. "Tell Daddy I'll be out shortly."

Before leaving the bedroom, I take a good look around.

The first thing to catch my eye is the large wedding portrait on the west wall. In the unlit room, made even dimmer by the snowy day outside, the photograph is in shadow. The picture is black-and-white—not hand-colorized as older photographs sometimes are, and not filmed with the color film that you see so much nowadays. Just a simple black-and-white photograph that looks as if it were intentionally taken a bit out of focus, as if to soften the image. Yet I can definitely make out my thirtyish self, along with a younger-than-now Lars—a little more hair on top, a little less girth around the middle. My white dress is simple, with capped lace sleeves, a fitted waist, and a full, tea-length skirt. Lars is standing slightly behind me, his arm around me, his hand placed lightly on my hip. I hold a bouquet of light-colored roses, perhaps pink or yellow, with sprays of baby's breath among the blooms. I cannot make anything of our whereabouts. Apparently we were posed for this portrait with a plain background, one that highlights the bride and groom but gives no clues about where the picture was taken.

Next to the wedding portrait is another black-and-white photograph, this one a street scene in what can only be Paris. I've never been to Paris; I've always wanted to go, but as of yet, my travels have not taken me that far from home. Unless you've spent your life in Siberia, however, Paris in a photograph is instantly identifiable. As in so many photographs of that city, there is a café in the background, a Metro stop, narrow streets. A bicycle with a large, flower-filled wicker basket attached to its handlebars leans against a wrought-iron fence. Stylishly dressed men and women cross the street, looking as if they are in a hurry to get somewhere both amusing and exotic.

Did we honeymoon there? I wonder.

I turn to the long, lean dresser. Stealthily, I open one drawer after another. They are filled with women's clothes, but they are not my clothes. As I've gotten older, my taste in clothing has gotten quite a bit more eclectic and—how shall I put this? *Haphazard*, I can hear Frieda filling in for me, oh-so-helpfully. My blouses are colorful, my scarves and jewelry plentiful. I wear slacks as often as skirts, though sometimes my customers—not to mention my parents—frown at this. "It's nineteen sixty-two," I tell my folks. (Of course, I would never say such a thing to a customer.) "Women are changing. Everything is changing."

However, in this 1962—if indeed it is 1962 here—my tastes are decidedly conventional. I run my fingers over delicate cashmere sweaters in shades of taupe and burgundy. Gingerly, I lift the neatly stacked rows of stockings to see if anything more interesting is buried underneath the nude and tan hose. Nothing is particularly jazzy or creative, but it looks as though I spend a good bit of time, not to mention money, on my wardrobe. Everything is well made; everything is neatly arranged in the drawers. When I open the closet's double doors, I find the same sense of organization on the racks. Rows of dresses, blouses, and skirts greet me, in order by color and degree of formality.

I envision the tiny bedroom closet in my duplex on Washington Street, the explosion of dresses and skirts and slacks hung any which way I can get them to fit in the too-small space. Every morning I go through the same ritual of digging through the closet to find a desired item, tossing aside everything else, and leaving a jumble of garments on the bed. I often come home from work to find Aslan curled in a cozy, purring ball amid my rumpled clothing.

This wardrobe, in comparison, looks as though nothing is ever out of place. With a closet as large and thoughtfully arranged as this, certainly one could find items to match any article of clothing, perfectly and appropriately, for any given occasion.

I slip on the blue bathrobe, which is comfy, as I noted last time I was here, but a bit subdued for my tastes. Belting it about my waist, I quietly open the bedroom door.

The house, as far as I can surmise, is a split-level. It's modern, definitely built after the war, probably within the past decade. Our bedroom, Lars's and mine (how odd that sounds!), is on the first floor, with our bathroom accessible only through the bedroom. You see that in these contemporary houses, a bathroom via the master bedroom. En suite, they call it. The sliding glass doors beside the bed presumably lead to a patio and the backyard. Peering out the bedroom doorway, I find a hallway to my left, with a door at the end that is ajar and looks as if it might lead to an office. To my right, I see the living room and the front door of the house. The walls are a pale gold and the door is aqua blue. Now, that's more like it, I think; at least I appear to have some color sense in my interior decorating.

Somewhere in front of me, blocked from my line of vision by the hallway, I can hear Lars and the children in what must be the kitchen. I know from my previous experience that the children's bedrooms are up the half flight of stairs just off the entryway. The stairs also go down a half flight, likely to a laundry or rumpus room, or possibly both.

Instead of heading toward the family and its noises, I slip down the hall to my left. The walls are decorated with photographs. All except the first one, the one that can be seen from the bedroom doorway, are pictures of people. That photograph—the mountain scene—still mystifies me. I step back to stare at it for a few seconds. But again, I cannot determine where it might be.

It's then, however, that I realize the placement of this photograph is no accident. While the other frames hold pictures of children, ancestors, family gatherings, this photograph has intentionally been positioned exactly where it is. From the bedroom—no, not just from the bedroom, but from the *bed*—one would be viewing this scene. Not looking at photographs of children or grandparents.

Pretty clever, I congratulate myself—if indeed this arrangement was my idea.

I study the other photographs. Surprisingly, I do not see Mitch and Missy. Instead, these are all black-and-white, and look as if they were taken a long time ago. Perhaps Lars's ancestors?

And then I stop and draw in my breath.

Midway down the hallway is a photograph that I know well. I cannot remember the actual event, though I am featured front and center. My blond hair falls in waves around my chubby face; my mother always said that I had the most beautiful curls as a small child. They only evolved into my maddening cowlicks when I entered my school years.

I am sitting on a picnic blanket, my parents on either side of me. My mother props me up—I couldn't have been more than six months old—and smiles her beguiling smile. My father is seated next to her on the blanket, his long legs stretched in front of him. We are picnicking in Washington Park, not far from my childhood home on York Street in the Myrtle Hill neighborhood of Denver. These days, people call Myrtle Hill "East Washington Park"—but back then the neighborhood had its own name, distinct from the park itself.

I know—because she told me some years ago—that at the time this photograph was taken, my mother was pregnant. She was expecting the first of three babies that came after me. All of them were boys, and all were stillborn. "The doctors never could figure it out," my mother said quietly, the day she told me this sad tale. "After it happened that many times . . . well, the doctors told your father and me that we ought to take steps to make sure we did not . . . that there was never another child." She shrugged, her eyes downcast, and said no more.

I don't remember her expecting the first two babies, but I remember the last one. I must have been about six or seven years of age. I remember my mother's protruding belly, how it got in my way when I wanted to climb on her lap and practice reading from my primer, the way my teacher expected us to do in the evenings. I remember my father taking Mother to the hospital, and my aunt May—who was young and unattached then, not yet Uncle Stan's navy bride—coming to stay with me. I recall that when my father came home, many hours later, his step was heavy. He sat on the sofa, wrapped his arms around me, and put his unshaven cheek against my smooth one. He told me in a very low voice that my baby brother had gone to heaven. "You mean the baby isn't going to come live here and grow up with me? He's gone forever?" I'd asked, keeping my cheek pressed to his scratchy face.

"Yes," he'd answered hoarsely, and I felt the wetness of his warm tears on my skin. "He's gone forever, honey."

I remember feeling angry with my mother's physician. He should have been able to save my baby brother, I thought. Weren't doctors supposed to save everybody?

Now, looking at the photograph of my young parents and my infant self, I feel as if something or someone is striking my heart. A small sob escapes my throat. I am, suddenly, awash in sadness.

"Mother, Daddy," I say softly. "Why is your photo in this house?" I look around. "Why am *I* in this house?"

I step quickly to look at the rest of the pictures. Yes, there are strangers here, old and young, children and grandparents, who knows who. But not all of the faces are unfamiliar. Some of these photographs are of my relatives. I see my aunt Beatrice, arm around my mother, in their teen years. There is a photograph of my cousins Grace and Carol Louise, with me sandwiched between them—me chubby, my swimsuit banding across my developing chest, and the two of them gangly in loose-fitting suits, all of us in rubber swim caps, squinting into the sun. There is a lake and a sandy beach behind us. I remember that time, remember the vacation our two families took that summer to Lake McConaughy in Nebraska.

There are my grandparents, stiff and formal in their wedding photograph, my grandmother looking more mature than the nineteen years she was at the time—and more grown-up by far than any nineteen-year-old you see these days. This picture, too, I remember. My mother showed it to me frequently, told me the story of their wedding day, how they almost didn't get married because the preacher was coming from Kansas City and a snowstorm delayed his train. "During the wait, Grandpa started to get cold feet—probably literally as well as figuratively," my mother would tell me, running her fingers over the photograph in its leather case. "But his brother—you remember Uncle Artie; he died when you were ten—gave Grandpa a firm talking-to. Told him good women did not come along every day, especially in eastern Colorado ranching country in 1899. Told Grandpa that if he didn't marry Grandma, then he—Uncle Artie—would do it instead." My mother smiled. "Well, that was all the convincing it took. Grandpa knew that Uncle Artie meant every word. The preacher arrived, and the deed was done." She smiled fondly at her mother's young face. "And the photograph taken."

Tears well in my eyes as I study the photographs. So many of these faces, like my cousins', are those I do not see often enough. Some, like Aunt Beatrice and my grandparents, are people who have passed out of my life already. I think suddenly about what it means to grow old. It means that all those that you loved as a youth become nothing but photographs on a wall, words in a story, memories in a heart.

"Thank heavens for you," I whisper to the picture of my parents with my baby self. "I don't know what I would do without you."

I make my way down the hallway and enter the room at the end of it. It is indeed an office, large and sunny, with a picture window on its east wall and a drafting board positioned beneath the window. Pencils and drafting tools overflow a metal tray attached to the board's right side. In the corner of the room is a small liquor cart, with a row of clean tumblers, several shot glasses, and an array of bottles—some clear glass, some green, all about half full—arranged neatly on its surface. The bottles and cut-glass barware catch rays of sunlight coming through the window.

A cherry desk sits in the middle of the room, with a telephone in one corner, two photograph frames in the opposite corner, and a blotter in the middle. There is a business-card holder next to the telephone, holding a stack of cards. I pick up the top one. "Andersson Architecture and Design. Lars Andersson, President," it reads. "Commercial, Business, Residential." I smile, remembering what Lars said years ago about planning more business-related structures than homes; I wonder if the third descriptor on the card is merely wishful thinking. The card shows an address in downtown Denver and a telephone number. I memorize the number, and then tuck the card in the pocket of my bathrobe, absurdly thinking that perhaps this small slip of paper will make its way back with me to the real world, where I might be able to dig deeper into the identity of Lars Andersson.

I lean over and study the picture frames. The first shows an eight-by-ten photograph of me. If it were real, and not simply a prop in my dreams, it would have been taken within the past few years; I can see the familiar lines around my mouth and eyes, the ones I see every morning in the mirror in the real world. I note a slight restraint in my face, as if I were hoping that I could smile sufficiently to look warm and friendly in the photograph, but not so much that the lines would noticeably deepen. My hair is smoothed down and curled under. I am wearing an indigo dress with a boatneck, pearls, and a matching pillbox hat. Very Jackie Kennedy, I think; in this dream world, clearly I am modeling myself after the First Lady. I let out a small laugh. I do like the Kennedys, and I did vote for Jack. I still believe firmly in his capabilities, despite the fears everyone has lately that he has no idea how to handle the Communists, and we're all going to be blown to bits before the year is out. Regardless of my admiration for her husband, however, it would be out of the question in my real life for anyone to confuse me with Jacqueline Bouvier Kennedy.

I pick up the other photograph frame. It is intriguing for the simple reason that it contains no pictures. Just three separate slots where pictures could be placed. Were these slots for photographs of the children? If so, why did Lars take the photographs out? And why three instead of two?

"Mama!" I hear Mitch shuffle down the hallway, and then he appears in the office doorway. "We've been waiting prayers for you," he says accusingly. "Daddy said to bring you this, and to carry it carefully." He holds out a mug that is three-quarters filled with coffee—almost black, as I like it, with just the slightest touch of cream. I smile and take a sip, enjoying the faintly sweet taste. Evidently, Lars also knows that I like one lump in my coffee.

"I'm sorry, darling. Tell Daddy I'll be right there."

"Okay." He takes off down the hall.

Chapter 4

I wake again to the yellow walls, to Aslan, to home.

"Lovely dream," I tell him. "But I'm not sure where you were, buddy." I scratch behind his ears. "You know, you may be there," I speculate. "It seems to be a rather large house. Maybe you're hiding in the basement."

I smile as I rise and begin my day.

Midmorning at the shop, while Frieda is in the ladies' room, I try calling the telephone number I'd memorized, the one on Lars's business card. I dial it furtively, feeling like a child sneaking a cookie from the jar while her mother is out of the kitchen. I have no idea what I'll do if someone comes on the line. But an operator's recorded voice tells me the number is not in service.

Next, I try Lars's residential number from eight years ago, the number he provided in his letter. Calling this number is a long shot—but it's worth a try, if for no other reason than to know whether the number is still in use. If it is, I expect I'll just hear the telephone ring indefinitely; the chances of him answering are slim, this time of day. Surely he would be at work at this hour on a weekday. Nevertheless, my palms are sweaty, dialing this number for only the second time in my life. After I have dialed,

I place my left index finger on the telephone hook, ready to hang up immediately if there is an answer. But I hear the same recorded voice, telling me this number is not in service either.

Quickly I pull the telephone book from the shelf under our checkout counter. I scan the business listings, looking for architectural firms with the name Andersson in them. There are none—not even an Anderson, the more typical spelling. And certainly no Anderssons.

I try the residential listings. Nothing for Lars Andersson or L. Andersson. Imagining myself as Mrs. Andersson, I even look for Katharyn Andersson and K. Andersson, thinking that perhaps our telephone is in my name. But no such luck.

I cannot think what else to do. My fingers drift into my dress pocket, finding my mother's daily postcard. I don't know why, but today I decided to carry my mother's words with me throughout the day, instead of filing them, as I have been up until now. I don't need to glance at the card to remember the picture on the front—a smiling hula dancer, her dark hair held back from her face by a gardenia crown, her grass skirt covering her long legs. Mother's words on the back—those, too, I have memorized.

Dearest Kitty,

I have been thinking about you all day today. I hope you are well, darling. You know, Aunt May keeps asking about you—whether you are happy, whether you have everything you want in life. And I tell her that of course you do. Of course. I tell her that if there was anything my Kitty wanted that she didn't have, she'd find a way to make it so. I believe this, darling. You can do anything you want. You can be anything you want to be.

I hope you know what I am trying to tell you.

Love,
Mother

"What, Mother?" I whisper aloud to the quiet shop. "What are you trying to tell me?"

Is there somewhere else I should look? Some clue I am missing?

I consider my personal ad, think about the newspaper in the fall of 1954. If I saw the paper from those days, would it give me a clue?

I need to do some research," I tell Frieda when we have our coffee break at ten o'clock. It's not truly a break, because we don't close the shop. If anyone came in, of course we would attend to the customer. But if no one is there, we settle on our stools behind the counter, sip our coffee, and have a chat. Sometimes we talk about business, sometimes about what we're reading. Sometimes we fall into idle Pearl Street gossip—who we saw coming out of the Vogue with whom the night before, what other shopkeepers are doing to attract business to our little street, how unkind it was of the city to take our streetcar line away.

Frieda blows on her hot coffee. "What kind of research?" she asks.

I feel myself blushing. "It's about a person. A . . . man." It sounds so foolish, saying it.

Frieda has a gleam in her eye. "You're holding out on me! Did you meet someone new? Where? When?"

I shake my head. "It's nothing like that."

Desperately, I want to confide in her. For over twenty years,

I've kept almost no secrets from her. But besides being silly, this just seems so . . . personal. Like it belongs to no one else. Just me.

"It's just someone I heard about," I tell her. And then, hastily, I lie. "An author. He writes historical books."

I know this will detach her interest immediately. Frieda can't stand history. In the eleventh grade, despite my efforts to tutor her, she nearly flunked America: Columbus through the Great War—without a doubt the easiest course I've ever taken in my life. But Frieda is all about the moment.

"Anyway, I'm going to take an early lunch and go to the library downtown, if it's okay with you." I drain my coffee cup and rise from my stool.

She waves her hand. "Certainly. I have nowhere else I need to be."

I walk over to Broadway and take the bus downtown, to the big central library that just opened a few years ago. In the research section, I ask the librarian to set me up with microfilm of the *Denver Post* from October 1954. It takes a while for her to find what I am looking for and set it up on a microfilm machine for me. I wait, browsing the stacks, thinking that the library is both the bookstore's enemy and our friend. They have everything here—why would anyone ever need to *buy* a book? On the other hand, there is nothing like the library to awaken a reader to the endless possibilities of the written word.

Finally, I am settled in with the microfilm I requested. I turn the hand crank gradually, scanning the pages until I reach the personal advertisements in the back of each day's edition.

Yes, my ad is there. I ran it for a week, from Sunday, October 10, until the following Saturday.

I smile ruefully, reading about my younger self, the self who still had hope for that part of her life.

I wonder what that self would think of me now. Would she be surprised that eight years have passed, and I have not changed all that much? That I still bop around my house listening to popular music in the morning? That I still root around in my closet for something to wear and leave a mess of clothes all over my bedroom, like a teenager? Would my thirty-year-old self *tsk-tsk* me about that? Would she be surprised that her personal ad got her nowhere, did not change her life one iota?

I don't know. But I do know that nothing in my personal ad gives me any idea what happened to Lars Andersson.

I browse the remaining pages slowly. At first I feel discouraged by the lack of information in my ad, but after a while, I get immersed in that world that was. Hurricane Hazel smashed into North Carolina on the fifteenth, working its way up the coast and taking down homes and businesses in its wake. In England, dockworkers were on strike. On the front page of the Saturday, October 16 edition is a photograph of a woman with a little boy on her lap. Tragically, the boy was killed by a self-inflicted wound from a handgun left unattended in the home. The caption informs me that the photograph is of the boy with his mother, taken some months before the accident. A prizefight, reportedly "the greatest match ever offered in Denver" took place on October 19 at City Auditorium Arena. The Trinidad Junior College homecoming queen and her attendants are shown in a photograph on October 20. They look carefree, joyous, and very, very young.

And then, in the October 21 edition, I come across the death notices.

Andersson, Lars, 34, of Lincoln St., Engle-
wood. Cause of death: cardiac arrest. Sur-

vived by sister Linnea (Steven) Hershall of Denver, one niece and one nephew. Preceded in death by his parents, Jon and Agnes Andersson. Services Friday at ten o'clock at Bethany Swedish Evangelical Lutheran Church, Denver. Interment immediately following at Fairmount Cemetery.

Chapter 5

So. There you go. Now I understand what happened. Lars Andersson did not stand me up, after all. Lars Andersson could not have stood me up, because he was not alive to do so.

Walking out of the library and slowly heading for the bus stop, I am not sure what to do with this information. I feel a terrible sadness for this man I never met—this man I've now met in my dreams. And I have to smile at my ridiculous imagination—at my crazy mind, which has come up with an entire dream life for myself with this person.

This man who, purely by a stroke of bad luck, I never got to see face-to-face.

I am almost eager to go to bed that night, curious what might happen and what I might dream. Laughing at myself, I pour a generous shot of whiskey just before bedtime, thinking it might put me to sleep sooner.

To my surprise, my dream places me not in the split-level house, but in a darkened restaurant. The tablecloths are checkered; the walls and linoleum floor are a deep red. The restaurant is crowded, and I can see several couples waiting for tables near the hostess stand. Judging by the hustle and bustle of the place, I think it must be a weekend evening.

To my right is Lars, in a suit and tie, looking respectable and happy, his left arm draped possessively around my bare shoulder. I am wearing a sleeveless forest-green dress made of broad silk; I can feel its slipperiness on my back and across my ribs. We are seated at a booth, facing the restaurant's entrance. The other side of the booth is empty.

"Welcome back," Lars says, his bright eyes gazing into mine. "You seemed to go off to dreamland there for a few minutes."

I smile awkwardly. "I'm sorry," I say. "I must have been day-dreaming."

"Imagining a more carefree lifestyle for yourself?" He grins.

My smile fades. "What makes you say that?"

He shrugs. "I don't know. Doesn't everyone do that some-times?" His smile is wistful. "Especially you and me."

What in heaven's name does *that* mean?

From speakers somewhere above our heads, there is music playing. The clear, lusty voice is unmistakable—it's Patsy Cline, one of my all-time favorite vocalists. Despite the fact that most of her songs are about heartbreak—or maybe it's because of that—I love Patsy's cadence, her musical approach. I love the way that you know, just through her songs, that whatever the reason for your sadness, Patsy would sympathize with you. If you could sit down with her over a drink in some smoky cowboy bar and talk about it, Patsy Cline would assure you that it—whatever *it* is—would be all right. She would pass a handkerchief to you and order another round. She'd tell you she'd been through the same thing, and worse, and she'd come out the better for it.

I have all of Patsy Cline's records. But I've never heard this twangy, melancholy song before. Like so much of her music, it's about breaking up. She's singing about how she would rather know now, would rather just get it over with, if her lover is thinking about leaving her.

If you got leavin' on your mind . . . Tell me now, get it over . . .

"Is this a new song?" I ask Lars abruptly.

"What, love?"

"This song." I frown. "This song that's playing—is this a new release of Patsy Cline's?"

He smiles. "I believe it is. In fact, I think it was you who told me that this is a new release—just a day or two ago, when it came on the radio at home."

Is that so? I smile inwardly. Now my brain is making up an imaginary hit parade. How very talented of it.

Lars looks toward the doorway, then glances at his watch. "They should be here any minute," he says. "Bill is generally quite prompt." He shrugs again. "I don't know anything about the wife, though."

Unsure how to respond to this, I simply nod.

Lars stirs his drink, then takes a sip. "Ah. Here they are."

He stands as a couple approaches our table. They are about our age, or perhaps a bit younger. The woman has jet-black hair, sleekly pulled back with a rhinestone headband. She wears a fur-trimmed cape. Her companion is tall, much taller than Lars; this is apparent when Lars stands up to greet them. The man has that square-faced jock look about him, the type who was probably a football player in high school. The type who always wanted to go out with Frieda, though she generally turned them down. Frieda has never been much for dating anyone, actually, no matter how good-looking a fellow is. Sometimes it seems like she tries to force herself to get out there—like when she contacted some of my personal-ad castoffs all those years ago. But in general, dating is not a big thing in Frieda's life.

"Bill, meet my wife, Katharyn." Lars turns toward me. I extend a hand over the table—it would be awkward to try to rise from the booth—and Bill takes it and clasps it tightly.

"And this is my wife, Judy," he says, releasing my hand. Judy and I exchange pleasantries. I am still trying to figure out who they are. Presumably business associates. Perhaps clients? I shake my head. This would be easier if I knew such details, but since it's a dream, I suppose it hardly matters what I say or do.

After we've placed Bill and Judy's drink order, and everyone's food order, we settle down to chat. I learn that Bill is indeed a client. He wants to build an office building downtown, but it will be more than that; the idea is that it will house offices on the upper floors and small shops on the lower floor. This immediately piques my interest, especially the part about the small shops. Ought Frieda and I to be considering downtown? It has never come up in our what-to-do-next discussions. I wonder what the rent would be on such a place. Perhaps, if the men keep talking, I will be able to find out.

"It's a brilliant move," Lars is saying approvingly. "It just makes business sense. We design it slick, we design it modern, but even so, we ensure that it's accessible on a smaller scale. We make it appealing to both the businessman and the passerby—something for everybody, as it were. You'll be at full capacity before you even open your doors, Bill. You'll be turning away tenants in droves. You'll see."

Bill sips his Scotch. "I absolutely agree, Lars." He sets down his glass. "And I must say that, after too many discussions with architects who seem to be living in the Victorian age, I appreciate talking with someone who understands foresight as much as I do."

Under the table, Lars squeezes my hand in triumph. I squeeze his back.

Judy slices herself a piece of bread and nibbles it without butter. "Enough business, boys," she says. "You can talk about that any time." She smiles at me, and I automatically smile back, although I am slightly ticked off. I actually wanted to hear more about the new building.

"Judy, you are one hundred percent correct." Lars nods at her. He's no dummy; he must realize that to get the husband's business, he also needs to chitchat with the wife. "Let's change the subject," he suggests.

"Let's," Judy agrees gaily. "I want to learn about Katharyn. Where did you two meet?"

Lars's eyes meet mine. "It's quite a story."

"Quite," I agree, and then, not knowing where to go from there, I add, "Why don't you tell it, dear?"

Lars places his hand over mine. "Believe it or not, this beautiful lady was looking to meet men through the lonely hearts section in the newspaper." He goes on to tell about my ad, about the letter that he spent days writing, in an effort to get it absolutely perfect. "I waited and waited for her to call," he says. "I was afraid I had taken too long to write. Perhaps she'd already met some other fellow." His eyes are downcast, but I can see that they are merry under his lashes. "And then one night the telephone rang."

"We talked for hours." I take up the tale. "And made plans to meet." After that, I don't know what else to say. The story is true so far, but only in a dream could it have ended here, in this restaurant, instead of where it actually did—with Lars deceased, with me sitting alone and unaware in a coffee shop.

"And then, as we were lingering over a few last words to each other on the telephone line, I began to feel a tight pain in my chest," Lars says. "I had trouble breathing. Katharyn must have heard it in my voice, because she asked what was wrong. I told her that I was having chest pains. 'Good heavens, where are you?' she asked, and the last thing I remember is giving her my address. Then I blacked out."

I stare at him, shocked. That did not happen.

In the real world, what happened is that we said good-bye and hung up the telephone. And two days later, he failed to appear at the coffee shop.

Now it all makes perfect sense. In the real world, Lars *did* have a heart attack and die, just as the newspaper obituary said he did.

What I hadn't realized—until now—is that it happened that very night.

It happened only moments after we got off the telephone.

So. This is the part where, if I were at a movie theater or watching a program on television, I might just laugh aloud. I would shake my head. Honestly, I might think, this is simply too absurd to continue. I would contemplate getting up from my seat, walking out of the theater, or turning off the television set.

But I can't do that. I am forced to stick around. Like a bug caught on flypaper, I don't have any choice in the matter.

Regardless of how absurd or unbelievable it may be, I cannot seem to leave. I cannot get out of this dream.

Judy leans forward. "My, what a story," she says. "Tell me, Katharyn, what happened next?"

And suddenly, in a rush—in the way things happen only in dreams, of course—I know exactly what happened next.

"I knew something serious must have gone on," I begin. "I knew I needed to act quickly. I'd scratched Lars's address on a piece of paper, and I picked it up and ran next door to my neighbor's.

I wanted to leave my telephone line open, you see, in case he regained consciousness. I knocked on the neighbor's door, and when she answered, I rushed for her telephone and called the police. When I explained what had happened, they said they'd dispatch a squad car and an ambulance right away. I explained briefly to my neighbor what was happening. Then I went back to my apartment and picked up the telephone and called his name, but he didn't come back on the line. Finally I could hear someone banging on his door, then breaking in. I heard lots of excitement and voices, and I could tell they were trying to do something medically with him, though of course I had no idea what."

Judy's eyes are huge over her martini glass. "Goodness, you must have been frightened out of your wits!"

"I was." Nodding, I continue. "I kept calling through the line, trying to get someone to talk to me. Finally a man picked up the telephone. When I told him I was the one who had rung for help, he said it appeared that Lars had had a heart attack. I asked where they were taking him, and he told me they were on their way to Porter Hospital.

"I didn't really think. I just grabbed a coat, called for a taxi—I didn't have a car back then—and went outside. When I got to the emergency room at Porter, I gave Lars's name and tried to get someone to tell me what was going on, but no one would. I didn't know what else to do, so I sat down in the waiting room. No one else was there. After what felt like an eternity, a man and a woman came in. The woman said her brother had been brought in because he'd had a heart attack. She was taken into the treatment area. The man with her was about to follow, but I caught his arm."

Lars's eyes are bright. "Quite forward of her, I might add."

" 'Forward' had nothing to do with it," I tell him sweetly. "I just wanted to know what had happened. I explained who I was, that I was the one who had called for help. The man introduced himself; he was Lars's brother-in-law, Steven. He told me to wait while he went inside to see what was going on. So I sat down again and waited. I was about to give up when Steven came back out. 'He's stable and conscious,' he told me. 'He'd like to see you.'

"So I was permitted to see him. He was lying on a cot in a treatment room, attached to all sorts of machines and monitors. His sister was seated at his side. When I came in, she rose and took my hand. 'Thank you,' she said, tearing up. 'You saved his life.'

"It was then that Lars opened his eyes . . ." And here I stare at him again, look into the deep blue. It's difficult to take my gaze away. Finally, I turn back to Judy and Bill. "Our eyes met, and he reached forward to take my hand. 'Thank you, Katharyn,' he whispered. 'Thank you.' "

I take a sip of wine, then smile delightedly around the table.

"And that," Lars says heartily, "was pretty much that. She visited me daily until I was released. When I went home, my sister Linnea was my official nurse, but Katharyn was the one who truly brought me back to health. I quit smoking—we both did—and started to exercise regularly. I love to hike, so we did that a lot, especially before we had children. And we took up tennis together; we still play in a doubles league. Of course, I have to take it a bit easy—I mostly play net, and Katharyn handles the back of the court." He chuckles. "Trust me, folks, you don't want to mess with this lady's backhand."

I stare at him, wondering if I look as confused as I feel. I have not held a tennis racquet since gym class in high school. I cannot imagine myself being even remotely skilled at something as athletic as playing tennis.

Lars squeezes my shoulder. "Katharyn and I were inseparable

from the day we met. We got married less than a year later, and we've been happy as larks ever since."

"What an amazing story!" Judy exclaims. "I don't believe I've ever heard anything quite so romantic."

Lars nods. "We ask each other all the time," he says, "what if we had never met? What if we'd gotten off the telephone just a few minutes before we did? The answer is chillingly simple: if it hadn't happened the way it did—why then, I would not have survived. We wouldn't be here tonight."

My hands are trembling. My whole body tenses at his words.

The dream continues. We enjoy a hearty spaghetti dinner and a bottle of Chianti. We get to hear how *they* met (not nearly as exciting; they were introduced via mutual friends in college), and then linger over coffee for all and cigarettes for them. As he'd mentioned, Lars does not smoke, and neither do I. He tells Bill and Judy that his doctors were ahead of their time in recognizing smoking's role in heart troubles, so at their insistence, he gave it up following his heart attack, and I did the same.

It is then that I remember something: I *did* give up smoking in the fall of '54. I could never explain to Frieda why I did it. At the time, it simply felt like something I had to do. Frieda says now that I must have had premonitions about the research they're doing these days linking smoking to cancer, heart attacks, all sorts of ills. She says she wishes she'd had the foresight to quit with me when I did. But she, a two-pack-a-day smoker, has never even tried to give it up, and I doubt she ever will.

Outside the restaurant, we bid Judy and Bill good night and walk to our car. I am curious to see what we drive. It turns out that we have a late-model Cadillac, silver-blue with a white interior. The Cadillac is probably Lars's, because unless it has been scrubbed clean that day, there are few signs that children ride in it all that often. Does that mean I have my own car, one in which I drive to the grocer's, run errands, cart children around? Either that, or the children and I walk everywhere, which seems unlikely. I wonder vaguely what my car looks like. The thought amuses me. I do know how to drive—my father taught me when I was in high school—but never once in my life have I considered the notion of buying, much less driving regularly, a car of any sort.

"Nice night," Lars remarks as he pulls out of the parking space. "What did you think?"

"They seemed to be enjoying themselves."

He nods. "I hope so. It would be great to land Bill's business."

Impulsively, I take his hand. "You will," I tell him. "I'm sure of it."

He squeezes my hand back, just as we did under the table in the restaurant. "I'm so thankful that you believe in me. It means the world to me. You know that, don't you?"

I hesitate, and then I reply, "Yes. I do know that."

The Caddy glides smoothly onto University Boulevard. I take careful note of our route. We drive south on University, taking the underpass below the Valley Highway. Entering the more populated area around the DU campus, we pass Evans Avenue; if we were to take a right there and go west, we would be heading toward my neighborhood. Instead, we continue on University for another mile or two, then take a left on Dartmouth, near the very southern edge of town.

There is a lot of new construction out here. I don't think the bus even runs this far south. It's dark, of course, but I can tell how pretty it is, almost like being in the country. The streets are named after midwestern cities: Milwaukee, Detroit, St. Paul.

We take a right onto Springfield Street. Houses are scattered on the block; not every lot has been built on. Some of the empty lots have signs advertising their availability. Among these, quite a few new houses are going up; I can see their shadows looming in the darkness, like long, lean skeletons across the sweeping vista.

We pull into the driveway of a finished split-level. I stare at the facade, trying to memorize what the house looks like from the outside. It's dark, so I can't tell much, but the brick seems to be a pinkish orange. I take note of the address—3258—which is in brass letters next to the turquoise front door.

Inside, we are greeted by a middle-aged brown-skinned woman in a maid's uniform. We have a maid? I hadn't caught that in my earlier dreams, but it doesn't surprise me. Nor am I surprised that our maid is likely from some Spanish-speaking country—probably Mexico, as so many people in Colorado are—rather than being some other race. Denver does not have large Negro or Oriental populations, and while I am in general uneducated about the world of domestic help, I would wager that white women rarely take jobs like this. Not if they can find something better.

Nonetheless, I am disappointed—not that my brain has fabricated a maid, because it makes sense that Lars and I would have help, living as we do in this large house, this fancy neighborhood. But I would have preferred my persona in this dream world to be a bit more enlightened. If I'm going to have a maid, I think, I could at least have the decency to let her wear street clothes, especially when she's babysitting after hours.

"Everything go okay, Alma?" Lars asks.

"*Sí*, señor. *Todo estaba bien.* Sleeping just like *los ángels.*" Alma takes her coat from the hall closet and shrugs her shoulders into it. She picks up a large bag with a magazine entitled *Vanidades* sticking out of the top of it.

"It's late," Lars says, opening his billfold. "Is Rico coming for you?"

"*Sí*, I call him when you pull in the driveway." She buttons her coat up to the collar and opens the door.

"Please wait inside," I say. I am not sure if this is protocol or not, but it seems cruel to send her out into the chilly night.

She shakes her head. "*Eso está bien*, señora. Rico is here any minute. And the fresh air, it feels good."

"Well, good night, then," Lars says, handing Alma a small stack of bills. "We'll see you on Monday."

"*Buenas noches*, señor, señora. Have a nice weekend."

You would expect the dream to end there, but it doesn't. After taking off our coats and hanging them in the closet, we watch from the front window as a car pulls up and Alma gets in. As Lars turns out the living room lights, I can't help stifling a yawn. Lars touches my shoulder gently. "Go get ready for bed," he says. "I'll check on the kids."

So I make my way to the sage-green bedroom and bath. In the medicine cabinet above the right-hand sink, I find all the things I'll need for an evening toilette. Baby oil to remove my mascara. Pond's Cold Cream for washing my face. A special night cream called Fountain of Youth, which Frieda discovered years ago at a cosmetic counter at Joslins; at her insistence, I tried it, too, and became hooked. The medicine cabinet looks as though I have personally stocked it. But of course I have, haven't I?

I carefully hang the pretty green dress in the closet and change into a nightgown that I find in a drawer of the long walnut dresser. I crawl under the covers to wait for Lars.

"They okay?" I ask when he enters the room.

"Fast asleep and dreaming deep." He smiles and goes into the bathroom, shutting the door behind him.

I am not sure what to do. Though I am drowsy from the wine

and the late hour—not to mention the fact, of course, that I am in an imaginary world—I resist closing my eyes. I fear that if I do, the dream will end and I will wake up in my own bed. And then I'll miss out on what might happen next.

As is no doubt evident, my lovers have been few and far between in the years since those events in the fall of 1954. After my experience (or rather, nonexperience) with Lars, I lost my motivation in the romance department. I canceled my personal ad. I rejected offers from friends to be set up with this fellow or that. If a friendly man came into the shop, one without a gold band on his left finger—why then, I would smile kindly, help him find the book he was looking for, and send him on his way. It didn't matter, I told myself. Never again would I force the issue.

There have been a few rare occasions—at a party or once in a while at a bar, out with friends—when there was a possibility for something quick and easy, and I allowed myself to be picked up. I will admit it: over the years, there have been a couple of one-night stands. These events were the result of physical desire and drinks flowing freely. I never cared if I saw such men again. I wasn't doing it because I wanted to find a husband.

And now I know why.

All these years, I believed it was a gradual shift, my transformation from hopeful, starry-eyed young woman to permanent old maid. But now I see that this change wasn't gradual at all. It was quite abrupt, really.

After Lars stood me up, I realize now, I never wanted to be attached. Honestly, I never thought about it again. It was as if that idea closed itself off for me permanently on that evening when he didn't show up to meet me.

But here I am, in his bed, waiting for him to come to me.

He opens the bathroom door and turns out the light. He is in pajama bottoms, but no top. His chest is covered with a beautiful reddish-brown fur. I want to run my fingers through it so badly that they ache.

He crawls into bed next to me. Taking me in his arms, he kisses me fully, deeply. "I have been waiting to do that all day," he says hoarsely when we come up for air.

It sounds corny, but as our nightclothes come off and our bodies come together—naturally, as if this has been happening regularly for years—I can see why no one else ever appealed to me again.

Because this is where I belong.

Chapter 6

And of course I wake up at home. A sense of melancholy comes over me. For the first time since I started having the dreams, I feel lonely in my own bed, my own home.

What an uncomfortable sensation, not to mention a ridiculous one. I rise and shake the covers off.

"Maybe it won't come anymore, this dream life," I tell Aslan. He follows me to the kitchen and winds himself around my legs, begging for food. I pour him a dish of milk, make myself coffee, and with a deep sigh force myself to realign with *this* world.

After an uneventful and, yet again, not particularly lucrative day, Frieda and I close the shop at five o'clock. As we are locking up, Bradley comes out the doorway that leads to his apartment above our shop. He pauses to button his cardigan, which is beige and tattered, with patches on the sleeves. His smile is friendly, but even so, Frieda and I exchange apprehensive glances.

Bradley is our landlord. He owns the building, living in one of the apartments upstairs, renting out the other, and leasing both our space and the small lawyer's office next door to us. Bradley is in his sixties, widowed with several grandchildren. When they visit him, they come into the shop and browse the children's section, and more often than not Frieda and I let them select something for free. Bradley is a good landlord, an honest man. It hurts my heart that we are so low on funds right now—and I know Frieda feels the same way. We have no idea how we'll make October's rent, which comes due in ten days.

"You girls have a nice evening, now," Bradley says. "Enjoy the warm weather while it lasts. Winter will be here before you know it."

He gives us a long look, one that I cannot read completely; nonetheless, it gives me a panicky feeling and makes my throat close up. Does he know? I wonder, swallowing hard. Surely he must. He has eyes; he can see out his window. Certainly he must see our shop's comings and goings—or lack thereof—every day.

In any case, Frieda and I both nod. "You, too, Bradley," Frieda says, and then we turn away and start walking south on Pearl Street.

We are both silent for a while. I don't want to talk about it—the shop, the rent—and I get the feeling that Frieda doesn't want to, either. After a few moments she begins to whistle—"Soldier Boy," by the Shirelles, I think, although with Frieda's off-key whistling, it's impossible to know for sure.

At the corner of Pearl and Jewell, we pause before parting ways.

"Have a good night," I tell her.

"You, too," she replies, fishing in her purse for her cigarettes and lighter. "Any big plans?"

I avert my eyes. "Nothing special," I mumble. "You?"

She shrugs, lighting up. "Just the usual old-maid-reading-and-going-to-bed-early routine."

I smile and give her a brief hug; hers in response is one-armed, the hand holding her cigarette dangling away from my body. "Well, enjoy," I say. "I'll see you tomorrow."

I walk east on Jewell, passing my own block at Washington. Glancing over my shoulder, I make sure that Frieda has continued on her way and can no longer see me. Then I walk the few blocks to Downing Street and turn right toward Evans Avenue. I cross the street to wait for an eastbound bus.

At University Boulevard I change buses, heading south. I am not sure where the bus line will stop; in the real world, this is not a part of town into which I've ventured. Although I've been aware that there is a lot of new construction out here, until now this area has held no allure for me. There is nothing out here but enormous new houses, with enormous new schools and churches to go along with them.

The bus goes as far south as Yale Avenue. "Last stop," the driver calls; I am the only person left on the bus. I hop off, then watch the bus turn around in an empty lot to make its way back north on University Boulevard. I walk farther south on University and after a few blocks turn east onto Dartmouth Street. A wrought-iron sign informs me that I have entered the Southern Hills neighborhood. I pass an elementary school on my left, a sprawling one-story brick building. Like everything else out here, it looks brand-new.

I keep going until I reach Springfield Street, and then I head south. All is as it was in my dream: freshly constructed houses, most of them ranches or split-levels, and lots of land being built upon. I don't remember the specifics of which houses existed and which didn't—it was so dark in the dream—but the feel of the neighborhood is just as I had seen it last night.

Even though I have never been on this particular street before.

I look for number 3258. I find 3248 and 3268.

But there is nothing between them except for an empty, tree-less, rather hilly lot.

I stare at the space. I can see the pink-orange brick house in my mind. I know exactly how the house would sit on the land, the low roofline of the attached garage and main section of the house and the higher roof over the upper level. I can envision the saplings planted in the yard, the juniper bushes by the front door. I picture the driveway where Lars smoothly rolled up and parked the Cadillac. My mind visualizes the wooden lamppost next to which Alma stood and waited for her ride home.

But there is no house here, not even any plan for a house—none that I can see, at any rate. There is nothing here except brittle prairie grass, dirt, and weeds.

A man strolls by, an unleashed spaniel walking quietly beside him. The man looks up and tips his hat at me. "Evening, ma'am." His bushy blond mustache lifts on each side as he gives me a small smile.

I nod. "Good evening."

He apparently reads the confusion in my expression, because he asks, "Can I help you, ma'am?"

I tilt my head and turn toward the empty lot. "I was just . . . perhaps I have the wrong address. I was looking for 3258 South Springfield Street."

He looks at the lot. "Well, this is where it would be, if there was a house there," he replies. "But as you can see, there's no house."

"No." I turn away, looking over the horizon, to the mountains in the distant west. "Tell me, do you live around here?"

He nods, glancing down the street. "On the corner."

"Have you lived there a long time?"

"Built in 'fifty-six. So a few years."

"You don't—there isn't a family around here named Andersson, is there? The Lars Anderssons?"

He shakes his head. "I can't say for sure I know everyone,

but the wife does try to make a point of meeting newcomers and introducing them around." He shrugs. "Can't say I've ever heard that name, though."

"And this lot—right here—there's never been a house here? Or any construction here?"

His mustache twitches again. "Not since 'fifty-six, ma'am."

I smile back. "All right. Thank you, then. I must have the street number mixed up."

"Well, good luck to you in finding the Lars Anderssons, ma'am. Have a nice night." And he strolls off, the dog at his side.

"Yes," I say to his retreating figure. "You, too."

There is nothing left to see. Feeling at once perplexed and a bit empty inside, I leave the Southern Hills neighborhood, walking slowly back to the corner of University and Yale. After waiting almost twenty minutes for a bus, I decide that they probably don't run into the evening this far out of town. Everyone out here has a car, anyway, I realize as I watch the late-model Fords, Chevys, and Dodges roll by. So I give up and continue walking north on University to Evans, where I catch the westbound bus. Altogether, I have probably walked three or four miles since starting this adventure, and I did not think to wear walking shoes. After taking a seat, I slide my heels partially off my blistered feet. I stare out the window until the bus reaches my stop. Then I put my shoes back on, step off the bus, and make my way up Washington Street.

As I walk, I start to move my arms. Before I realize what I am doing, I am swinging my right arm as if I'm holding a tennis racquet. It actually feels rather satisfying to move my arm that way—and instinctive as well, like it's something I have the natural strength and ability to do well. My feet don't even hurt anymore; it's as if I never even took that long walk tonight. I laugh at myself, shaking my head. Nonsense. It's all nonsense; my head is playing tricks on me, and using my body as a clever prop.

It's a crisp, just-start-of-fall evening, and some of my neighbors are out on their porches. "Hello, there, Miss Kitty," Mr. Morris on the corner calls out. He is smoking a cigar and rocking back and forth in his decrepit wooden rocking chair with its cane back. He is close to a hundred years old. He migrated here from Ohio with his parents and sisters in the 1870s, went to one of the first secondary schools in Denver, and graduated from DU when it was in its infancy. He worked as a newspaperman, raised a family, and now lives with his widowed son, who is no spring chicken himself. Mr. Morris says that he remembers his daddy coming home from the Civil War—though you have to wonder, doing the math, if the man who showed up was actually the man who fathered him or not.

"Good evening, Mr. Morris." I wave, but I don't step up on his porch to chat, the way I sometimes do. I have too much on my mind.

Other neighbors also smile and greet me as I pass. I am well known in the neighborhood. I can imagine how someone from this area might describe me to a newcomer: *Quirky old maid, to be sure, but nice enough, and she runs such a lovely bookshop on Pearl Street! Really, you should stop in and browse.*

As I walk toward home, I can't help noticing the contrast with Southern Hills. So much land out there, so much space between the houses. And so few tall trees. Most of the yards had a sapling or two, but none of the soaring spruces and cottonwoods that line my street.

Platt Park, the neighborhood I call home, has been here since the early part of the century. It was settled by religious families who emigrated from the Netherlands to Little Holland, as the area is still sometimes called. It shows in the Dutch-gabled roofs of many of the houses, not to mention the plethora of Christian Reformed churches. Nowadays this is mostly a blue-collar neighborhood, populated with maintenance and cleaning employees at the university, people who work in the factories on South Broadway, and some who, in the old days, would take the trolley to secretarial and retail jobs downtown.

These days, of course, folks take the bus. The bus that doesn't run by our shop, and therefore doesn't provide us with any customers.

I know that I should be pondering a solution to that problem. I know that Frieda, these days, is thinking of little else.

Still, I can't get my mind off Springfield Street and those long, lean houses. I can see the appeal. All that space. All that air to breathe.

As I approach my duplex, I spot Greg Hansen out front. He is the son of my neighbors, who own the duplex. The Hansens' only child, Greg is perhaps eight or nine years old. He is bouncing a large, red rubber ball against the brick side of the building—*my* side, I note with some annoyance. He better watch it around the windows.

Jeepers, I sound like a curmudgeon.

"Hi, Greg." I climb the steps and retrieve my afternoon *Denver Post* from my doorstep. I'm a newspaper addict; one paper a day isn't enough for me, so I read the *Rocky* in the morning and the *Post* in the evening.

"Hey, Miss Miller." Greg continues bouncing.

"Whatcha doing?" I ask him, fishing in my purse for my keys.

He shrugs. "Ma sent me out. Says if I'm not going to do my homework, I might as well get out from underfoot."

I find my keys and close the clasp on my purse. "Why aren't you doing your homework?"

He shrugs again. "Don't like it." The ball bounces against the wall once, twice, three times. "Don't like school, ma'am." He peers up at the sky. "Wow, what a fine color the sunset is," he remarks. "I don't think I've ever seen it so orange."

I set my purse on the green-and-yellow nylon-weave aluminum rocking chair that I keep on my side of the porch, then walk to the railing and lean over it. Greg is right; the sunset is brilliant tonight, the orange and pink hues weaving together to the west as the sun sinks in a scarlet blaze behind the mountains. But it seems an unusually keen observation for one so young, and for a boy. Perhaps, I muse, Greg is an artist in the making.

I take a good look at him. He is lanky, dark-haired, freckled. His grubby white T-shirt and dungarees hang loosely on his body. His bangs fall into his eyes.

"Greg," I say. He glances at me, back at the sky, and then at the wall. "Are there *any* subjects you like in school?"

He considers this, and throws the ball again. "Math is okay. I do all right in math, sometimes." *Bounce, bounce.* "The rest is really hard."

"What's hard? What do you find the hardest?"

He looks up at me. "Reading," he says flatly. "I just . . . I don't know, ma'am, I just don't get it. I read real slow, and . . ." He looks away, embarrassed.

"Have you . . ." I am not sure how to word this. "Surely your teacher could give you some extra help."

"Ma'am, no disrespect, but my teacher has a mess of kids in her class. I don't know how many there are, but it's lots. Sometimes she doesn't even remember my name."

I nod, thinking about that. I remember that feeling from my teaching days. So many kids, all needing so much from their schoolteacher, even if they were loath to admit it. All those eyes staring at the teacher. Some of them blank, a few of them not. A few of them following what the teacher is saying. But so many not.

But for all of them, regardless of their ability, the responsibility for their education falls to the teacher. And who can fulfill that for every single kid? What teacher is capable of that?

But what if Greg doesn't learn to read? What does he have to look forward to, if he can't even read?

"Greg," I say firmly. "I've got some wonderful kids' books in my apartment. Some swell books for boys. Hardy Boys—do you know those?—and some very funny books about a boy named Henry Huggins and his dog Ribsy. Would you like to come over tonight and take a look at them? Perhaps we could look at them together and see if there is something you'd enjoy reading." I smile at him. "I could help you," I say quietly, coaxingly. "I think . . . I think it would be fun for both of us, actually."

He bounces the ball a few more times, biting his lip. "Let me think about it."

He doesn't look at me. After a minute or two, I go inside and close my door.

After dinner, I resolutely push Springfield Street and the dream man—and his dream children and even his dream housekeeper—out of my head. Keeping my mind on young Greg Hansen, I go through my bookshelves and pull out all the children's books I have that are appropriate for beginning readers. I am not sure exactly how much trouble Greg has with his reading, how far behind he is, or even what difference I could possibly make. But if he is willing to give it a whirl—why then, I am willing to help.

Just before eight, there is a knock on my door. I dash over and open it, and Greg is standing there in the half darkness, looking small and anxious in my porch light.

"I thought . . ." He looks down. "I thought maybe you could show me some of those books."

"Of course." I smile and usher him inside.

Chapter 7

I am floating in a pool of green. My eyes are half closed, but through the slits of them I make out that the room I'm in is dimly lit. I wiggle around a bit and feel warm water rush over my body.

I open my eyes all the way, expecting to see the sea-green bathroom in the house on Springfield Street. Instead, I find myself in a much smaller bathroom. Like the bathroom in the split-level house, this one has green walls and fixtures—in this case a toilet, a pedestal sink, and the small bathtub in which I lie, half covered with warm water. The bathtub faucet is marked with elaborately engraved letters, swirled versions of a *C* and an *F*. A thick yellow candle in a clear glass dish sits on a wooden shelf next to the sink, its flame flickering in the shadowy room. A white towel is neatly folded on the closed toilet-seat lid, waiting for me to dry off when I finish bathing. On a hook on the back of the door hangs a short peignoir—lacy, tiny, and ruby-red. Good heavens, I think, who is going to wear *that*?

The frosted-glass casement window is slightly opened, and from outside I can hear the sounds of street vendors and music—an *accordion*? How odd!—drifting toward my ears.

I stretch my arms forward and wiggle my hands in front of me. I smile, admiring the rings on my left hand. I take a closer look at them today than I did the first time I noticed them, the first time I entered this dream world. The wedding ring is a wide gold band; along with it, I wear a brilliant diamond ring with an etched gold setting. I am no expert on diamonds, but this stone seems respectably sized. It is not so huge that it is gaudy or flashy, but it's certainly large enough that it doesn't look cheap.

My hands themselves look better than I've ever seen them— devoid of their customary ragged cuticles, the nails polished a pale pink. These hands, too, are decidedly younger and less wrinkly than they are in real life.

There is a knock on the door, and Lars hesitantly sticks his head in. "Just wanted to check on you, love," he says. "Make sure you didn't fall asleep in here."

I smile at him, my heart filled with adoration. "Come in and keep me company."

He laughs. "I don't think I'd fit in that little tub." He steps into the bathroom, closes the door, and looks around the tiny space. "The French sure don't make anything oversize, do they? Except meals." He pats his stomach. "What a dinner that was! I can't remember the last time I ate so well."

"Just take it easy on the pastries," I warn him playfully. I have no idea what I am talking about, or why I am saying such a thing. It just comes out.

It is then that I notice Lars looks younger, too. He has more hair on his head, and only a few strands of gray. In casual slacks, a white shirt, and no tie, he seems leaner, his body relaxed and comfortable. When he smiles, there are creases around his blue eyes, but they are not as deep as those I remember from my other dreams.

"You look amazing," I tell him. "You look so young and healthy."

He leans over and kisses me. "You look pretty amazing your-self." He deliberately looks me up and down, naked in the tub. "Every inch of you."

Suddenly I remember the photograph on the wall of our bedroom on Springfield Street—and I understand. We are on our honeymoon. We are in Paris. "Oh!" I exclaim.

He laughs again. "Have an insight? Something you want to share?"

I smile. "Not really." I look around. "I'll tell you this, though," I say. "I want a green bathroom like this someday. I want all the fixtures in my bathroom to be sea green like this. It's the loveliest color I've ever bathed in."

"Sounds like a good idea to me." He glances around the room, then back at me. "Maybe a bathroom that's a little bigger than this, though, don't you think?"

I wiggle in the water. "Maybe a little."

"You're going to turn into a prune if you don't get out."

"You're right. I'll be out in just a moment." I sneak a peek at the lingerie hanging on the back of the door.

He smiles tenderly at me. "I'll go pour us a nightcap." He goes out and gently closes the door.

I remember the last dream I had, when we were in bed and I was afraid to shut my eyes—afraid that if I did, I'd leave this lovely, imaginary world and wake up at home. Floating here, bathed not just in water but in happiness, I feel that same way again. I do not want to wake up from this dream-within-a-dream.

Despite this, I apparently drift off, at least for a moment or two. But when I open my eyes again, I am in the other green bathroom, the one in Denver. The one in the house that doesn't exist, that I share with the people who are not real.

I look at my hands. The rings are there, all right—looking a bit less glittery, to be sure, but nonetheless the same wedding set.

I notice with dismay that the wrinkles are there, too. I glance at my stomach, see stretch marks on the sides of my body. We must be back in 1962.

There is another knock, on another bathroom door. I hear Lars's voice. "You okay, Katharyn?"

"Yes," I reply. "I'm fine."

"Can I come in?"

"Sure."

Lars enters the bathroom, looking like the middle-aged Lars I am now used to. Nonetheless, he looks gorgeous to me. He may be balder and paunchier, but his blazing blue eyes haven't changed. And I can tell that when he looks at me, he doesn't see wrinkles or stretch marks. He just sees me, and what he sees is still beautiful.

"I love you," I blurt out. "I absolutely and positively love everything about you."

He smiles. "Hey, now, don't get carried away." He pulls a towel from the bar and places it on the edge of the vanity, where I can more easily reach it when I'm done. "You've been in here a long time," he says. "You'll turn into a prune."

I laugh. "You and your prune jokes."

He looks at me quizzically.

"Do you remember our honeymoon?" I ask. "Remember the green bathroom in Paris?"

"Of course. You said that's why you wanted a green bathroom. You wanted one just like that one. Except larger."

"I did say that," I concur. "And you know what, Lars? I *remember* saying it. I remember!" I know I probably sound childish, gleeful. But I can't help it.

Lars laughs. "I'm glad to hear you sounding more like yourself." His voice lowers. "I've been so worried about you, Katharyn," he says. "We all have been."

"Why?" I ask. "Why are you worried?"

"Honey." He comes forward and kisses the top of my head. "Just relax and finish your bath. The important thing is that *you* try not to worry."

"I'm not worried. I'm in love."

He shakes his head. "You're cute tonight." He turns toward the door. "Finish up, and I'll pour us a nightcap."

A dream inside a dream. A dream of a minor—albeit pleasant—incident that never happened. All inside a dream of an entire life that never happened.

When I wake up at home, alone in my own bed, I realize something quite unsettling.

I have fallen in love with a ghost.

Chapter 8

I have to stop thinking about it. I have to put these dreams out of my waking mind. They are confusing and pathetic, and they do me no good whatsoever.

Fortunately, I have other concerns with which to occupy myself. Forcefully pushing Lars out of my head—it makes me feel smugly self-satisfied, like refusing a second helping of dessert when I am trying to trim unwanted pounds from my hips—I instead turn my mind to the previous evening with young Greg Hansen.

We began with Hardy Boys and Beverly Cleary books, but he struggled with the first few pages of each. "Use the pictures as clues to what the text might say," I'd advised him—remembering how he'd noticed the sunset, I figured that Greg likely learns best when there are visual cues. But as soon as I provided this counsel, I realized how useless the suggestion was. Mine would have been fine advice if Greg were reading a picture book, something akin to the *Madeline's Rescue* story that young Missy was reading the first time I dreamed about my other life. But books like the Hardy Boys series and Cleary's novels, books with topics that might interest Greg, have only a few pictures scattered throughout, not one on every page.

Setting the advanced books aside, I pulled my old Dick and Jane readers off the shelf. Greg scoffed when he saw the covers.

"Those are baby books. They're boring," he proclaimed.

"Can you read them?"

Greg shrugged. I opened one and tapped the first page. He squinted at the words. " 'Spot has the ball,' " he recited. " 'See Spot run with the ball.' " He looked up at me. "There, you see? I can read that."

"Greg." I closed the book with a swoosh of the pages. "Why do I get the feeling you've seen this book before?"

He reddened. "Maybe I have, maybe I haven't. But I still read it!" he said defensively.

"Okay." I placed the book on the side table next to my davenport. "Let me poke around for something else." I looked into his eyes. "Will you come back another time, if I can find something more interesting for you to read?"

He shrugged. "Maybe."

Remembering the conversation with Greg last night, I am eager this morning to get to the shop. My mail is arriving just as I leave my duplex; hastily I grab my mother's postcard and read it while walking.

Kitty, darling,

We've had a turn of foul weather here. I must say that tropical storms are much more frightening than landlocked ones. The way the waves whip up, the debris that lands on the beach—yesterday, after the storm passed, I went walking and found a woman's necklace on the sand. Just

*a string of clear beads, very simple and humble. I left it
hanging in on a bush by the beach's entrance, though I
doubt anyone will return for it. Such incidents make one
wonder what other mysteries lie deep under the sea.*

*Such dark thoughts for a mother writing to her daughter
from paradise! I hope your day is sunnier, my dear.*

> *Love,*
> *Mother*

Poor Mother. I am distressed to hear her sound so melancholy; it's not like her at all. As I unlock the shop door, I resolve to write her a long letter this evening, after work.

Frieda and I don't have a large selection for kids, just a few classics and some newer children's books from the publishers' catalogs, books that we find interesting and salable. But surely, I think as I comb the children's section, there must be something that would appeal to Greg, at a level he can comprehend.

To my surprise, I discover nothing appropriate. The books he'd find interesting would be too difficult for him to read. And those he *could* read are too lackluster to hold his attention.

On my lunch hour, I walk over to the Decker Branch Library, just a few blocks from Pearl Street. It's the same story there as at our shop. Plenty of beginning-reader books . . . as long as one assumes that the beginning reader is five or six years old. I check out a few Dr. Seuss books. I know they will not satisfy him, but I need to start somewhere.

"This isn't much better than the one from last night," Greg complains that evening, after a few pages of *Green Eggs and Ham*. "I'm sorry, Miss Miller, I know you're trying to help me, but . . ." He looks down at his feet, embarrassed.

"Greg," I say, an idea suddenly forming in my head. "If you could read a book about any subject, what would it be?"

"Baseball," he says without hesitation. "I would love to read a story about baseball."

I nod. "I'll see what I can do."

Of course, there are no baseball stories for nine-year-olds who can't read. I look through our catalogs, I go back to Decker, and I even make a trip to the downtown library—my second time there in as many weeks, I note, and the reasons couldn't be more different. But I find no stories that would appeal to Greg.

So I decide to write some for him.

I start by asking him questions. "How exactly does the game work, Greg? What are the rules?"

He rolls his eyes. "Everyone knows the rules of baseball, Miss Miller."

"Well, pretend that I don't. Pretend you're explaining it to someone who's never heard of baseball. Maybe someone from another country, where they don't play baseball."

He looks astounded. "Don't they play baseball everywhere?"

I smile and shake my head. "Actually, they do not."

It's a warm evening, and we're sitting on my porch, he on the railing and me in my aluminum rocker. I have a notebook in my lap. As he talks, I take notes on what he says.

"In major-league baseball, there are two leagues, the American League and the National League," he tells me. "The best team in the National League right now is the San Francisco Giants. They're a shoo-in for the series."

"The series?"

He scoffs at me. "The World Series, Miss Miller." He looks up, thoughtful. "You know . . . it's funny that they call it the World Series, if they don't even play baseball all over the world." He shrugs. "I've never thought about that before."

I smile again. "Neither have I, actually."

"Anyway," he goes on, turning back to me. "My favorite player is Willie Mays. He's colored, and some kids at school say you shouldn't like him because he's colored, but that's just stupid, if you ask me." His eyes narrow. "If a player can hit the ball, who cares what color his skin is? Not me. You should see Willie Mays hit. He can send it screaming out of Candlestick Park—that's where the Giants play, in San Francisco." Greg looks up at the twilit sky. "I would give anything—*anything*—just once, to sit in a major-league ballpark and see Mays hit a home run."

"Anything," I repeat, scribbling in my notebook. "Wouldn't that be something?"

Two nights later, I knock on the Hansens' door. Greg answers.

"I'm sorry the pictures are so basic," I tell him as I hand him a set of stapled, handwritten pages. "I'm no artist. But I thought you'd enjoy this story anyway." I smile. "And even if the drawings are terrible, it's nice to have some pictures to go with the story." Unlike the first books I tried to read with him—the books by Beverly Cleary, and the Hardy Boys stories—in the book I've written for Greg, I have included drawings, minimal as they are, on each page.

Greg shuffles through the pages. "It's about baseball," he says, scanning the artwork and maybe—*maybe!*—even the words.

I nod.

"It's about Willie Mays." He turns page after page. "I know how to read his name from the headlines in the sports section of the newspaper. You wrote a story about Mays . . . and . . . and . . ." He looks more closely at the pages. "And *my* name is in it, too." He looks up. "What am I doing in the story?"

"Well." I smile. "I guess you'll have to read it to find out."

"I've never seen a book about baseball that I could read." Greg is beaming. "And I've never seen a story that had Willie Mays and me in it."

I reach into my dress pocket and pull out another item: a stack of about twelve index cards. I have punched a hole in each card and tied them together with a string. On each card, I've written a single word: *bases*, *pitcher*, *strike*, *catcher*. For each word, I've drawn a picture—again, terribly basic—that illustrates what the word means. "These cards will help you read the book," I explained to Greg. "If you get stuck on a word, look in this stack of cards and see if you can find it. Once you learn to recognize these words every time you see them, reading will get easier, because you won't have to stop to think about words you already know."

He takes the card stack I hold out to him, closes the book, and puts both items under his arm. "Thank you, Miss Miller," he tells me. "I can't wait to get started on this."

His words are music to my ears.

Besides the joy of teaching a child to read, there is another benefit: for more than a week now, the dreams have disappeared. Each night of that week, I sleep well, solidly, like a stone, without any dreams.

During the day, my energy level skyrockets. I hustle around the store, rearranging everything and creating a fall display in the window: leaves that I cut from red, yellow, and brown construction paper and scatter artistically (or so I tell myself) about the window shelf, best sellers that I set up in display racks, and a banner I've made: COLD WEATHER IS COMING! COZY UP WITH A GOOD BOOK!

Frieda rolls her eyes and tells me I'm getting downright annoying. "I liked you better when you were as grumpy as me," she says.

"I'll take it into consideration," I reply.

Greg tears through his book in a single day. "I read it start to finish," he tells me proudly. "The words on the cards really helped. I know them all now. After I read the book, I read it again, and then I read it to my mother. She . . ." He looks down, sheepish, his face reddened. "She said she was really proud of me."

"I'm proud, too," I say. "Very proud." I put my hand lightly on his shoulder. "Shall I write another one?" I ask. "Would you like that? I can make more cards, too. We can add to your collection of words you know."

"I would love that," Greg replies. "Thank you, Miss Miller. Thank you very much." He rewards me with a big smile, then hops enthusiastically across our shared porch and goes inside his own house, cheerfully banging the door behind him.

Chapter 9

And then, after over a week of dreamless sleep, my nighttime visions return.

We are out of the house again, Lars and me. Goodness, we socialize a lot in this fanciful world. In my real life, I go out in the evening two or three times a month, perhaps. Every now and then I go see a movie with old friends from my teaching days, but many of those friends have to plan weeks in advance to get a night out of the house without their husbands and children. Frieda and I dine in a restaurant now and again, and once in a while we attend a book signing at one of the bigger bookstores or department stores around town. These stores are always the venues for such events; our little bookshop does not attract celebrity authors—or even noncelebrity ones, for that matter.

But most evenings I'm at home, curled up on the sofa reading or watching television, Aslan at my side. Thinking about this, I wonder if my subconscious wishes I spent more time dressed up and running around, like I do in my dream life.

In any event, I find myself standing next to Lars at a cocktail party. He is in a suit and tie, and I am in a satin party dress—coral-hued, a color I actually like quite a bit in my real life, too—with a sweetheart neckline, a full skirt, and a wide bow at the waist. It reminds me of something I saw Jackie Kennedy wearing in *Life* not long ago; clearly, when doing my clothes shopping in this world, I follow the First Lady's trends. On my feet, I am wearing pointed heels in the same shade as the dress.

Music is playing from the speakers of a gleaming hi-fi stereo cabinet in the corner of the room. The Kingston Trio is singing about how they don't need booze to be high; apparently, seeing their woman smile does the same thing for them as a good stiff drink.

Well. I'm not sure my dream persona can say the same for herself. In my hand is a half-empty martini glass. Unlike Frieda, who adores a good martini, I rarely drink martinis in real life; nonetheless, I take a sip. It's surprisingly sweet. It must have something else in it, besides the usual gin and vermouth. I sip again, thinking that I could get used to this—if it were real, of course.

Lars and I are standing with a redheaded woman who is wearing a black satin sheath dress and holding a martini like mine. The room is crowded with couples, the men in suits and the women in cocktail dresses. I scan the room for Bill and Judy, our dinner companions from a few dreams ago. I smile inwardly; even here in a dream, a recognizable face would be a fine thing to see. But I don't see them.

We are in a house, but it is not our house. Like ours, however, this home is contemporary and lean. The living room stretches the width of the front of the house, with a bank of floor-to-ceiling windows looking toward the street. Over my shoulder I see that the dining area is open to the kitchen, which in turn has a sliding glass door that presumably leads to the backyard—which is no doubt as expansive as everything else in this world.

"Katharyn, that color is gorgeous on you," the redhead says, bringing my attention to the conversation in front of me.

I smile and sip my fruity drink. "Thank you . . ." Of course,

I have no idea what her name is, so I cannot call her by it. This bothers me greatly. My mother always impressed upon me the importance of learning—and using—other people's names. "You'll always have plenty of friends and social invitations if you remember names," Mother told me throughout my formative years. I'm not sure she's right about that, because I am quite good at names—yet in the real world, at least, I have a fundamentally nonexistent social life. I give a little laugh, and suddenly realize I feel a bit light-headed. I wonder how many martinis I've already put away.

Gently but firmly, Lars takes my elbow. "Jean, I always tell Katharyn that she's pretty in pink." He raises his eyebrows. "Of course, I told her that tonight before we left home, and she insisted that it's *coral*, not pink, that she's wearing." He lifts his shoulders in the playful shrug of a hapless male. "What man could be expected to know a thing like that?"

I laugh merrily. "Jean," I say, planting the name in my mind. "Would you call this more of a coral, or more of a peach? The saleslady called it peach, but . . ."—I finger the sateen fabric of my skirt with my free hand—"I think it's more of a coral."

"It's coral," Jean says firmly. "Peach would be lighter, which wouldn't be suitable for this time of year. But that . . ." She looks me up and down. "It's perfect, my dear." She glances toward the darkness outside the front windows. "Just make sure you bundle up before going home. What a storm! You didn't walk, did you two?"

"Sure we did," Lars replies. "It's only a block."

A mustached man walks up and hands Jean a fresh drink. "You looked thirsty," he says to her, taking her empty glass from her hand. I notice that their fingers touch for a few extra seconds.

"Ah, George." Jean looks impishly at the man over the rim of her glass, her green eyes large behind false eyelashes. "Such an attentive host."

Suddenly I realize who he is. It's the man with the dog, the one I saw on the street when I walked alone past where our house would be. When I walked there in the real world.

So actual, live people reside in the dream world, too. This strikes me as amusing, and I laugh aloud. Everyone looks at me, puzzled. "Did I say something funny?" Jean asks.

"No, of course not," I reply quickly. "I'm just in a happy mood tonight." I raise my glass. "It's so nice to be here with you all!"

Lars still has a solid hold on my elbow. "Katharyn, do you need to sit down?"

Suddenly, what I need to do most is use the bathroom. How is that possible, when I am not even awake? I laugh again, absurdly wondering if I am wetting my bed in the real world. "No, thanks," I say to Lars. "I'm off to the little girls' room." I extract myself from his grip and weave toward the back of the house, figuring there must be a bathroom somewhere in the vicinity, if I just keep my eyes peeled.

In the kitchen, a gaggle of maids is preparing food and placing it on trays. To my surprise, I see Alma, our own housekeeper, among the workers. Like Alma, the others are all Mexican. Even in my imaginarily inebriated state, I find the situation distressing. This world, this place in which brown-skinned people wait on white-skinned people—this is not how I live in my real life. I'll concede that in the world where I'm Kitty, I don't personally *know* many people of other races. But I do believe in conducting myself equally toward everyone. We have the occasional nonwhite customer at the shop, and I go out of my way to treat these patrons the same as I would a white person. It's how I was raised. It's just a matter of good taste and of being a decent human being, my mother would say, and she's right. My father worked with men and women of all races at his job; my mother cares for babies in a rainbow of colors in her volunteer work at the hospital. I may have graduated from college, and I may travel in more educated circles than my parents ever did, but my blue-collar upbringing has made me who I am.

Who I am in my real life, that is.

In any case, I am thrilled to see a familiar face at the party. "Alma," I hiss, catching her eye. She comes over to where I stand next to the dining room table, one hand on it for support.

"You okay, Señora Andersson? You enjoying *lo borlo*?"

I giggle. "I'm fine. I'm having a terrific time!"

"*No bronca*? No trouble, señora?"

I wave my arm about and almost knock over a tray of hors d'oeuvres on the table. Alma quickly reaches forward and catches it.

"I just have a . . . lil' . . . dilemma," I slur. "I cannot . . . for the life of me . . .'member where it . . . where it is." I look around. "The bathroom, I mean. Do you happen to know?"

Alma smiles. She has a kind face, Alma—a warm smile with large, white teeth. Like me, she gets crinkles around her eyes when she smiles, and I wonder vaguely if she is as self-conscious about that as I am. "*Sí*, señora. Follow me."

I follow her down the hallway. I hazily make out several large abstract paintings on the walls, lit with small artist's lamps bracketed above the canvases. There are a number of sleek doors with no panels on them, all of them shut. Closets, I suppose, and bedrooms. The woodwork is rich and dark-toned. At the third door on the right, Alma knocks gently. No one answers, so she opens it for me. "*Lo baño*," she says, as if to reassure me. "You are all right?"

"Sure, honey. Just dandy." I slip inside and close the door behind me.

After taking care of my business, I wash my hands and splash a little cold water on my face. I fish in my purse—it's quite a cute little thing, gold-sparkled, with a rhinestone clasp—and find a compact and lipstick. I powder my nose, notice the high flush in my cheeks, and carefully fill in my lips with lipstick that matches the color of my dress. I note that my hair looks unusually fabulous. The cowlicks have been tamed and pressed into big waves, held in place with lots of spray. I must have had it set this afternoon, I think, and then I thank the dream gods, or whoever puts me in this crazy world, for at least letting my hair look stunning when I am out of the house for the evening.

I stumble back to the darkened hallway and bump into a shadowy figure making its way toward me. "Lars?" I ask.

"Nope," says a cheery voice. "Just your friendly host, coming to check on you." He gets closer, and I see it is George, of the mustache and the spaniel.

"I'm fine, thanks," I say, but he blocks my way before I can sneak past him.

"Katharyn," he says in a low voice. "You look beautiful tonight." He places a hand lightly but persistently on my right hip.

Startled, I back away from his touch. "Yes, my husband said the same thing." That word, *husband*, feels peculiar on my lips; it's like speaking a foreign language. Yet I recognize the power in it. I am reminded of how satisfied I felt in high school Spanish class when, called upon to recite by Señora Torrez, I uttered some Spanish turn of phrase confidently, completely, and correctly.

George lowers his arm. "Oh, come on," he says. "I'm just paying you a compliment. Don't take it so seriously."

"George." A sharp voice rises behind him, and he steps aside. A woman in a slim-fitting dress, dark-colored with pinstripes, steps quickly down the hallway. "Katharyn, are you all right?"

"Of . . . yes, of course." Is this my hostess? Good grief, what a sticky situation.

"George, you go on back," she says. "We need more ice from the cooler on the patio."

He gives her a guilty look and slinks away.

The woman takes my arm. "Shameful," she says, shaking her head. "That husband of mine has an eye for pretty women, I'll tell you that. But you'd think, in his own house . . . and with what you've been through, too." She gives me a long, worried look. "Tell me, dear, how are you coping?"

How am I coping? Does she mean with being drunk? Good heavens, how mortifying.

"I . . . I'm just fine," I say. "Really. I probably just need some water."

Her look softens. "Of course. Let's go back to the kitchen and get you a nice tall glass of ice water." She takes my arm and steers me down the hall. "And Katharyn," she says, leaning toward me. "I can't thank you enough for lending me Alma. What a worker that girl is!"

I do not know Alma's exact age, but I would guess she is a good five or ten years my senior—and I would guess that I am at least that many years again older than my hostess. Thus I'm unsure how Alma could be considered a "girl." Nonetheless, I just smile and say, "Any time."

Not long afterward, the party breaks up. The hostess—whose name, maddeningly, I never did learn—rounds up ladies' boots and men's galoshes. The maids bring coats from the bedroom and hand them out; most people take them without a word. Alma hands me mine. "Why, thank you, Alma! *Muchas gracias!*" I tell her, probably a bit too loudly. People stare at me. I don't care.

The snow is swirling around us as Lars and I step down

the drive. "Easy, there," he says, holding my arm. "Perhaps we should have brought the car." He steers me into the street, and we shuffle through the snowpack. It is less than a block to our house. I cannot think of anything sillier than the idea of driving to this party.

At our door, Lars waits outside while I go in. The babysitter, who appears to be high school age, rises from the couch and walks over to the television. "Hi, Mrs. Andersson," she says, switching it off. Before she does, I catch a glimpse of Paul Newman and Joanne Woodward in a steamy embrace. I think the movie might be *The Long, Hot Summer,* a film adaptation of a Faulkner novel that was made some years ago. Must be *Saturday Night at the Movies*, a program with which I am unequivocally familiar in my real life. Most Saturday nights I am at home alone, watching whatever movie NBC is showing.

"How was your evening?" the girl asks me.

"Just fine." I am wondering why Lars does not come inside, and also whether I am expected to pay the girl. And if so, how much? I haven't a clue about such things.

"How was *your* evening?" I ask her. I glance out through the storm door and see that Lars is shoveling the front walk with rapid, efficient strokes.

"Everything went well. No problems." She smiles at me. "They really are good kids, you know," she says kindly.

Instead of reassuring me, this makes me wonder if other people think they really *aren't* good kids. And if so, why?

"Well." I slide out of my coat. "Thank you." Through the storm door, I can see that Lars has finished shoveling and is now motionless on the covered front step, staring out into the swirling snow. His shoulders rise and fall quickly with his breath, and I think anxiously about his heart. Again, I wonder why he doesn't come inside, and then I realize that he must be either walking or driving the babysitter home.

The sitter opens the coat closet and selects a brown girl's woolen jacket with SPARTANS stitched in gold felt letters across the back. Several small pins that look like they represent various sports and activities—softball, field hockey, cheerleading—decorate the left chest area of the jacket. On the right, TRISHA is embroidered in script of matching gold.

"Thank you, Trisha," I say. "Oh, and would you ask Mr. Andersson to pay you? I don't have enough in my wallet." Silently, I congratulate myself on this inspiration.

Trisha buttons up her coat and slips on her boots. "Sure thing, Mrs. Andersson. You have a nice night."

"You, too. Stay warm out there." I open the door for her, and she goes outside to where Lars is stamping the shovel against the concrete step to drive off the packed snow.

"I'll be back in ten," he says, leaning in to give me a quick kiss. I point at my purse and shake my head, and he nods in understanding. I marvel at this silent communication between us; if you didn't know any better, you might think we've been doing this for years. I watch as he ushers Trisha down the snowy walk.

After hanging my coat in the closet and taking off my boots, I weave toward the bedroom. The room is dimly lit by a small lamp on the dresser. To my surprise, Aslan is napping on the bed. The relief I feel at seeing him is enormous, as if I have been reunited with a dear friend after years and years of separation.

"My sweet kitty." I rush over, sit next to him, and stroke his soft yellow fur. He looks up at me with his big green eyes and purrs loudly.

I am still sitting there when I hear Lars come in. I stay where I am, contemplatively petting Aslan and listening as Lars goes up the half flight of stairs, opens one door briefly and then closes it, and then does the same with another. He comes back down. I hear water running in the kitchen, and then stopping. I can see into the hallway as one light after another is turned off, until the only illumination left in the house is the faint glow from the lamp on the dresser. It is into this light that Lars steps, meeting my eyes as I wait for him in our bedroom.

"You feeling any better?" he asks. He has a glass of water in his hand, and he walks over and gives it to me. "I thought you might need this."

"Thank you." I take the glass and drink it. I suddenly feel embarrassed by my wooziness, even if it is not real. "I'm sorry I drank so much."

He shrugs. "It's understandable, Katharyn."

I do not know how to answer that, so I remain silent. I watch as he loosens his tie and unbuttons his collar button, opens the closet door, and hangs up his jacket and the tie.

When he turns back to the room, I am looking at myself in the mirror over the dresser. "Lars," I say softly.

He sits beside me. "What is it?"

I touch my dress, still looking at my reflection. In the soft light, the dress's color is dazzling, like something an actress or a ballerina would wear on opening night.

"Do you know where I got this dress?" I ask.

He looks at me quizzically. "You got it at May-D&F," he says. "Where you buy most of your clothes."

I nod slowly. "And my hair?" I ask, touching the perfect curls. "Who does my hair? What beauty parlor do I go to?"

"Katharyn." He smiles, puzzled. "You go to Beauty on Broadway, of course. It's the beauty parlor where Linnea works. She's done your hair ever since we met."

"Linnea." I ponder for a moment. "Your sister, right?"

"Katharyn." He puts his arms around me. "You really did drink a lot, didn't you?"

I shake my head and laugh a little. "Well, I guess I did," I say. I squeeze him tightly and raise my chin, my lips open and ready for his kiss.

Chapter 10

Beauty on Broadway is not at all difficult to find. What is difficult is getting an appointment with Linnea Hershall. "I'm sorry, but Linnea is booked solid until a week from Thursday," the receptionist tells me on the telephone when I call to set up an appointment for a wash-and-set—profusely apologizing in my head to Veronica at Modern Hair, who I've been seeing regularly for at least a dozen years.

"Can I give you my number, in case Linnea has a cancellation?" I ask. "Really, I can come in any time." I pause. "She was highly recommended to me."

"Let me just check." The line goes dead, and I wait a few minutes, then the receptionist's voice returns. "Can you come in Tuesday afternoon at one thirty? I think she could squeeze you in, if it's quick."

I smile and raise my fist in a little gesture of triumph. "I can do that," I tell the girl, and give her my name.

While waiting for my hair appointment, a few days hence, I amuse myself by going downtown to May-D&F and heading straight for the formal-wear section. I look through every rack, but I do not see the coral-colored dress. "Can I help you find something?" a saleslady asks me.

"I'm looking for a dress that . . . a friend had on." I describe the dress, carefully noting its color as "coral, or maybe you'd call it more of a peach."

The saleswoman looks thoughtful. "Honestly, it doesn't sound familiar," she says. "Are you sure your friend purchased it here?"

"Well, that's what I was told."

"And when was this?"

It occurs to me that I have no idea when it was. Given the blinding snowstorm, it must still have been winter. But for the first time since the dreams started, I realize that they might not necessarily be taking place in 1962. It's obviously not now, not the first week in October. Denver does get snow in October sometimes, but not big storms like that—and not one storm after another, the way it is in the dreams. Our big storms, our snowiest days, tend to come toward the end of the winter season, February or March. So if the dreams are happening in the present day, why then, it's either a few months from now, or else it's last winter.

Then again, it could be an entirely different period altogether. It's a *dream*, for heaven's sake! It could be any time, or no time at all.

"You know," I say slowly. "Now that I think about it, maybe it wasn't May-D&F that she said carried it. Perhaps it was somewhere else."

"Well, we do have a gorgeous new line, just in time for holiday parties. Some of the first items have come in already, and we're expecting more very soon. If I could interest you in something else . . ."

"No." I shake my head. "Not right now, thanks." I turn toward the escalator. "Thank you for your time."

"Certainly. Come back in a few weeks, dear. All the Christmas and New Year's wear will be in by then."

Walking into Beauty on Broadway, I am as nervous as if I'm on a first date. The decor is mauve, with dark purple accents. The shop is large; I count eight hairdressing stations. Women are seated at most of the stations. There is a bank of hair dryers along the back wall, nearly all of them humming happily. A manicurist carefully applies polish to the nails of one of the hair-drying women; others under the dryers busy themselves with fashion magazines or the entertainment section from the newspaper.

The receptionist takes my name, leads me to an empty station, and walks away silently. I wait, looking at my reflection. The lights on either side of the mirror emphasize my pale skin. I pinch my cheeks, trying to bring some color to them. I should have put on more lipstick.

While I am agonizing over this, a middle-aged, brown-haired woman appears in the mirror, approaching me from behind. I put my heel down and spin the chair slightly so we are facing each other. She takes my hand. "I'm Linnea Hershall," she says, a slight lilt in her voice—the remnants, no doubt, of her girlhood Swedish accent. "You're Kitty, is that right?"

I nod, gulping and speechless. Up close, her resemblance to Lars is remarkable. She has the same striking blue eyes, the same wry smile, the same rounded nose. Tears spring to my eyes at the sight of her. I cannot believe that I am looking at a real flesh-and-blood relative of my dream man.

Seeing my distress, Linnea softens. "Let me guess," she says. "First time with a new hairdresser in entirely too many years." Her eyebrows rise, then lower. "Am I right?"

Despite myself, I smile. "Ummm . . . yes. That's right."

"Well, relax." She turns my chair so I am facing the mirror, and then lightly runs her fingers through my crazy cowlicked hair. "It's easy to get in what I call a 'hair rut.' And when you're in one, it's hard to make a change. It can be upsetting." She tilts her head, looking thoughtfully at my reflection. "My guess, however, is that you'd like a way to tame this unruly look and give it a bit more elegance."

I nod. "Please," I say. "That is exactly what I want."

And so I take a deep breath, trying to calm down and enjoy the experience for what it is. Even Linnea's hands remind me of Lars's: strong, capable, like you could put your whole life in them and nothing bad would ever come of it. I am halfway in love with her before she finishes my shampoo.

Back at her station, she pensively runs a comb through my hair, then rummages in a side cart for rollers. Eyeing my head critically, she tries first one size, and then another, finding just the right small curlers for some areas, the larger pink rollers for big waves on top. She dunks her fingers into a large vat of green Dippity-Do, smooths it into my hair, then expertly rolls each curler and pins it into place.

Once she appears at ease with her work, I open my mouth and venture a comment. "Linnea," I say hesitantly. "That's a pretty name. And unusual."

She looks up and smiles at me in the mirror. "It's Swedish," she explains. "I emigrated here from a small town not far from Borås, which itself is not so big; most Americans have not heard of it. I came here as a girl."

I clasp my hands together tightly to keep them from trembling. "That's a long way to move," I say finally. "Your family . . . they moved here with you?"

She nods, arranging a small blue curler around a wisp of my hair and attaching it with a roller clip. "My parents and my brother." She bites her lip. "They've all passed, however."

"Oh. I'm sorry." I can feel myself shaking. "How sad for you. Were they . . . ill?"

Linnea nods again. "My parents did not do well here," she says. "We started out in Iowa, where we had distant relatives. But it was the Depression, the work that was available was hard, and my mother's heart . . . well, her heart could not withstand it." She looks away, and then back at my hair. "More or less the same could be said of my father, I suppose."

It is hard for me to fathom. I cannot in my wildest imagination envision losing my parents. Perhaps it is because they are so young—my mother is not even sixty yet—but it's hard to picture my life without them. Even this two-month period in which they are so far away is proving much more difficult than I anticipated. The whole idea of them being thousands of miles from home is starting to wear on me. I think about the postcard I received from Mother this morning.

Kitty, my dear,

We are so far from home. Yesterday, I asked May how far it is from Honolulu to Denver, and she said over 3,000 miles. Think about that. The earth is about 25,000 miles around; so we are almost 1/8 of the earth's circumference from home.

Some mornings, I get up with the sun, face east, and think about you. By the time I do this, you are halfway through your morning, probably having coffee with Frieda in your lovely little bookshop.

Do you know how proud I am of you, darling Kitty?

Love,
Mother

Reading those words at home this morning, I had an almost uncontrollable urge to pick up the telephone and call, different time zones and overseas charges be damned. I just wanted to hear my mother's voice. I actually lifted the receiver and started to dial—but, knowing that it was several hours earlier there and they would still be asleep, I forced myself to hang up before I could complete the call.

Turning back to the conversation with Linnea, I am afraid of my next question. But it must be asked. Taking a deep breath, I ask, "And your brother? What happened to him?"

Linnea shakes her head. "Heart troubles again," she replies. "Very sad . . . he was young, only thirty-four."

"I'm so sorry," I whisper. "Linnea, I am so sorry."

She steps back and shakes her head as if to clear it. "Listen to me," she says, smiling. "Breaking the first two rules they teach you in beauty school. Rule number one: don't tell the customer about yourself until you've learned all there is to know about the customer. And rule number two: if you do talk about yourself, make sure you speak only of happy things."

I smile in return. "I'm sorry we got off on the wrong foot," I say. "So tell me some happy things about you."

She wags her finger at my reflection. "Oh, no, you don't, Kitty Miller," she says firmly. "Not until I learn all about you first."

And so I tell her. We talk about my parents, and I tell her about their big trip. She says it must be heaven for them, to be able to travel to an exotic place like Hawaii, and be able to visit family and have a free place to stay. Thinking of my mother's words, I just smile and nod.

Linnea says she has always dreamed of traveling, but with raising two children, buying a house, and paying their bills, the best she and her husband managed through the years was an occasional auto trip. The children, Joe and Gloria, are now twenty and sixteen. "Joe is at the university up in Boulder." Linnea shrugs. "Nice up there, I guess. Pretty campus. I hope he's learning something, is all I am thinking." She shakes her head. "And that Gloria. Goodness, between school, friends, clubs, boys— that girl is busy. Runs around like a chicken with its feathers cut off."

I look at her quizzically in the mirror.

"Did I say that wrong?" She shrugs again. "You know, I've been in this country and speaking English for close to thirty years, and I still do not get the expressions right."

I smile and laugh, and she laughs with me. I love Linnea's laugh. It sounds just like a female version of Lars's.

I tell her about the bookstore, about Frieda and how we got started in it after being disenchanted with our original career plans. "What a marvelous thing," Linnea says. "Following your hearts that way. Tell me, what sorts of books do you carry?"

"All sorts." I reach into the pocket of my slacks for a Sisters' Bookshop business card. "Fiction, travel, history, poetry, art."

"Classics?" Linnea asks, taking the business card from my hand. "I love the classics."

"Do you?" I smile. "Who is your favorite author?"

"Oh." Linnea waves her hand, the one that is not holding my card. "It's difficult to pick one favorite. Shakespeare, perhaps. I love reading Shakespearean sonnets, and some of the plays, though others are quite so sad. I'm a great admirer of Henry James; I loved *The Portrait of a Lady*. Of more recent authors, I suppose John Steinbeck is my favorite. I just now finished reading *The Winter of Our Discontent*. This is a book that I know a lot of readers did not care for, and I understand; it's not a happy story. But I think it shows the disappointing side of American life." She furrows her brow. "Maybe Americans do not want to read about that," she says thoughtfully.

I nod. I had the same impression of *The Winter of Our Discontent*, which I read last year when it came out. After reading several reviews that proclaimed that Steinbeck's barefaced morality was putting him on the downward slope of his career, I wondered the same thing as Linnea: is it the author's moral high ground that we find disagreeable—or is it that he is spot-on, but the theme of his new novel makes us uncomfortable?

"I learned English by reading," Linnea tells me. "It's the best way, really."

"Well, we have plenty of Shakespeare, plenty of James, and plenty of Steinbeck," I say. "Anything else you want, too. And anything we don't carry in the store, we can order for you. You ought to come by sometime." I hear the pleading in my voice, and I pray that Linnea is too engrossed in her work to notice it herself. "It would be my pleasure to show you around."

She places the Sisters' business card carefully on her side table. "I'll do that," she promises. "I'll bring Gloria. She, too, loves to read." Linnea steps back, eyeing my curler-covered head, nodding her approval. "All right, then, Kitty, I think you're ready for a dryer."

Back at Sisters', Frieda exclaims over my new look. "It's stunning," she says, staring at me. "Honestly, Kitty, I have never seen you look so good." She fishes under the counter for her purse and pulls out a compact, dusting her nose. "You make me want to freshen up," she explains, grinning apologetically. Closing the compact with a firm click, she says, "Haven't I told you for years to get rid of that Veronica and go see someone new for your hair?"

"You have." I am looking at my reflection in the mirror over the counter. I cannot stop staring at myself. I look exactly like I did in the dream. Except a lot more sober, and with much less ritzy clothes on.

"Oh, I almost forgot to tell you." Frieda comes from behind the counter and bends down to retrieve a book that has fallen over on the Classics shelf—*The Canterbury Tales* by Chaucer, a substantial volume if there ever was one. The *Tales* should, by all means, be expected to hold themselves up. That cheeky old Wife of Bath is probably to blame.

Frieda uses both hands to adjust the book. I think about Linnea and wonder, since she likes Shakespeare, if she has read Chaucer. I make a mental note to go through the stacks and put aside a selection of books for her—Chaucer and maybe Edmund Spenser if she likes classics, Joseph Conrad, perhaps George Bernard Shaw, if she enjoys turn-of-the-century writing, and possibly some contemporary female authors like Katherine Anne Porter and Flannery O'Connor, since it appears Linnea has primarily read works by men.

"That Hansen kid came by," Frieda says. "The one that lives next door to you. Said to tell you thanks again, said he 'just keeps reading it over and over.' Said he can't wait to read more." She stands back, waiting to see if the Chaucer will fall again, but it appears to be grounded now. Frieda turns to me. "What's *that* all about?"

Chapter 11

Mama."

I open my eyes and look around. Everything is so blurry.

"Mama, can you hear me? Are you all right?"

There is a small pat on my right sleeve. I concentrate, and Missy's face comes into focus. She is looking at me with trepidation. Her look reminds me of an actor I once saw playing a psychiatrist on television. In that story, the patient was a woman who had stumbled on the sidewalk and hit her head on a stone wall; she lost her memory entirely and could not even recall her own name. In the scene I am now thinking about, the doctor was looking at the patient as if he felt not only concerned about her situation, but also overwhelmingly sorry for her.

Missy is giving me the exact same look. Her strawberry blond curls are in pigtails on either side of her head, tied with red bows that match her plaid dress. Her little brow is furrowed, making her appear much older than the age she is—which, I realize with alarm, I still don't actually *know*. I have assumed the children to be about five or six, but I have no idea of their exact age, or when their birthday is. Moreover, I still assume that they are twins— nothing so far has led me to believe otherwise—but I don't know that with any certainty. What a preposterous imagination I have. To keep dreaming about an entire made-up family, one's *own* entirely made-up family, and not even know the children's ages, birth dates, or birth order.

"I'm . . . I'm fine, sweetie." I look around. My vision has cleared up, and I can now see that we are in the shoe department of a large store. It is not a store with which I am familiar. I do most of my shopping at Monkey Wards on Broadway or May-D&F downtown, the store where I went in real life to seek out the coral-hued dress. This store looks a bit like May-D&F, but not like any part of May-D&F that I've ever been in. I can tell by the vivid yellow, red, and blue display racks, the carefully arranged patent leathers, tennis shoes, and rubber boots, that we are in a department that carries only children's shoes. In all my years of shopping at May-D&F, I don't think I have once set foot in the children's shoe department—but I do know where it is, on the second floor, near the better dresses and coats. I see neither of those departments anywhere nearby, which leads me to believe we are in a different store entirely.

A salesman briskly approaches us, his arms loaded with brightly colored cardboard boxes. RICHARD, his nametag reads, and above that I see the familiar blue May-D&F logo, with its tiny sketch of the downtown store's iconic triangular roof standing in for the hyphen. So this *is* a May-D&F store—but unless they've rearranged recently, I don't believe we're downtown. I wonder exactly where we are, but of course there's no way to ask without sounding absurd.

"I've brought several styles for each of the children," Richard informs me, and for the first time I look to my left and notice that Mitch is seated there, quietly swinging his stockinged feet and glancing around the store. "You've come at the right time for school shoes. Most of last fall's styles are on clearance, and our spring shoes are not in yet. So you'll find some excellent values, ma'am."

I smile. "Well, there's no telling when children will outgrow their shoes and need a new pair." This statement—as is the case with so much of what I say in these dreams—falls into the "How on God's green earth do I know a thing like that?" category.

"First, for the young lady . . ." Richard opens a box and pulls out a pair of brown Mary Janes. Charming and delicate as Cinderella being presented with the glass slipper, Missy lifts a foot. The salesman slips on the shoe and buckles it across her instep. Missy has lovely, dainty feet, similar to my own. My feet have always been a source of pride; they're one of my best features. Judging by the graceful fit of the shoes, my imaginary daughter will likely follow suit.

Richard pinches Missy's toes through the shoe. I wonder why he is doing that; no one does a thing like that when you buy adult shoes. I realize he must be checking the fit. "How do they feel, honey?" I ask her as he adjusts the second shoe on her other foot.

"Nice," she says, standing. "Comfortable."

"Take a walk," Richard suggests.

Missy walks from one end of the shoe department to the other. "I also have those in black, if you prefer," Richard tells me.

I shake my head. "No, the brown is fine."

Missy returns and sits next to me. "They're good," she says. "But can I try the others, just in case?"

I smile. That is exactly what I do when I shop. Even if I am satisfied with the first thing I try on, I always have to try all my selections, just in case something else turns out to be more to my liking.

After trying two more pairs, Missy goes back to the brown Mary Janes. Just what I would have done, I think, nodding my approval.

Once Missy is outfitted, Richard and I turn to Mitch. He tries on several pairs of lace-up shoes, all of which he says are uncomfortable. I look at his eyes as he uneasily watches Richard lace one pair after another onto his feet.

"Mitch," I say, scanning the displays in front of us. "How about a pair of loafers?" I smile at him. "They would just slip on your foot. They'd not need to be tied."

Relief is visible on his face. "That would be perfect, Mama."

This parenting thing isn't so hard, I tell myself. I could do this, if I had to do it all the time. All you need is a little intuition, and the wherewithal to pay attention to the details.

"Betty at the counter will ring you up," Richard says when we are through. He stands and picks up the discarded boxes. "Lovely children, madam. You must be proud of them."

I smile. "Indeed I am."

And it's true. I *am*—totally and irrationally—quite proud of these two imaginary little people.

I fish in my handbag and find a checkbook with both "Lars K. Andersson" and "Mrs. Katharyn Andersson" printed in the top-left corner of each check. Writing a check to May-D&F for the shoes, I realize I have no idea what the date is; I scribble some illegible numbers on that line.

I tear the check from the book and give it to Betty, the sales-girl at the counter. "You don't want to use your account, Mrs. Andersson?" she asks me as she takes the check.

"My account?"

"Yes—your charge account."

"Oh." I can feel my face turn slightly red. Of course I would have a charge account here. "No, not today." I smile sweetly at her as she hands me the receipt.

Mitch tugs at my coat sleeve as I'm placing the checkbook back in my purse. "Were we good?" he asks me.

"Excuse me?"

"Were we good? Missy and me, were we good?"

"Of course you were good." I smile down at him, thinking about what the babysitter said in my last dream. *They really are good kids, you know.* Of course they are; isn't it obvious? So what in heaven's name was she talking about?

Mitch hops up and down excitedly. "Yippee!" he says. "Then we can go, can't we?"

I have no idea what he means, so I just shake my head in confusion.

"To Bluebell Toys," Missy explains. "Don't you remember, Mama? You promised that if we were good while we got our shoes, we could go to Bluebell Toys and . . . well, you know. Look around."

I promised that? Did I promise to buy them something? Do they get a toy for being good on an errand like this? I have no idea what the protocol is. I wish Lars was here to help me navigate these peculiar waters.

"Well, so I did," I say. "Lead the way, children."

We take the escalator down. I scan the first floor as we descend, my eyes instinctively seeking out a book section. The May-D&F downtown has a rather substantial book department. They host visiting authors and book-signing events—something Frieda and I would love to do, but it is impossible to get any writer with a national or even regional reputation to visit our small shop; we have tried, and always come up short in our appeals to the authors' publicists. It's discouraging. In many ways, the book departments at the big stores—those, and the drugstores that peddle dime paperbacks—are more our competition than other small bookshops.

The children and I get off the escalator, then walk toward a large doorway, which evidently leads outside to the smaller stores in the shopping center. This whole shopping center experience is foreign to me; I don't shop this way in my real life.

Right before we reach the door, Missy points toward the women's formal wear section. "Look, Mama, there's your dress," she says. "The one you wore the other night." She smiles. "Well, not *your* dress exactly," she explains. "Yours is at home, of course, in your closet. But it's the same dress as yours."

She's right. There, on the racks, is the coral dress that I couldn't find at the May-D&F downtown the other day. It's undeniably the exact same dress—although I can't help noticing that it's on a clearance rack.

"Do you remember when I bought that dress?" I ask Missy.

"Sure," she replies. "Just after Thanksgiving. You wore it to Daddy's office Christmas party. And then you wore it the other night to the party at the Nelsons' house."

I nod, thinking that over. The dress must be part of the holiday line of formal wear that the saleslady downtown mentioned. If it's on clearance now, that means that in this dream world we've moved into the future, as I suspected.

How far into the future? I wonder. Are we only into 1963, just a few months from now? Or have we moved even further beyond that?

"Here's a quiz for you," I say to the children as we go outside. The air is cold, but the bright sunlight warms our faces. "Can you tell me who's the president of the United States?"

Both Mitch and Missy burst into peals of laughter. "Of course we can, Mama," Mitch replies. "It's Mr. Kennedy. And Mr. and Mrs. Kennedy have a little girl. And a baby boy too."

"And you're always saying that all you want in life is to be as fashionable as Mrs. Kennedy," Missy adds, enthusiasm pumped into her breathless words like water pouring from a broken faucet.

I shake my head, realizing how absurd it is to quiz the children in this manner. The name of the president proves nothing.

It could be 1963—or 1965, or even 1968. Despite everyone's concerns over Cuba and those appalling Communists, I have no doubt that Jack Kennedy will be reelected in 1964. No one doubts that. So this could be any year in which he is still president.

I ought to have just asked Mitch and Missy straight out what year it is. But that seems too harebrained a question to ask. They might think I'm more loopy than they already do.

We walk along the concrete pathway of the shopping center. Music is piped in from somewhere above us; I think it is that song about the flowers and girls and soldiers, that song Pete Seeger wrote and several artists have recorded. It is pleasant and lyrical, and even on this slightly chilly day it puts you in the mood for strolling and browsing—and with any luck buying, as no doubt the merchants desire. I wonder if Frieda and I ought to consider playing some soft background music in our bookstore. Would that make customers more apt to browse, and consequentially to buy?

The children eagerly lead me along the wide boulevard. Large juniper bushes in beige stone planters are positioned every few feet. Women chat animatedly with each other as they gaze into the sparkling storefront windows. Children run screeching down the broad passageway, only to be sharply reprimanded and drawn back by their mothers. I see very few men walking about. Clearly, this is a women's world.

I can see now what Frieda is talking about when she brings up closing our Pearl Street shop and moving to a shopping center like this. We are in the wrong place. That world—the streetcar world in which she and I grew up—it's gone now. This is the new world—this bright, clean shopping center with its fresh stores and gleaming walkways. Perhaps Frieda is right. Perhaps if we want to survive, this is where we are meant to be.

"Here it is!" Mitch and Missy gape at a brilliantly lit sign: BLUEBELL TOYS, in large, cobalt letters. Below the sign, a double doorway, opened wide despite the slight nip in the air, leads to lavish, irresistible displays of playthings. The displays are placed just inside the doorway; it almost seems that they are alive, with long arms reaching out to smoothly pull the children inside.

"Come on, Mama!" Mitch and Missy tug impatiently on my hands, and we step into the store.

Bluebell Toys is a child's paradise. Board games, baby dolls, pop guns, and all manner of dress-up clothes, from princess costumes to Western wear. Mitch heads straight for the cars and trucks section, and begins zooming a large metal dump truck across the carpeting. Missy dreamily enters the Barbie doll aisle, studying the racks of clothes designed especially for the fashionable plastic teen. I can see both children from the front entrance, so I stay where I am, looking over the store's minuscule book section. These are all the books they carry? I didn't see a book department at May-D&F, though there may have been one on an upper floor. I wonder if there is another bookstore in the shopping center, with a bigger selection for both children and adults.

I am about to ask the checkout girl this very question when a voice behind me loudly proclaims, "Katharyn! Fancy meeting you here!"

Turning, I am confronted by my hostess from the snow-blown cocktail party of my last dream. Instead of the pin-striped satin dress, today she is modestly attired in a brown coat and a burgundy silk scarf. She wears a pair of glasses on a chain around her neck. This makes her look older—although, as I noted at her party, I actually suspect she is a good ten years younger than I. Holding her hand is a small boy—bigger than a baby, but not as old as my children.

"Hello." Of course, I still don't know her name. I catch Missy's eye and motion her toward us. Maybe she can rescue me.

Missy skips over obligingly. "Hi, Mrs. Nelson." She bends down to greet the toddler. "And hi there, Kenny. How are you today?" She reaches toward the little guy and pinches his cheek, the way a grandmother might. Gracious, this girl is an old soul if I ever saw one. She reminds me so much of myself as a child, I cannot contain my emotions. I want to hug her, hold on to her forever. I have to resist an impulse to bend down, grab her around the waist, and bury my face in her hair.

Watching her, I am struck by a thought. I would give anything—anything in the world—for this child of my heart to be real. To be real, and to be mine.

Missy's calling the woman Mrs. Nelson, however, is of absolutely no help. Mrs. Nelson and I are neighbors and adults—and, as an aside, her husband made a pass at me the other evening in their dimly lit hallway. Of course we'd be on a first-name basis. But Missy, being a child, and a polite one at that, would naturally address this woman by her surname. How exasperating.

"Shopping or just browsing?" Mrs. Nelson asks me. Missy looks up expectantly, waiting for my response.

I don't have to think about that for long. Suddenly I don't care what Lars would think, or what the protocol is. These are good children, and they deserve a treat.

"Shopping," I answer firmly. "Missy, go pick out one of those Barbie outfits for yourself. And tell Mitch that he can get a car or truck. Nothing over three dollars." I have no idea what three dollars buys in the way of toy trucks, but it seems like it ought to be enough to get something significant.

"Special occasion?" Mrs. Nelson asks, as Missy skips off. "It's not their birthday, is it?"

Aha. So they *are* twins, just as I'd suspected.

I shrug. "No special occasion," I reply. "Sometimes you just need to spoil them a little . . . right?" I say this last weakly, my resolve flushed away by my inexperience, like so much trash in a rainy gutter. Maybe I am taking a huge misstep here.

Mrs. Nelson raises her eyebrows. "Well, under the circumstances, I'd certainly agree." She places her hand on my arm. "You know, Katharyn," she goes on, her voice lowered. "I must mention, I saw your Lars taking the children over to the golf course on Sunday afternoon, the day after our party. All bundled up and with their sleds dragging behind them. Delightful. And I didn't see them return for a good two hours. Now, I know Kenny here isn't much more than a baby . . ." She looks down at him affectionately; he tries to pull away from her, but she tightens her grip. "But even so, I cannot imagine George taking over Kenny's care for a *whole* afternoon that way." She shrugs. "It just wouldn't happen, you see, not in my house."

Kenny starts to whine, and Mrs. Nelson reaches down to hoist him to her hip. "Your Lars is a good man," she tells me—as if I didn't already know this. "You got a good one, Katharyn. They aren't—" Kenny's wails become louder; he clearly wants to run around the store with the bigger kids. Mrs. Nelson sets him down again. "The husbands aren't all like yours," she finishes. "You're very lucky, you know."

"Lucky." Yes, I suppose I am. Or I would be, if any of this were real.

"Oh!" Mrs. Nelson puts her hand to her mouth. "Oh, I didn't mean . . ." Her face turns red. "I'm sorry. It wasn't kind of me to say that."

Wasn't it? It sounded kind to me.

"I mean, after . . . everything." She shrugs, and I can see that she feels she's backed herself into a corner, though I have no idea why. "I just meant that Lars is a good man, a good father," she says hastily. "I know that we all—every one of us—we all have some things to be thankful for, and some things . . . some things . . ."

Young Kenny saves her from further embarrassment. He starts crying so loudly that neither of us would be able to continue our conversation even if we wanted to. "I'd better take him out of here," Mrs. Nelson says, picking him up. "This boy needs an early dinner and an early bedtime."

"Yes." I nod. "I understand."

"I'm sure you do. Look at me, with just the one. I cannot imagine what the toddler years must have been like in your house!" Mrs. Nelson lifts her fingers in a small wave. "Bye, now, Katharyn. You enjoy the rest of your day." She is gone before I can say anything else.

After we have purchased their selections—I can tell that Mitch and Missy think they've hit some sort of jackpot, getting a new toy for no reason—we walk back along the concrete pathway toward the parking lot. I look around. Suddenly I know where we are. This is the University Hills Shopping Center, out on Colorado Boulevard, on the east side of town. This shopping center has been in operation for a decade or so, but May-D&F only opened their store here a few years ago. I have been here once or twice, but honestly, for me it's easier to take the bus downtown or walk over to Broadway. This place is only convenient if you have a car.

Which, in this life, surely I must. "Do you two remember where we parked?" I ask Mitch and Missy. The sun has disappeared behind a cloud, and I lean down to button her coat, to adjust his woolen cap more tightly on his head against the wind.

"Silly Mama." They swing their toy-shop bags happily, and with their free hands each take one of mine. Balancing the shopping bag with the shoe boxes in it over one arm, I let them lead me to a dark green Chevrolet station wagon with wood-paneled doors.

"I call front seat!" Mitch yells. He opens the passenger-side front door and scrambles happily onto the brown vinyl seat. Missy whines that it isn't fair. I shoot her an ominous look, and she grudgingly opens the rear door and slides in, opening her bag to inspect the evening gown she's chosen for Barbie.

After finding keys in my purse, I get into the driver's seat. It feels odd to sit there. I haven't driven a car in years, not since Kevin and I were together; he used to loan me his car occasionally, if he didn't need it. Praying that I will remember how to shift the gears and simultaneously operate the clutch, I turn the key in the ignition.

I am going along just fine, making my way across the parking lot, when a wave of panic hits me. I punch my foot down hard on the brake. In doing so, I forget all about the clutch, and the car stalls.

"Mama!" Both children are hurtled forward, and I instinctively reach my arm across the front seat to prevent Mitch's forehead from hitting the dash.

"Are you all right?" I ask them. "I'm sorry . . . I didn't mean to stop suddenly like that. It's just . . . it's just . . ."

And then I don't know what to say. They wait, eyes large and questioning.

"It's just . . ." I continue weakly. "All of a sudden . . . I just can't remember . . . where is Michael? Why isn't he with us?"

Michael? Who is Michael? What am I talking about?

Missy shakes her head. "Silly, silly Mama," she says, reaching forward and affectionately patting my shoulder. "Did you really forget? Daddy came home from work early today, so you could take Mitch and me shoe shopping." She releases my shoulder and leans back in her seat. "Everything is fine, Mama," she reassures me gently. "Michael is safe at home, with Daddy."

Chapter 12

Heavens, how disturbing," I tell Aslan when I awake. "It's nice to be back here, where everything makes sense." Aslan looks at me blankly, then stands, turns twice, and settles back into the covers, purring loudly.

It's raining lightly but steadily. A rainy morning in Denver generally means it will rain all day. More common here are abrupt afternoon thunderstorms, especially in the summer and early autumn, but those are sudden and violent—brief downpours that sluice off the rooftops in buckets and occasionally cause the South Platte River and some of the neighborhood gulches to flood. A gentle, all-day rain is a rarity here. We get so few of those days, I actually find them to be a bit of a treat.

I get up and pull on my cotton robe, which is quite a bit more threadbare than the blue quilted number of the dreams. But it is also more colorful, bright purple with a fuchsia cherry-blossom pattern all over it. In the bathroom, I untie the kerchief I've been wearing over my head at night to protect Linnea's exceptional work. It's only been a few days since my wash-and-set, but I plan to call and make another appointment soon. I am beyond a doubt going back. I am a Linnea Andersson Hershall convert.

Going out to get the mail, I am saddened to find there is no postcard from Mother. I fetch my damp *Rocky Mountain News* from the welcome mat and shuffle through it as I step back inside. I have taken to reading the sports page before anything else. Greg was right; the Giants did win the pennant, beating the Los Angeles Dodgers last night with four runs in the ninth inning. The World Series, which will pit the Giants against the New York Yankees, starts immediately. This surprises me. I would have thought they'd give the players some time to rest first. But what do I know of sports? I've learned more about baseball in the past few weeks of talking to Greg than I've ever known before in my life.

Going into my kitchen to make breakfast, I think dreamily about the stories I can write for Greg, once the World Series is under way. Mitch, Missy—and the mysterious Michael, whoever he is—are erased from my mind.

At the shop entrance, I shake out my umbrella. Once inside, I take off my slicker and rain bonnet and hang them in the back room. Glancing in the mirror above the restroom sink, I admire my hair once more. I brush a bit of rainwater from the hem of my indigo-blue skirt, which I have paired with my favorite chartreuse sweater and a long string of blue and yellow glass beads; a bright outfit to cheer up a damp day.

Frieda is at the counter, drinking coffee and smoking. I wave my hand in front of her. "I really wish you wouldn't smoke in the shop."

She inhales, then puffs out. "And a good morning to you, too."

"Honestly." I pour myself a cup of coffee, deliberately place my stool beyond the reach of her fumes, and sit down. "It turns away customers, Frieda."

She lets out a laugh. "Since when?"

"Since always." I don't know why I'm picking a fight with her. I just feel irritable. And uneasy.

Frieda has the newspaper spread in front of her on the counter. She is scanning the help-wanted section. "Looking for a job?" I ask, glad for an excuse to change the subject.

She shakes her head. "Looking for inspiration." She glances around. "We have to do something, Kitty. We barely made the rent this month; I don't see how we're going to make it in November. And if we're not staying, we ought to tell Bradley immediately."

She's right. We did make the October rent, but we had to scrape to do it. Frieda says we will have to delay our loan payment this month, hoping to see a little capital come in before the loan is past due on the fifteenth. But I'm glad we at least paid Bradley. I always feel bad when we are late on our payment to Bradley.

Even so—even though we sometimes pay late and a few times we did not pay at all—I know Bradley would be disappointed to lose us. Chances are, another tenant would not come along easily, not with the lack of business on Pearl Street these days.

"Maybe we can negotiate a lower rent," I suggest. "That would be better for Bradley than having us leave, wouldn't it?"

Frieda shrugs. "I don't know," she says snappily. "And anyway, what good would that do?" She looks around again. "How long can we stay here, anyway, with no business? Ask yourself that, Kitty."

I think about University Hills, the shopping center in my dream. Except, of course, it is not made up. That shopping center actually exists. "Have you ever been to University Hills?" I ask Frieda. "The shopping center way down south, on Colorado Boulevard?"

"Once," she says, stubbing out her cigarette. "It seems so far out of town." She looks thoughtful. "But everything is far out of town, these days, isn't it?"

I nod. "May-D&F has a store there, and they probably carry books. But I wonder if there is any other bookstore in the shopping center."

Frieda looks at me carefully. "Would you even consider it?" she asks. "You've shot down the idea of moving to a shopping center—you've shot it down numerous times, Kitty." She stands and looks out at the rain. "Why the change of heart?"

I shrug. "Things are changing, aren't they?" I ask her quietly. "The world is changing." I step closer to Frieda, feeling the heat of her body next to mine, smelling her smoke-and-perfume scent. Stinky, but familiar. "We have to keep up," I say. "Or else get out of the way and let someone else pass us by."

That afternoon, Frieda and I close early and take a little excursion to University Hills. We have to ride two buses to get there, and it's still raining, so we are both soaked by the time we arrive. Stepping off the bus, we scan the large parking lot. "All these cars," Frieda says, shaking her head in wonder. "Where do they come from?"

I point to the west, the south, where new neighborhoods and houses are cropping up like dandelions in a garden plot. "Out there," I say. "You wouldn't believe it if you saw it."

Frieda glances at me. "Have *you* seen it?"

I nod, hoping she won't ask more. The rain is letting up, and the sun is starting to poke through. We turn and begin walking along the pathway. The shopping center is exactly as I remember it from my dream. The outsize concrete planters, the piped-in music. The strolling mothers and children. I half expect to see my own self, with Mitch and Missy in tow, walking toward us.

There's a shopping center directory posted next to one of the planters, and Frieda and I scan the listings, looking for a bookstore. We find none. "Let's see if there are any available spaces," Frieda suggests, almost in a whisper.

As we walk along, she suddenly takes my hand. "Kitty," she says. "Thank you for doing this with me."

I shrug. "I know it's what you want." I gently squeeze her hand. "And we're just looking, right? Don't get your hopes up."

Frieda nods slowly, but I see the sparkle in her eyes. "Just looking," she says dreamily. "We're just looking."

Chapter 13

I wake up alone in the sage-green bedroom. Lars's side of the bed is empty, the covers rumpled. Putting my hand out and feeling the warmth under the sheet where he was lying, I guess that he arose not long ago. I leave my hand there for what seems like a long time.

After rising and putting on my robe, I enter the hall and turn into the living room. To my left, I can see the dining room. It isn't a separate room but rather an extension of the living room, the way it was at the Nelsons' house and the way it so often is in these modern houses. Both the living and dining rooms have pale, faintly golden-hued walls and coved ceilings. The low-pile aqua carpeting matches the color of the front door, I note with self-approval. The dining room features a lustrous oak table; six chairs surround it, upholstered in nubby turquoise fabric. Near the head of the table, under the window, is a small wooden school desk, not unlike those that filled the classroom back in my teaching days. There is a faintly sour smell in the air, but I cannot make out what it is.

Along the back wall of the dining room are several sets of dark wood, shutter-style doors; two are cabinet-height with a counter jutting out below them, and the other is a saloon-style doorway, leading, presumably, to the kitchen. The cabinet-height shutters are closed, but I can see that when opened, they would provide access from the kitchen to the dining room. Quite handy, I think, should the cook be preparing a meal in one room and serving it in the other.

From behind the shutters, I hear a man's cheery whistle—off-key, just like Frieda's. The thought makes me smile. I cross the room and push through the swinging doorway. Lars is there, with all his brightness and his blue eyes. I walk quickly to him and embrace him, my body pressed against his. "Well, hello, there, beautiful," he whispers. "Feeling better this morning?"

"Feeling just fine." I tilt my head up to receive his kiss. It's a long, lingering, full-mouth kiss, one that I don't want to end. I can tell that Lars doesn't, either; it's with reluctance that he finally draws his lips away from mine.

"Wow," he says breathlessly. "That was quite a welcome."

"I just missed you," I replied. "I just . . . wanted to . . . feel you." I give him another squeeze. "Feel how real you are."

He laughs. "I'm real, all right." He turns back to the countertop and lifts an olive green electric percolator. "Ready for coffee, love?"

"Yes, please." While he pours it, I look around the kitchen. The countertops are orange Formica; the stove and refrigerator are both beige. A window over the sink lets in morning light; on its sill is a large mason jar, half filled with coins. The curtain over the window exactly matches the wallpaper; both show a cheery pattern of fruit slices—bananas, apples, oranges, limes—on a taupe background. The cabinetry is dark brown, very simple, with sleek brass handles and no ornamentation on the wood. My first thought is how easy it must be to keep it clean. I am forever scrubbing the ornate trim on the kitchen cabinets in my Washington Street duplex, and no matter how I try, I can never get the decades-old gunk out of the crevices.

I wander back through the swinging doors, cross the dining room, and enter the living room. My eyes are drawn to the large picture window that faces the street, and I step over to take a look outside. It's a bright, wintry morning. Why is it winter here and autumn in the real world? I cannot reconcile this. The clean white snow against the dark of the leafless trees, the startling blue of the sky, the mountains in the distance, and the long, lean houses—all together, they make me take a deep breath, relishing their freshness.

"Here's your coffee." Lars comes up behind me and hands me a warm cup. I wrap my hands around it. "See anything new and exciting?"

I shake my head, sipping the coffee. "It's pretty, though."

He puts his arm around my waist. "Sure is. I love this view."

I laugh. "Of the neighbors' houses?"

He shakes his head. "Of potential," he says. "Of the future." Squeezing my shoulder, he goes back to the kitchen.

Just as I am wondering why Lars is making breakfast instead of me—isn't that the wife's job?—I am attacked.

"Mamamamamamamamamamamama!" I manage to hang on to my mug, but the hot coffee goes flying. It does not land on my attacker or me, thank goodness, but it splashes all over the picture window and the carpeting.

I turn to see a small, bespectacled boy with an enormous grin on his face. But there's something off about his smile, and with a start I realize what it is: although he is beaming, he's not looking directly at me. He is looking sideways through his thick lenses—at the couch, the coffee table, perhaps the floor.

At nothing.

"Jesus Christ!" I yell at him. "What do you think you're doing?"

And then a noise arises from the boy that doesn't even sound human. It's the shriek of an animal in pain—one caught in a trap, perhaps, about to be devoured by a predator and fully aware of its fate. I've seen some disturbing fits by children, in restaurants and the like, but never in my life have I heard a child scream like this. I stagger backward and stare at him.

Lars rushes in from the kitchen. Simultaneously Mitch and Missy arrive, tumbling down the stairs and into the living room.

Lars firmly takes the screaming child by his shoulders. He holds him tightly, but I notice he does not actually hug the boy, nor move in any closer than arm's length. Instead, he starts softly repeating, "Go to the river, go down to the river, go to the river, go down to the river . . ."

I step back, transfixed. Mitch quietly walks over and stands next to me. "Is he always like that?" I whisper to Mitch.

He nods, and we both continue to stare. Finally, after what seems like an eternity, but is likely only a few minutes, the screaming subsides into whimpers. And then there is silence.

Lars slowly releases the child's shoulders. "Mitch," he says, turning toward the other two children. "Why don't you and Missy take Michael back upstairs?" He presses his lips together. "I'll have breakfast ready in just a few minutes."

One on each side of him, like pint-size, protective parents, Missy and Mitch walk the third child across the room. Their hair color is identical; their three heads are at exactly the same height. I watch as they quietly climb the stairs.

Lars stares at me without speaking. His blue eyes are narrowed; for the first time ever in this world, I see a blaze of anger in them. The eyes that focus on mine are unblinking, and I realize, quite abruptly, that Lars's fury is not aimed at the child who has just left the room.

It is aimed at me.

"Katharyn," he says finally. "What the hell is the matter with you?"

Chapter 14

And again, before I can react—it's over. I am back in my apartment.

It's dark and silent when I awake. I look at the little green-lit alarm clock beside my bed. Four in the morning. Aslan purrs contentedly beside me.

I turn over, adjust the covers, and tell myself to go back to sleep. "Just a silly dream," I murmur to Aslan. "These are just dreams. They don't mean anything."

But they are so *real*. I feel like I truly experience everything in that world. I know precisely how snug the quilted robe felt, wrapped around my body. I can recall the touch of Lars's kiss, the warmth and softness of his mouth on mine. The snow on the ground outside the window—I see it in my mind's eye. I can still taste the coffee in my mouth.

I can see those three children.

The two delightful ones. And the frightening one.

I shake my head in the darkness. That's not fair, I tell myself. You have no idea why that child acted that way. True, something was off with him. Something was not right in that boy's head. You could tell by looking at him, by how his eyes did not meet yours. By how he seemed to lean to one side, as if he were having trouble holding himself up.

And that scream. I have never heard anything like that scream.

But the child—like Lars, like Mitch and Missy—is a figment of my imagination. All of this is nothing but my head playing tricks on me. If I had even the slightest doubt of that before, I have absolutely none now.

Because what mother could completely fail to remember her own child? What kind of mother would I be—if I actually was a mother, and that world was real—if I had somehow forgotten that Michael even existed?

It does not occur to me to question whether Michael is my child. I know—have always known, since the dreams started—that in the imaginary world, Mitch and Missy are mine. And I know now that Michael is, too. I don't know how I know these things, but I do. In that world, that world that doesn't exist, those three children are mine. Lars's and mine. And they are all the same age; they are triplets. I am certain of it.

I put my hand out and stroke Aslan's warm fur. I feel his solid weight under my hand. I ground myself in his simple authenticity.

I must put that other world to rest. I must sleep it off.

I close my eyes and fall into slumber, deep and blackened.

Later at the shop, I am paging through the newspaper while Frieda runs errands at lunchtime. Skimming past the latest news about the Communist takeover in Cuba—a Senate subcommittee has determined that at least one State Department official should have known, and should have warned his superiors long before—I move on to the sports section. Great news: after four days of delays causes by torrential rainstorms, game six of the World Series finally happened last night in San Francisco. The Giants won, tying the series at three games to three. Greg must be over the moon, I think, scanning the details of the game. I begin picturing the book I can write for him about this game, about how the fans in San Francisco—Greg included, of course—were properly rewarded, after days of patiently waiting for the game to take place.

After a while, I put the paper aside. Impulsively, I pick up the telephone and dial Aunt May's number. Long distance to Honolulu. Frieda will have my head for making a long-distance personal call at the shop, but I don't care.

"To what do I owe this honor?" Mother asks, upon hearing my voice.

I laugh a little. "Nothing at all," I reply. "I just miss you, Mother. I can't wait to see you."

"I can't wait to see you, either," she says. "This trip is wonderful, it truly is—but I guess I am finding that I am a homebody." She pauses. "I miss home. And I miss you."

The bell over the door jangles, and a customer comes into the shop. It is a woman in a blue hat and suit, not unlike those I was wearing in the photograph in Lars's office. Jeepers, everyone wants to be Jackie Kennedy, don't they?

Holding the woman's hand is a little girl, perhaps a bit older than my children in the dreams. The girl has blond braids; she wears a pink dress and a matching cardigan with pearl buttons down the front. She gazes to one side, then down at the floor.

I smile and wave at the customer, and she nods. She begins to browse, the child in tow. I turn back to the telephone. "Well, your trip is almost over," I say to my mother. "And it sounds like you're ready to come home."

She laughs. I love my mother's laugh; it is the most delightful sound in the world. With its quick up-and-down tones, it's like listening to a whole host of bells from different churches, ringing as one.

"Yes, I'm ready," she replies. "Although I can't say I'm looking forward to winter, after being here. And neither is your father. But we'll weather the storm. Or storms, I ought to say. It will be good to be back in our own house, with our own things." I hear a rustle, as if she has shifted the receiver to her other ear. "Are you watering my plants?"

My mother is not much of a green thumb, but she does have several houseplants—a spider, an ivy, and a philodendron—and I am their official caretaker until she returns. "Twice a week," I tell her. "They're all thriving."

"Good girl, Kitty."

I hear a crash, and then a sharp, long wail from the stacks where the woman and child are. "Mother, I've got to go. I have a customer." Before hanging up, I add, "I'm counting the days, Mother. I miss you so."

After we ring off, I head for the stacks. The child is still crying, a high-pitched scream that reminds me of the one I heard in my dream the night before. She is seated on the floor, the child, legs crisscrossed awkwardly as if they belonged to a flopping frog instead of a girl. She is rocking from side to side. In front of her, about a dozen books are strewn on the floor. The books are the former elements of a pyramidal display I'd set up a few days ago—rather awkwardly, I realize now—on an open shelf at the end of an aisle. There are a number of copies of *Silent Spring*, which arrived at the end of September as expected, and another up-and-coming title, the near-future thriller *Seven Days in May*, in which the military takes over after a fictional president signs a disarmament treaty with the Soviet Union. Both of these books are attracting a lot of attention right now, and my objective in setting up the display had simply been to make them easier for my customers to locate—and purchase, of course. I hadn't considered the precarious nature of the arrangement.

Her back to me, the woman leans over her child and says, "It's all right. Please stop. Please, just stop."

The child screams more loudly.

I stand still, not sure whether or not to interrupt. The woman, apparently sensing my presence, turns slightly and gives me a pained look. "I am so sorry," she says loudly over the din. She begins picking up the books, which makes the child shriek with more fervor and clutch her mother's arm. The books the woman has gathered spill once more onto the rug.

"Don't worry about the books," I say. "Is there anything I can do?"

The woman shakes her head. "She—they—she knocked them over accidentally, and I think the noise startled her." Her lips are pursed. She wraps her arms around the child, and after a few moments the girl seems to settle down. She closes her eyes and leans her head against the woman's shoulder.

"I ought not to have come in," the mother says, almost in a whisper. "It's just that we were having such a good day. *She* was having such a good day. And I thought . . . I only thought, for a minute . . . there was a novel I wanted to find, something new by Katherine Ann Porter; it was recommended to me. And I thought, just quickly . . ." Her voice trails off.

"You must mean *Ship of Fools*," I reply. "I've read it. It's quite good, everything the reviewers say it is. I have a copy over at the counter." I wave my hand in that direction. "I can wrap it for you . . . just let me check the price . . ."

The woman shakes her head. "I think it's best if I leave," she said. "Perhaps I can come back another day." She heaves her too-large child into her arms; the girl collapses into them like a rag doll and wraps her bare legs around her mother's waist. "I'm sorry about the books on the floor," the mother calls over her shoulder.

I rush ahead of her to open the door. The girl is playing with her mother's hat, still moaning softly. "Is she . . . I know it's terribly rude of me to ask, but is your daughter . . ." I stop talking, because I don't know what else to say.

The woman gives me a sharp look. "She's autistic," she says. And then she strides through the doorway and does not look back.

Autistic.

I have heard of that, I think. I know it is some sort of mental disorder. But I am not sure exactly what it means.

Luckily, I have a convenient facility at my fingertips for finding out.

The store is silent as I head for the psychology section. This is not a big section; we are an all-purpose shop, but a small one, and we carry only the basics in most nonfiction. Only those items that might appeal to the general reader. We can order anything, and often do for our regulars. But as for the stacks, we keep them stocked with what appeals mainly to the browser, the woman reader, the casual intellect. Nothing too studious.

I scan the psychology volumes. Unlike our fiction section, which is organized by author, Frieda and I arrange the nonfiction shelves in our store by category—such as psychology—and then by book title. Over the years we have learned that customers are more likely to find what they seek there by title rather than author, because the names of many nonfiction authors are unknown to the general reading public.

I select a book entitled *A Basic Introduction to Modern Psychology.* Turning to the index, I locate the topic in question and find a few paragraphs that suit my purpose.

Autism, also called infantile schizophrenia, is a disorder exemplified by limited social and communication skills in infants and young children. In numerous documented cases, sufferers also exhibit excessively constrained, overly rhythmic behavior. Autistic infants and toddlers generally do not respond when called by name. Such infants and toddlers rarely smile or make eye contact; nor do they imitate other children or adults. As autistic children grow, they appear to be incapable of understanding basic social cues and norms. They frequently find it difficult to share and take turns with others. They generally do not understand or enjoy imaginative play. Autistic children are often subject to emotional outbursts when no clear cause for such outbursts exists.

Fair enough. Sounds like Michael, and like the little girl in my store today.

The next line, however, stops me in my tracks and leaves my heart cold.

The causes of autism are unclear. However, autism is commonly thought to be caused by emotionally distant parenting, generally on the part of the mother.

Chapter 15

Mama."

I am startled into consciousness.

"*Mama*." This time, the tone is more insistent.

I turn my head and see him. The frightening little boy. Michael. I attempt to meet his eye, but he refuses to look directly at me. Nonetheless, I can tell that behind the glasses, his eyes are blue—like Lars, like Mitch and Missy. Evidently, no one in this dream world inherited my hazel eye color. I don't know if it's the thick lenses or if Michael's eye color is simply not as saturated as that of the others—but in either case, behind the glasses, his eyes seem cloudy, unfocused.

He shakes my shoulder. His long, thin fingers dig into me; it feels like tiny knife blades burrowing in my flesh.

I reach up and rub my shoulder. "Ow. Michael, that hurt."

He ignores this. "Mama, I was saying your name and you weren't answering."

"I'm sorry," I tell him, although I don't feel sorry at all.

I look around. We are sitting on a bench near a playground, with a small lake to our left. I swivel my head, looking for the mountains to the west—that is the best way to orient oneself in Denver. Finding them, I trace directions for the nearby landscape. The lake is north of us. To the east and the west, I see residential streets, rows of houses. To the south is a barren field, patched with snow, and another, equally small lake beyond it. I can barely make out the tall chain-link fences around a cluster of tennis courts at the southern lake's far end. In the distance, a red-brick clock tower rises above the trees.

I realize we are in Washington Park. The clock tower belongs to South High School, the secondary school from which I graduated more than twenty years ago. The school is across the street from the southern edge of the park; we students used to walk across to the park for our PE classes, to run laps on the roadway that winds through the park or take practice shots on the tennis courts.

It is probably a good five or six miles from here to the house on Springfield Street that I share with Lars and the children in my imaginary life. But it is only a few blocks from the park to my parents' house on York Street. The photograph hanging in the hallway of the Springfield Street house—the picture of my parents, with me as a baby, picnicking—was taken in this park. I haven't been here in years, but I spent many a happy hour in Washington Park as a child, both at this playground and swimming in the lake. Smith Lake, it's called; when we were kids, the neighborhood children and I would scare each other with tales of sea monsters who lived in Smith Lake. "Don't go out too far," we'd tease each other. "A one-eyed monster will get you."

The park and playground have changed over the years. The swings look new, and the city closed the swimming beach a few years ago; the lake was too small, too many people were using it, and the water had become murky. Perhaps, I think now, my friends and I were right about a monster living in that dark, dim water.

Michael and I are the only people at the playground. The lake is partially frozen over, the air is cold, and the sky is gray. Snow is not falling, but it hangs in the clouds. I lift my nose and smell it, the way a watchdog might sniff out an approaching intruder.

Whatever are we doing here? And where are the other children?

"Michael," I say. "Where are Mitch and Missy?"

He rolls his eyes—not at me, because he doesn't look at me, but at the swings a few feet from us. "You know where they are, Mama. Where they always are during the daytime."

"And where is that?"

Now he grins; he must think I am joking with him. "Honestly," I implore. "Where is that?"

"Mama!" He laughs out loud. To my surprise, I find the sound delightful. His laugh has a joyous, ringing tone; it reminds me instantly and incongruously of my mother's laughter. "Silly Mama. They're in school, of course."

"Oh." I place my kidskin-gloved hands on either side of me, on the green bench. "And you?" I ask. "Why aren't you in school, too?"

He laughs again and hops clumsily off the bench. "Well, now you're just being crazy," he says. "You know I don't go to school, Mama."

Oh.

He trips away from me and walks over to a swing. He gets on and sits still. It's clear he doesn't know how to pump and get himself going. "Push me, Mama."

I rise from the bench and walk over to him. From behind, I give him a push, my hands light on his back. I am not sure how high he wants to go, but I keep pushing just a little more each time. He laughs gleefully. Once I find a pace that he seems to enjoy, I settle in, maintaining just enough tempo to keep him going without variation.

"Wheeeeee!" Michael cries out with joy as the swing sails through the air.

I take a good look at him. He wears green corduroy pants, a checkered woolen jacket, and a chunky, navy-blue knitted cap that covers his ears. I wonder vaguely if my mother made his hat. His thick-lensed horn-rimmed glasses are sturdily positioned on his head. I have the feeling he doesn't go far without them.

He is thinner than Mitch and Missy, who have clearly inherited their stocky builds from both Lars and me. Michael is willowy; I can see how stick-thin his legs are through his pants, how his elbows poke out against the sleeves of his jacket. Is this his natural build, I wonder, or is he simply a picky eater? His hair color and features are similar to Mitch's; it is entirely possible that they are identical twins. I have no idea what the odds are of conceiving triplets, or whether it is typical for two of them to be identical. These are issues that have never crossed my mind back in the real world.

I close my eyes and put my fingers lightly on my belly. I am trying to imagine what it would feel like to have three babies inside me, all at the same time. I cannot fathom it. It makes me think of high school plays, of how Miss Potts, the drama coach, always told us, "*Feel* your character. *Be* your character." Frieda loved that advice and took it to heart, enthusiastically becoming the tragic Lady Macbeth or the spunky, aspiring actress Terry Randall from *Stage Door*. But I was never particularly good at it. I was always too aware that no matter who I was playing on-stage, underneath the detailed costume and the thick makeup I was still just plain old Kitty.

That's how I feel right now, imagining myself as someone who has been pregnant with triplets. Like it's a part I *could* play if I had to, but I wouldn't be fooling anyone. They'd all know that there were no babies inside me, that it was just a pillow under my skirt. I remove my hand from my stomach and continue pushing the swing.

Suddenly, I have an inspiration. "Hey, Michael."

He does not turn his head. "What?"

"When Mama was being silly . . ." I know I am going out on a limb here, and I hesitate. I do not know, have no idea, how I would handle him having a scene, out here all by myself. None-theless, I take a deep breath and plunge in. "When Mama was asking those silly questions . . . did you like that?"

His shoulders move up and down slightly. "I don't know," he says dully.

"Can I . . . is it okay if I ask you some more silly questions?"

He shrugs again. "I don't know."

I think we are both glad that we are not facing one another.

"Let's give it a try," I suggest. "How about this? How old are you, Michael?"

He doesn't say anything, and I wait, breathless, praying that he won't explode.

"Michael? Did you hear me?"

"I'm thinking!" he yells. "Can't you see that I'm thinking, Mama?"

He is coming in for a push, and my hands snap back in aversion, missing a beat. "I'm sorry," I whisper.

Neither of us says anything for a few minutes. Recovered, I continue pushing. Then Michael pipes up. "Do you know what time it is?"

I look at my wrist to see if I am wearing a watch, and indeed I am: a tasteful jeweled one with a black velvet band. "It's ten thirty."

"Ten thirty exactly?"

I laugh. "Okay. It's ten thirty-two."

"Well, then," he says. "I am six years, three months, fourteen days, twelve hours, and eighteen minutes. Mitch is six years, three months, fourteen days, twelve hours, and fifteen minutes. Missy is six years, three months, fourteen days, twelve hours, and eleven minutes. I'm the oldest!" he finishes proudly.

I am speechless.

He turns his head slightly, so he is looking to the west rather than southward in front of him. "Mama? Do you have any other questions?"

"Yes," I say. "What day is it?"

"It's Wednesday, February twenty-seventh."

"What year?"

He giggles. "Nineteen sixty-three, Mama."

Nineteen sixty-three. So we *have* only moved a few months into the future.

Shifting topics, I ask, "What else are we doing this morning? Besides playing here at the park, I mean."

His shoulders stiffen. "Mama, it's Wednesday."

I wait.

"It's *Wednesday*," he repeats, with a little more edge in his voice.

"Remember, Michael, this is a game," I say. "So let me ask you: What do we do on Wednesdays?"

"Oh!" He giggles again. "We go food shopping, Mama."

Aha. "Does Mama make a shopping list?" I ask.

"Well, of course," he replies. "All mothers make shopping lists."

I suppose they do. Incidentally, thirty-eight-year-old unmarried women do not make shopping lists. They pop into the food mart when their cabinets and refrigerator are bare, buy whatever looks good and doesn't require a lot of preparation, and take it home.

"Who cooks at our house?" I ask. "Alma or me?"

"Sometimes you, sometimes Alma," Michael says.

"And Alma . . . does she come to our house every day?"

He chortles, as if what I've asked is extraordinarily ridiculous. "Of course not," he says. "She comes three times a week. Mondays, Wednesdays, and Thursdays. She arrives at nine o'clock in the morning, and she leaves as soon as she has dinner ready. Except sometimes she comes on Friday instead of Thursday, and then she stays in the evening, if you and Daddy are to go out. But you never go out . . ." He pauses. "Until I'm in bed."

Hmm. Interesting. I decide it's best to change topics again. "So Alma is not there in the mornings before Daddy goes to work . . . or Mitch and Missy go to school." I consider this. "Does Mama make breakfast?" I can't imagine preparing a good, healthy breakfast for five people. Many mornings in the real world, I barely get my own egg, toast, and juice on the table before I find myself running late for the shop. In this world, I probably serve Froot Loops every morning.

Nonetheless, Michael nods. "You make breakfast," he confirms. "Except for the weekends. Daddy makes breakfast on the weekends." I can't see his face, but I can feel it brighten, the way you can sometimes feel the sun through a thin bank of clouds. "Swedish pancakes on Saturdays and waffles on Sundays."

"Is that right?" I smile, picturing it: Lars, an apron around his waist, pancake batter on a griddle, expertly flipping at just the right golden-brown moment. It must have been a weekend, the last time we were in the house. The morning I first saw Michael, when Lars was in the kitchen.

This leads me to another question. "Michael," I say quietly. "You love Daddy a lot, don't you?"

Michael gives a happy sigh. "Yes," he replies. "Oh, *yes*."

And me? I want to ask. Do you love *me*, Michael?

But I cannot ask that question. I fear its answer too much.

Instead I say, "One more silly question." I look around. "Do we come to this park a lot, Michael?"

He leans forward, into the cold air. "We didn't used to," he tells me. "But lately we do."

I close my eyes and concentrate on pushing. I am waiting for the dream to end, because these dreams always seem to end on critical moments like this one. But this time, it does not. I open my eyes, and I am still in the park, still feeling the chill of the air through my coat, still pushing skinny Michael on his wooden swing.

"Mama, is it eleven o'clock yet?" Michael asks.

I check my watch. "Almost."

"We go shopping at eleven," he informs me.

"Oh. Right. Well, hop off then and let's go get in the car."

He skips in front of me, leading me to the parking lot and the Chevy station wagon. He climbs in shotgun, and I turn the key in the ignition.

Glancing sideways at Michael, I say, "Ought we to . . . do you think we ought to go by Grandma and Grandpa's house, since we're in the neighborhood?"

He doesn't look at me—not that I expected him to, of course. "If you want to," he mumbles, staring at the floorboard.

So I drive carefully out of the park. The only other driving I've done of late was as imaginary as this—the few moments in the car with Mitch and Missy, before I slammed on the brakes, wondering where Michael was, and thus ending that dream. Today the dream does not end; my time behind the wheel continues. The roadworthy lessons my father taught me years ago come back more easily than I would have expected. Just like riding a bicycle, I guess. That thought makes me smile, because in the real world I do ride my bicycle—quite often, in fact, whenever I am not walking or taking the bus. I wonder if I even have a bicycle in this life.

I head east, then turn south on York Street. A few blocks later, I pull up in front of my parents' small brick bungalow on the west side of the street.

The house is still. The shades are drawn. Someone has shoveled the sidewalk in front of the house, but not the four concrete steps leading up from the sidewalk, nor the walkway to the front porch; these are covered in patches of icy snow that look like they've been there for quite some time. I've become used to the house having a quiet calm about it. It's been that way since my parents left on their long vacation, every time I go over to water the plants. But shouldn't I be done with that by now?

I had been planning to park the car, go inside, see my parents' faces. Driving over, I'd felt a lightness at the thought of their familiar voices. My nose had been lifted in anticipation of the particular smell that always pervades the house—I've never been able to nail down precisely what it is; the best I can come up with is a peculiar cross between roasted butternut squash and dried lavender. I'd been looking forward to the way my father's eyes would twinkle at the sight of Michael and me walking up the steps. I'd thought about how my mother's hug would feel: solid, warm, with a brush of soft wool against my cheek—the handmade yellow shawl she throws around her shoulders in the house, because my father keeps the furnace turned low to save money.

Do my parents get along with Michael? Do they know how to say the right things, do the right things, not set him off? I can't know for sure, of course, but I feel confident that they do. I don't know how I know it, but I am certain that Michael loves my parents, that he feels safe and comfortable around them, just as he does with Lars.

Suddenly a memory comes to me, the flash of an imaginary episode.

It is the height of summertime, the sun blazing, the air warm, the bushes heavy with their fattest warm-weather foliage. I am walking up the steps to my parents' house, all three children in tow. Lars, behind us, is coming around from the driver's side of my car. Lars and I are both in tennis whites, racquets in tennis bags slung over our shoulders.

We all grin as the front door bursts open and my father comes out. He steps briskly off the front stoop and bends down to take all three children in his arms at once. They wrap themselves around him, hugging him eagerly.

Even Michael.

"Ah, my darlings," my father says breathlessly, releasing them. "When did I last see you? It seems like forever."

Missy giggles. "It was last weekend, Grandpa."

"Only last weekend?" He gives her a look of exaggerated shock. "Surely that can't be so, Missy. It had to be last year. Maybe the year before."

Michael laughs, and I notice that he looks directly at my father. Looks him straight in the eye. "Grandpa," he says seriously. "You are *such* a kidder."

My mother comes outside, glancing at Lars and me, and then at her watch. "Scoot, you two," she says. "Don't be late for your game." She places one hand on Michael's shoulder and the other on Mitch's, steering them gently toward the house. My father takes Missy's hand in his.

"We'll all be fine," my mother assures me. "As always, dear . . . we will be just fine."

I nod. "I know you will."

Lars and I give out kisses all around, and then we walk down the block hand in hand, heading toward the park. I sigh happily, feeling carefree and lighthearted. "What would we do without them?" I say, glancing back at my parents' house. "Whatever would we do without my parents?"

He nods and squeezes my hand a bit tighter.

Thinking about this now, I can't help but smile. Nonetheless, I find that I don't want to go inside my parents' house at all. Not today. I am not sure why, but suddenly this is the last place I want to be.

"On second thought, maybe we ought to just go on with the shopping," I say to Michael, taking my foot off the brake and pulling away from the curb. He does not look up, nor does he reply.

I turn left on Louisiana Avenue, then wait at the light at University Boulevard. "Since you're so good at answering questions, Michael, let's see if you can answer this one: What's the best way to get to the food store from here?"

He directs me to a Safeway store not far from the University Hills shopping center where I went with Mitch and Missy, and not far from the house on Springfield Street, either. We pull into the parking lot, and I search my purse for a list. Sure enough, there is one. On the right-hand side of the paper, I have carefully written a week's worth of dinner menus, the name of each day underlined and the main course and side dishes listed below it. On the left-hand side, divided by categories such as Fruit/Vegetables, Dairy, and Meat, I have written what I need to prepare the listed suppers, as well as breakfast and lunch staples such as bread, peanut butter, and eggs. Marveling at my impressive organizational skills, I usher Michael into the store.

We're doing quite well, working our way through the aisles, when I turn a corner and hear my name. "Katharyn, is that you?"

Naturally, I have never before seen the woman who addresses me—neither in real life nor in any of my previous dreams. Her hair is dark and pulled back into a large, elaborately braided bun at the nape of her slender neck. She wears a dark blue car coat with a black fur collar. Her lips and nails are a startlingly bright red.

"I thought it was you. Delightful to see you." She smiles at Michael. "And how are *you* today?"

He looks at the floor and mumbles.

The woman looks back at me. "I'm sorry," she whispers, loudly and dramatically. "I never know what I'm meant to—"

"I can hear you!" Michael yells at the top of his voice. "I can hear you, I can hear you. I—can—hear—YOU!"

During this outburst, he continues staring at the floor. Carts stop in the aisle; heads turn in our direction.

"It's okay," I say, getting down to his level. "The river," I say frantically, remembering what Lars did. "The river, the river, Michael . . ."

"You're not saying it right!" He breaks away from me and tears down the aisle, knocking over a display of on-sale Wheaties cereal boxes as he turns the corner. He bolts for the door.

"Oh, my, I'm—" Without finishing, I rush out of the store, leaving my cart in the middle of the aisle.

Cars screech as Michael runs headlong through the parking lot. I expect him to run toward our station wagon, but he goes in the opposite direction. He is astonishingly fast; I would not have expected that of him. I would have thought him too weak and clumsy to be much of an athlete, but his legs seem to have taken on a life of their own. Terrified, I get in the car and drive toward him, praying that no vehicle will hit him before I get there. I cut him off and he almost slams into the front bumper of the Chevy. I get out, grab him by the arm, and drag him into the car. He is screaming incoherently, and I pray for the dream to end. I buckle him into his seat, hoping he won't know how to unbuckle it. I lock the passenger-side door and scoot around the car. Sliding in on the driver's side, I slam the door shut and pull out of the parking lot.

Having a pretty good sense of where I am now, I make my way home to Springfield Street. Though the drive is short, these are among the worst minutes of my life—real or imagined. The screaming is fever-pitched; I cannot hear myself think, and my head is pounding by the time we pull into the driveway. This has got to end soon, I think. I'm going to wake up any second now.

But I don't. I turn off the car's engine and wait to see what Michael will do. He continues to scream. There are no words, just high-pitched screeches issuing from his lungs. I don't know whether to try to bring him inside or leave him here until he calms down.

While I am thinking about it, the front door opens and Alma appears, pulling her arms into her coat sleeves. I open the car window and lean out. "Señora Andersson," Alma says. "*¿Estás bien?*"

I can feel tears welling in my eyes. "I'm just fine," I say. "Just dandy." I glance over at Michael. "Please tell me how to make him stop," I beg Alma.

She shrugs her shoulders. "Señora, I do not know," she says starkly. "You know that you do not let me near *el niño*."

I don't? Whyever not?

"Well, then," I say, opening my car door and standing next to her in the drive. "If he were your child, what would you do?"

She shrugs. "I guess I do what Señor Andersson does."

"The river song, you mean? I tried that, and he didn't like it."

"Did you . . ." She wraps her arms around herself. "*¿Abrazarlo?* Hold him?"

"I was afraid to touch him!"

"Señor Andersson . . . señora, I know you are not comfortable doing it, but Señor Andersson holds him."

Damn right I'm not comfortable.

She shakes her head. "Señora, the iron is on inside. *Por favor*, I go back in?"

I nod. "Yes, Alma, go on."

"You want me *llamar por teléfono* Señor Andersson?"

I take a second to think about that. Do I want her to telephone Lars? Do I want to admit to him—even if all of this is imaginary—that I cannot handle it myself?

"No," I say slowly. "No, thank you. *Gracias*, Alma."

She goes inside.

Wobbly on my heels, I walk around the car to Michael's side. I use the key to unlock the door, but before I open it, I tap on the window. "Michael, honey, can you hear me?"

Rapid-fire, with astonishing strength, he pounds his small fists against the window. I am almost afraid he'll break the glass. He may be undersize, but I realize now that that doesn't mean he's weak. I open the door and lean in toward him.

He keeps pounding, but now instead of the window, he begins hitting me. I step back, rubbing my upper arm. How am I expected to hold him, when any time I come near him, he lashes out at me?

Finally I go around to the driver's side of the car. Quickly, before he can hit me more than a few times, I reach in and unbuckle his seat belt.

"You want to scream, stay out here and scream as long as you want," I tell him. "But the seat belt is undone and the door is open if you want to come in."

And then, letting the screams subside behind me, I go into the house, leaving the front door standing wide open.

Alma is ironing in the living room, the television tuned to *Guiding Light*. She looks up when I enter. Neither of us says anything.

I go down the hall to Lars's office. I make a beeline for the bar and pour myself a sizable glass of whiskey. Taking it to the kitchen, I add water and ice, and then stir my drink with a clean butter knife that I find in the dish rack. I brush past Alma and stand in front of the picture window, waiting to see what Michael will do.

For a while, nothing happens. I can hear his muffled screams through the plate glass. Probably the whole neighborhood can. But I don't care.

"How long do you think he can keep that up?" I ask Alma, sipping my drink.

She shrugs, her eyes downcast. "We have seen longer, señora. *¿Sí?*"

Yes, Alma. I'm sure we have.

I press my lips together. The whiskey is starting to mellow me. I take a deep breath. "I tried to touch him," I say, still looking out. "He hit me."

Alma nods, but does not reply.

I face her. "He won't run away, will he?"

"So far he has not. *¿No?*"

"No." I take the last swallow of my drink. "Well," I say. "I'm all out of answers. Time to call my husband."

Chapter 16

But I don't get the opportunity to call Lars, because the dream does end at last.

"Well, that one was a doozy," I tell Aslan, who yawns, showing off his cracked, yellowed teeth. He stands, executes a full-on kitty stretch, and then resettles himself on my bed. You're long and lean, I always tell him—a yellow-striped fighting machine. It's a joke between us, because he is anything but a long, lean fighting machine. My aging, chunky Aslan couldn't so much as catch a fly.

So here I am, where it's nice and quiet and I have private jokes with my cat. Back in the genuine, real world.

I smile to myself, thinking that it doesn't seem bad here at all.

You're in a good mood," Frieda observes, a few hours later. I am humming as I dust the back upper shelves at the shop. She's at the counter, working on inventory.

"I haven't been sleeping well—but I guess I finally got enough sleep last night." The idea amuses me; in truth, I am sure I did not sleep well at all. Anyone who dreams the kind of madness that I do is clearly not sleeping well. This train of thought causes me to break into peals of laughter. Frieda smiles, shakes her head, and returns to her books.

We have, at my suggestion, installed a phonograph, one that I purchased in a pawnshop on South Broadway. We both brought stacks of records from home, and now we have soft background music playing every day. At the moment, it's an old Ella Fitzgerald tune, about how nice it would be if falling in love was one's sole occupation.

I cock my head as I dust, listening to the lyrics. Sounds good in a song, Ella, I think—but honestly, in real life, it all depends on the circumstances, doesn't it?

I turn my gaze to Frieda. Next to her on the counter, propped on a wooden display rack, is the copy of *Ship of Fools* that I wanted to sell to the woman who came in the shop the other day. The one with the autistic daughter. In careful letters, I've printed a small sign and placed it in front of the book: RECOMMENDED! BEST SELLER!

Katherine Anne Porter, the short story writer and journalist, wrote that book. I read it earlier this year. In my view, the narration, like the ship itself, seemed rather adrift at times—but I think that was intentional, and it certainly didn't dilute the impact of the characters' struggles. Rather, Porter did an excellent job of exploring how people in a confined space can come to know more about each other than they might wish.

There's a scene in *Ship of Fools* in which one of the characters says something like, "Please do not tell me about yourself; I will not listen. I do not want to know you; I will not know you." Those aren't the exact words, but it was something like that. It makes me think of my imaginary family. The family who, in my dream life, I'm getting to know, whether I want to or not.

From what I have heard, at some point in the 1930s Katherine Anne Porter was on a ship similar to the one she portrays in the novel; apparently she spoke little to the other passengers, but took copious notes. She let the notes lie dormant for years before writing *Ship of Fools*. I have long admired Porter's work. Perhaps I feel a kinship with her because she lived in Denver for a time. In fact, I've heard that she almost died here in 1918, the year of the Spanish flu pandemic.

I consider this. If Porter had died in 1918—why then, she would not have written *Ship of Fools*. In that case, the woman would not have come into my shop, seeking it. I would not have had the rather embarrassing opportunity to ask her what ailed her child. And thus I would not have learned—at least not in this way—what clearly ails my own child in my dream life.

How odd—events turn so easily on a dime, don't they? In much the same way, if Lars and I had stayed on the telephone a few moments longer that night—if I had heard him having his heart attack, if I had been his savior—why then, none of this right now would be happening. Nothing in this life would be real. Instead, the life I have with him and the children would be my reality.

I shake my head and climb down the stepladder. I walk over to the counter and pick up the newspaper, turning to the sports section. I need to find out what happened last night in the final game of the World Series. "Darn it—they lost!" I exclaim.

Frieda looks up. "Who lost?"

"The Giants. They lost the series in game seven. Now what am I going to write for Greg?"

She shakes her head. "What are you talking about?"

"Never mind." I give her a scowl and turn toward the door. I need some fresh air.

I go outside to sweep the front steps. It's a beautiful fall day, and I'm glad to be enjoying it, back here in the real world. I don't know why the dreams take place in the future; now that Michael has been so accommodating as to give me dates, I can see that it's just a few months from now. It doesn't make any sense. But then again, it's not real, so why should it make sense?

"Want to go out to dinner tonight?" I ask Frieda when I come back inside.

"What for?"

I shrug. "No reason. We just haven't had a 'date' in a long time, sister."

Frieda and I have been calling each other "sister" for most of our lives. That is where the name of our store comes from, of course—it was a natural choice for the store name, something we came up with simultaneously when we first discussed opening a bookstore together. Our use of the expression started in high school, when we wished we were real sisters. She was the oldest of four and the only girl in her family; I was an only child who, but for my mother's loss of those three baby boys, would have grown up with the same family structure. What each of us wanted most in her childhood was a sister.

Frieda and I first met on a September day in 1938. We were freshmen at South High, and it was our first day of school. South was nearly new then; only a decade or so had passed since its groundbreaking. The linoleum hallways were still gleaming, the windows bright and uncracked, the bricks a vivid, school-proper red, without the toll that weather and years would eventually take. We freshmen filtered in that first day, following upperclassmen who seemed to know their way around as if they'd been born inside that building. Those older students spoke animatedly to one another. There were shouts of joy as students hugged one another, many of them thrilled to be reunited after a summer apart. Still others laughed over memories of a summer spent together: "Remember the Fourth of July? Will we ever have that much fun again? *Ever?*"

As freshmen, we envied those older students. Though some of us knew each other from our humble grammar schools, we all felt disjointed. Our exchanges with one another were awkward and brief. "I hope your summer was nice." "Do you know how to find room 106?" We immediately grasped, as the crowd jostled inside the building, that our place in these huge halls was yet to be determined. And we were not at all sure that the fates bestowed upon us would be those we'd choose, if given the choice.

Into this mix of insecurity and unfamiliarity strolled Frieda, head held high, long brown hair pulled back from her high forehead with a tortoiseshell band. She wore a straight taupe skirt and an ivory sleeveless blouse that showed off her shoulders, which were tanned and becomingly freckled. Her dark eyes gleamed with mystery and magic. Not just freshmen but even older boys gazed at her as she made her way through the hall. I couldn't take my eyes off her; I stared until she entered a classroom and disappeared.

As luck would have it, I found that I was headed for the same room. As I stepped in, I noticed that—miraculously—the seat to her right was vacant. Boldly, not knowing where my courage came from, I took the seat and held out my hand.

"I'm Kitty Miller," I told her. "It's nice to meet you."

She nodded. Her grip was warm and firm. "Frieda Green. Nice to meet you, too."

We compared our schedules, which had been mailed to us from the school's office the week before. We found that we had nearly every class together. "What a relief," Frieda said. She leaned toward me and whispered conspiratorially, "I was a little afraid of finding my way around alone—weren't you?"

Yes, of course I'd had the same fear. But I was astonished at her candidness in admitting it. Recovering, I nodded and smiled at her. "Let's find our way together, shall we?"

She grinned back. "Indeed we shall, Kitty Miller."

Over time, I got to know everything there was to know about Frieda. She came from money; her maternal grandfather had made a fortune in railroads in the 1880s, and her father's family owned a large construction firm. His family had gotten in on the ground floor when Denver was a young city, just being built up, and they'd stayed on top ever since.

Frieda had gone to private school through eighth grade, but her father felt that she needed to round out her education at a public high school, where she would meet and mix with people of all classes. He had a theory that his children, despite their advantages, would best build their characters by interacting with others of different backgrounds. While attending our solidly middle-class high school, Frieda lived with her parents and brothers in a large three-story brick house in the Country Club section of town—an elite development of palatial houses a couple of miles north of the modest Myrtle Hill district in which my family resided. The first time I went to Frieda's house, I impulsively called it a "mansion," which made her giggle. "You are so *cute*, Kitty Miller," she said, grabbing my arm affectionately.

All these years later, I still remember how her grip felt on my arm, how possessive it was—and yet gratifying as well. Despite all that she had, all that she was, Frieda Green—somehow, inconceivably—wanted to be my friend.

It took months before I finally worked up the courage to ask her about this. What, specifically, made Frieda want *me* to be her dearest and closest friend, when she could have been best friends with any freshman girl in the school, or even with an upperclassman girl, if she'd wanted to?

Frieda had laughed at the question. "You are *you*, Kitty," she said simply. "I could tell from the first moment I met you that you would be loyal, that you would be truthful, that you would stand by me."

It was an unusually warm day for November, the day I asked

that question, and we were standing on the school lawn between classes. Frieda waved her slender arms dramatically, as if to take in the entire student body, most of which milled around outside with us, enjoying the sun and warmth. "I didn't see that sincerity in anyone else. Not at first glance, anyway." She shrugged. "So, no point in letting myself be disappointed when others let me down."

How could I keep from loving someone who spoke so highly of me? No one else, save for my parents, had ever done so in my entire life.

And as for Frieda—how could she not love someone who was so faithful to her? For she was right. Never, no matter what, would I do anything to betray her.

And how amazing, I think as I walk toward her at the counter of our little shop—how amazing that all these years later, we still love each other more than anyone else, outside of our own families.

We are sisters.

Suddenly, I realize something disturbing: in the dreams, I don't know where Frieda is. Obviously, in my last dream, when I was with Michael, I was not spending my weekday morning hours at the shop. Does that mean I don't spend *any* hours at the shop? Do we even *have* the shop in that world?

I shudder, thinking about it. I can't imagine my life without the shop. Without being around Frieda all day, every day.

Thank God, I think, as she starts throwing out restaurant names—"Rockybilt? Could you go for a burger? Or what about C.J.'s Tavern? I know it's an expedition to get there, but I would adore Mexican food, wouldn't you?"—thank God I'm just making up that other world in my head.

C.J.'s Tavern, despite its name and despite having a small lounge that opens into the dining room, is not actually a tavern. It's a Mexican restaurant on Santa Fe Drive. We have to take three buses to get there, but, as Frieda says, it's worth it. You can't grow up in Denver without learning to love Mexican food, and C.J.'s has the best chiles rellenos in town.

Frieda and I are both upbeat at dinner. I am eternally grateful to be here with her, without having to think about that other world. As for Frieda, she simply seems happy and carefree. I know she's been worried about the shop, so it's reassuring to see her so animated.

We talk about the vacant storefront we saw in the shopping center at University Hills. A few days ago Frieda called the manager and set up an appointment for us to look at its interior. "It's not that unreasonable, you know," she tells me. "Yes, it's more than we're spending now for rent. A lot more. But when you run the numbers . . . I've been going over it, both in my head and on paper, and I think that it would only be a few months before we'd start turning a profit."

"And what until then?" I ask. "Where would we get the capital?"

She sips her wine. "I can't go to my parents for money. We'd have to get another bank loan." Before I can open my mouth to protest, she goes on. "I know my father cosigned our last loan. And I know that the bank might turn us down without his cosignature on a new loan. And yes—we still owe on our current loan. I know all that." She sets down her glass. "But if we could convince the bank that we're going in the right direction, that this move would keep us from going under . . ." She shrugs. "Don't you think they'd prefer to extend us just a little bit, rather than have to foreclose on us?"

I take a big gulp from my wineglass. It sounds so daunting. It sounds like the big time. Like really going out on a limb, much more so than we did when we opened our little shop eight years ago.

Frieda's eyes are dreamy. "We could be big, you know," she says, leaning toward me. "This could be just the start. There are shopping centers like that cropping up all over the place. And the stores that make big money—they have a formula, you know, a style, something that people come to expect when they walk in." She shrugs again. "Now, that hasn't been done much in the book business, at least not in Denver. But that could change, right? Who's to say a chain of bookstores couldn't work? If it works for hamburgers and hardware, why not for books?"

Why not indeed? She has a point. A truly good point. I can't deny it.

Still—this feels like *her* gig, not mine. Like she could do this whether I was there or not. She could take all that glowing confidence she's always had; she could use it to sail into whatever success story she wanted to write for herself.

"You've really thought this through, haven't you?" I ask.

Frieda shrugs. "I've been thinking this through for years, Kitty."

I don't know how to answer that. I take a bite of my chile relleno and push the rice about on my plate.

Frieda glances over my shoulder. "Don't turn your head," she whispers. "But I have to tell you who I see sitting alone at the bar."

"Who?"

She raises her eyebrows. "Kevin."

Kevin? Good grief, I haven't seen him in more than a decade. "How does he look?" I ask Frieda.

She watches him from the corner of her eye. "Tired," she says finally. "And old." She smiles. "He looks old, Kitty. You ought to be happy about that."

I laugh. "Well, I look old, too."

Frieda drains her wineglass and lights up a Salem. "Not with that dazzling new hairstyle, you don't."

I put my hand to my head. Linnea's work has held up well, although I do have an appointment to see her again next week. It's true that when I look in the mirror these days, I see a fresher, more attractive Kitty than I've seen in a long time. But how much of that is a new hairstyle? And how much of it is the fact that—at night when I'm asleep, anyway—I am madly in love with my perfect dream husband?

"I think Kevin just noticed me," Frieda says. "And you, too. He's getting up." She lowers her voice. "Take a deep breath, sister. He's on his way over."

She looks up at him and smiles, and that gives me an excuse to turn my head. I feign surprise, but I'm sure he's not fooled.

"Hey. I thought it was you two." Kevin leans over our table. He is as long and gangly as he was back in the day, with those sloping shoulders of his. Still built like an adolescent boy. I realize that I have become used to Lars's broad back and shoulders, his stockiness, which complements my own. Kevin and I were never a very good match physically. He was too tall when we danced; the top of my head barely made it to his collarbone, and I felt like I was straining my neck looking up at him. He always tried to get me to wear the highest heels possible, to get us closer in size. That only made things worse; my feet would be killing me by the end of the evening. He also thought I was too chubby, although he did appreciate my bountiful breasts. Despite these noteworthy assets, he was constantly urging me to go on a diet.

Unlike Lars, Kevin has managed to hang on to his hair all these years. He always had a lot of it, dark and wavy, and he still does. His eyes are the same warm brown they always were, but they look glassy. I can tell he's had too much to drink.

Frieda motions toward the empty chair between us, then stubs out her smoke in the ashtray by her side. "Have a seat, Kev."

He pulls out the chair and sits. I give Frieda a questioning look. She glances down at her hands, which are folded neatly in front of her; she ever-so-slightly motions with her right pinkie toward her left ring finger. I sneak a peek at Kevin's left hand and see that it is ringless.

Aha. Did she see that from all the way across the room? Or did she just guess it, since he's here all by himself this late at night? Married men—happily married men, at any rate—are not sitting alone in a bar at this time of night. They are at home with their wives, their children, and probably in most cases the pro-verbial family dog.

"Long time," Kevin says. He has brought his drink, and he empties it and motions to the waitress to bring him another. "You girls fancy a round on me?"

Now this is a surprise. He was always a cheapskate. Not that he didn't pay for our dates, of course, but I always felt like he took me to the most inexpensive places he could get away with, and spent as little on me as he could. Even for my birthday and Christmas, his presents were things like a tiny bottle of perfume or a cut-rate scarf or hat. He always said he was saving for our future. Well, that didn't turn out to be all that accurate, did it?

Frieda nods at the offer of a drink. The waitress brings Kevin another Scotch and the bottle to fill our wineglasses. "On my tab," Kevin says pointedly. The waitress smiles stiffly at Frieda and me, and withdraws from the table.

"How is life treating you girls?" Kevin relaxes back in his seat, and for a moment I think he's going to fall over backward.

Good heavens, how many has he had? You'd think, on a week-night, out in public—and him a doctor now, too; I can't forget that. You'd think a doctor with a drinking habit would be more discreet.

"We've been quite well," Frieda replies. "We have a book-store on South Pearl Street."

Kevin nods. He pulls a pack of Pall Malls from his jacket pocket and lights one. Frieda immediately joins him by selecting a Salem from her pack on the table. He holds out his lighter to her, and she leans forward to accept the flame he offers. I watch them both silently, trying to relax my heated face and my fur-rowed brows.

"I've heard about your bookstore," Kevin says, clicking his lighter closed. "Been meaning to stop in for ages."

A likely story. I glare at him and take a sip of wine. I cannot explain why I feel such animosity toward him. It was a long time ago. And look at him now. Would I really want to be married to this man?

No. Of course not. I want to be married to the man who doesn't exist.

I force myself to soften, give Kevin a smile. "And you? How have you been?"

He looks at me for a long time, as if trying to decide how to answer. "Oh," he says finally. "I guess I get along all right. Got a good practice, internal medicine, working out of Saint Joe's Hospital." He shrugs. "And I'm on my own now. Maybe you've heard that."

I shake my head. "No. I hadn't heard."

"Well." He stirs his drink with his finger. He always did that, I remember. "Some things are just not meant to be." He smiles grimly. "Got a couple of good kids out of it, though. Want to see pictures?"

I don't, really, but Frieda replies kindly, "Of course we do." Kevin pulls out his wallet and flips it open. Two smiling little girls peer out at us from school photographs; the smaller one is missing her two front teeth. "This one's Becky; she's ten," Kevin says, pointing to the elder. "And Nancy here is eight."

"Lovely." Frieda comes in for a quick look, then leans back and takes a long drag on her Salem, watching my eyes carefully.

"Yes, lovely," I echo. "I'm sure you're very proud of them, Kevin."

He nods. "Well, what little I see of them—their mother keeps them under lock and key—yeah, they seem to be doing all right." He shrugs, stubbing out his cigarette. "They have a stepfather; he's a decent guy, actually. Better for them than me, really."

Goodness, it all seems so clichéd, like some B-grade movie. Made the wrong choice, did you, buddy? And look where it got you. Drunk and alone in a bar—and running into your college girlfriend, who clearly would have appreciated you more than that shrew you married ever did.

This strikes me as quite funny, and I stifle a laugh. Mortified, I put my hand over my mouth, hoping Kevin won't notice.

But he does. Gazing darkly at me, he asks. "Something funny, Kitty?"

I shake my head. "No, of course not. I'm sorry your marriage didn't work out."

He takes a long swallow of Scotch. "Yes," he says coolly. "I'm sure you are." He stands and drains his glass. "I shouldn't have come over," he says crossly. "I don't know why I did. I'm sorry I interrupted your dinner, girls." He slams his empty glass on our table and stalks back to the bar. We watch in silence as he pays his tab, picks up his overcoat and hat, and strides out the door without a backward glance.

"Well, for heaven's sake," Frieda says softly. I nod, and we both watch the door where he's disappeared.

"Poor chap," Frieda says after a few moments. She watches me over her wineglass. "Must make *you* feel good, though."

"Actually," I tell her, "it doesn't." I put my face in my hands. "Freeds, I'm tired," I say. "I had too much wine. I need to go home."

She nods. "Me too, sister. Me too."

Chapter 17

At home, I crawl into bed, adjust the covers evenly around myself, and then pull Aslan toward me and snuggle him close to my chest. I turn off my bedside lamp and take a deep breath, enjoying the stillness and my solitude.

I am convinced that the dreams won't return. I've seen it all now, haven't I? I've seen what kind of child Michael is. I've seen what I would have to contend with, if the dream life was my real life.

"I get it," I say aloud in the darkness. It seems silly, saying it out loud, but I want to make sure my subconscious understands. I want to be sure it knows that *I* understand.

There is no such thing as a perfect life. It's not perfect here, and it's not perfect there.

I truly don't expect that I'll wake up there again. In the house with Lars, the children, and my other life.

But I do. This time we are eating what appears to be lunch, seated around the dining room table. The shutters to the kitchen are open, and I spy the cheery fruit-motif wallpaper, sunlight shimmering through the south-facing window. The entire family is at the table with me: Lars, Missy and Mitch, Michael.

I look across the table, meeting Lars's eyes.

"How was it, in that other world?" he asks.

"What?" I startle myself, and everyone else, with the sharpness of my reply. The children stare at me, half-eaten sandwiches in their hands. Lars gives me a curious look.

"Sorry," he says. "You just seemed like you were a million miles away. In some other world."

"Oh." I smile. "I suppose I was."

The children go back to their sandwiches. Peanut butter and grape jelly, it looks like, judging from their purple-smeared faces. On each child's plate is a small stack of carrot sticks and the remains of a pile of potato chips; evidently they ate the chips first, before the sandwiches and vegetables. Mitch and Missy eat delicately, holding their sandwiches with their fingertips, like little bear cubs licking a handful of honey. Michael is not eating his sandwich at all; instead he is pulling it apart into small bits that he rolls into balls, then arranges neatly around the perimeter of his plate. I turn my gaze away from him, hoping my distaste doesn't show. And hating myself for feeling this way about my own—albeit imaginary—child.

I look down at my plate, and glance at Lars's. He and I are eating chef salads. Did I make this? It's quite elaborate, with carefully arranged slices of Swiss cheese, hard-boiled egg, olives, and delicatessen ham and turkey on a bed of iceberg lettuce. In real life, I would never make something this fancy for lunch. Frieda and I usually have a sandwich from the shop down the street, or else I brown-bag it with what the children are eating today, peanut butter and jelly.

"So, what's on the docket for the afternoon?" Lars asks. He sets his fork on his empty salad plate and wipes his mouth with a blue-flowered paper napkin.

"Celebrity Lanes, Daddy!" Mitch cries, and Missy enthusiastically nods in agreement.

Michael, I note, remains expressionless.

I've heard of Celebrity, although I've never been there. It's on Colorado Boulevard, the same street as the University Hills Shopping Center, several miles north. It opened a few years ago. I believe its official name is Celebrity Sports Center, and in addition to bowling, they have a swimming pool, arcade games, and other amusements. I'm sure it's delightful if you have children, or like bowling. Since neither of those is true in my real life, I have not found occasion to visit Celebrity. Besides, like the shopping center, it's difficult to get to without a car.

"Maybe Mickey will be there," Missy says, and I remember reading in the *Denver Post* that Walt Disney owns the place, and his characters make regular appearances.

Lars tilts his head thoughtfully. "It will be busy there. It might take a while to get a lane."

"We'll be patient," Missy promises. "Anyways, there's lots to do while we wait."

"Anyway," I correct her. "It's not 'anyways,' Missy—it's 'anyway.'"

She ducks her head, chided. "Sorry, Mama."

Lars smiles. "Mama the schoolmarm." His eyes twinkle at me across the long table. "Once a teacher, always a teacher. Right, Katharyn?"

I raise my eyebrows. "That was a long time ago."

He lifts his glass and takes a sip of water. "A whole other lifetime ago."

I don't reply. Instead, I get up to clear the table. As I am rising, Michael swings his arm in front of himself, and his milk glass tumbles over.

"Michael!" I say harshly. His face crumples, and I can tell he's about to start shrieking.

I put my hand to my mouth. "It's okay," I tell him, softening.

"It happens. We'll clean it up." Lars comes around the table and puts both hands on Michael's shoulders, trying to calm him before he explodes.

I go through the swinging doors to the kitchen. While I am getting a dishcloth from the sink, Lars appears behind me and puts his arms around my waist. "Everything okay in there?" I ask.

"Yes, he's fine. I got to him in time."

I nod, relieved. Lars nuzzles my neck. "You don't seem too enthused about our afternoon plans."

I shrug.

"Honey." He spins me to face him. "Let me take them. You take the day off. Go do something you enjoy."

I can feel my face brighten. "Really? Are you sure?"

He laughs. "Of course. You need it, love. You've had a hard week."

I bite my lip. "I really have," I reply. "And there are things . . . I need to do some things, so yes . . . thank you, Lars."

"You take all the time you need," he says. "Take the Cadillac. Go shopping. Go see Linnea, get your hair done."

But shopping and getting my hair done—even by Linnea, who I'm dying to see in this world, if for no other reason than to see how she compares with the Linnea in my other world—these are the last things on my mind. Although I do plan to go to one shop in particular.

If indeed such a shop exists.

I wanted to ask Lars what day it is, but I would have felt silly doing so. Since he's home during the day, it must be the weekend. I'm hoping it's Saturday, not Sunday. If it's Saturday, Sisters' ought to be open. A few years ago, Frieda and I decided to open on Saturdays. It cuts off our weekends, certainly, but it makes good business sense. With so many women in the workforce these days, we want to cater to not only the housewife but also the working girl. So now Sisters' is open Tuesday through Saturday each week. We are still closed on Sundays, of course, as are all the businesses on our street. We're also closed on Mondays, making those our own personal Saturdays.

After bidding good-bye to the family, I head to the garage and slide behind the wheel of Lars's car, backing it carefully out of the garage.

The Cadillac is a dream to drive. It seems to have every imaginable convenience: firm but cushiony Naugahyde seats, a heating system that cranks to life and warms me within minutes of turning on the ignition, and an automatic transmission. All I have to do is shift the car into R to back down the driveway and then D to move forward. The steering is remarkably responsive; as I make a left onto Dartmouth Avenue, the car turns with a flick of the wheel. It must be the new power steering that my father has mentioned, wistfulness in his voice; my hardworking father hasn't had a new car in a dozen years or more. I smile, wondering if, here in the dream world, Lars lets him drive the Cadillac. My father would be in heaven, driving this car.

I turn on the radio and tune it to KIMN. They're playing that new song by Patsy Cline, the song that Lars and I heard in the restaurant the night we were there with his clients. I hum along softly.

The car glides smoothly up University Boulevard. I take a left on Evans and head west. Everything looks the same as always. The same University of Denver taverns, drugstores, and filling stations, the same buildings on campus. I note this with slight surprise; the world has not turned upside down just because *my* life is different.

On Pearl, I turn right and head north. There's not much auto traffic. It's a crisp, clear day—no snow in the skies and I'm guessing none in the forecast, at least not here in town. The mountains in the distance to my left are bright with freshly fallen snow; even from here, I can see the sheen that the sun puts on them.

When I reach our block, I cruise by slowly. I'm dismayed, but not entirely surprised, by what I see: Sisters' Bookshop is not there. Bennett and Sons, Attorneys-at-Law, still have their office in the right-hand side of the building. But the display windows on Frieda's and my side are boarded up, and there is a hand-printed FOR LEASE sign on the door. Bradley's telephone number is printed beneath the words. The sign is faded and weathered; it looks as if it's been there for a long time. Months, at least, perhaps years.

I park across the street and walk toward what used to be my bookshop.

I don't know exactly what to do. The glass-fronted door has no board over it, so I peer inside. It's empty. All of our shelves, our countertop—everything is gone. The linoleum floor is bare; the Turkish rugs that we bought secondhand at a thrift store have disappeared. The posters on the wall announcing the latest books and movies—vanished. The door to the back room hangs open, but it's too dark to see past it. But I know what would be there—nothing.

I turn toward the doorway at the side of the building. It leads up a flight of stairs to Bradley's apartment above the store. His number is on the FOR LEASE sign; that means he must still own the building. Does he still live upstairs, too? I tread carefully up the stairs and knock on his apartment door.

No one answers for a full five minutes. I am about to leave

when finally the door slowly opens. Bradley looks older here than he does in the other world. He is hunched over, his kind brown eyes behind their spectacles sunk deep into ashy sockets. It takes him a moment to figure out who I am.

"Well, as I live and breathe," he says finally. "If it isn't Miss Kitty."

Hearing someone speak my name—my real name, in this unreal world—almost moves me to tears, and I blink rapidly a few times. "Bradley." My voice cracks a bit. "It's good to see you."

He opens the door wider. "And to what do I owe the pleasure?"

I shrug. "I was . . . in the neighborhood, and I just . . ." I lower my eyes, look away, then back at him. "I thought I'd stop by."

"Well, come in." He opens the door the rest of the way. "I was just making tea. Would you like some?"

"That would be lovely. Thank you, Bradley."

While he is in the kitchen, I look around. His apartment, I note with relief, has not changed. Same old gray sofa with the stuffing coming out, same tweed armchair by the window, pulled a little closer to the television set than I remember. Same small, battered wooden dining table with four chairs. Enough space, he always said, for himself and his three grandchildren to sit there at the same time.

Bradley appears, a teacup held shakily in each hand. I step forward and take one of the cups. Our hands touch; his are rough from the cold of winter and the depths of old age.

"Please, sit," he says, pointing toward the table.

I take a seat, and Bradley sets down his tea and pulls out the chair across from me. "How are you?" he asks, settling himself. "And that nice husband, and the children—how is everyone?"

I smile and sip my tea. "We're all fine, Bradley. Just fine." I put down my teacup. "See here, I'm a bit confused, and I hope you can help me out. I'm not sure what happened or why we don't have the shop anymore." I look down at the floor. "And where Frieda is," I say, looking up. "I don't know where Frieda is."

I can't believe I'm having this conversation—but truthfully, what do I care? It's going to end soon anyway, and I'll be safe at home in my apartment. So I may as well say what I wish.

Bradley looks at me for a long time. "You don't know where Frieda is?"

I shake my head.

"Did something happen, Kitty? Something to make you not . . . remember things?"

"I don't know!" I burst out. "I think I'm dreaming, Bradley— this is a dream, right? This is not real, this is just made up in my head, and I'm just going along with it. But some parts of it . . . some parts . . ." I shake my head, not sure what I want to say. "Some things in this world make perfect sense, and are wonderful," I go on. "Lars—my husband—he's amazing. Truly amazing. I've never met anyone like him. I love him, with all my heart." I feel my face warm with bliss when I say this, and I smile in spite of myself, picturing my beautiful dream man. "And the children—well, two of them, Mitch and Missy, they're darlings. Michael is . . . Michael is . . ."

Bradley nods, and when I can't continue, he speaks softly. "It's all right, Kitty. I know what Michael is."

This acknowledgment, this gentle understanding from this gentle man, gives me more relief than anything—with the exception of Lars's clear devotion—that I've experienced thus far in this dream world. I want to hug Bradley, and I have to put my arms down firmly at my sides to keep myself from doing so. "Thank you," I tell him quietly. "Thank you for . . ." I don't know what to else to say, so I just finish, "the tea."

Bradley smiles. "Any time."

"You're okay . . . without a . . . tenant downstairs?"

He shrugs. "I'm okay. Building's been paid for a long time now. Just gotta keep up with the taxes and utilities, and the Bennetts' rent and the apartment next door mostly cover it. My sons want me to sell, but I like it here. I don't want to get kicked out, and I don't—" He grins. "God knows, I love my grandchildren. But I do *not* want to live with them."

I smile in return, then reach forward and take his leathery hand. "Where is Frieda?" I ask him softly. "Tell me, where is Frieda, and where is our shop?"

Bradley squeezes my hand, then releases it. He stands and picks ups his empty teacup. "She's moved on," he says. "Bigger and better things, Kitty." He shakes his head, looking out the window. "I can't tell you exactly where, because I don't know," he goes on. "She closed here and opened in that newfangled shopping center on Colorado Boulevard." He looks back at me. "But I think—and this is just what I hear from others, because God knows she doesn't come around here anymore—I think that was just the beginning."

I leave Bradley's apartment and get in the Cadillac. Placing the key in the ignition, I take one last look at the quiet old building. But there is nothing more to see there, so I turn my head, put the car in gear, and pull away from the curb.

I drive around the corner and turn south on Washington Street. A few blocks later, I park across from my old duplex. Here, too, things are silent. Absent are the shimmery purple drapes that hang in my front windows in the real world. Instead, the curtains are light blue with daisies printed on them. I find them fussy-looking, not like anything I would have selected.

Over on the Hansens' side of the building, the shades are drawn. I wonder if they still live there. In the real world, the Hansens' home was dark last night by the time I returned from my dinner with Frieda, so I didn't get to see Greg and commiserate with him about the Giants' loss in the last game of the World Series. I wonder what I can interest him in now. Perhaps football? Let's hope so. I laugh at myself, thinking about this. I couldn't care less about football. But if Greg is interested—why then, I shall become interested, too.

I wonder how Greg is doing with his reading, in this dream world. I am curious whether someone else is helping him, since in this life, I'm not here to do so.

Kevin and I saw a film a couple of years after the war, a Christmas story called *It's a Wonderful Life*. Jimmy Stewart starred as a man who, contemplating suicide on Christmas Eve, was given the opportunity to see what the world would have been like if he'd never been born. As we emerged from the theater after the show ended, Kevin said he thought the film was hugely sentimental, with an obvious plot and far-fetched characters. He scoffed at the storyline as Christmastime sappiness, with a singular intention: selling movie tickets.

True, I conceded, but you have to admit that it gives you something to think about. "It does give you pause, thinking about your own life," I'd added, "and who you've affected over the years."

Kevin shook his head and rolled his eyes. "Movies like that are made for women," he said. "Your gender is entirely too romantic, Kitty."

I smile now, remembering this conversation, remembering the movie. I think about seeing Kevin at C.J.'s last night. And I wonder if he'd still feel that way, were he to see that movie now, all these years later.

And I? What do I think? Am I having the effect on others that I want? I'm helping Greg, in the real world. Moreover, I'm thoroughly enjoying it.

In fact, nothing else going on there right now—not Sisters', not Frieda, not even thinking about my parents coming home soon—gives me as much pleasure as seeing Greg learn to read, seeing the world of literature open up for him.

I take one last look at the duplex, then pull away from the curb. When I drive past Mr. Morris's house down the block, I slow down, turning my head to see if my nonagenarian neighbor is sitting in his rocking chair on the porch. But he is not there, so I speed up again. Keeping my eyes and the long hood of the Cadillac facing forward, I hastily leave Washington Street and the old neighborhood behind.

At the shopping center, I head directly for the storefront that had been empty, the one Frieda has her eye on. Of course, I don't imagine it will be empty in this world.

Not only is the store a bookshop, but it's twice the size of the available space in the real world. Frieda must have taken over the unit next door, as well. Over both units is a large sign: Green's Books and News.

Of course. This store is hers, not ours. This bookstore belongs to Frieda Green. It does not belong to two would-be sisters. It's no surprise that she changed the name.

I peer through the glass, trying to be inconspicuous, looking at the displays inside. The store is bustling; customers browse dozens of stacks filled with books, magazines, newspapers, reading material of all sorts. Toward the right-hand side, I see a young male clerk helping someone reach a book on a high shelf. Nearby, in the fiction area, two middle-aged women huddle, comparing the covers of novels, evidently trying to decide what looks interesting. One of them is holding a book with block lettering and a Jewish star on the cover. Squinting and learning forward, I can just make out the title—*The King's Persons*. The woman opens the book and scans the first few pages, then speaks to her friend, who shrugs and takes the book in her hands. She flips through the pages and says something to her companion before tucking the book under her arm, in all likelihood intending to purchase it. The two women—shoulders pressed together, heads bent toward one another, talking books—remind me of Frieda and myself. Of Frieda and myself in my real life, that is. It saddens me to look at them; I bite my lip and turn away.

I glance at the checkout counter. My heart beats rapidly in my chest. I expect to see Frieda, all her confidence and swinging hair, running her show. But that doesn't happen. Frieda is not there at all, at least not anywhere that I can see. Instead, a young shopgirl sits behind the counter on a tall stool, her eyes down, reading something in front of her on the counter.

I take a deep breath and step inside. Walking toward the register, I put on what I hope is a spirited smile, and face the shopgirl.

"Can I help you?" she asks.

Despite my bravado, I am at a loss. "I was just . . . I was looking for . . ." I glance around helplessly, as if the answer will appear before me if I sweep my eyes around the brightly lit shop. I turn back to her and shrug. "I think I'd just like to browse."

She smiles and waves her hand. "Go ahead, ma'am. If you have any questions, be sure to let me know." She turns to wait on a customer who has queued up behind me.

I walk to the front stacks. The two women have moved on, and I have this area to myself. The stacks are filled with best sellers, romances, books with colorful covers. I immediately spy the new anthology by J. D. Salinger, which we've heard is coming out in early 1963. In this bright new bookstore, Frieda has almost a full row of copies of the new Salinger on display, highlighting its mustard-colored cover, its title in simple, modern text with no other artwork. There are numerous copies of *Seven Days in May*, the military thriller that was just gaining momentum back in my real world. I spot a shelf stocked with another nuclear-war-themed novel, *Fail-Safe*. In the real world, Frieda and I have preordered twenty copies of that book, which is due for release any day now. Clearly, *Fail-Safe* is making its mark in my imaginary 1963. Maybe, I think with amusement, I should increase our order quantity, back in the real world.

I pick up a copy of the book that the two women were looking at, and one of them bought—*The King's Persons*, by Joanne Greenberg. About dozen copies are lined up on the shelf. To their left, a small poster is propped up with an easel: NEWLY RELEASED! LOCAL AUTHOR! On it is a photograph of a rather serious-looking young woman, along with a glowing review of *The King's Persons* from the February 17, 1963, *Denver Post*. I've never heard of this novel, nor of Joanne Greenberg, but I make a mental note to find out more about her when I return to real life. And then I smile inwardly; how entertaining it is to be able to predict the future—albeit an imaginary future—in such a vibrant, meticulous way! Perhaps if I let go more often in these dreams, simply rolled with them as I did at first, I would enjoy them more.

A large copy of a Henri Matisse paper cutout—its vivid black, blue, green, and yellow hues attracting my eyes—hangs between two tall bookshelves. I recognize it immediately; I even know its name, *The Sorrows of the King*. Matisse created this work in 1952, toward the end of his life, when he worked with cutouts instead of painting. I have no idea how I know this; I've never seen it before. It's very to-the-moment, exactly the kind of thing Frieda would adore.

And then, suddenly, I realize that I *have* seen it before. A lithograph of *The Sorrows of the King* was displayed in the window of a gallery in Paris, when Lars and I were there on our honeymoon. I remember standing on the street with my new husband, my arm tucked into his, staring at it. Both of us were silent, overcome with the beauty of the simple figures, the colors, the blackness in the center. "It just stays with you," Lars whispered. "Close your eyes, Katharyn, and you can still see it in your mind's eye. You can still see the colors."

I closed my eyes and squeezed his arm, taking it in. "Frieda would love this piece," I said, opening my eyes. "I must tell her about it when we get home."

Yes, I remember that.

I glance at the counter, where the shopgirl has finished ringing up the customer who was waiting earlier. I walk back over. "What a lovely store," I say. "Have you worked here long?"

She shrugs. "A few months. It's a nice place to work, especially if you love books." She smiles again; she has a pretty smile, with very white teeth. "My friend who works at the Bear Valley Green's told me about it. Said I should apply. So I did, and I was fortunate to get the job."

"At the . . ." I shake my head, confused.

"Bear Valley," the girl says patiently. "You know, the shopping center in Lakewood."

I frown. "I'm sorry, I haven't heard of it."

The girl gives me a curious look. "Well, it's one of our six."

"Your six?"

"Six Green's Books and News locations," she explains.

What she says doesn't register for a moment. "I'm sorry, did you just say . . ."

"There are six stores," she says, handing me a brochure. "This one we're in, this is the original."

I glance at the brochure. It lists the shop here in University Hills, plus a location in downtown Denver; the one the shopgirl mentioned at Bear Valley; another one in Thornton, a Denver suburb to the north; and two in Colorado Springs. The photographs of the other stores show gleaming new locations in shopping centers or on busy commercial streets.

Of course there is no photograph of the tiny, dingy, long-closed Pearl Street store.

"This place has become soooo popular." The shopgirl sighs. "Miss Green put out a letter to all employees last week about another store that's opening in the spring, in Boulder. She says we're only going to get bigger and bigger."

"Miss Green . . . do you mean Frieda Green?"

"Yes, that's her. Do you know her, ma'am?"

"I used to," I say slowly. "It was a long time ago." I straighten up a bit and tap the brochure in my hand. "Tell me, where would I find Miss Green these days? Does she work in one of these other stores?"

The shopgirl laughs. "Of course not," she says. "She's got a big office downtown. A—what's it called? A corporate headquarters. It's on the same block as the downtown Green's. I went there for the company Christmas party." She smiles shyly. "I felt like a church mouse; they were all so glamorous."

I take another breath and plunge in again. "Do you know . . . maybe this is a silly question, but do you know about . . . Miss Green used to have a business partner. A Miss Miller. Kitty Miller . . ."

The shop girl's face sours. "*Everyone* knows about Miss Miller."

"Oh," I breathe. "Oh, is that true? What do they know about her?"

She looks around. "I shouldn't gossip like this to a customer, but okay." She leans forward. "Miss Miller and Miss Green had a terrible fight some years ago. Miss Miller—well, she was married by then, her married name was Mrs. Andersson, and honestly, I don't know the whole story, but I think that had something to do with it—her getting married, having a family, all that." Her voice lowers. "Anyway, they had some little bookshop that didn't make any money. They were in a lot of debt, and they quarreled about it. And Mrs. Andersson just walked away. Left the whole mess in Miss Green's hands." She shrugs. "Miss Green picked up the pieces and made a success of it, as you can see. But I heard that Miss Green never forgave her old partner." She looks down at her book, obviously embarrassed at having said so much, then quickly returns her gaze to me. "But I have no idea what happened to Mrs. Andersson. Or Miss Miller, if you want to call her that."

I sit in the driver's seat of the Cadillac, my forehead in my hands. The thought I had while browsing Frieda's store, my notion that the dreams mean nothing—that they exist purely for my amusement and entertainment—has been crushed, like a fallen leaf buried under the first heavy snow of winter.

Frieda, Frieda, what have I done? What did I do?

What happened between us?

Chapter 18

I wake with a start. It's pitch-black in my bedroom. The clock reads 2:45. Aslan is there, of course, purring blissfully, happy as a clam. Sometimes I wish I were Aslan.

Rising from the bed, I don my purple dressing gown and slippers and stumble through the darkness to the living room. At my desk, I turn on the lamp and have a seat. I reach for the telephone and dial Frieda's number.

She answers on about the seventh ring. Frieda is a heavy sleeper; always has been. "Huhhh . . ." she says, something between a grunt and a hello.

"Freeds," I say urgently. "Freeds, I'm sorry it's so late—"

"Kitty? What's wrong? Are you all right?" Her voice is instantly alert, and this warms me. Knowing that she could shift from bottomless sleep into enormous concern for me, just at the sound of my voice—I am comforted by this, and I feel my entire body relax.

"I'm sorry," I say again. "I'm all right. I just . . ." I hold the receiver closer to my mouth and whisper, "I had a bad dream." It sounds silly when I say it, so I add, "A really terrifying dream." And then I have to smile, because of course my dream was not terrifying in the typical sense: no monsters, no masked men with handguns, no tornadoes whipping off the roof above my head.

"Oh," Frieda breathes, and I hear her settling herself. I can picture her curled up in a mound of blankets in her bedroom—the shades drawn, the bedside lamp turned on. I hear the click of her lighter and the long inhale of smoke. "Do you want to tell me about it?"

Do I want to tell her about it? What an interesting question. I have no idea whether I want to tell her about it. On the one hand, it would be wonderful to unburden myself. Especially to a person like Frieda, who would listen and offer practical advice—and then perhaps the whole ordeal would end once and for all. On the other hand, the complete and utter foolishness of it makes me hesitate to put it into words. Even to Frieda, who I'd trust with my life.

"Kitty? Are you still there? Did you dream about the troubles in Cuba? What the president said on the news, about the Russian missiles? Is that what scared you?" She sighs, and I can almost feel her clenching her teeth. "Because, honestly, that whole situation is downright petrifying."

My mouth lifts into a tiny faux smile, the smile you make when you don't feel like smiling. "Actually," I tell Frieda. "I'm not scared about that at all."

I can't explain to her why I'm not anxious about Cuba. Everyone else is frightened to pieces by that. And yet I feel an inherent calm about it. I don't know why, but I'm certain it's going to blow over—and soon, too.

"You aren't scared by that?" Frieda sounds surprised. "What is it, then?" She pauses. "Are you all right, sister?"

I stare out at the darkness of the street in front of me. I can't tell her. I just have to hope the dreams go away on their own. Perhaps they simply have more of the story to tell me. And once the story is over, the dreams will end.

"I'm all right," I say finally. "I just . . . I had to hear your voice. I had to know that I'm back here. That I'm safe."

"Your doors are locked?" Frieda asks, exhaling cigarette smoke.

I laugh; of course locked doors can't keep out what is making its way inside my world. "Yes," I tell her. "Aslan and I are snug as bugs."

"Well, then. Go back to bed and try to get a good night's sleep. I'll see you in the morning."

"Okay," I say, feeling like a child who has been comforted by her mother. "Frieda . . ."

"Yes, sister?"

"Thank you," I whisper. "I'll see you in the morning."

Chapter 19

I return to bed and close my eyes, waiting for sleep. I hope it will be a sleep of darkness, of blankness, of nothing. But that is not to be. Coming into dream-consciousness, I'm back there again. Back in the other world.

I am no longer shocked at my return to the dream life. What is surprising is that I am still sitting in the Cadillac in the shopping center parking lot. It seems to be the same day, even the same hour. The sun is sitting identically low in the western sky. I am wearing the same camel-colored coat and matching gloves, and the car is in precisely the same parking space. It is as if no time has passed. But of course, there is no reason time *should* pass here. Not here, where everything—good and bad—is imaginary.

I turn on the engine, pull out of the lot, and drive back to Springfield Street. Lars and the children have returned; the station wagon is parked in the driveway. I go inside and shake off the cold, hanging my coat in the front hall closet. I place my hat, gloves, and handbag on the shelf above the closet's clothing rod.

"Mama!" I am hugged around the waist by both Mitch and Missy. I bend down to their level and return their affection. I am surprised at the fierceness with which I hold them, with how deeply I bury my nose into their flaxen heads and inhale the profound, clean smell of their hair. In my real life, I do not hold children like this. I had no idea, before now, how good it feels to do so. There are so few children in my life. There is Greg Hansen, of course, but our relationship is that of instructor and student, not one of physical affection. Occasionally I see Frieda's nieces and nephews, and Bradley's grandchildren regularly make an appearance in the shop. But none of those are children I'd feel comfortable holding with this fervor. Were I to suddenly do so, the discomfort would undoubtedly go both ways.

But these two—clearly they not only desire but expect this connection with me. The thought makes my heart pound just a bit more quickly.

Finally I release them and ask, "Did you have fun, darlings?"

"*So* much fun," Missy says. "I won the first game. Daddy won the second."

"And I got a strike!" Mitch adds, hopping up and down. "Mama, I got all the pins down at one time!"

"Good for you both," I tell them, and then I ask, "Where are Daddy and Michael?"

"Upstairs," Missy says. "Daddy is giving Michael a bath."

This seems odd, in the middle of the day. I make my way up the half flight of stairs and knock on the bathroom door. "It's me."

"Come in," Lars says. He is slowly, rhythmically pouring water from two plastic cups over Michael's thin, naked back. I can see the tiny round bones of Michael's spine, like beads under the skin. Michael has his eyes closed and a smile on his face, and he is humming. I look at Lars, searching for understanding. "He was having a rough time," Lars says in a low voice. "So we came home. You know how warm water helps him settle down."

I nod, not because I was aware of this tactic for calming Michael, but because it makes sense. I, too, find a warm bath beneficial when I'm not at my best. The heat, the gentle splashes of water—it's soothing in a way that nothing else can quite equal.

"Did you have a nice time?" Lars asks.

"Yes, it was . . ." I sit down on the closed toilet seat lid and take a look around. This bathroom, though smaller than the one I share with Lars, has the same slanted-front cabinets on the vanity; here, they are painted white. The walls are sky blue with white fish decals swimming the length of the longest wall, stuck-on bubbles arranged merrily above them. The sink, tub, and toilet are a robin's-egg color, and the floor is a spotless white tile.

I watch the water stream down Michael's back. "I went to the shop," I finally venture. "Frieda's and my . . . our old bookshop."

Lars looks at me. "Did you now?" His voice is even, and I cannot decode his opinion about this information.

"It's closed down." I can see myself in the mirror over the vanity, and my eyes look hollow. "She's closed down the Pearl Street shop. She has six other stores, and she changed the name to Green's Books and News, and she wasn't even there when I went to the one at the shopping center, and . . ." I stop talking. I must sound ridiculous to him.

Lars keeps his eyes steady on me. "Katharyn," he says finally. "All that happened a long time ago." He returns his gaze to Michael. "You know this. You remember it, right?"

I shake my head. "I don't remember it. I'm sorry, Lars, I still don't . . . I don't . . ." I bite my lip, looking at my gloomy face in the mirror. "I just don't remember a lot of . . . details."

"Well." His voice is neutral, but soft. "That's understandable, love."

"Oh, Lars." And suddenly, I feel myself breaking down. Tears start streaming down my cheeks.

Lars stands and comes to my side. He puts his hand on my shoulder and rubs it gently. "It's okay, love," he whispers. "It's okay. I know you feel bad about it. Even all these years later."

"What did I do?" I ask him, and I know he thinks the question is rhetorical. But of course it's not.

"You did what you had to," Lars says evenly. "You did what you had to for your family, for your child . . ." He tilts my chin up, so I can look in his eyes. "I know everything you gave up . . . for us . . . for him." His voice is a whisper, and he turns his eyes toward the bathtub, where Michael is still humming, quietly playing with the two cups. "I know what you sacrificed. Don't ever, ever doubt, Katharyn . . . how incredibly grateful I am to you for that."

I go to our bedroom to lie down. If I fall asleep, I will wake up back where I belong. Where things make sense and nothing is confusing like this.

But I can't sleep. I close my eyes, but sleep doesn't come.

Instead, to my surprise, memories do.

It's like the time when I was in the green bathtub, or the evening in the restaurant with Lars's client and his wife. All of a sudden, I remember things with clarity.

I remember what started out as a routine visit to the obstetrician. I even remember the date: July 6, 1956. I was a few weeks into the second trimester of my pregnancy; Lars and I were expecting a Christmastime baby. I expressed concern that I was so big already. I felt tired and out of sorts, I told the doctor, as if I were ready to give birth now, though of course I had months yet to go.

"Let's check for a heartbeat again," Dr. Silver said. "I know we tried to hear it early on, and we checked again when you were here a few weeks ago. But we should definitely hear it by now." Putting the stethoscope to my belly, he listened, then moved it, listened again, moved it again. This went on for a full five minutes, while he didn't say a word. Finally he stood. "I'll be back in a moment, Mrs. Andersson," he told me. "I want to have Dr. Enright take a listen here, too."

I lay there, sweating bullets, my mind numb. No heartbeat, I was thinking. He can't hear a heartbeat, and he's afraid the baby is dead. He wants the other doctor to confirm it.

The two men entered the room, and Dr. Enright poked all over my belly with his stethoscope, too. They looked at each other and nodded, then conferred with each other, their backs to me. I started to cry; I couldn't help it. How will I ever tell Lars that the baby has died? I wondered. He's going to be devastated.

The doctors turned around simultaneously. Seeing my face, Dr. Silver took my hand in both of his. "Mrs. Andersson, please don't cry. It's good news. Let me be the first to congratulate you. Both Dr. Enright and I are quite sure you are expecting twins!"

I floated home from the doctor's office. My mind was reeling with excitement. Twins! How lucky could we be? To have met each other so late in life—when both of us had, for all intents and purposes, given up on ever finding a mate. To almost *not* have met, had we not stayed on the telephone long enough for me to hear his emergency and rescue him. To find ourselves so compatible, to fall in love so rapidly. To marry so quickly, to start a family so soon. And now this! It could not be more perfect.

I was convinced it was a boy and a girl.

I was still working at Sisters' in those days, of course, but I telephoned Frieda and told her the appointment had worn me out and I had gone home to rest. Of course, I did not tell her the news that there were two babies. I was dying to, but that was Lars's to hear first, not Frieda's.

Back home, in the kitchen of our small apartment, I made a batch of white cake batter, which I separated into two bowls. I dyed one with a few drops of red food coloring, turning it pink; the other, I dyed baby blue. I poured them into two pans. When the cake layers had cooled, I stacked them and frosted the entire thing generously with white icing.

I prepared dinner: salad with garden-fresh vegetables, pork chops stuffed with bread crumbs and spinach, and mashed potatoes. After dinner, I brought out the cake. "Slice into it," I said to Lars. "It will tell you if we're having a boy or a girl."

Lars gave me a quizzical look. "I thought you went to the doctor today, not a fortune-teller." Nonetheless, he smiled and took up the knife. I watched his face carefully as he pulled a slice from the cake, then looked at me in confusion.

"Congratulations, Papa," I said. "We're having twins!"

He laughed and shook his head. "Amazing." He pulled me onto his lap, my big belly protruding between us. "And how, my beautiful wife, do you know for sure that it's not two boys? Or two girls?"

I smiled. "I just know. It's here." I tapped my heart. And then I put my hand on his chest and whispered, "Here, too."

I wish I could remember Frieda's reaction to the news that I was having twins. I am sure that would speak volumes about where we are now. But I cannot remember what she said. I do remember that before the big news, back when we thought it was only one baby, I had planned to bring my infant to Sisters' with me while it was small. Frieda, as I recall, thought that would be fine. I had it all pictured in my mind: a cradle in the corner, where the baby would sleep peacefully while Frieda and I tended our shop. "Once he or she is more active, I'll hire a babysitter," I'd assured

Frieda. "It will be fine. Everything here will stay the same as always."

She'd nodded. "I'm glad." She squeezed my hand. "Don't leave me, sister. Don't abandon me."

"Never," I told her firmly. "We'll work it out."

"I'll help you find someone, when the time comes," she offered. "With all my parents' connections . . . You want someone really qualified, Kitty. Someone competent, someone you can trust. I'll help. I want you to be sure of what you're doing."

I'd nodded gratefully. "That would be wonderful, Frieda. Thank you."

Yes. That conversation, I remember well.

After pronouncing me expectant with twins, Dr. Silver warned me against working too hard. He convinced me to cut back my hours at the shop to mornings only. I promised Frieda that I would be back full-time as soon as possible. With two babies, it seemed impractical to bring them to the shop, but we would simply accelerate the hiring of a babysitter.

Because of this promise, Frieda was not overly upset when the doctor put me on bed rest at twenty-eight weeks' gestation. It was not a strict bed rest; although I could not leave our apartment, I was permitted to get up from the bed in the morning and go to the couch. I could take occasional small walks from room to room, just to stretch my legs, and I was allowed to fix myself lunch, if I were alone.

But I was rarely alone. My mother was there almost every day. Taking care of me, preparing my meals, keeping me company. I remember thanking her almost daily for this, and I specifically remember her reaction: "No thanks are needed, sweetheart. What mother wouldn't do this? What do you think I've been waiting for all these years? At last I'm going to be a grandmother!"

Lars's return from work every evening brought kisses, smiles, and often flowers. He frequently brought me novels or paperback books of crossword puzzles, something to keep me occupied. He called a dozen times a day, just to check up on me. "Just to hear your voice," he'd tell me over the line.

Aslan, dear Aslan, was my companion at all times, purring contently beside me. "If Aslan had his way," I'd joked to Lars and my mother. "I'd stay on this couch gestating babies forever."

Did Frieda visit my couch-prison? I cannot recall ever seeing her there—although of course she must have made an appearance every now and then. How often? I have no idea.

I pored over baby-name books, and every night Lars and I would consult on the subject. I refused to select more than one girl name and one boy name, so sure was I that the babies would be what I thought they were. After much discussion, we agreed on Mitchell Jon and Melissa Claire. Mitchell's middle name was after Lars's father, and Melissa's middle name was after my mother. We'd call them Mitch and Missy.

Despite my best efforts to carry those babies to term, I made it to only thirty-four weeks—just over seven and a half months. On the evening of November 12, as I lay on the couch watching television with Lars, I felt warm water rushing from my body. And then I felt the first painful contraction.

"Lars, the babies . . . I think they're coming," I gasped.

"They can't come!" he said. I could hear panic in his normally calm voice. "It's too soon."

I shrugged. I even laughed. "Tell *them* that."

At the hospital, we were told that the babies would need to be born via cesarean section. "They would not survive a natural birth," Dr. Silver told Lars and me sternly.

I tried to tell myself rationally that the doctor didn't mean to sound as if he were scolding me—but that is exactly how he sounded.

I remember Lars holding my hand before I went into the operating room, then slowly releasing it as I was wheeled away. I remember the anesthesiologist, a kind-looking older man. "Count backward from ten, my dear," he told me. I got to six, and that's the last thing I remember.

When I woke up, I was in a regular hospital room. My abdomen was on fire with pain, and I winced, turning my head and closing my eyes again. I opened them and saw Lars sitting at my bedside. I whispered feebly, "The babies—are they okay?"

He smiled wearily. "They're fine. They're in intensive care, because their lungs are small and they need some help breathing. But they're doing great, and the doctor thinks they'll be just fine."

"And I was right, wasn't I? A boy and a girl?"

He shook his head. "You were *almost* right."

"Almost? What does that mean?"

"A girl, my love. And a boy. And . . . a boy."

I didn't say anything for a moment. I wasn't sure I understood what he meant. Then it started to sink in. "Are you saying it was . . . *triplets?*"

"Was and is. Yep. Triplets. The doctor thinks one was hiding behind the other two, which is why he only heard two heartbeats." Lars let out a long breath, then took my hand. "So we have our Mitch and Missy. Now, what will we name that other fellow?"

Lying on the bed in our green bedroom, I remember all of this as if it happened yesterday.

As if it *really* happened.

I think about Michael, and how he was always "that other fellow."

The unintended one. Not expected at all, really.

And, once he was here, certainly not expected to be as he turned out.

Chapter 20

When I wake up, I am at home—if indeed you can call this home; this quiet apartment with the hopeful yellow walls and the false sense of serenity.

Is it false? I think about this as I rise from the bed. A small part of me has started to wonder what is true and what is made up. It's beginning to seem impossible that something as real as the world I share with Lars and the children could actually be imaginary.

I shake off the thought and fix myself some brain-tidying coffee. It's Monday morning. Yesterday, thank goodness, the Soviets agreed to remove their nuclear weapons from Cuba, and the United States breathed a collective sigh of relief. I joined in the exhalation, of course; I walked over to Frieda's house, and we watched the rebroadcast of the news on her television set, sitting side by side on her couch and drinking black tea with honey and no cream. Frieda never has cream in the house, much to my aggravation.

"Thank the Lord," Frieda said, chain-smoking Salems and barely touching her tea. "Thank the Lord."

Despite the relief I share with the nation, it's true, what I said to Frieda in the middle of the night last week—I was never truly frightened about the Cuban situation. Perhaps it just seemed too unbearable to fathom, that World War III could actually be about to start, and there wasn't a thing any of us could do about it. Or perhaps my mind is just too muddied these days by the peculiarity of my dream life, leaving me little room to think on a broader scope. Whatever the reason, I never thought the threat was as vast and imminent as everyone else seemed to believe. Turns out I was right.

As I drink my coffee, I consider this chain of events. I remember calling Frieda in the night; I remember her words of comfort. I remember, yesterday, hearing the news about Cuba and going to Frieda's house to watch television. But what of the days in between? I shake my head. I can recall nothing of these days. I have no idea what I did or who I spoke to or what I thought about.

Feeling a bit panicky, I gulp the last of my coffee. How can this be? I search my mind for recent memories, but none appear. I look in the dustbin for newspapers from last week, but all I can find is yesterday's *Post*, wrinkled and crumpled beneath a layer of bread crumbs and the wrapper from a Hershey's candy bar. I don't even remember eating a candy bar. When did this happen? Where was I, what was I doing, where did I buy a candy bar? It seems terribly important that I remember these details, but my mind is blank.

I need to gather my wits, I think as I go outside for my mail. There's a postcard from Mother—one that was obviously written well before the Cuban situation came to an end yesterday.

Dear Kitty,

I suppose by now you've heard the news about the weapons in Cuba. It's dreadful, isn't it? I must say we feel very isolated here. And I am terrified for you, darling. I

don't think that madman Castro could fire his missiles all
the way to Hawaii. But on the mainland—even though you
are, thankfully, thousands of miles from the east coast—
even so, your father and I are concerned.

Dad is looking into flights for you to come here to us,
instead of us coming home next week. Think about it, darling.

Love,
Mother

I shake my head. I adore my mother, and I love how anxious
she is about me. But honestly, does she truly think I could just
up and leave? Get on a plane and fly away from Frieda, the shop,
Aslan, my entire life? It's a good thing the whole Cuban incident
has blown over, making it a moot point.

Today is, luckily, my day off from work. I have planned to
spend it opening my parents' house and airing it out. I will give
it a good dusting, and I hope to have time to rake the leaves in
their yard, too. I want everything to be perfect for them when
they get home. With the Cuban situation resolved, there will be
no change in plans; my parents will leave Honolulu on Wednesday night and arrive here on Thursday.

I put on old pedal pushers and a frayed denim blouse, tie
my hair back with a kerchief, and retrieve my bicycle from the
shed behind my duplex. It's a cool, cloudy day, and after crossing the Valley Highway on the Downing Street bridge, I ride up
the slight hill, turn right, and pedal on Louisiana Avenue, along
the southern edge of Washington Park—the park I went to with
Michael in the dream life, a few dreams ago.

I ride past South High School, my alma mater. Its bell tower
rises above the houses and trees, the clocks on each side displaying
the eight o'clock hour. There is a low buzz of students making their

way into the building, starting their school day. They seem unusually subdued for so early an hour—a time, at least in my memory of high school, when everyone and everything was overflowing with noisy anticipation of the day ahead.

Deep in thought, I watch the students as I cycle past. As a student here—with characteristic teenage angst—I thought of the school as something like a torture chamber, designed specifically to heighten my suffering. *Nothing* ever goes my way, I would say to myself, more morose and downtrodden than any Dickensian character had ever been. Few boys noticed me, and I did not have a gaggle of girlfriends, the way so many of my female classmates seemed to. Even some of my teachers barely knew who I was. I remember one particularly embarrassing incident in which my algebra teacher, Miss Parker, mistakenly called on me in class using the name of the most unpopular girl in our grade, Melvina Jones, who was not even in the room at the time. Melvina was slovenly, overweight, wore glasses; add to those strikes a name like Melvina, and the poor girl was doomed to social failure. Unfortunately for me, Melvina also had curly strawberry blond hair, similar to my own. There was no mistaking it when the teacher looked directly at me and called Melvina's name. "Oh!" Miss Parker said quickly, realizing her error. "You're not Melvina. I meant Kitty . . . I'm sorry, Kitty. Would you answer question twelve on page ninety-eight? Come up to the board and show your work, please." When I did so, my face flushed with embarrassment, Miss Parker smiled apologetically; I nodded submissively. But—as my classmates' mirth made all too clear—the damage had been done.

If not for Frieda, those years would have been unbearable. I think about what Frieda was like back then, how that confidence of hers rubbed off on me, like so much magical dust on the proverbial timid girl in a fairy tale. I was certain that my friendship with Frieda was the only thing that separated me, at least a little, from the Melvina Joneses of the world.

At one point during those years, I remember reading a passage in the psychology section of my health textbook that said as long as a person has just one good friend, he is not abnormal. I finished the passage with a satisfied sigh; I had Frieda, and as long as I held on to her, I was going to be all right.

Thinking about these times makes me wistful. I wish I could go back and tell my fifteen-year-old self that the passage was right. All *would* be well. I would grow up to be happy. Someday, I would have everything I wanted.

But do I? I am not so sure anymore about this "everything" business. Yes, I am content. I've had to face some heartache, some loss, but what I have—the shop, Frieda, my parents, Aslan, my uncomplicated life—it feels like enough.

And in the other life? What of that?

I shake my head and set my right foot firmly down on the bicycle pedal, speeding up my journey. I am eager to get to my parents' house, eager to get dirty and sweaty. I need to focus on the concrete, real world in front of me. I need to stop all of this idle speculation.

Inside the house, everything feels closed and heavy, casketlike. The gloom disturbs me, and I open all the curtains and window sashes.

The windows look dirty, so I mix warm water, vinegar, and lemon juice in a bucket and start rubbing them with an old cloth. The late-fall weather is cool and dank, so my efforts don't show much, but I continue working nonetheless. A slight breeze, combined with the lemon scent from the bucket, gives the house a sweet smell, like a baby after a bath. I smile at this random thought. What do I know about how a baby smells after a bath? I have never in my life bathed a baby.

As I'm working, I see Frieda walking up the street toward the house. She's arriving unannounced, but this doesn't surprise me. She knew I'd be cleaning over here today, and even on our days off, we are often together for at least part of the day. I lean out the window and call her name when she gets closer; she waves and her gait accelerates as she steps from the sidewalk up the walkway to the house. I leave my post to greet her.

"How are you, sister?" I reach up to give her a tight squeeze around the shoulders.

"Swell," she says, returning my hug, then releasing me after a moment. "I'm enjoying the clouds, actually. Isn't it funny how that's a nice change of pace after so many sunny days?" With nary a pause, she says, "Look, I bought the most perfect apples in the world." She fishes in her large, gray leather handbag and draws out two red-green apples. "Did you ever see anything so divine?"

I shake my head. "Gorgeous." She hands one to me, and we sit side by side on the sofa to enjoy them.

"All ready for the big homecoming?" Frieda asks.

I smile. "How pitiful is that?" I ask. "I'm thirty-eight years old, and I'm excited that my parents are finally coming home from vacation."

She shrugs. "I don't think it's pitiful. I think it's rather nice, actually."

Frieda is not as close to her parents as I am to mine. It's not that she's had any sort of falling-out with Margie and Lou; it's more that she doesn't have a good deal in common with them. Margie never understood Frieda's drive to be a businesswoman. She was disappointed that Frieda never made a "proper marriage" with some eligible, well-heeled young man in Denver society; many have asked Frieda out over the years, and Frieda's parents would have welcomed any of those fellows into their family. "It's not right," Margie has said on more than one occasion. "A pretty girl like you, a girl with everything going for her, wasting away in a little shop like that." She never says it directly, Margie, but you can tell she thinks it's all right for *me*.

As for Lou, he's much more interested in his sons and their families, especially the grandsons, than in Frieda's bookish world. Lou played football in college and was even second string for the Bears, Denver's first professional football team, before quitting professional sports and becoming a businessman. At family gatherings, you'll most likely find him out in the yard, throwing a ball with the boys. Frieda's life, which centers mostly on the shop, books, and me, makes little sense to him. Frieda has on more than one occasion attempted to merge these two worlds by bringing him books about sports, fishing, or hunting; these, he politely thanks her for and promptly casts aside. Frieda has told me she later finds them carefully arranged on the bookshelf in her parents' den, gathering dust.

Despite all that—there is their money. Without her parents' money, Frieda and I would not be where we are today.

When we first opened Sisters', my parents put up a small sum for us, more as a gesture than to make much difference financially, since their savings were meager. It was Frieda's parents' contribution that truly got us started. I remember the day we signed our loan paperwork, remember sitting in the bank next to Frieda, her father on the other side of her, the loan officer looming large over his desk in front of us. "So, Lou, you're going to take a chance on these girls," the bank man said. "You sure that's a wise idea?" His mouth twitched playfully, but you could tell that he was only half joking; I was pretty sure that he didn't think it was a wise idea at all.

Lou answered gruffly. "Wife agrees with you," he told the man. "But let's do this thing anyway."

We pay our loan faithfully each month, although sometimes we're late with the payment because of a simple lack of cash flow. We paid our parents back, Frieda's and mine, as soon as we possibly could. After that, we never asked anyone for another dime. My parents didn't have the money to spare, and Frieda's—well, their money made her uncomfortable. She would have much preferred, if there'd been any way to do it, for us to get started all on our own. "Just this once," I remember her hissing as we left the bank the day we got the loan, her father and the banker shaking hands behind us. "Just this once, Kitty. Never again."

There was a time, a few years ago, when we were getting into a bit of hot water with the bookstore's finances. It was shortly after the bus line left; we saw a sharp decline in business and mounting debt. I remember that I asked Frieda if she'd be willing to ask her parents for another loan, and she shook her head. "We'll figure out something else," she'd said firmly. "We'll have to."

Take it as coincidence or destiny, I don't know—but soon after, my maternal grandfather died, leaving a thousand dollars to each of his grandchildren, including me. That money kept Sisters' afloat, allowing us to catch up on the loan and pay Bradley the two months' rent we owed him. We reorganized our stock, ran a few advertisements in the local papers, and also had a bit of random luck—a sandwich shop opened a few doors down from us, and a full-service restaurant on the next block. Those establishments brought in new customers, some of whom became regulars. Fortunately, we were able to stay in business.

My small inheritance also kept Frieda from having to ask her parents for money. She was grateful for this, I know. "Anything I can do to keep from being indebted to them," she told me. "Anything is a help." Across the countertop at Sisters', she'd taken my hand and held it tightly, massaging my fingers between her own. "Thank you, Kitty," she'd said.

Now, at my parents' house, I bite thoughtfully into my apple. Then I ask Frieda, "Do you remember me eating a candy bar yesterday? Or perhaps the day before?"

She shakes her head. "What are you talking about?"

"A Hershey's bar." I hear the urgency in my voice—idiotic, illogical. "A Hershey's Milk Chocolate bar. Did I eat one in front of you, sometime in the past day or two?"

Frieda smiles and takes another bite of apple. "I honestly cannot recall such an event."

"What *do* you recall, then?" I query her. "What do you remember of the past couple of days?" I look around my mother's familiar living room—the slumped but comfortable velvet chairs, the scratched but tidy Victorian side tables, the shabby rug. "Because I can hardly remember a thing."

Frieda shrugs. "You came to my house and watched television with me all day yesterday. You remember that, don't you?" She grins. "Please tell me you remember that the country is no longer threatened by direct nuclear attack."

I nod. "I remember that. But nothing else. What did we do on Saturday, or Friday? Or the few days before that? I don't remember anything since we ran into Kevin the other night."

Frieda faces me. "You okay, sister?" she asks softly.

Again, I'm overwhelmingly tempted to tell her everything. All about the dreams, all about my mixed-up memories. But I cannot. I shrug. "Sure. I'm fine. Let's talk about something else."

Frieda glances around the room. "The place is in good shape."

I groan. "I have hours of work ahead of me."

She shakes her head. "No, it looks nice. They'll be pleased." She grins again. "You know they wouldn't care, don't you?"

I do know that. But there is something about pleasing your parents, even when you're grown up, even when you're almost middle-aged yourself. It never goes away, at least not for me.

Frieda nibbles the last of her apple. "Well, I'm off," she says, standing. "I have shopping to do. Penney's is having a sale. I want a new coat for winter."

I nod. "I wish I could come. Have fun."

She hugs me. "You, too, sister."

After Frieda leaves, I'm frenzied in my work, and by midafternoon the place is spotless. I look around, a satisfied smile on my face. I've done a good job. They *will* be pleased.

I think about that rambling house on Springfield Street. I wonder how my other self keeps it clean, even with the faithful Alma to help out. And then I laugh a little.

It's easy to keep an imaginary house clean, isn't it?

Despite my intentions not to dwell on the dream life, I am drawn to Southern Hills again.

I tell myself it's just something to do, a way to pass an evening that's chilly but not yet wintry. I bike home from my parents' place and, too weary for much more exercise, take the bus, getting off at Yale and walking south and then east.

Slowly I meander through the neighborhood streets. I imagine the people who live in each of the houses. I think about their lives, their families, their children. That house there, the redbrick one with the juniper bushes by the driveway, they must have teenagers. There's a basketball hoop hung above the garage door and a pile of bicycles, all of them too big for young children, lying on the lawn by the front porch. The family in the house with the brown shutters—I think their car must be brand-new. It's red with a white top, and it gleams with a just-off-the-showroom-floor sparkle. The man of the house stands next to the car, stroking its side panel affectionately, the way one might the cheek of a newborn.

These people have names, although I don't know what they are. They have histories. They were probably raised in old-time neighborhoods like Myrtle Hill, where I grew up. They went to high school, perhaps to college. They met their husbands and wives; they had children. They decided this neighborhood of newly built houses would be a comfortable, homey, secure place in which to raise their families.

Lars and I, in the imaginary world, must have decided the same thing.

If that imaginary world were real, these would be my friends and neighbors. I walk by the Nelsons' house, irrationally grateful that I know at least one family's name, though in this life they do not know me. George is in the yard, raking leaves. Mrs. Nelson—I still don't know her first name—is just coming out the front door, handbag over her wrist, car keys jangling. Their little spaniel runs up to me and barks.

"Buster," George calls, and the dog runs back to his master's side. "Sorry about that, ma'am," George says.

Both George and his wife give me little half waves as I walk by. Their waves are the type you give a stranger. Not the type you give your neighbors.

I shake my head as I approach the bare lot where my own house would be. And then I quicken my pace.

I have *got* to get out of this silliness, I tell myself.

I am so glad my parents are coming home. Clearly I need the distraction.

Chapter 21

And then I'm standing on the street, right where I was standing in real life, in the exact same spot. But it's not real life anymore. Now the house is in front of me, and I'm looking at it, and my family is with me. It's a warmish day, but it still must be winter; there is no snow on the road, but it is melting into slushy puddles on the lawn. From the angle of the shadows on the snow, I can tell it's probably midafternoon.

But how did I get into the dream this time? I don't remember taking the bus back to my own neighborhood. I have no memory of making dinner, of reading or watching television or tutoring Greg, the things I usually do in the evening at home. I don't remember turning off the front porch light, feeding Aslan, getting dressed for bed. I don't recall closing my eyes, and I certainly don't remember falling asleep. But I must have done those things.

Or I did something. Something.

Mitch and Missy are wobbling on bicycles—two-wheelers, his green and hers pink. Lars is walking beside the two of them, working with one and then the other to teach them how to ride. I think the training wheels must have recently been taken off the bikes, because both children are falling. A lot.

Missy goes down and lands on her elbow. "Ow!"

Before I have time to react, Lars reaches down to help her

rise. Gently, he bends her arm back and forth a few times to make sure the elbow is functioning normally. "Don't give up," he tells her, righting the bike and helping her back onto it. "It takes a lot of practice."

Lars catches my eye and smiles. Then he turns sideways and swings his arm, as if he's batting a tennis ball. Automatically I do the same thing, also turned sideways. Lars is a lefty and I'm right-handed, so our positions pose us as partners, as if we were playing doubles against imaginary rivals. This pantomime, I suddenly understand, is one that Lars and I frequently perform. It's our silent way of communicating to each other that we are on the same team—not just in tennis, but in everything. I nod at him, and he turns his attention back to Mitch and Missy.

It's then that I realize Michael is not riding. He's sitting in the driveway, staring down at the fabric of his bunched-up pants. A blue boy's bike stands in the drive next to him; this one still has its training wheels on it.

I pause for a moment, and then I walk over and sit next to Michael.

Hesitantly, I ask, "Michael? Don't you want to ride?"

He shakes his head, not looking up.

"You can try, you know," I tell him gently. Because I believe this. There are a lot of things that, perhaps, he can't do. But he *can* learn to ride a bike. I am sure of it.

He shakes his head again, and won't answer and won't meet my eye.

I inspect his bike. It's beautiful and looks brand-new—still gleaming, with nary a scratch on it. I recall that the triplets' birthday is in November; perhaps these bikes were birthday presents when they turned six.

I glance back at the garage, which is standing open, the large double door raised. "I'll be right back," I say to Michael, standing and dusting off my skirt.

I go into the garage and look around. The station wagon is parked in here; the Cadillac, too. It's a big garage, with room for a lawn mower, sleds, and bikes in addition to vehicles.

I find my bike easily. It's the same battered red Schwinn that I have in real life. I suspect that at some point during our marriage Lars would have proposed purchasing a new bicycle for me. But I would have resisted that notion. He may be able to buy me a car and fine clothes and a diamond ring, but this is my bike. We've been together for a long time, my Schwinn and me; I bought it myself during the early days of my teaching career, so I could bicycle to school. I would not have abandoned it heedlessly.

I wheel it out and climb on, gliding down the driveway. I stop in front of Michael, pressing the brakes gently with my feet. "Mama will ride with you," I coax.

Michael doesn't respond.

I know I ought to let it go, but I simply cannot. It seems terribly important—for reasons that I cannot fathom—that I make this connection with him.

That he rides with me. That biking becomes "our thing." Something we share.

I reach out for him, try to pull him up by his arm.

Oh, I should know better, shouldn't I? By now, I should know better.

The howl that comes out of him makes me step back, drop my bike, put my hands over my own mouth, as if by doing so I can silence his. Missy and Mitch stop riding and stare at us wordlessly. Lars strides over, glaring at me.

"I was hoping . . . I thought I could convince him to . . ." I trail off.

Lars bends down, does the shoulder-hold, and begins to hum.

After a moment, Michael stops screaming and hums with Lars, until they are both in a little singsong trance. No one else in the world except the two of them.

Biting my lip, I turn away.

I pick up my Schwinn and wheel it over to Missy and Mitch. "Daddy will manage Michael," I tell them, climbing on my bicycle. "Now, you two show me what you can do."

Chapter 22

On Wednesday afternoon, I have a hair appointment with Linnea.

I wonder, as I walk toward Linnea's beauty parlor, how I got from Monday to Wednesday. Again—as was the case a few days ago, when I didn't remember getting from the middle of last week to the beginning of this week—I don't remember a lot of details. I can't recall transitioning from my last dream, from bicycling with the children, back to the safety of my own bed. I don't remember waking up on Tuesday morning. Indeed, I must have arisen and made breakfast and fed Aslan. I must have gone to the shop and worked. There would have been customers; there would have been book orders and shelf arrangements and conversations with Frieda. What did we discuss? I don't remember. I *think* there was more conversation about the vacant space in the shopping center. I *think* we went over the financial aspects, trying to figure out how we could make it work moneywise. Did we decide to make an appointment with the bank to talk about an extension to our loan? Perhaps we did, but I can't recall any particulars about the discussion.

Waiting for the light to change so I can cross the street, I pull my coat collar tightly around my throat, protecting myself from the windy, overcast day. I know this absence of memories ought to concern me, but when I give it more thought, I realize how very few actual moments—whether yesterday, last week, a month ago, last year—I can truly recall in detail. We remember so little of our lives, really, insofar as the finer points go.

Living, I think as I cross Jewell Avenue at Broadway, is not made up of details, but rather of highlights. Can I remember what I had for lunch last Thursday? Can I recall every word of my latest tutoring session with Greg? Do I know what the weather was like three weeks ago on Sunday? Certainly not. It all just flies by, the big and the small, and some of it stays in our minds, but much of it disappears the moment after it occurs.

I open the door to Beauty on Broadway and walk inside.

At her station, Linnea greets me with a smile. "It's nice to see you again, Kitty. I'm sorry I haven't made it to your bookstore yet. I really do want to see it." She touches my hair gently, frowning at me in the mirror. "Goodness, you ought to come here to see *me* more often, though. If you don't mind my saying so."

I grin. "I don't mind at all. You're right; I ought to."

After my shampoo, she settles into her work with the rollers. I lean back and relax. It's Halloween today, and Linnea has her station decorated with a little paper black cat taped to the mirror and a bowl of tiny pink-and-white boxes of Good & Plenty candy on the vanity.

In the mirror I watch Linnea's hands, those lovely hands that remind me of Lars's. I want to reach out to them, and I have to press my own hands together, as if in prayer, to control myself.

I'm glad she's touching me, however. It feels wonderful to have Linnea touch me.

"You made the right move, going into a line of work where you use your hands." It sounds silly the moment I say it, and I close my mouth, embarrassed.

Linnea smiles. "Oh, I've got strong peasant hands," she says.

"They've done plenty of tough work over the years. My brother Lars and I, when we first moved to Colorado . . . we were kids, we had nothing, we took any job we could get. Dishwashers, potato diggers, bakers. He was a bricklayer for a while, and then he got a job as a streetcar repairman. Put himself through college doing that job." Her brow furrows. "He was the real worker, Lars. He could fix anything, build anything. Loved to work with his hands."

I nod. Though I have not witnessed this directly, I can imagine it. I can imagine how, given the time and capacity, he would build things, fix things.

And then something comes to me. A memory, or a thought, or something I made up. I have no idea where it comes from, but when I know it, I know it.

Naturally, Lars designed our house's distinctive layout. Certainly, given his line of work and his enthusiasm for custom residential design, he would have done that. But he also personally constructed all the cabinetry in our house. Those slanted bathroom cabinets, and the slick-faced ones in the kitchen— Lars built all of those by hand.

I do not know how I know this, but I do. I close my eyes, letting reflections and memories from my made-up life envelop my mind.

When we first married, I gave up my duplex, Lars gave up his small studio apartment, and we moved together into a two-bedroom apartment on Lincoln Street, I could walk to the shop from our new place, and Lars took the Broadway line to the office he'd rented downtown for his fledgling architectural firm. The apartment was temporary, he assured me, just until his business showed a profit. "Then I'll build you a house," he'd said, looking around at the apartment's bright but small living room. "I'll build you a wonderful house, Katharyn."

The apartment on Lincoln was where I spent my bed rest. It was the home to which we brought our babies when they were ready to leave the hospital.

After the surprise of triplets instead of twins, Lars had hastily switched the bedrooms, moving our double bed and bulky dresser into the smaller bedroom—which, months earlier, we had painstakingly set up as a nursery for a boy and a girl. I remember the pale yellow walls, the nursery-rhyme mural that I hired an artist friend of my mother's to paint on the wall over the area where we placed the changing table. It was a lovely nursery, and adequate for two babies, but it was too small for three cribs and everything else that three would need. Lars selected another crib at Guys and Dolls, the children's furniture store where we had purchased the other two cribs. He set up the three cribs, the changing table, and the rocking chair in what had once been our bedroom. I had been told that he'd made these changes, yet I remember my dismay, seeing the arrangement when the babies and I were finally discharged from the hospital. There had been no time for repainting; our bedroom walls were a sophisticated mauve that had gone wonderfully with my bedspread, but was not at all suitable for three babies. Although the children's furniture fit in the room, it was a tight squeeze, and we had to shuffle sideways to fetch Mitch from his crib.

The setup was equally awkward in Lars's and my "new" bedroom. The nursery-themed mural, of course, made no sense in a master bedroom. The way our furniture had to be arranged in the small room, the mural was directly over my head when I lay in bed—the cow jumping over the moon was the last thing my worn-out eyes saw before they closed at night. But we were too exhausted and overwhelmed to do anything about it. All we were trying to do was get through one day and one night at a time.

Within months we were overrun with baby things everywhere in the apartment. It wasn't long before we needed three high chairs and three walkers. We kept the pram—enormous, large enough for two babies side by side and one more at their feet—in the living room, where it would be handier than if we kept it in our storage unit out back. Long ago, in the naive days when we thought we were having only one baby, Lars had constructed a beautiful, highly polished wooden cradle. That, too, we kept in the living room, and it made a handy spot to place one baby when my arms were full with two more.

Poor Aslan hid anywhere he could to stay out of the fray. Sometimes I forgot to feed him, and he would meow loudly in my ear at night, just when I'd finally fallen asleep. It would have been better for Aslan if I'd shipped him off to some nice unmarried woman like I used to be, allowing him to resume the quiet life he'd once had. But Frieda was allergic to cats, and I didn't know anyone else who would take him. So we kept him, and I hoped he wouldn't get so angry with me that he'd run away.

"We need that house," I'd said when the babies were three months old. "We need that house, Lars, and we need it soon."

We were feeding the babies their bedtime bottles. I was holding Missy; Lars had Michael. His turn already finished, Mitch was curled up and snoozing beside us in the cradle in the crowded living room.

Lars nodded. "I've been thinking the same thing."

"I know we wanted to wait awhile, but I just don't see how we can," I went on. "If we can't afford to build right now, we ought just to buy some other house and build in a few years."

Lars shook his head firmly. "Nothing doing," he said. "We

only need to find the right plot of land." His look was pensive. "We'll know it when we see it."

He looked so dreamy, his blue eyes lost in imagination. "But can we afford it?" My words were hesitant; I didn't want to break him out of his reverie.

He shrugged. "If we do it right, we can. The house doesn't have to be enormous. Just big enough to comfortably raise these three little folks."

"Still, a custom-built house . . ."

"And some things I could do myself," he interrupted, looking over at Mitch. "I built that cradle, didn't I?"

I didn't want to be discouraging, but a cradle is hardly a house.

"I helped my father build, back in Sweden," Lars went on. "And I did construction here, too, in those early years." He looked thoughtful. "I've let them go, those skills. But I don't think they go away forever. It's like riding a bicycle."

This made me shake my head wistfully. Only several months past giving birth to triplets, I had not been on my bicycle in close to a year. But it was still in the storage unit of our apartment building. I could never give it up.

"And your heart?" I questioned. "What of that? I don't think you ought to be doing heavy construction, Lars."

"I'll leave the heavy work to others," he assured me. "I'll just do the inside things, the finish work." He shifted Michael gently to his shoulder for a burp. "Just the fun parts, I promise." He smiled at me. "I'll build you that green bathroom you said you wanted, when we were in Paris."

I smiled, too, remembering that. It had not even been a year and a half since our honeymoon, but already it seemed like a long time ago.

I looked down at Missy's sweet face. Her eyes were half closed and the bottle's nipple fell out of her mouth, dribbling formula down her chin. I wiped it with a burp cloth. "I'd say she's done," I whispered.

Lars laughed. "Him, too." He rose slowly and kissed Michael's forehead. "Time for bed, little ones."

Once we'd made the decision, we looked at plots of land west and south of town, where so much new construction was going on. It took us a while to find the right lot.

"It doesn't feel right, not yet," Lars said on more than one occasion, as we climbed back into the car after walking an empty property—the babies at home with my mother and father, because who wants to lug three infants along on such excursions if they don't have to? Thank goodness for my young, energetic, do-anything-for-me parents.

I remember finding the property on Springfield Street. We had looked at several other lots in Southern Hills, but when we found Springfield Street, we knew it was the right lot for us. We loved the way the lot was situated slightly on a rise; Lars said we could build a split-level house on such a plot of land, with the higher part of the house nestled against the hill. It was only a few blocks to a newly opened public elementary school. The neighborhood had only a few houses then, but there were others under construction; we would be in good company. "The kids can grow up here," Lars said with satisfaction as we walked around the empty lot. "This will always be home for them." He looked into the distance, the empty spaces between us and the mountains. "They'll have what I never had."

I took his hand. I wanted so badly to give him this opportunity, to give him the chance at something permanent, something he could build for our family and hold on to forever.

Once we had purchased the land, Lars worked night after night on the house's design. He pored over sketches and blueprints in our small living room on Lincoln Avenue, going over every detail. I tried to stay out of his way, ensconced in our tiny kitchen or the bedroom, but sometimes a trip through the living room was necessary for one reason or another. Whenever I passed by him, Lars would look up, his eyes shining with eagerness and love.

The day we broke ground, we were all there: Lars and I, the babies, my parents, the job foreman, and the construction crew. Everyone clapped when the diesel engine on the backhoe roared to life, when the first shovelful of earth was removed to dig our basement.

I remember that the neighbors strolled by, the Nelsons. George and—well, of *course*, her name is Yvonne; how could I forget that? George and Yvonne came by, introduced themselves, pointed out their house at the end of the block. "Such beautiful babies," Yvonne said longingly, admiring the triplets. Yvonne was young, in her early twenties, I guessed, and pretty, with brown, curly hair, long eyelashes, and indigo Elizabeth Taylor eyes.

"When it comes to family, Kitty—I mean, Katharyn—hit the jackpot," Mother said, snuggling Missy against her bosom. I smiled; my dear mother was trying her best with the Katharyn business, but I was pretty sure that I would always be Kitty to her. "My go-getting daughter went from career gal to mother of three in just over two years."

I winced. I knew she meant well, but at the time I was unsure where that "career gal" business was headed. I was working at the shop full-time, with my mother and various hired babysitters taking over the triplets' care during my working hours. We had tried a few full-time nannies, but none worked out; they generally left after a few days, proclaiming the job too difficult. Each time that happened, my mother swooped in until I could find someone else. But this revolving-door arrangement was taking its toll—on me, on my mother, on the babies, and, though he never said so, certainly on Lars.

Not to mention that Frieda was getting fed up with my wishy-washy stance on what I wanted to do with the rest of my life. And I couldn't blame her, really. "You just need to decide," she'd said more than once—hands on hips, lips pressed together in exasperation—when I was yet again being summoned home from the shop early by one family crisis or another. "You just need to figure it out, Kitty. What do you want? Because here's a news flash—you can't have it all, sister."

Yvonne broke me out of these weighty thoughts. "We're still hoping to be blessed with a bundle of joy . . . someday," she said longingly, reaching out a tentative finger to stroke Mitch's little blond head.

I nodded and asked her if she wanted to hold Mitch. She did . . . gratefully, as if she'd been given an unexpected gift. Mitch rewarded her with a sweet smile, a giggle, and the tug of a fistful of her dark hair into his mouth.

Later, back in our apartment, I remember praying—a little appeal to whoever might be listening—that Yvonne might have a child soon. It was several years before my prayer was answered and Kenny came along for them, but he did finally come along.

Oh, it's all falling into place for me. I remember so much that I didn't understand before.

But how is it possible that I can remember events from a life that never even happened?

Linnea's voice brings me back to the present. "Goodness, you were off in dreamland," she said. "I've been busy as a bunny here, and you've been a million miles away in your thoughts, madam."

Busy as a bunny? I look at her quizzically, then remember how she mixes up American expressions. She must have meant a bee.

Linnea smiles playfully at me in the mirror and ties a plastic kerchief over my head. "Under the dryer you go, and then I'll have you finished and out of here in a snip."

"Linnea." I reach over my shoulder and take hold of her warm, firm hand. She is startled into silence.

"I just wanted to say . . . I just . . . I'm sorry," I tell her.

"Sorry for what, Kitty?"

"Sorry about your brother," I go on hastily. I need to say this, no matter how absurd it might sound to her. "I feel . . . I don't know, Linnea, I don't know why, but I feel a connection with him, with you . . . and I'm just . . ." I look down, then back in the mirror, meeting her eyes. "I'm just sorry . . . I never met him. He sounds like a wonderful man. I think . . . I think we would have liked each other."

Linnea nods slowly. "Lars should have had someone like you in his life," she says. "I wish that he had. It would have made all the difference."

She shrugs sadly and withdraws her hand from mine.

Chapter 23

Once again, I don't remember going to sleep, but when I come to wakefulness, I am in Lars's office in the house on Springfield Street, standing next to his desk. A pair of scissors is in my hand. For a moment I stare at them, wondering what I was planning to do with them.

I look around, confused, and then it comes to me. Of course. I look at the desk and see Mitch and Missy's school photographs lying there. I sort through them and find the sheets that contain three-by-five-inch photographs, the right size for the frame on Lars's desk, the one meant to hold three photographs.

In the school pictures, Mitch and Missy are a matched set. Mitch wears a mustard-colored button-down shirt under a brown vest. His hair is combed carefully to one side, the curls cropped close. Someone, probably Linnea, must have cut his hair not long before the photograph was taken. Missy is wearing a brown dress with a white collar and a wide bow that matches the dark yellow of Mitch's shirt. Her hair is in pigtails, tied with brown ribbons. Both children are smiling merrily, their eyes no more than slits in their round faces.

I cut out a photograph of each of them and carefully place them in the frame, Mitch on the left-hand side and Missy in the center. And then I look through the photographs and papers on the desk for a picture of Michael.

The photograph I find makes me melancholy. Michael does not have a school picture, of course. But I—to be sure, I am the one who would have done this—have dressed him in the same outfit as Mitch's and taken a photograph of him against a blank wall in the house. Likely I snapped a whole roll to get this shot, and this was the best of the bunch.

The photograph is not terrible. Michael is not looking at the camera, and he's not smiling, but at least he's not scowling. His expression is blank. His collar is straight and his hair is neatly combed. His eyes, behind his glasses, are impossible to decipher; they look neither glad nor glum. But at least he doesn't seem to be in distress. I hope I didn't put him through too much, trying to get this photograph taken for Lars.

I place the picture of Michael in the right-hand slot in the frame, then gather up the scraps and extras. I am standing back to admire the effect when I hear the doorbell ring. This is followed by Missy's excited voice shouting, "They're here!" There is a trampling of children's feet down the staircase, then Lars calling down the hallway, "Katharyn, where *are* you? They're here!"

Wondering who "they" are, I hurry down the hall. As I do so, I glance at the photograph of the mountain scene, the one across from the master bedroom door. I don't know where the thought comes from, but suddenly I know exactly where this photograph was taken: at the top of Rabbit Ears Pass, near Steamboat Springs in northwestern Colorado. But that location means nothing to me; I've never even been there. I shake my head, trying to make sense of it. No flashes of clarity come to me, so I continue walking and join my family at the front door.

Just coming inside are Linnea, followed by a thin, pleasant-looking man and two gangly young people, a boy and a girl. Linnea's arms are full with a cookie tray covered with tinfoil. "I brought the rolls," she says, passing the tray to me. "They just need heating for about twenty minutes." She leans in and kisses my cheek. "You look beautiful, as always."

I smile and kiss her back. "It's all your work, you know."

"Oh, pish, it's not me at all. You'd be lovely if you never combed your hair out and only washed it once a month."

I laugh merrily and am surprised at how happy I feel. "I hardly think that's true."

Linnea ignores this. "Here's that book back," she says, handing me a hardback volume. I glance at the cover: *The Age of Innocence*, by Edith Wharton. "I really enjoyed it. Thanks for loaning it to me."

"You're welcome. I thought it might be your style." I balance the book underneath the pan of rolls.

"Well, come on in, everyone." Lars ushers the crowd into the living room. "Kids, you go downstairs and play. Mama will bring Cokes in a bit."

I will? Fine, then, I will.

"Gloria, you go on down with them," Linnea says, taking off her coat. "Play with the little ones, won't you?"

Gloria rolls her eyes. "I'm not a child, Mother," she says. "I'd rather be in the kitchen with you and Aunt Katharyn. Must I go downstairs with the children?"

Linnea nods firmly, opening the front hall closet door to hang up her coat. "You must. You know how they love playing with you, *käresta*." Linnea reaches for her husband's coat while Gloria heaves a heavy, dramatic teenage-girl sigh. I get the distinct feeling we've been through this routine before.

The boy—I believe his name is Joe; I remember Linnea telling me that in my other life—slips out of his jacket and loafers, while simultaneously ruffling Missy's hair. "Don't worry, sis, I'll come, too," he says, looking at Gloria over the children's heads.

He hands his coat to Linnea while all three of my children—even Michael, I note with pleasurable surprise—jump gaily around him.

"Cousin Joe! Yippee, we get to play with Cousin Joe!" Mitch cries.

Mitch, Missy, and Michael fly down the basement stairs with Joe in hand. Gloria, still sulky but at least compliant, takes off her jacket and shoes, places them in the coat closet, and then heads slowly down the stairs. Before long, I hear what sounds like all five of them talking at once, likely figuring out what they want to play. Their voices are elated and loud, though muffled by the distance and the carpeting. I'm not sure what the game is, but it seems that everyone—even Gloria, even Michael—is having a good time.

"Come with me to the kitchen," I say to Linnea. "I'll put these rolls in as soon as the roast comes out. Boys," I call over my shoulder. "Can you fix us gals some drinks?"

Good heavens, who *am* I? For the first time ever in this world, I feel a complete sense of confidence. I know exactly what to say and what to do. Why is that? Is it because Linnea is here? I have to admit that her presence, looking and acting just as warm and sweet as she does in the real world, buoys my spirits like nothing else I have experienced here so far.

Linnea leans on the counter and sips the Brandy Alexander that Lars has brought her. She stirs the ice with the red plastic swizzle stick that Lars placed in her glass. "How are you holding up?" she asks me.

My confidence, my sense that I have acutely grasped everything that's going on here, abruptly falls away. For a moment I think Linnea is referring to how I am holding up in the peculiar situation of being in an entirely different life in my dreams—as if she knows I am dreaming. Perhaps she does. Why not? With the exception of Bradley and our neighbors the Nelsons, Linnea is the only other person who has been in both worlds with me.

But when I look at her, I can tell she's not talking about the dreams. Her look is serious, as if we're continuing a discussion we've recently left off. For all I know, we are. Perhaps I saw her earlier today to get my hair done. I put my hand on my head; it does feel marvelous, as if every strand is exactly where it should be.

Well, then. She must mean Michael. "We've had a good week," I reply. "Nothing too out of the ordinary. A few moments . . . but overall, okay." I open the oven door and, mitts on both hands, remove a hefty roasting pan. I adjust the temperature a bit higher to brown the rolls. How do I know to do this?

"You and Lars . . ." Linnea ventures. "Things are okay?"

What in heaven's name is she talking about? I think about the few occasions when Lars has been angry with me in this imaginary world—each time, it had to do with Michael. Goodness, does that mean that we—sometime that I can't remember, sometime recently—have had an all-out disagreement about Michael? Inwardly, I shake my head at my own idiocy. Who cares if you did, Kitty? I chide myself. This is all made up. What difference could it possibly make, in the grand scheme of things, if you and Lars have quarreled?

Nonetheless, I find I can't meet Linnea's eyes. "Sure." I shrug, my gaze fixed on the orange countertop. "We're fine."

Linnea says nothing in response. After a moment, she asks if I have the potatoes cooking.

"Of course. Lars wouldn't consider it dinner without them." I remove the lid from a large pot at the back of the stove and poke the potatoes with a fork. They're almost ready to drain and mash. Jeepers, could I truly be making an entire meal for nine people? From scratch?

I reach into the refrigerator and bring out five Coke bottles. Do I really let my kids drink Coke? Yes, I suddenly realize. On special occasions, like when the cousins are here for dinner, they can have one. Well, then. "Let me run these downstairs," I say to Linnea, grabbing a bottle opener from a drawer. It barely registers that I don't have to think about which drawer it's in.

Linnea straightens up. "No, you have your hands full. I'll do it." She gathers the bottles and opener, disappearing through the swinging doors.

I look around. It seems I have everything under control. Meat, potatoes, rolls, and now I see there is also a pot of peas simmering on the stove. Gravy, I can start in a few minutes. Is the table set? I draw back one of the wooden shutters and see that it is. I can also see Lars and Steven in the living room. The television is tuned to a drag race; both men are leaning forward, drinks in hand, keenly studying the action. Occasionally one of the men turns toward the other to remark on a car's features or a racer taking the lead. From the basement I can hear the children's eager squeals; Linnea must be passing the pop bottles around.

It seems such a sweet state of family and domesticity. So this is what other people do on Sunday afternoons.

Suddenly I wonder where my parents are. Do they get along with Linnea and her family? Of course they must. Linnea is lovely, like my mother. And Steven seems like a calm, kind man. Like my father.

I wonder if sometimes we have the whole family here—both sides, Lars's and mine. Neither of us has much family, but small as it is, certainly they all get along, and here is where we would gather.

This is the place.

I sigh a contented smile. I smell the good smells of the meal I've prepared; I watch the men engaged in their drinks and sports talk. I see Linnea appear at the top of the stairs, meeting my eye and making an "okay" sign with her thumb and index finger—well, at least she got that one right. Someone must have taught her, probably Gloria.

Yes, Linnea, you are correct. Everything is A-OK in this world.

Chapter 24

Despite the familial bliss in my last dream, I am eternally grateful to wake up the next morning in the real world. It is Thursday, finally, the day I am to take the bus to Stapleton to meet my parents' airplane. We will take a taxicab home—they'll have all of their luggage, too much for the bus—but for me it's just as easy, not to mention more economical, to hop on the bus to go out there and meet them. I considered taking my father's car; with my newfound driving expertise in my dream life, I thought I might be able to handle it. My father had left the keys at home and told me I could use the car any time I wanted. But at the last minute, I decided I wasn't up to driving that far.

As it turns out, their flight, a connection they made in Los Angeles, is delayed. I wait anxiously for almost two hours, browsing the airport's notions store and wishing I'd brought along a book to read. I purchase a copy of *Woman's Day* and glance through it, sitting restlessly in one of the airport's plastic seats. There is a whole section about Christmas crafts, and I wonder vaguely if the self in my other life would have made some of these items as gifts—since, apparently, I am a skillful seamstress in that world.

I sigh and place the magazine on the seat next to me. I can't concentrate on it anyway; perhaps the next passerby will get more out of it than I can.

I pull a postcard from my handbag. It shows an aerial view of Honolulu, a range of high-rise hotels on the beach, one taller than the next, like the rows of tall books Frieda and I keep on a bottom shelf in the shop—the art and travel books, those too big for the regular stacks.

This card is the last one I will receive. My mother says as much.

> *Dearest Kitty,*
>
> *This is the last time I will write to you from here. We are packing to leave, and we board the overnight flight on Wednesday evening. I must say I am a bit apprehensive about flying. Who knows what all those Communists are doing these days, and where they are? Who is to say they are not in some ship in the Pacific, just waiting for us? Your father says the idea of the Russians shooting a plane out of the sky, especially one full of tourists, is preposterous. I suspect he's right.*
>
> *What gloomy thoughts! I hope that by the time you see me, I will be all smiles again. Certainly I will—how could it be otherwise, when I will be seeing my girl after much too long a separation?*
>
> *All my love,*
> *Mother*

I read and reread the card until finally I hear an announcement that the Los Angeles flight is landing. I rush to Gate 18.

Eagerly, I stand by the window at the gate as the airplane taxis. I can see my parents as they descend the stairs from the airplane and walk across the tarmac. I jump up and down and wave through the big pane windows. Mother sees me and waves back. She is wearing her navy blue coat and matching hat, which she holds against her head in the wind.

"Kitty!" My mother's hug, after she comes through the doorway, is exuberant. I hold her tightly, breathing in her perfume—Chanel No. 5, which she's worn for as long as I can remember. I wonder if she still feels that rush of warmth when she holds me that I feel when I hold Mitch and Missy. (Who knows how it would feel to hold Michael? Or if I will ever get an opportunity to hold him at all?) I wonder, as my mother and I cling to each other, if holding one's child is always so warm, so powerful—even when one's child is grown. I suspect it is.

Reluctantly, when I sense that people will probably start staring at us soon, I release her. Then it's my father's turn. He's wearing a suit and tie for the special occasion of airline travel, his clothing a bit rumpled now after the overnight ride from Honolulu and the layover in Los Angeles. His buttons press against me as we hug. His shoulders, curved from years of hunching over an assembly-line table, straighten gallantly in my embrace.

We all three hold hands, me in the middle, as we make our way to the baggage claim—childish, I know, but I am more than overjoyed to see them. I've never been as elated in my life to see someone as I am to see my parents at the airport this afternoon.

Suddenly, I wonder if the self in my other life missed my parents this much when they went on this trip. For that matter, did they go on the trip at all? Surely, they must have; it's something they've talked about doing for years, ever since Uncle Stanley and Aunt May moved to Honolulu more than a decade ago.

"Well, that long delay was unexpected," my mother says as we wait for the luggage to come around on the carousel. "But worse things have happened. Did you hear about Tuesday's Honolulu flight?" She shakes her head. "Not the Russians, but

Mother Nature can be equally as dreadful. I almost didn't get on the plane when we heard the news, but your father reminded me that it's a long boat trip from Hawaii to the mainland." Her eyes light up, and she changes the subject. "Tom, there's my train case—don't let it get away." My father reaches for it, and then both of their suitcases come round, one right after the other. "Lucky!" my mother says triumphantly, as my father heaves the large bag. I take the midsize one, and she clutches her train case.

We go outside to hail a taxicab. "We didn't plan to get here so late." My mother glances at her watch. "Goodness, it's nearly suppertime."

"It's all right. I expected to have supper with you." Noticing how tightly I'm gripping her hand, I try to relax, loosening my grasp but not letting go. "But I thought you'd get a few hours to unwind first." I shrug as a cab pulls up in front of us.

"I hope you didn't plan to cook." My father hands his bag to the cabbie and holds the taxi's back door open for my mother and me. "Because I want nothing more than a steak at the Buckhorn." His look is wistful. "You can get all the mai tais you want, but you can't get a good steak to save your life in Hawaii."

Unlike my mother, with her frequent postcards, my father wrote to me only twice from Honolulu. What his communication lacked in quantity, it made up for in quality; he wrote letters, not postcards, pages and pages describing his favorite holes at the golf course, the hike he took with Uncle Stanley up a mountain called Diamond Head, the surf on the beaches on the north side of the island. And the food; he told me all about the meals he'd been eating, the fruit salads and grilled fish and sweet rolls. In both letters he remarked that while the Hawaiian food was "interesting," he missed eating "good old-fashioned red meat."

Now, however, at his mention of going out to eat, I let my face fall slightly. "I have a delicious home-cooked supper planned."

"Do you now? What a shame." He shakes his head dramatically as he climbs in after my mother and me, a little smile playing around his lips.

I grin, too. I can't get a joke over on him; he knows me too well. "Now, Dad, you didn't let me finish," I chide him affably. "*My* supper is planned for tomorrow night."

He takes my hand. "That's my girl." Looking up, he informs the driver to take us to his favorite steak house.

The Buckhorn Exchange is the oldest restaurant in Denver, dating back to 1893. It is also one of the most famous; there was an article about it in *Life* magazine some years ago. I remember my father proudly showing me the glossy magazine page and saying, "Look, honey, Denver is on the map now!" The editors, I suppose, took note of the Buckhorn's long history, its delicious steak dinners, and its Western ambience. In its small, darkly paneled rooms, old photographs line the walls, and saddles and horse memorabilia are spread about. There are rustic tables and chairs for dining, and comfy velvet sofas in the lounge. It's kitschy, but my dad loves it. "Ah, home!" he says as we are seated at a table in the back room. "Back in the wonderful, wild, wild West."

Supper is marvelous. We linger over cocktails, followed by two bottles of wine—much of which, I am ashamed to admit, I drink myself. My parents are alive with stories of Hawaii. "It was exceptionally beautiful," my mother says, her voice hushed, as if describing a cathedral. "I've never seen anything like it. Flowers as big as dinner plates. Palm trees everywhere. Brand-new, high-rise hotels cropping up everywhere in Waikiki. And the ocean . . . you should have seen how blue the ocean was . . ."

"And the girls," my father says. "You should have seen how gorgeous the girls were."

"Tom!" Lightly, my mother punches his upper arm.

He's teasing, of course. He's never had eyes for anyone but her. Once, when he and I were watching a beauty pageant together on television, he told me that if Miss America walked into the room and offered to run away with him, he'd send her packing. "Even if she had legs to the moon, she couldn't hold a candle to your mother," he said, his eyes luminous. "Not when your mother was her age, and not now, either."

I remember feeling a bit melancholy, wondering if anyone would ever adore me like that.

After dinner, my father has the hostess call another cab to take us home. The wine has gone to my head; vaguely, I hear my dad saying something like, "We're living it up—this is the last night of vacation!" I climb into the backseat of the taxicab, sitting in the middle. How safe I feel, snuggled between my parents, and how easy it is to nod off in the secure little haven that they create for me.

Chapter 25

And then I'm singing to my children.

Lay thee down now and rest . . . May thy slumber be blessed . . .

I'm in the boys' room, a space I haven't previously occupied in the dreams. The room is, predictably, painted blue, somewhere between the hue of the sky and that of a king's royal robe. Side by side are twin beds, with blue-and-red-plaid coverlets on them and matching shams that are currently on the floor, as the boys are in their beds and ready for sleep. Above Mitch's bed are several small framed prints of ships and trains—no doubt painstakingly selected by yours truly—as well as an assortment of crayon sketches on the same subjects, most likely done in his own hand, taped beside the framed works. His bedside table is piled with picture books; his bed is crammed with stuffed animals of every sort. In the center of the bed, Mitch sits in rumpled splendor, his covers already disheveled despite the fact that he has likely just been tucked in.

Michael's side of the room holds nothing. No artwork on the walls, no toys on the bed, no books to look at if he wakes early and can't get back to sleep. The only thing on his bedside table is his eyeglasses case. He is sitting up very straight in bed, his pillow carefully arranged behind him, his covers neatly pulled up on his lap. His eyes without his glasses are open but unfocused, and he is swaying slightly, silently.

Both boys wear forest-green flannel pajamas with contrasting blue piping. But other than their attire and their vaguely similar coloring and features, they could not be more different.

I am seated in a rocking chair between the beds. I have a sudden flashback to this chair in this same room, same position, but between two cribs, when the boys were toddlers. Even then, the contrast was stark. Mitch would stand up in his crib, leaping gleefully about, until I was terrified that he would fling himself out of the crib in his excitement. His crib then, like his bed now, was filled with stuffed animals. Some of the same ones, no doubt.

Michael, on the other hand, would position himself quietly in the middle of his pristine, animal-less crib, not moving a muscle, while I sat in the rocking chair and read a bedtime story. Michael would not look at me, nor demand to see each page as I turned it, the way Mitch did. He'd stare at his feet in their fuzzy footed pajamas, betraying no emotion toward the story, Mitch, or me.

Now I rock slowly, humming Brahms's Lullaby. Mitch lies back under his covers and closes his eyes. In the light from the small, dimly lit lamp on the dresser his mop of blond curls gives off a faint sheen. His hair looks slightly damp, as if he has just been bathed, and I can't resist leaning in to sniff the Johnson's Baby Shampoo smell of his clean head. He smiles and opens his eyes, meeting mine. *I love you*, he mouths.

I love you, too, I mouth back. Mitch closes his eyes again and snuggles into his blankets.

I turn toward Michael. He is still sitting upright; his eyes remain wide open. I notice, for the first time, that his eyes are as strikingly blue as everyone else's in the family. It must be the glasses, I decide, that make them appear hazy most of the time.

I'm afraid to suggest that he lie down, because I'm quite sure that whatever he is doing is part of his nighttime routine. I don't want to touch him, for fear of setting him off, but I feel like I ought to do something. I settle for pressing my palm against his bedspread, far from his body. "Sleep well, Michael," I say quietly. "I love you."

He doesn't move a muscle, or look my way. I turn off the lamp, leaving the room lit only by a nightlight plugged into an outlet near the rocking chair. Going out silently, I shut the door behind me.

I meet Lars in the hallway, coming out of Missy's room. "Sleeping?" he asks me.

"Close." Even though neither boy is asleep, I have an instinct that where they are right now is where each of them needs to be to get himself to sleep. I nod toward Missy's door. "How about her?"

"Fast asleep." He smiles. "That bike riding takes it out of her."

"She's getting good, though. They both are."

Lars does not respond, and I know what he's thinking, because I'm thinking the same thing. About how I—mindlessly—used the word *both*. Because two of them are "getting good." And one of them might never "get good."

"Want a drink?" Lars asks, as we make our way down the stairs.

"Now you're talking."

He goes to his office to pour, and I wait in the living room, sitting on the sofa. Like so many things in this house, the sofa is sleek and modern, new. Its fabric is a nubby beige tweed with a faint striped pattern. To liven it up, there are throw pillows in solid colors of orange, yellow, and cobalt blue.

Lars returns with two glasses of Scotch on the rocks. Handing one to me, he sits beside me and drapes his arm over my shoulder, massaging it gently. "You look so tired, love," he says, and the concern in his voice makes me tremble.

I close my eyes. "I'm exhausted," I admit. "I'm overwhelmed." It seems ridiculous to say such a thing in a dream, but since it's true, I may as well say it.

"Well, it's understandable," he says. "There's not much that's more stressful than this."

I shake my head. "I guess I don't know . . . quite what you mean."

He sips his drink. "I felt the same way, you know," he says. "When it happened to me." His voice lowers. "Mine weren't together, of course, but . . . you know that mine were only days apart."

I have absolutely no idea what we're talking about, so I just nod and wait for him to go on.

"He couldn't live without her," Lars says, his voice breaking. "He couldn't go on without her. So he . . ." His lips tighten. "So he . . . didn't."

I put my hand on his. "I know." Of course, I *don't* know, but I want him to keep talking. "Does it help . . ." I hesitate. "To talk about it?"

He looks up. "It helps to talk to you about it," he says. "It always has." He swirls the ice in his glass. "You were so understanding and so . . . *not* shocked, when I first told you how . . . how horrendously things had gone for my family. *Horrendously*. There's really no other word for it—and because of that, I didn't share this story with many people in those days. But I knew from the start, when we first met, that I could tell you about it, and it would be okay." He smiles, but his expression is forlorn. "It made me feel like I could tell you anything."

"You can," I say softly.

"She was so sick," he goes on, entwining his fingers in mine.

"Heart palpitations, coughing, chest pains. You know, she was probably the same as me, probably had an irregular heartbeat like I do, but back then, such things were not diagnosed. Still . . . it exhausted her, sucked the life out of her. Every bit of life she'd ever had. And she *had* had life in her, even though hers wasn't easy. She worked so hard, they both did, and . . ."

I squeeze his hand.

"I was just glad she didn't suffer long," he says. "You know, in those days and in those times especially, and where we were—rural Iowa, of all places, and we hardly knew a soul and could barely speak English—well, she'd been having chest pains and she should have seen a doctor, but it's not like her treatment options were plentiful." He finishes his drink and sucks on an ice cube. "At least it was over quickly for her. There was nothing we could do for her." He shakes his head. "My mother's life was shorter than it should have been," he says grimly. "Short and not so sweet." He stands up. "I'm going for another," he announces, holding up his glass. "You want one?"

I hold out my glass to him, and he takes it and strides down the hall.

When he returns with fresh drinks, I'm worried that he'll let the story go and turn to some other subject. But he continues. "She'd only been buried a few days when he decided he couldn't bear it," Lars says. "Took a shotgun and went out to the shed. Linnea found him." He takes a long swallow of Scotch. "Linnea was only sixteen years old, still just a girl. No one, no *child*, should have to face something like that."

Oh, no. Linnea had hinted at some of this, but she hadn't told me any of these grim details.

"What did you do?" I know I shouldn't ask this question; certainly, I would already know what he did. I am hoping he is so involved in his story that he won't register my asking.

"I did what any big brother would do," he says. "I took charge. We buried our father next to our mother. We sold everything we had, which wasn't much. We got on a train going west, because neither of us ever wanted to see Iowa again."

"And ended up here."

"And ended up here. It was early morning when our train arrived at Union Station. We had only bought tickets as far as Denver. We would have had to buy another ticket and change trains if we wanted to go farther west. We didn't, though. We got off the train and looked around; we saw the mountains in the distance and the sun shining on the buildings of the city just as it was waking up. And we looked at each other and decided that here was as good as anywhere else."

"You've come a long way since then," I say. "And so has Linnea."

Lars nods. "We've been lucky," he says. "Lucky that, after all the dreary, desperate jobs she and I took just trying to scrape out a living, Linnea found work in a bakery. Lucky that Steven walked into that bakery one day and liked who he saw behind the counter enough to return again and again, just to see her. And lucky that Linnea found Steven as appealing as he found her."

Oh, now I remember that story. I remember Linnea telling it to me, her eyes shining with a spark she still felt for her husband, even after all those years together. She told me about it the first time she gave me a wash-and-set, back in October 1954. Not in my real life, not when I'm Kitty. No, it was here, when I was Katharyn. It was the first time I went to see her at Beauty on Broadway. Lars was still in the hospital then, recovering from his heart attack.

"And it was Steven who convinced you that you could do better than being a streetcar repairman for the rest of your life," I say now to Lars. "Steven helped you apply for college." I can feel my heart quicken, remembering this. *Knowing* this.

Lars nods. "He encouraged me to stick it out when I wondered whether it was worth all the hassle and expense. Yep, without him, I'm not sure my career would have happened. I might still be fixing streetcars on the Colfax line."

"No, you wouldn't," I say a bit ruefully, thinking about Sisters' and deserted Pearl Street. "There are no more streetcar lines. You'd be repairing buses now."

Lars chuckles. "Well, that's probably true. So you see how lucky I was that Steven and Linnea met." He takes my hand. "And of course, I was very, very lucky that you came along when you did, Katharyn."

"Lucky," I parrot softly. "I guess in many ways we *have* been very lucky."

His eyes are pained. "I know it doesn't seem like that right now," he says. "I know it's hard to imagine that there could be any good outcome after what happened last fall."

What happened last fall? I remain silent, waiting.

"You know I'll always be here for you," Lars says, squeezing my hand. "You know that I know how hard it is to lose your parents."

To . . . what?

Now I shake my head in a frenzy, trying desperately to wake up.

I'm sitting on the sofa, rocking back and forth and crying. Lars holds me by the shoulders, hands me his handkerchief, presses his cheek against mine.

"I need to get away from here," I tell him, squeezing my eyes shut. "I want to go home."

"Katharyn, you *are* home. This is your home."

"No." I shake my head. "No, you don't understand. This isn't where I belong. This is all made up, and I need to go back where I belong." I stand and start pacing the living room floor. My left heel gets caught in the aqua carpet. Perhaps, I think, pulling it loose, the heel has a torn edge and needs repair. If I'm not careful, it will become hooked in the carpeting and I'll fall. What an absurd thought to have right now.

Lars stands and tries to put his hand on my waist, but I push him away. "You've been kind," I tell him. "More than kind. You've been the man I always dreamed would come along someday." I laugh, and I can feel the bitterness in my throat. "The man of my dreams, right? But this is not real. This is all just a dream. And in the real world, my parents are not dead. Do you understand me? They are not *dead* there, and I need to go back to where my parents are alive!"

"Mama?" a small voice calls from the landing upstairs. "Mama, is everything all right?"

Lars hurries to the bottom of the staircase. "It's fine, buddy," he says. "Go back to bed."

"Mama sounds upset," Mitch says, and despite myself, my heart fills with love for him, this delightful, imaginary child of mine. "Mama, are you all right?"

I wobble toward the staircase, wiping my eyes. Standing at the bottom of it, I look up at him, his mop of clean hair, his cozy green pajamas. "Mama's fine, sweetheart," I manage. "Just feeling a little sad tonight."

"Because of Grandma and Grandpa?"

I can't help it; an enormous sob escapes my throat. Mitch rushes down the stairs and puts his arms around my waist. I bend down to his level and squeeze him tight. Lars stands next to us, silent.

"I just . . . I didn't think I'd lose them . . . this soon," I whisper to my son.

He holds me tighter. "I know, Mama. I'm sorry. I know it must be really hard for you." He sniffles. "Even if you are all grown up."

I nod into his hair. "Yes," I say. "Even if I am all grown up."

I close my eyes and wait. Surely this is the moment when I ought to be going home. I've accepted it, haven't I? I've accepted this crazy news the dream has thrown at me, and I'm being the adult here and doing the right thing. Surely that ought to earn me a trip back to my own bed in my own apartment—oughtn't it?

But I remain where I am, holding my son against me. After a moment, I let him go.

Lars steps forward. "Let me tuck you back in, buddy," he says, taking Mitch's hand. To me, he says, "Go back and sit on the sofa, Katharyn. Just relax and I'll be back soon."

But I don't go to the sofa. Instead I walk to the hallway and stand in front of the photograph of myself with my parents when I was a baby. I am still staring at it when Lars returns.

"She was twenty then," I say hoarsely. "She had me at twenty. He was twenty-two." I do not turn to face Lars. "She is only fifty-eight; he just turned sixty. I know they'll die someday. I know that. Everyone loses their parents someday. But not yet. Not this soon."

"Katharyn . . ."

"Don't call me that!" I whirl on him. "My name is not Katharyn. It's Kitty. My name is Kitty Miller, and I am an old maid who owns a bookstore with her best friend. My life is very simple. There are few surprises. It does not resemble *this* life whatsoever."

"Okay." Tentatively he places a hand on my shoulder and steers me toward the living room. "Let's sit down again."

We go back to the sofa, and he gently presses my shoulder until I am sitting. After he has seated himself beside me, I say, "Tell me exactly what happened to them."

"Katharyn." His eyes are sorrowful.

"No." I sit up straighter, resolved to hear this out. "Tell me. I don't care if you think I already know. I *don't* know. You have to tell me."

He sighs and sips his Scotch. "They were flying here," he says. "They were coming home from a big fortieth-wedding anniversary trip they took to Hawaii. There was weather, a storm, and . . ." He sighs again. "Their airplane went down, Katharyn, in the Pacific. Everyone onboard was killed."

I shake my head. "That's not true," I say. "They did go to Hawaii, but they arrived home just fine, safe and sound. Their airplane did not go down. Nothing of the sort happened."

He doesn't answer. He is waiting.

"When was it?" I ask. "Tell me the date."

He frowns, considering. "It was a Wednesday," he says. "It was Halloween. They'd flown over Tuesday night; that must have been the night of the thirtieth. Their Honolulu flight was scheduled to arrive in Los Angeles on Wednesday morning, and then they were to take a connecting flight back to Denver. It would have been the morning of Halloween."

"Well, there you go." I stand up. "They did not come home on Halloween. They came home the day *after* Halloween. I remember it distinctly."

"No." Firmly, he shakes his head. "No, it would have had to be Halloween day, because they wanted to be here for Halloween. To see the children in costume."

I laugh. I can't help it. I shake my head, and I laugh and laugh. It's almost too hysterical for words.

"Are you all right?" Lars asks.

"Of course," I say, practically gasping for breath. "Of course, but you see how absurd that is. My parents would not come on Halloween to see the children in costume. Because in the real world, Lars, there *are* no children! Don't you understand?" I sweep my hand around the room. "None of this is here, Lars. None of it. No house, no Mitch and Missy, no Michael. No you."

And then my face falls, as I think about what that means for him. He is so lovely and so beautiful and so perfect, and the last thing I would ever want is for such a divine man to have died as young as he was on that October evening in 1954, when we talked on the telephone.

I turn to face him. "I'm sorry," I whisper to him. "I'm sorry. I don't want it to be this way for you." I laugh again, a bit cynically this time. "I would rather you'd turned out to be who I always thought you were—the rat who stood me up. Not someone who died alone in his apartment."

His brow furrows. "What in the world are you talking about?"

"You died," I whisper. "I'm so sorry, truly I am, but in the real world, Lars, we didn't continue talking on the telephone. We made plans to meet each other, said good-bye, and hung up. I went to meet you for coffee two days later, and you never showed up. You had a heart attack and died that night. Right after we got off the telephone."

He swallows the last of his drink. "That's the craziest thing I've ever heard in my life."

"But it's not!" I put my hand on his knee, pressing into the flesh through his trousers. "*This* is what's crazy, Lars. All of this. You are a figment of my imagination. This house and this family and Alma and the neighbors and not speaking to Frieda anymore and my parents *dead*—all of that is crazy, Lars. Not the real world. Not the world I live in, where everything perhaps is not perfect, but at least it makes sense."

I lean forward, wrap my arms around his neck, and kiss him deeply. I want to burn the memory of his lips, his touch, into my mind and heart. I never want to forget—but I never want to be back here again, either.

Finally, we break apart. I give him one last sorrowful look. "I'm going to bed now," I say, standing up. "I'm going to go lie down in that imaginary bed in this imaginary house, and I am going to go to imaginary sleep, and when I wake up, I will be back in the real world." I touch a curl of hair behind his ear—tenderly, as if he were one of the children. "Good-bye, my darling," I whisper.

Chapter 26

When I wake up, I'm not sure where I am. The room is dark, and the bed is narrow and high. Curtains close off two side-by-side windows. The coverlet that envelops me is chenille, soft and cozy.

And then the smell hits me, that roasted-squash-and-lavender smell that I would recognize anywhere, and I realize that I'm at home. Not *my* home, not my duplex, but my parents' home. I am in my own childhood bedroom in the house on York Street.

Throwing off the covers, I pad to one of the windows and open the drapes. It is still dark out, and misty. I can't tell if the sun has not yet risen or if we have a cloudy day in store. I have no idea what time it is; there is no clock in this room. I make a mental note to remind my mother that she needs to add one.

Some years ago, after I moved out, my mother depersonalized this room. She pulled down my South High School banners and my movie posters—Clark Gable and Vivien Leigh in *Gone with the Wind*; Deanna Durbin in *It Started with Eve*; William Holden and Martha Scott in *Our Town*. My mother painted the walls, which had been sea green, a more impartial beige. She replaced my old pink-and-yellow patchwork quilt and matching curtains with this austere colonial-blue chenille spread and coordinating drapes. On the walls, she hung several small reproductions of

French Impressionist paintings: Degas ballerinas, Renoir café scenes. "It's perfect for a houseguest," my mother proclaimed when it was finished. I honestly can't remember my parents ever having a houseguest here, though my mother is right; the room would be lovely and ideal if a guest were to arrive.

I glance down at my body, which is covered in a too-large white nightgown, high-necked with a lace collar. Doubtless it belongs to my mother. What happened? Was I so drunk they couldn't even get me home to my own place? Good heavens, how humiliating.

My mother has thoughtfully placed a glass of water on the bedside table, and I gulp it in its entirety. My head is pounding softly. I open the bedroom door and creep into the hall.

I glance at my parents' bedroom door, which is closed. It's all I can do to stop myself from flinging it open and hurling myself into bed with them, as a six-year-old might. As a six-year-old *has*, I remind myself wryly, in that imaginary world.

And then the horror of what Lars told me in the dream comes back to me. A small, barely audible cry escapes my throat. I stop walking and stand motionless in the dim hallway, my arms wrapped around my body for warmth.

My mother had mentioned something about the Honolulu flight on Tuesday being "dreadful," so it seems likely that Lars's information was correct. An airplane coming from Hawaii must have gone down in a storm, though I hadn't heard about it here in the real world. I feel an overwhelming sadness for those who lost their lives and those who lost loved ones. And then I feel a vast sense of relief that my parents were not on that plane.

I try to imagine this life, my real life, without my parents. I know it happens—airplanes crash, people die. And I know that unforeseen death, whether via illness or accident, *could* happen—to my parents, to Frieda, to anyone I love. But the point is, it did *not* happen. Not to my mother and father. Not in my life.

I make my way down the hall in the darkness, heading for the kitchen and the coffee percolator. It's no matter. I am not going back to that imaginary world. I am not sure exactly how I am going to keep it from happening, but one thing is certain: I'm not going back there again. I simply can't let my mind go there again, I tell myself as I fill the percolator with water.

The truth is this: I am terrified that if I end up there again, I may never be able to get back home.

I can't tell my parents, of course. Who would want to hear such a thing about themselves? I fix breakfast and wait for them to wake up. The day before yesterday, I went to the market and stocked their refrigerator with a few staples so they would have what they needed on their first morning at home: orange juice, a loaf of bread, cream, eggs. The smell of coffee wakes them and they both emerge from their bedroom, robes belted around their waists, noses in the air.

"Kitty." My mother takes a long look at me. "Did you sleep at all, darling? Look at those sandbags under your eyes." She reaches for a coffee cup and pours from the percolator. "I'm sorry we didn't take you back to your apartment," she goes on, her voice even. "We just felt that you—"

"It's all right," I interrupt, embarrassed. "I'm sorry."

"No need to be sorry." My father sits at the table as my mother fills the familiar rose-patterned china creamer—a staple in this house for as long as I can remember—and sets it, along with a cup of coffee, in front of him. "We've all been there, honey." He pours cream into his coffee, adds a lump of sugar, and stirs. Then he sneezes the way he always does—loudly, sounding less like a person sneezing than like some large dog, a Labrador or a Great Dane, saying *woof*. The sound, though familiar, catches me off guard. I realize that the self in my other life—were I to go back there, something I fully intend not to do—would never again hear what for me is a very normal, everyday noise.

My father pulls a handkerchief from his robe pocket and blows his nose. "We just wanted to make sure you were okay, so we thought you'd be better off here," he says, tucking the handkerchief back in his pocket.

I sit next to him and run my fingers through my hair. "Well, I'm mortified, all the same."

"Honey." My father places his hand gently on my shoulder. "This is *us*," he says. "You don't ever need to feel that way around your mother and me." He takes a sip of coffee. "You know that, Kitty."

After breakfast, my parents drive me back to my duplex. The day is still cloudy, but warm for early November, and they wait on the porch while I go inside to freshen up. I look like death warmed over, so there's not much I can do, no matter how much makeup I use.

After I've changed clothes and done what I can with my haggard face, my parents walk with me to the shop, so they can say hello to Frieda. It's still cloudy, and rain falls intermittently on our heads as we walk. Nonetheless, the door to the shop is open, letting in the warmish breezes. "Probably getting toward the end of the season when we can leave the door open," Frieda says as we enter. She and I exchange glances, and I know we're thinking the same thing: it may be the last time forever in this little space. When and if we move our bookstore to a shopping center, there will still be a door to open, but it will be a big sliding glass door leading to a pristine concrete walkway, not a crumbling city sidewalk.

Frieda stands up from behind the counter and comes around to kiss both my parents. "You look wonderful, darling," my mother tells her, holding her at arm's length. I grimace, knowing that I look about the opposite of wonderful right now.

"You and Tom do, too." Frieda tucks a stray hair behind her ear and turns to my father. "Tom, you must tell me: Is Hawaii the fountain of youth?"

I can't help it; I'm pained to hear these words. On so many levels. One, because Hawaii probably *was* the fountain of youth for them. The winters in Colorado can get harsh, especially for older people—and while I don't consider my parents elderly, they're not getting any younger, either. In so many ways, I know they'd be better off living somewhere warm full-time, the way my aunt and uncle do.

And two, because in that other world, all of it—Hawaii, their wonderful memories of this trip of a lifetime, not to mention everything they have back here at home—gets ripped away from them.

And from me.

After a brief visit with Frieda, my parents leave. The sky is still threatening a full-blown storm, and they don't want to get caught in it. Besides, my mother tells us, they have unpacking to do, and there will be mountains of clothes to launder.

When they're gone, I turn to Frieda. "I have to tell you something," I say to her. "It's going to sound crazy."

She grins. "Then let's put on a pot of coffee first."

When we're settled behind the counter with our cups, I face her. Frieda lights up a Salem and inhales deeply. She turns away to exhale, then looks toward me again. Her eyes are dancing; she's in a good mood. I realize how often my moods follow hers.

If she's feeling dark, then I am, too. When her spirits are up, then mine are, too. But while I'm glad she's so cheerful today, I can't follow suit.

"Something strange has been happening to me for the past few weeks," I begin. "When I go to sleep, sometimes I dream I'm in another life." I take a breath. "A totally different life, but I'm still me and it's still now . . . actually, it's a few months hence, the beginning of March, I think, and . . ." I trail off. I cannot think of any sensible way of explaining this to her.

Frieda sips her coffee and taps her cigarette into the ashtray on the counter. "Everyone has dreams like that sometimes," she says. "Last night I dreamed I was an actress singing on Broadway. You should have heard me . . . I did a tear-jerking rendition of 'Soon It's Gonna Rain' from *The Fantasticks*."

I smile. "It's not quite like that. These dreams, Frieda . . . they're so real. It's hard to explain. But here's the thing: it could have happened. My whole life, in these dreams, turns on an event that happened eight years ago."

She shakes her head. "Sorry, honey, I'm not following you at all."

So I tell her. I explain about Lars and the telephone call, and about how in the dream world, we stayed on the line long enough for me to, in essence, save his life. It sounds corny when I say it. Probably because it is, I remind myself.

Frieda has lit and smoked a second cigarette during my long discourse; now she stubs it out and regards me playfully. "Must be your long-lost husband who died."

I frown. "What do you mean?"

"You don't remember?" She twirls her empty coffee cup on the counter. "Years ago, we had a conversation in which we speculated about why we hadn't met the men of our dreams. And you cracked a good one. You said—and I think I am directly quoting you here—'Well, the only explanation that could possibly make sense is that he died before I had a chance to meet him.' "

I am silent for a moment, taking this in. I *do* remember that conversation. We had it over drinks downtown one night; I think we were celebrating our five-hundredth book sold, or something such. "I can't believe I actually said that."

"Oh, you said it, all right." Thoughtfully, she fingers her coffee cup. "So, how does this fairy tale end?"

I shrug. "As you would expect it to," I tell her. "We fall in love and get married. Quite quickly, within a year, and not long after that I get pregnant and we think it's twins, and when they're born, it turns out they're triplets."

Frieda bursts out laughing. "Jesus H., this gets better and better," she says. "Tell me you get fat as a pig from having them—*please*."

"I'm already fat," I point out, smiling.

Frieda shakes her head. "You are not fat, Kitty." She pours herself more coffee, and holds out the pot to me. "You're generously endowed, sister."

I roll my eyes, accept a refill, and wait for her to sit down. "The thing is," I tell her, "the thing is, at first it did seem perfect. He was perfect. The house was perfect. The children were perfect—well, sort of, but that's another story. But now, the more time I spend there, the less . . ."

I trail off, because I don't know how to explain any of it. Not Michael and my guilt about his condition—which I can tell, even from this distance of an entirely different world, wears on me greatly in my imaginary life. Not what happened with Frieda in that life. How can I explain that we aren't even on speaking terms there?

And certainly not my parents. I can't tell her what happens to my parents.

"The less perfect it seems," I finally finish, and let it go at that.

Frieda puts her hand on mine. "Oh, honey," she says. "I don't know why you're letting it get to you like this." She looks out the window, then back at me. "It's been a tense time for everybody lately—the thing in Cuba, the uncertainty about what's going to happen, both in the larger world and here in our own little world. But this dream life of yours . . . it's just an escape, Kitty. It's not real."

"But it *feels* real!" I cry. "It feels absolutely real, and when I'm there, I can't help feeling . . . I can't help worrying . . ." I shake my head and look out the window. "I'm terrified that one of these nights I'm going to fall asleep and end up there permanently. And I will not be able to get back here again."

There. I've said it.

Frieda stands and goes to the window. She beckons me to join her. "Put your hand here," she says, pressing hers against the glass. I do the same. "Feel how warm?" she asks. "Feel the sun?"

She's right. When did it get so sunny out? The cloud cover we had this morning seemed like it was going to last all day, but now the sun has broken through, and the glass feels almost hot. I look at Frieda and nod.

She takes my hand and turns to a bookcase. She places my fingertips against a new hardcover, sleek in its gold-hued paper casing and crisp along the edges of the pages. "You can feel that, too, right?"

I nod again.

She leads me to the doorway, and we walk out onto the sidewalk. A truck passes, filling our nostrils with diesel fumes. "You can't tell me you didn't smell that," Frieda says. "And the coffee. You tasted that, right? You felt your mother's good-bye kiss, your father's hug. You can feel your stockings against your legs, you can feel your earrings pressed to the fronts and backs of your ears. Right?"

I sigh. "Frieda, I can feel all of that. But the point is, I feel those things in the other life, too."

She shakes her head. "No," she says. "You have a very active imagination, Kitty. That's a great thing. An active mind—even in sleep—that's a sign of intelligence." Her look, when my eyes meet hers, is kind. "But that dream world is not reality. This . . ." She sweeps her long, lovely arm around, taking in the space, *our* space. And then she puts her arm around my waist and holds me close. "This," she whispers. "This is where you belong."

Chapter 27

I am—as I told Frieda I would be—frightened to go to sleep that night.

I put it off as long as possible. As promised, I make my parents a full dinner: lasagna, garlic bread, salad. I have wine on hand to celebrate, but I am careful to drink only one glass myself. The three of us stay up late—talking, remembering old times, and giggling at pictures of clumsy me and so-young them in the photograph album I keep on my desk.

Finally, at eleven o'clock, they yawn and say it's time to leave. At the door, they both hug me tight. "Welcome back," I whisper. "I'm so glad you're home."

After they've climbed into their car and driven off, I sit upright on the sofa, scratching out a draft of Greg's next book. It will be about what baseball players do in the off-season, I've decided. Of course, what they do is make personal visits to their most loyal fans, people like Greg Hansen. I get through the middle section, where Willie Mays shows up on the doorstep of our little duplex on Washington Street. I underline words I want Greg to memorize: *season, street, taxi.* Not sure how the book will end, I chew thoughtfully on my pencil, considering. But I can't concentrate.

Finally I put the draft pages aside and begin reading *Fail-*

Safe, the novel about nuclear war that we just got in at the shop. It received a marvelous review in last Sunday's *Denver Post*, and I expect customers to begin asking about it. The story is not particularly interesting to me, but I need to read it so I can answer customers' questions.

As I stare at the pages, rereading the same lines over and over, my eyes cast longingly toward the end table, upon which rests a copy of *The Prime of Miss Jean Brodie* by Muriel Spark. I read it last year when it first came out, but it was so good, I want to read it again. Well, I tell myself, despite my need to keep up with frontlist fiction—those newly released titles that are popular with customers—the more important thing right now is that I stay awake. I set down *Fail-Safe* and pick up *Miss Brodie*.

Another half hour passes. But despite the switch to a book that's more to my liking, I am unable to keep my eyes open. I go to the kitchen and brew strong black tea. Cup at my side, I settle back on the sofa with the Spark novel. I sip my tea, read a few more pages, and fight to keep from nodding off.

When I awake, I cannot say I am entirely surprised to be in the house on Springfield Street. But even so, a moan catches in my throat as I open my eyes and see the green bedroom. I close my lids, hoping I can make it go away, knowing full well that I cannot. Heaving a sigh, I open my eyes again.

Judging from the light coming through the patio doors, it seems to be late morning. I glance at the clock on Lars's nightstand—yes, it's after eleven. I am alone in the bed; the bedroom door is closed. I rise and make my way silently through the quiet house to the kitchen. Alma is there, sitting at the table. It must be coffee-break time; she's reading the newspaper, a cup on the table in front of her.

Alma looks up when I enter. "How do you feel, Señora Andersson?" she asks, and I'm touched by the genuine concern in her voice.

"I'm . . . I feel all right." I pour a cup of coffee from the percolator. "Where are Mr. Andersson and the children?"

"Señor Andersson, he take a day off from work. Let you rest. He take Mitch and Missy to school. Say to stay out with Michael as long as he can. This way, the house is quiet." She stands up. "I try to do quiet tasks this morning," she says. "Not disturbing you. No?"

"No," I say, shaking my head. "You didn't disturb me at all. I appreciate it."

"Señor Andersson, he say your night, it was *difícil*."

I nod and sit at the table.

"You want me fix you something? Some eggs and toast?"

"Yes," I say, sipping my coffee. "That would be nice. *Gracias*."

She busies herself at the stove. I glance at the front page of the newspaper, which is dated Monday, March 4, 1963. "Slide Near Ouray Buries 3 Persons," the headline proclaims. A photo fills most of the page, showing workers trying to rescue avalanche victims on a mountain pass in the southwestern part of the state.

"Alma," I say as she places a plate in front of me. "Can you sit a minute and talk with me?"

She shrugs. "*Sí*. If you like."

"Get yourself more coffee."

She raises her eyebrows, but complies.

"I need some information," I tell her as she settles into her seat across from me. "The things I'm going to ask you will probably sound crazy, because they are all things that I ought to already know. But I can't remember them, and I need you to help me."

She tilts her head curiously and waits.

"First, can you tell me when you started working for us?"

"Hmmm. I think May. It is nineteen fifty-eight. The house, it is *nuevo*," she said. "You and Señor Andersson and *los niños* just move in. You hire me because this house, it is too big for you to manage without help. Especially because you are working in those days, señora."

"Was I? And what can you tell me about that?"

"You have *tienda de libros*. A bookshop. With the other lady, Señorita Green. You go to the bookshop every day and leave *los niños* here. They are *bebés* then, not even two."

"And you cared for them?"

She laughs. "Not me," she says. "They are handful, those three. Cannot be managed by someone with a household to run. Meals to cook. No, señora, you have *la niñera*. You do not remember Jenny?"

I shake my head. "Even if I did . . . tell me about her as if I didn't."

"She think she is high and mighty, that one. But you ask me, she is *chafa*. No good." Alma's lips pucker. "Jenny has fancy college degree in *psiquiatría infantil* . . . I do not know the English for this; it means taking care of *los niños'* heads inside. But she finds no job doing that. You ask me why, I do not know. But later, when I come to know her, I think I can guess. So she come here, work for you and Señor Andersson." Alma hesitates, and then says, "*No es mi lugar,* señora, but I told you then, and I say again now. I had lots of *güisa*—girlfriends—who raised *los niños,* their own and others, and they fight for the job of raising yours. But Jenny, she is 'professional.' This is what you say then, señora." Alma snorted. "*Los niños pobres.* Their own *mamá* can't be here. Okay. Then they need someone else to be like *mamá*. They do not need someone to act like they are *ratas de laboratorio*."

I can feel my face fall, and Alma puts her hand tentatively on mine. "*Lo siento*," she says quickly. "I should not say this. It is cruel, to say this."

I shrug. "It's okay. Just go on."

"Jenny works for you longer than me. She thinks she knows everything about this family. But I think that Jenny was *estricto* on *los niños*." Alma withdraws her hand. "Especially Michael. Jenny thinks . . ." Alma sips her coffee and hesitates. "She thinks there is something wrong in his head. That he is *loco*. *Sí*. Okay, she is right about that. *Lo siento decir*, señora, but she is. But she also thinks she can cure it. Michael does not want to do things *los otros niños* do. Things *todos los niños* do. Throw a ball, listen to music, read books. These things do not interest him. He sits in a corner and hums. And Jenny pulls him by his little arms and makes him join *los otros niños*. She takes his hand and holds it *apretado*." Alma puts one hand in the other and grips it tightly, causing her skin to redden beneath her fingers. She lets go and sighs, and I find that I sigh along with her.

Alma continues. "Jenny forces Michael to join their games. She tries making him sing. 'Ring Around the Rosie.' She pulls him, *que todo se derrumbe*. When he cries, she . . ." Alma bites her lip. "Really, you do not remember this, señora? You do not remember any of this?"

I swallow hard. "Just keep telling me."

"She slaps him," Alma says softly. "Señora Andersson, *mi corazón*, it breaks, seeing that. Jenny slaps him and he cries louder, and she picks him up and puts him in the corner and holds his mouth closed so he does not scream. He is *un niño pequeño*, such a small boy. *Los otros niños*—so sweet, same as now—they stand there, hold hands, they do not know what to do. They come to me and tug at my skirt. They do not have much words, but I know what they try to say: *Alma, do something!*

And I put up my hands, because what can I do? *¿Y qué?* That woman, she is *mono*, but it is none of my business. My job is to clean *los baños* and cook, not raise *los niños*."

"Did we . . ." I say softly. "Did Mr. Andersson and I . . . did we have any idea?"

"Well, *el niño* was *loco*, not right in the head. *Lo siento decir.* And everybody knows. Señor Andersson knows before you. He begs you to take Michael to doctor. But you say Michael is fine, just a little shy and *lento*, cannot do things fast like *los otros niños*. You say he comes around, in time."

"But we didn't know . . . that he was being . . . that she was . . ."

Alma shakes her head. "No. You do not know about that. I should tell you. I should tell you long before I did." She lowers her eyes. "Like I say, Jenny came here before me. Me, I am the new girl. In those days, I am afraid to speak up. Afraid to lose my job."

"But you did . . . eventually."

"*Sí*. More than a year pass. Then I speak up." Her look is grim. "And when I speak up, you fire that Jenny *como un rayo*, like . . ." She waves her arm, making a zigzag pattern like lightning in the sky. "Me, I am glad of it. *¡Adiós!*" She sets down her cup. "And then you take Michael to the doctors. See what they think."

"What did they tell me?"

"They tell you it is your fault, señora." Alma stands up. "They tell you he has a disease—autism—and they cannot cure it. And they say it is because he needs his *mamá* when he is small. But she is not here when he needs her."

I can feel my face pucker into a frown. "Do you believe that, Alma? Do you believe it's my fault?"

Alma clears my empty plate. "Señora, I say too much. There

work to do. I run the vacuum cleaner, now that you are up. ¿Bueno?"

Okay, I tell myself. I want to close my eyes, go to sleep, and wake up at home, but I know that I won't, not yet. Okay, this is only one person's opinion. Granted, Alma is about as credible a witness as you could find. But still. That couldn't be the whole story.

If it was, I reason as I rinse my coffee cup in the sink, why are Mitch and Missy just fine? If Michael is autistic because I am such a horrible mother—why, then, wouldn't my other two children be autistic, too?

Immediately I scorn this easy response. It doesn't work that neatly, my interior critic tells me. If it did, there would be a lot more autistic people in the world. Because there are plenty of horrible mothers.

The truth is—and I know this as I walk back to the master bedroom to dress—the truth is, there must be some element of hit-or-miss. And whatever hit Michael—*Let's be honest, Kitty, "whatever hit Michael" is your awful mothering*—somehow it missed the other two. They dodged a bullet, and they will be fine.

But will they? Alma had stopped her story with the firing of Jenny, followed by Michael's diagnosis. But I could pick up the pieces from there. I must have left Sisters' Bookshop then. I must have left Frieda, probably quite abruptly. I'd settled in here, staying home with the children and doing my penance. And hoping, praying, that it wasn't too late. That whatever damage I'd done to Michael could be undone. Hoping, as well, that it wouldn't strike the other two.

In the bedroom, I glance at the bed. It's still unmade, the

sheets jumbled as if those sleeping there were restless. Perhaps we were, Lars and I. Crossing the room, I smooth the sheets and bedspread, fluff the pillows. I sense that making the bed is likely not my job, at least not on the days when Alma is here. Nonetheless, I feel compelled to do it.

Opening the closet door, I inspect the clothes in front of me, trying to select something to wear. But the clothes won't come into focus. Instead I start seeing little snippets of my life from the past few years.

I remember some of those days. Not all days, but some of them.

My children were two and a half when I fired Jenny and determined to throw myself, body and soul, into the raising of my family. I was sure I could make amends. I could make Michael love me. I could make him be normal, be like the other two.

I decided that being outside in the yard, working with the earth, would be good for all of us. That spring we planted a vegetable garden: tiny lettuce and carrot seeds that we carefully placed in neat rows in the crumbly soil; leggy tomato plants that we bought from the garden store near my old duplex and transplanted into a plot along the back fence. I had to stop Mitch and Missy from having sword fights with the tomato stakes, but eventually we got the job done, and the tomato plants thrived. "Fresh food," I told Lars with satisfaction when he came home from work. "Fresh food and fresh air. That will change everything."

I remember how he smiled appreciatively, clearly enjoying this new version of his wife. "Farmer Katharyn," he called me. "And her farmhands."

The triplets and I put flowerbeds in the front yard. I let the children pick out the seed packets, and we waited with anticipation for the flowers to pop through the ground and bring patches of brightness to our yard. Mitch and Missy loved the muddy, colorful messes, the warm earth filtering through their fingers. Michael abhorred it; he would shriek when dirt got under his fingernails.

When the fall came, and we had to spend more time inside, I figured that imaginative play would help Michael find a way outside his own head—and besides, Missy wanted to grow up to be a princess. So we played dress-up. On Saturdays, when Lars relieved me of child-care duties for a few hours, I'd rummage through the Salvation Army store, bringing home treasures in satin and lace. These I'd transform into costume after costume, with a little magic on my sewing machine—another new acquisition, and one that was further converting me, I hoped, into the domestic whiz I was sure I could be.

Missy loved the costumes; she changed outfits twenty times a day, becoming Cinderella and Sleeping Beauty and a princess she made up herself, a princess named Claire after my mother and Missy's own middle name. Princess Claire wanted to marry Prince Jon—her name for Mitch—and she would force him, both of them giggling, into a tinfoil crown and a little velvet jacket. She tried the same with Michael. "A princess can marry as many princes as she wants," Missy told us with authority. But Michael brutally ripped off his royal trappings and ran from the room, cowering in the corner of his bedroom, behind his bed.

I thought that being out in public might give Michael the opportunity to learn to interact with different types of people. So we went on outings: the zoo, the park, the library. Even though I had my station wagon, we sometimes rode the bus, because Mitch, as young as three, had already begun his love affair with transportation. But they were exhausting, those trips, because

I never knew how Michael would behave, never knew what, if anything, would set him off. It was like the woman in Sisters', the one who had come in with the autistic daughter. I know now how that woman must have felt, because my feelings when I took my child out of the house were the same. We'd be having a good day, and then suddenly, with no warning, something would happen—Michael would be hungry and I'd have packed a different snack than the one I'd promised him, or another child at the park would climb onto the swing that Michael had been heading toward, or the weather, which had promised to be sunny according to the television forecasters, would unexpectedly turn cold and cloudy. And then it would start. The screaming, the howling. The other two children would be in tears, and so would I. It was all I could do to get everyone back to Springfield Street in one piece.

By the time Lars came home in the evening, I was spent. The best I could manage by then would be to sit quietly on the couch and read stories to Mitch and Missy, who snuggled next to me.

Michael, as I recall, I was all too happy to hand off to Lars each night. I made it clear to Lars that the moment he walked in the door, Michael was his responsibility.

Despite my desire to make it up to Michael—to change him, to cure him—by the end of the day, I couldn't stand to spend another second with him.

The September before they turned four, Mitch and Missy began attending nursery school three mornings a week. Logically, that ought to have made things better. Caring for one child, albeit one child like Michael, ought to have been much easier than caring for three, right? To my surprise, I found that things were more difficult on the days that Mitch and Missy were in school. Michael and I both missed them, and the time that we spent one-on-one did not satisfy either of us. Although he did not have the words to say so—he spoke very little, and what he did say, we usually had to work to decipher—Michael did not understand why he could not join his brother and sister at school. Barring that, he could not understand why Mitch and Missy ought not to be prevented from going. "Michael go," he'd insist when I dropped them off each morning. He shook his head violently, clawing at my arm as I held him at the doorway, as I tried to steal a moment to kiss my other two children good-bye, rarely getting the opportunity to do so. "Michael go, too! Or no go. No, no, no go!" He'd break into a fit and pummel me with his little fists as I dragged him to the car, the other mothers staring and whispering as I made my hasty retreat.

On the short drive home, I would be silent as he whimpered and fussed beside me. I knew it was my job to help him, to comfort him. But nothing I said or did—no touch, no word, no gesture of any sort—seemed to matter to him. So I learned to keep my eyes on the road, choking back the guilty tears. There was nothing, I told myself, that I could do for my child. The damage had been done; it was too late. And it was my fault.

Eventually I started having Lars drop the other two off at the nursery school. That helped, but I still dreaded pickup time; I was never sure how Michael would act in that gathering of children and mothers and end-of-schoolday confusion. But there was no way to avoid it; Lars was at his office at that hour.

The hours between Lars leaving to take the other two to nursery school and my driving to the school for pickup felt like an eternity. I did my best to entertain Michael, trying to engage his interest as I read him stories on the couch, walking around the block at his slow, methodical pace, and taking him to the playground on nice days, where I'd swing him for hours—something he loved, and that gave me respite in a way, a chance to clear my head, the orderly, reliable pace of the swing on its chains a small comfort to both Michael and me.

Mitch and Missy were aglow with all they learned at nursery school. They adored music hour, and they would insist I turn on the car's radio on the way home, so they could sing along with the catchy tunes. They learned in full detail the name and sound of each letter in the alphabet, and they quickly became skilled at counting to twenty. These accomplishments made me smile, thinking that even at their tender age, they already displayed an extraordinary ease with and love of learning, much like my own.

Still, my joy was bittersweet. While they flourished in this introduction to school life, Michael and I both withered.

Kindergarten the next year only made things worse. I was thankful Mitch and Missy had had the nursery-school experience; they were a few months shy of age five when they started kindergarten, and thus younger than many of their peers. But having each other, and having a little bit of schooling under their belts, they did splendidly. They learned to write their own names, and they could recognize a number of words in their picture books. Their drawings transformed from scribbles to stick figures and recognizable houses and suns and stars. They remembered to hang up their jackets and carefully line up their boots in the coat closet when they got home, as they did at school. Lars and I marveled at these wonders, at how smart and accomplished Mitch and Missy were.

And then we would both be silent, thinking about Michael.

There was never a question of sending him to school. Not regular public school, at any rate. The public school was not required by law to educate him, and we did not feel it would be fair to anyone—the teacher, the other children in the class, or Michael himself—to force him into a typical classroom situation. He would be disruptive, we knew, and he would learn little; a teacher with a room full of other young children to manage would not be able to give Michael the type of one-on-one attention he so clearly would require.

Of course we researched other options. We looked at a few special schools, private schools designed for children who could not function in a regular school. But the children at those schools were either high achievers who were completely out of Michael's league, or else children with much more severe disabilities, for whom the schools seemed little more than babysitting services, somewhere such children could be during the day, giving their mothers a break.

"I can teach him at home," I told Lars. "I have the credentials; I have the experience."

He gave me a skeptical look.

"I can do it," I insisted. "I had the occasional difficult child in my classes, you know."

"But none like Michael, right? And none that were your own."

"True," I conceded. "But really, Lars, what other choice do we have?"

I didn't bother giving Michael formal lessons during the kindergarten year, but we began working on some basic skills. Knowing that forming accurate circles, squares, and triangles is the foundation for writing letters, I encouraged him to draw. This he appeared to enjoy on occasion, although his drawings were generally indecipherable as any particular objects. Quite often I read to him, hoping that he would eventually fall in love with stories, as most children do when frequently read to. Michael did not relish these sessions, the way most children would, but he tolerated them for short periods.

Not until Mitch and Missy started first grade did I decide it was time for Michael's lessons to start in earnest. His learning might be delayed, but, I reasoned, I had as long as it would take to teach him.

Whatever it took.

I set up a little desk for him in the dining room. I would sit him there, put paper in front of him, and work with him on writing his letters. We started with *A*. I didn't ask anything else of him—just to write *A*'s and to look for *A*'s when we read books. At first he was willing, but as time went on, he became less and less interested.

I was in despair. I thought he'd never learn a thing. He could recite the alphabet, but it had no meaning for him. Words on a page meant nothing. He'd shake his head if I asked if he recognized an A, or any other letter. He was a compliant student, if not an eager one; he did not protest when I said it was time for lessons. Instead, he would sit at the little desk and write his A's, staring at the blank wall, waiting wordlessly for me to say it was all right for him to rise from his seat, that lessons were over for the day. Which I would do, eventually—sometimes two or three exhausting hours later, when I was ready to give up.

I couldn't understand it. "He knows how to do it," I told Lars. "He just doesn't want to."

"He'll get it, in time."

That was mid-October of last year. Right before Halloween. Right before . . . that week.

Now, standing at the closet door, I select a pair of dark slacks and a gray sweater. They match my mood. I slip them on, find knee-highs and a pair of black leather flats, brush my hair and pull it back with a headband.

I return to the living room. Alma has vacuumed here, making neat lines in the carpet from the picture window to the dining room table. As I cross it, my feet leave prints in the pile. I stand by the window and watch for Lars's car.

When Lars pulls up and opens the car door for Michael, I see my son emerge sullenly, sniffling. This surprises me; he always seems more cheerful around Lars than he is around me. I go to the door to greet them.

Lars helps Michael off with his coat. "Go on upstairs," he tells our child, and Michael complies, wordlessly.

Lars shakes his head. "I don't know how you do this all day, every day."

I shrug. "Me, neither."

He goes to the kitchen and pours coffee from the still-warm pot. "Want some?"

"No, thanks." While I get myself a glass of water, Lars heads to his office. I drink my water, then go to the bottom of the stairs and listen. It's silent up there; perhaps, I think, Michael is resting on his bed. I follow Lars to his office.

Standing in the doorway, I watch him speak into the telephone. "Right, but I can't make it in today," he says. "Okay . . . no, I understand." He glances at me. "Hold the line a moment, Gladys." He covers the receiver and turns to me. "They really need me this afternoon," he pleads. "Will you be all right if I go in?"

I shrug again. "It's fine by me. I just need to . . . I'd like to talk to you for a few minutes first."

He puts the receiver back to his mouth. "Gladys, tell them I'll be there by one thirty." He hangs up and brushes past me. "I've got to change," he says. "Can we talk while I do that?"

I nod and follow him to our bedroom.

We have a club chair in the bedroom, tweed, dark green, a nice contrast to the sage-colored walls. I sit in it, watching Lars while he finds trousers, a crisp white shirt and tie. Even from across the room, I can smell the clean-laundry smell of his fresh clothes as he dresses. I watch him button the shirt over his broad shoulders, his solid chest. He is such an attractive man. So lovely, so perfect, and I know I should feel nothing but gratitude to be here with him.

Whether it be real or not, I should be happy for what I have.

He looks at me in the mirror. "You feeling any better?"

"I'm hanging in there."

"You were pretty upset last night."

"Lars." I stand and cross the room, joining him by the mirror as he puts his tie around his neck. "I need you to do something for me. It might be hard."

He turns and puts his arms around me. "Anything you need."

I close my eyes for a moment, relishing the feel and smell of him so close to me. Wishing I could just take pleasure in that and forget everything else. But I can't. I open my eyes.

"Just . . ." I sigh. "Just tell me what happened," I whisper. "To them. To my parents."

He tilts his head. "Honey, you know this."

I shake my head. "No, I mean afterward." I break away from him and step back. "How did we find out? What did we do? How did we tell the children? How . . ." I bite my lip. "What was the funeral like?"

He looks at me for a long moment. Then he ties his tie—slowly, cautiously, taking his time.

When he is satisfied with his appearance, he leads me back to the club chair, gently pushing me down into it. He sits on the bed opposite me. "It was rough," he says, shaking his head.

I nod. Of course it was rough.

"I took the morning off from work, and we'd kept Mitch and Missy out of school for the occasion. We went out to the airport in your car," he went on. "Piled in and ready to pick up Grandma and Grandpa from their flight. The kids had on their Halloween costumes; they were delirious with excitement." He looks at me sadly. "You, too, honey." He puts his hand on my knee. "Katharyn, maybe I shouldn't say this, but that morning in the car . . . I think that's the last time I saw you truly happy."

I look out through the patio doors to the snowy backyard. I don't remember that, but I can picture it in my mind. I know how the children would be dressed. Missy would be a princess, because Missy is always a princess. Mitch would be a hobo or a magician or a train engineer or perhaps a cowboy—Mitch's imagination could take him anywhere in the world, so the possibilities were endless. Even Michael would have gotten into the spirit of it; perhaps I would have convinced him to dress up, just a little. I would have outfitted him in something comfortable and not too confining—yes, I know what it would be, a puppy-dog costume, with floppy ears that I made out of felt and attached to a soft, loose hood, worn with a regular pair of brown pants and a brown sweatshirt, the spotted tail I'd fashioned from more felt pinned to the seat of his trousers.

I can see myself, too. My face would be flushed with anticipation. I would lean over to check my reflection in the rearview mirror as we drove to Stapleton. I would be fussing over my hair, although it would no doubt be picture-perfect from Linnea's skilled hand.

Lars would be at the wheel, whistling and cracking jokes with the kids. The weather would be overcast, the same as it was in the real world on that day, but that would not destroy our jovial moods.

I can imagine us reaching the airport, parking, going inside. Passersby would smile and nudge each other, gazing at our delightful children in their costumes. I can see us finding our way to Gate 18.

The same gate from which I picked up my parents in the real world, just a few days ago.

"They were to make a connection in Los Angeles," Lars continues. 'The connection came in on time. We waited, watching at the window, waving to everyone who got off the airplane and stepped onto the tarmac. We waited while they all came through the gate. And then we waited until the gate area was empty.

" 'They must have missed their connection,' you said. 'I'm surprised they didn't telephone.' "

"Yes," I whisper. "They would have telephoned."

Lars nods. "There was a stewardess at the gate, so we asked her. She directed us to a service desk. They . . . they seemed to be waiting for us there. Several people, a man and two women. 'The Anderssons?' " one of the women said as we approached. 'We tried to telephone you at home, but you must have already left for the airport. We're sorry to inform you that Mr. and Mrs. Miller's airplane from Honolulu . . .' "

And here Lars stops. "Well," he says after a moment. "You know what they told us."

"Oh," I breathe. "Oh, not in front of the children?"

He nods. "I was angry about that. I thought . . . they ought to have pulled us aside or something . . ." He shakes his head.

"What did . . . what then?"

"Well, it was bad," he says. "Everyone was crying. You, the children, even me. I . . ." He holds up his hands. "They were fine people, Katharyn. I loved them, you know, as a son loves his parents."

He pauses, and I remember our first telephone conversation, when Lars told me he was 4-F and didn't serve in the war, and I wondered what my father would think about that. And then I know—I realize I have always known, of course—that my father would not have cared at all. I understand that my father, that both my parents, would have adored Lars. That they would have seen how much he loved me, how devoted he was to our family, and that would be all that mattered. And Lars would have felt exactly the same way about them.

"My own parents had been gone for such a long time . . . and I always felt . . . I felt . . . that with Tom and Claire, I received a second chance to have parents."

And suddenly I discover something about grief that I had not known before. When I was a child and a young adult, when I'd lost grandparents, pets, friends during the war—not to mention that awful day when my father told me that my baby brother had died—those grievings were huge and sad, nearly immeasurable in my young mind. But they were my own. There were times when I had to attend funerals, offer condolences, send sympathy cards. But I did not have to think too much about anyone else's grief. I could go home and fall apart; I could cry and cry, for as long as I wanted to. I did not have to hold it together for anyone else.

In that other life, I am the center of my world. Of course, I love and care about other people—many other people. But at the end of the day, my thoughts and actions are mainly about managing my own life and my own emotions.

Here, that is not the case. My life, and my love, are bigger than that. Even in grief, I have to hold other people close.

I reach forward and clasp Lars's hands. "Tell me . . . if it's not too hard . . . tell me about the funeral."

He shrugs. "No . . . um, no bodies, of course. No caskets. Nothing but . . . well, we put up some photographs and flowers." He smiles. "Lots of photographs and lots of flowers, as a matter of fact. It seemed you couldn't get enough of either."

"Because that was all that was available," I say, not really wanting to think about what that means.

He shrugs. "Anyway, it was a nice service. The church was packed." He looks away, then back at me. "So many people,

Katharyn. I couldn't believe all the people. Men and women that your father worked with over the years. Everyone your mother knew from all her volunteer time at the hospital, all the community work she did. All your neighbors from Myrtle Hill and our neighbors from here. So many people that you went to school with—high school, college. People you knew over the years, when you had the bookstore." He smiles at me. "Everyone, Katharyn. Everyone was there."

I am appreciative of this. But there is only one name I really want to know about. "Lars," I say softly.

"Yes?"

"Was . . . was Frieda there?"

Lars stands abruptly. He puts his hands on mine. "Katharyn," he says. "Don't torture yourself like this."

I shake my head, incredulous. "So she didn't come," I say. "She didn't even come to my parents' funeral."

"My love." He kneels in front of me. "My love, there are things in our past . . . that we just can't change." He stands. "I don't think there's anything you could have done . . . not a single thing . . . that would have changed how things turned out with Frieda."

I lean back in the green chair and blink away tears.

Lars puts a hand on my shoulder. I see him glance toward the clock on the nightstand.

"It's okay," I whisper. "I know you have to go."

"I don't want to leave you like this." He looks into my eyes. "Katharyn," he pleads. "I think you should talk to someone. A psychiatrist. Please, let me make some calls . . ."

A psychiatrist. A doctor. I think about the things doctors have said over the years—all their "truths." Telling my mother not to have any more babies. Telling Lars and me that our child has an incurable disease, and it's my fault. Telling me, I think ruefully I as remember Kevin's rebuff all those years ago—not in so many words, but telling me by his actions—that I was not good enough to be a doctor's wife.

I shake my head and look up with resolve. "No doctors. I'll be fine." I stand and put my arms around him. "Thank you for telling me," I say. "I know it sounds crazy . . . that I can't remember."

He nods. "You just tell me what you need," he says gently. "Whatever you need, Katharyn . . . anything . . . I will do it for you."

I smile. He is so amazing, so perfect.

But he can't give me the one thing I want.

He can't give me back the people who—in my real life—I love the most.

After Lars leaves the house, I go to the kitchen and ask Alma to fix lunch for Michael. "What for you?" she asks me, frowning.

"Nothing," I tell her. "I'm not hungry." I go to the staircase and call Michael. He appears in the doorway to his room. "Come down and eat lunch now, honey," I say. "Alma will sit with you." I turn to her. "After he's done, he can watch television," I say. "Then he won't be in your way. Is that all right?"

She shrugs and nods. I tell her I'm going to lie down.

In the green bedroom, I lie on the bed and cover myself with an afghan that matches the colors in the wallpaper. I don't recognize the afghan itself, but I recognize my mother's favorite knitting pattern. She must have made it for us after we moved into this house. It would have been like her to make me one that matched my perfect new master bedroom.

I close my eyes and wait, knowing exactly where I will be when I awake.

Chapter 28

It's sunny when I open my eyes. I am in my own living room, lying on the sofa. Across my body is my familiar, cozy afghan—also my mother's pattern, of course, but this one purple and blue, colors I chose. Aslan is curled alongside my stomach.

To my surprise, my mother is sitting in the armchair to my right. Her knitting needles click quietly; it looks like she's making a baby sweater. Blue, for a boy. "Hi," I say. "What are you doing here?"

She looks up and smiles. "Well, good morning, sunshine." She turns her wrist and glances at her watch. "Actually, good afternoon. It's almost two."

"Oh, good heavens." I throw off the afghan and sit up. Aslan, disrupted by my sudden movement, also rises. He arches his back and then settles down at the end of the sofa, where he has a good view of my mother's flashing knitting needles. "How could I have slept so long?"

Mother shrugs. "Frieda rang us when you didn't come in to the shop by eleven. She had called here several times, and there was no answer. So she asked us to swing by." She frowns. "Your door was unlocked, Kitty. That's not safe, you know, not for a woman living alone. It near about gave me a heart attack, when I saw you lying on the davenport. Dad and I thought perhaps you'd been strangled by a burglar and left for dead."

I grimace. "Yikes, I'm sorry. I guess I was sleeping really hard." I rub my eyes. "I suppose I fell asleep reading, after you and Dad left last night."

"I suppose you did, all right. You must have been exhausted. When your father and I saw how soundly you were sleeping, we decided not to disturb you. We telephoned Frieda and explained the situation. She said it was all right, that you should take the day off and rest. Then your father left; he wanted to get the brakes checked on the car, said that the car sitting idle in the garage while we were away had not been good for it. The brakes weren't responding quite right to his foot . . ." She shrugs again. "In any case, you slept right through all that. So I just settled down here, and I've been knitting and waiting for you to wake up."

It is exactly like my mother to have the foresight to grab her knitting bag when she has been called to her adult daughter's home to check whether she's dead or alive.

"You were sleeping so deeply. It's like you weren't even in there," she says, tapping my forehead teasingly with one of her needles.

I duck away, smiling. "Who are you making that for?"

She looks down at her work. "My neighbor Rose's daughter," she tells me. "You know Rose and Harry; they're the couple that moved in to the Freemans' old place, around the same time you moved over here. Their girl, Sally is her name, she's expecting in January." She shrugs. "Now, Rose insists it's a boy. Sally already has a girl, so Rose says this one *has* to be a boy." My mother winks at me. "But I'm making a pink one, too, just in case."

I wink back. "Good thinking, Mother." I look out the window. "You don't always get one of each."

My mother shakes her head. "Now, that is certainly true," she says, not meeting my eyes. And I know she must be thinking of my brothers, those three babies who never breathed a single breath of life.

"Mother." I turn to face her, tucking my legs under the afghan. She looks up at me. "Are you ever . . . does it ever bother you . . ." I hesitate, then go on. "That I didn't marry and have children?"

My mother casts her glance back to the needles in her hands. "Now, that's not a fair question," she tells me. "Bother me? What a strange way to put it." She finishes a row and looks up, meeting my eyes. "Did I *want* you to marry and have children? Of course I did. What mother doesn't want that for her daughter? But am I 'bothered' that it didn't happen? Well, that's just silly. I want you to be happy, and you seem . . ." She starts the next row. "You and Frieda . . . you both seem happy."

I laugh aloud. "Talk about a strange way to put it!" I stretch my arms, releasing the tension in my shoulders. "Frieda and I aren't lovers, Mother."

Her face reddens. "No, of course not. I didn't mean . . . that wasn't what I meant, Kitty."

"Some women are, you know," I say playfully.

"I know that, too, darling. I wasn't born yesterday."

"But not Frieda and me. That's simply not the way we feel about each other." This discussion has taken a surprising turn, and now I find that I am the one to blush. My mother and I have always been able to speak openly with one another, but I think I can say with assurance that in the thirty-five-odd years I've known how to verbalize my thoughts, she and I have never discussed lesbianism, on either a personal or a purely social science level.

"Well." Thoughtfully, she puts down her needles. "You and Frieda are true companions. That's not easy to find, you know. Some people search their entire lives for it. Some people—many people, really—marry, and don't get that with their husbands or wives."

This makes me wonder about Lars and myself. Do we have that, in the other world? Are we "true companions," as my mother puts it? I believe we are, actually. He seems to read me so well, like he's known me forever. The way that Frieda does, in this life.

Who do I lean on in that other life, if not on Lars? Certainly, I lean on him more than any other person. Without Lars, how would I manage Michael? If the memories that return to me in my dream life are any indication, it's clear that I have done, and continue to do, a poor job of parenting Michael. And it would be all the poorer if it were not for Lars.

But suddenly I realize who else I must lean on, in that world.

My parents, of course. They are my champions there.

Mine, and—more importantly—Michael's.

Another memory comes to me, or maybe something I'm making up in my head. Who knows anymore? In either case, I can see us in my mind's eye: my children, myself, and my mother.

We are at the library. It's the Decker Branch Library, the one that's within walking distance from my duplex and from Sisters'. Is there no library closer to Southern Hills? There is so much new construction out that way; you'd think there would be a library. But perhaps one has not been built yet. Or perhaps one *has* been built, but in that life, I prefer the old-time library in my former neighborhood.

We are in the children's section, and it's story hour. All of us—Mother, Mitch, Missy, Michael, and myself—are sitting cross-legged on the carpeting. A number of other mothers and their children are settled in to listen, too. The children all seem similar in age to mine, perhaps three or four.

The librarian holds up a book and begins to read. The book

is called *Ann Can Fly*. It tells the story of a girl who gets to fly with her father in his single-engine airplane. He is flying her to, of all places, her summer camp. Lucky girl.

The children listen thoughtfully—a twitch or a wiggle here or there, but the story is mesmerizing, and the librarian is an animated reader. She has everyone's attention.

Everyone except Michael.

He is seated next to me, with his knobby knees up around his chest and his eyes on the floor. His upper body sways side to side. I know, because I've seen him do it before, that this helps him concentrate and block out any sensations that disturb him. His swaying is rhythmic, steady, and silent, but I note that his movements are getting wider and more dramatic. He doesn't seem to realize that he is moving more and more rapidly as the story goes on.

I am not the only one to notice. Several of the other mothers, those in close proximity to me, turn to glare. Two of them lean toward each other and whisper, then look my way again. I can tell exactly what they're thinking: What's *wrong* with that child?

My mother is looking straight ahead at the librarian, Mitch on one side of her and Missy on the other. She has her arms around both of them, and they snuggle against her.

Michael's swaying gets even more exaggerated; he almost reaches the floor with each shoulder as he moves his torso from left to right. It *is* distracting, I have to admit. I duck my head, feeling ashamed—not of Michael, but of myself. I am ashamed for wishing so desperately that my son could simply be *ordinary*.

One of the mothers leans toward me. "Please," she whispers loudly. "Your boy's swaying is distracting. It's hard for the children to concentrate." She gives me a long, pointed look. "I don't really think he belongs here, do you?"

I stare at the woman, unable to answer. I find that I am blinking back tears.

Before I can say anything, my mother—still spry despite her fifty-odd years—slides on her bottom until she is between Michael and me on her left, and the other mothers and children on her right. She puts her arm around me and reaches her hand to gently ruffle Michael's hair. "*This* child," she whispers fiercely to the woman, "has as much right to hear the story as any other child. He and his mother belong here, the same as any other mother and child." She glares around at the women. "The same as all of you and your children." She raises her hand and points her index finger directly at them. "Don't forget," she says to the other mothers, "that all children are God's children."

My mother reaches into her pocket and hands her handkerchief to me. "Dry your eyes, beautiful girl," she tells me. "These people are not worthy of your tears."

Now, recalling that moment, I gaze appreciatively at my mother. I am grateful for this memory, for this understanding that in the other world, she is not only my advocate but my child's as well.

And then I remember that in that world, she is no longer there. That she will never be there again.

I don't want to think about it. I wrench my mind back to the current conversation. What were we talking about? Not children, because in this world I have no children.

Oh, yes. Now I remember. Companionship.

"I agree," I say softly. "I can see that if one were married, companionship would be the most important part."

She nods, studying the sweater in her lap. "It is," she concurs. "You know, the other part . . . the physical part . . . that's not always all it's cracked up to be."

Jeepers. She really is telling it all, isn't she? "Do you mean . . . you and Dad . . ."

"Gracious, Kitty, that's hardly something I'm going to discuss with my daughter." She pulls yarn from her bag, and Aslan bats at it. "Get away, you." She pushes his paw away, and he jumps down, heading for the kitchen, no doubt wondering if there is any food left in his bowl.

"But you're all right, aren't you?" I face her, my slippered feet on the floor. "You and Dad—everything is all right? You're happy, aren't you?" My voice becomes a hoarse whisper. "Please tell me you're happy."

She smiles. "Your father and I have been married for a good many years, and we are lucky that we still like to spend time together. We're lucky that we know how to find common ground. Do I want to be with him all day long? Does he want to be with me all day long? Goodness, no. He has golf and reading; he has friends and plenty to do. And I have my knitting, my ladies' club, my volunteer work at the hospital. In the evenings, we have each other. True companionship? Yes, we have that. But that doesn't mean we need to spend every waking moment together. And that"—she pulls more yarn from her bag—"is how it ought to be." She frowns. "You want a companion, yes. But you'd never want someone to be your whole world, Kitty."

"No," I say slowly. "No, even if one is married . . . there ought to be more. Not just your husband, not even just your children." I blink a few times. "Family is important, it's the most important thing. But it can't be everything. If it is . . ." I look away, toward the front window. "If it is, when your family life doesn't go as you expected it to . . . why then, you're in for a huge disappointment. If that's all you have."

"Exactly." My mother gently folds her handiwork and places it in her bag. "Why do you think I work with all those poor ailing children at the hospital?" she asks me. "Why do you think I've spent so much time there? Do you think I would have done that if things had gone differently? If you had not been an only child?"

I have never considered this before. She is of a generation in which married women in the workforce were a rarity—not that there are loads of mothers working outside their homes nowadays, but certainly more than when I was a child. That lifestyle was out of the question for my mother—indeed, for most women of that time. But as a mother of just one child—and a mother who had hoped for many more—what was she to do with all her time, once I was past infancy, once I was in school? She had more than enough time to spend on me; she lavished time on me. And yet I was a good kid, an easy kid. She always said so, they both said so. With just one easy kid, she would have had buckets of spare time. So she spent that time on other children, on babies who took the place of the babies she did not get to raise.

"In either case," my mother says briskly, rising from her chair, "now that I know you're perfectly all right, I'm going to call your father. He ought to be home by now, and he can come back down here and pick me up."

After my mother leaves, I call Frieda to say I'm sorry. "It's all right," she says. "I'm just glad you're okay."

"I'm coming in," I tell her.

"You don't have to, Kitty. It's slow."

When isn't it slow, these days? "All the same," I insist. "I'll be there in ten minutes."

I'm still thinking about the conversation with my mother as I walk to the shop. It makes me wonder about my other life, about what I have there and what is missing. Leaving Frieda, leaving the shop and that entire lifestyle behind to devote myself to the children—it had been the right thing to do, the only thing to do.

I can see that now, having spent time there, having seen what I've seen and remembered what I remember. I can see that there was no other choice.

Nonetheless, in that life I've undoubtedly dug myself into a hole. And that hole includes guilt over Michael's condition, shock that Frieda really seems to be gone from my life for good—and, of course, the desolation of losing my parents. That heartbreaking triumvirate overshadows everything good there.

I shake my head. Even from here, from a whole other world, it's painfully clear that I cannot get past that triumvirate. It eclipses everything else.

That evening, after we close the shop, Frieda and I go out for a drink. It's Saturday night, but neither of us feels like venturing far from our neighborhood, so we just go to the Stadium Inn, a tavern on Evans, near the university. When Frieda and I were in college, this joint was always filled to the brim on Saturdays, after DU football games. You couldn't get a table—you could barely even move. But the university disbanded the football program last year, much to the dismay of many in the DU community— neighborhood watering hole proprietors included, no doubt.

It's early, just after five o'clock on a slow night, and we have the place nearly to ourselves. We sit in a booth toward the back. There doesn't seem to be a waiter or waitress, so I offer to go up to the bar to get us drinks. The bartender, a smiling older man, reminds me a bit of Bradley. I order Frieda's martini and a glass of wine for myself. "On the house," the bartender says, putting both glasses in front of me.

I raise my eyebrows. "On the house? Why?"

He shrugs, his eyes deep and tender. "Consider it my good deed for the day, ma'am."

I shake my head as if to clear it. "Well, thanks," I say, leaving a dollar for his tip.

Back at our table, I place the glasses in front of Frieda and tell her what happened at the bar. "Strange," she says. "Well, no sense looking a gift horse in the mouth." She takes a sip of her martini and closes her eyes. "Mmm, I needed that."

I smile, but do not reply. I plan to nurse this one glass of wine. I am doing entirely too much drinking these days, both here and in the other world.

Frieda sets down her glass and lights a cigarette. "Kitty," she says, her voice level. "We need to decide, you know. Our lease is up at the end of November. We could tell Bradley right away that we don't plan to renew. I know we're a few days past the first of the month, but he'll understand." She takes another sip of her drink. "I rang yesterday," she tells me. "The management company at the shopping center. I telephoned them, and the space is still available." Her eyes look dreamy. "We could open in time for the Christmas shopping season."

Knowing I ought not, I take several long sips of wine. The hell with it. I need my courage.

"Freeds," I say finally. "What if . . . what would you think . . . if I didn't want to do this anymore?"

She stares at me. "What are you talking about?"

I sigh. "The thing is," I say. "The thing is, I know it's progress. I know it's the wave of the future. I know that Sisters' has no future where we are. I know all of that." I drink more wine. "But I've been thinking a lot about it," I go on. "And even though all of that is true . . . I don't know, Frieda, my heart just isn't in it."

"Your heart?" She inhales, then blows smoke toward the ceiling. She looks back at me. "This is business, sister."

"I realize that. But even if it is business . . ." I look around desperately, as if the right words will appear before me, perhaps on a cue card or something. "You have to love it," I say finally. "You have to love what you do. And I don't think . . . I don't think . . ." I lower my voice. "I just don't think I would love it there."

Frieda finishes her drink. A waiter has materialized, leaning on the bar; he must have just come on shift. He's a young college kid, gangly like Kevin was, back in the day—like Kevin still is, as Frieda and I discovered not long ago. Frieda signals him to bring us another round.

"You're afraid of change," she challenges me, as the kid nods at her and ambles behind the bar.

"I'm not. That's not it at all. In fact, I *do* feel ready to make a change."

"Oh, really? To what?"

I finger my empty wineglass. "I was thinking . . . well, two things. One would be tutoring, like I'm doing with Greg Hansen. Working with students who are having trouble learning to read. There are so many of them, and they don't learn. But they *need* to learn; that's how you get by these days. Kids can't get by in the world anymore if they grow up illiterate, Freeds. And I could . . . I could help them. I'd be good at it. I *am* good at it. I could start a private service, or maybe work in the schools; they have situations now where someone—a teacher or someone else with the right background—specializes in teaching reading, one-on-one or with small groups. I could do that."

Our second drinks arrive—I wonder, will these be free, too? Frieda takes a sip of hers. "You could do that. You could specialize like that," she says, and I can hear that she's trying to keep the emotion out of her voice. "You could do that, Kitty, and you would be good at it." She sets down her glass. "What's the other thing?"

"The other thing is . . . well, I've been writing these books for Greg, these books about sports, but with simple text that he can read and comprehend, not too advanced. And you know, it really makes a difference. Having something to read that he is interested in, but the writing is at his level . . . it's made all the difference for him. I think . . ." I look away, then back at her. "I think there is a need for children's authors who can write books like that."

"Well." Frieda presses her lips together. "Well, these are really good ideas, Kitty."

I nod. Neither of us says anything for a while.

She twirls her martini glass thoughtfully with both hands. "If I tell you something, will you be mad at me?"

I laugh. "Of course not. What would I be mad about?"

She ducks her head. "I . . . I've met someone, Kitty. A man."

"Really?" I sit up straighter. "Where? When?"

"Now, before you get all worked up," she says. "I don't even know if the romantic part is going to happen. I'm not sure how I feel about it." She smiles. "He's made it clear how *he* feels about it, but I'm not sure yet. But here's the thing." Her eyes are bright. "He's an investor, Kitty. He invests in small businesses. Puts up the cash to get a business started, and helps it become a success."

"Oh," I say. "Oh, that . . . it certainly has potential, Frieda."

"But I didn't want to put you at risk," she says. "I was afraid to say anything, because I know it's a risk. A business risk, a personal risk. It's everything, and it wasn't fair to ask you to tag along with that. But if you want out . . ." She looks away. "Well. That would make it easier. It would be *my* responsibility. *My* risk."

"Where did you meet this man?"

"At my brother Rob's house, if you can believe that—at Donny's birthday party. He's the father of one of Donny's school friends. Divorced. But took his kid to a birthday party on a Sunday afternoon. Isn't that great?"

"Sure," I say. "It's swell. What's his name?"

"Jim Brooks. He's . . ." She seems suddenly shy, which is unlike Frieda; I find it rather endearing. "He's a good man, Kitty. A very smart man, a successful man, but also a truly good man. I never . . ." She looks up and smiles. "Meeting someone now, at thirty-eight . . . I never thought that would happen to me. I thought that chapter was closed."

But how could it be? She is still as lovely as ever. Yes, there are lines around her eyes. There are strands of gray in her dark hair. But she still carries herself like a queen, just the same as she did back in high school. What smart, successful, good man wouldn't take notice?

The only reason it hasn't happened earlier, I tell myself, is because of chance. Up until now, pure chance had not put her in the right place at the right time.

Chance has not done that for me, either. Not in this world, anyway.

I put my hand on hers. "I'm happy for you," I say. "Whether it turns out to be just business or something more. Either way, it sounds like a good thing." I drain my wineglass; so much for *that* resolution.

She smiles. "It could be a good thing, Kitty. It could be." She removes her wallet from her purse and starts to put a few bills on the table, but the waiter catches her eye and shakes his head, gesturing to her to put her money away. "Odd," she says, frowning and tucking the bills back into her wallet. She turns back to me. "A good thing . . ." she repeats thoughtfully.

"But you're not going anywhere, right?" I hear the pleading in my voice. "This man, this Jim Brooks—he lives here, he has a child here. Even if . . . even if we didn't stay in business together anymore, we'd still be as close as we are now. Wouldn't we?"

She shakes her head good-naturedly. "Now, what about those

dreams of yours? In that world, who goes off and has another life? Who deserts who?" She laughs. "Don't worry, my darling," she says, squeezing my hand. "My heart will always be yours." She finishes her drink. "But I've got a big heart," she goes on. "There's room to share."

Chapter 29

The master bedroom on Springfield Street is dark when I wake up. I don't know what day it is, or how much time has passed. I'm no longer dressed in the gray slacks and sweater I had on when I laid down here. Instead, I'm wearing a burgundy skirt and a white blouse. This tells me that at some point, I must have risen and gone about my life. I laugh, thinking of this. Because this isn't really a life. This is all imaginary.

I go to the living room. Lars is seated on the tweed sofa, reading *One Fish, Two Fish*, all three children huddled around him. It's dark outside; light snow is falling. I wonder if I've slept through dinner. Not the dinner that I missed in the last dream, of course; this would have to be some other dinner at some other time. Who knows how time flows here? It could be the next day, or two weeks from now, or the following month. This thought makes me laugh recklessly, and when Lars looks up at me, I ask, "What day is it?"

He glances at his watch. "Do you mean what time? It's seven o'clock, love."

"No." I giggle. "I mean, what day?" I perch on the arm of the sofa, next to Missy. "I can't keep track of days when I'm sleeping," I tell him. "I wake up, and I barely know where I am."

"Katharyn." He lays the book on the coffee table and gently

pushes Mitch aside, making room for me next to him. I sit between Lars and Mitch, with Missy next to Mitch, and Michael on Lars's other side. It occurs to me that we would paint a delightful family picture.

"You're overwrought, love," Lars says softly to me.

"Daddy, what does 'overwrought' mean?" Mitch asks.

"Worried," I tell him. "Daddy thinks Mama is worried, is all."

"What are you worried about?"

I laugh again. "Nothing, sweetheart. Not a thing. Because there is nothing here to worry about. Nothing at all."

"Mama doesn't think we're real," says a quiet voice from Lars's other side.

"What?" Lars asks sharply. "What did you say, Michael?"

We all look at Michael. "She thinks she's making us up," he says, tapping his forehead. "Inside her brain."

I am stunned into silence. The last person in this house I ever would have expected to understand me—he's hit the nail on the head.

"That's enough," Lars says, rising. "It's time to get ready for bed, everyone."

And so I find myself in the bedtime hustle: baths for all, pajamas for Mitch and Michael, nightie and hair brushing for Missy. She is remarkably patient with this last chore, despite her mop of curls. Remembering how tortured I felt as a child when my mother attempted to detangle my own crazy head of hair, I try my best to go easy on my daughter.

Lars and I apparently switch off the girl-boy thing, because tonight I get Missy for tucking in. She settles under her covers, her eyes large, looking at the snow falling outside her window. "Do you think we'll have school tomorrow?"

I shrug. "Depends on how much we get overnight."

And will I be here to know the difference? It's impossible to be sure of that, one way or the other. I find myself saddened by that bit of actuality.

We read *Cinderella*—her favorite, she tells me—and then after hugs, kisses, and two songs, I press the covers around her chin and bid her good night. "Sleep well, Princess Claire," I say softly.

Missy opens her eyes wide. "I haven't used that name in a long time, Mama."

"No." I shake my head. "But you'll always be a princess to me."

I remember the thought I had on the day—it now seems very long ago—when Missy, Mitch, and I went shoe shopping. The thought that I would give anything in the world for Missy to be real, and to be mine.

Anything, Kitty? You would truly give up anything for her?

My fingers tremble as I brush a lock of hair from Missy's forehead. I lean toward her ear and whisper tenderly, "I love you."

She smiles. "I love you, too, Mama."

Downstairs, I wait while Lars finishes with the boys. It's quiet in the living room, and I pick up the *Denver Post* from the coffee table. A headline on the right-hand side of the front page cries out, "Air Crash Kills Three Opry Stars."

My hands tremble as I pick up the paper and look at the date: Wednesday, March 6, 1963.

Quickly, I scan the story. The crash occurred last night—Tuesday, at around six o'clock in the evening. Those killed included country music singers Cowboy Copas, Hawkshaw Hawkins . . . and Patsy Cline.

"No," I whisper to the silent room. "Oh, no. Please, no."

They were in a small airplane. Randy Hughes, Patsy's manager, was flying the plane.

There was bad weather, a storm. Everyone on board was killed.

I feel hot tears in the back of my eyes. It's so unfair, I think. Good people, people with so much to live for—they should not die that way.

"Patsy, I'll miss you," I say aloud in the silent living room. I make a mental note to keep an eye on Patsy Cline's performance schedule when I get back to the real world. Perhaps, I think, I will get an opportunity to see her in concert before she dies.

And then I shake my head, feeling a slight fondness for my own silly imagination. You're making this up, I remind myself. It would make perfect sense for you to invent a plane-crash death for one of your favorite singers. It's merely a way, I tell myself sternly, to mentally sort out those same false circumstances for your parents. That doesn't mean it's actually going to *happen*, Kitty.

Lars comes down the stairs and quietly joins me on the sofa. I show him the paper. "Patsy Cline died," I say, my hands trembling.

He nods. "I know. We talked about it before dinner tonight. Don't you remember?"

I shake my head. "I have no memory of that whatsoever. All I know is, this paper says that one of my all-time favorite singers is dead."

Lars nods again. "I'm so sorry, love. I know how much you adored her."

"But I'm making it up, anyway," I say, brightening. "She's not going to die. None of this is happening, so it's of no consequence, really."

He sighs. "Katharyn . . ."

I squeeze his hand. "You know, in some ways, I wish this *was* real," I admit. "There are parts of this world that I wish desperately were real. But other parts . . ." I shake my head, tapping the paper. And thinking of my parents.

He takes my face in his hands and turns it toward his. "How can I help you, Katharyn? How can I convince you that this is real life?"

I break away from him and shake my head. "You can't. Not any more than Frieda can convince me of the same thing back there." I am thoughtful for a moment. "Tell me," I say. "What am I like here most of the time? You say we talked about Patsy earlier this evening; I don't remember that. But I can't be like this all the time, can I? Not remembering? Thinking I have another life?"

"You're not like this all the time," Lars confirms. "Generally, you do the things you've always done. Take care of the children, manage the household. You don't . . ." He bites his lip. "You rarely mention your parents, Katharyn. When their names come up, you usually change the subject. The kids have asked me about it, and I just say . . ." He shrugs. "I just say that Mama needs some time."

I nod. I have no memories of that whatsoever. I try to picture myself—Katharyn, that is—coping in this life. Going about her day, caring for her children. Running into her neighbors at the shopping center and knowing their names. Going to the grocery store without having to be reminded of how to get there. It is hard to envision.

And yet a part of me longs for it. A part of me is desperate to know what that feels like. What it feels like to truly be me—the me who resides all the time in this world.

"And have I . . . how long have I been . . . acting this way?" I ask.

He furrows his brow. "A few weeks," he says. "You seemed fine for a while after . . . it happened . . . We had the kids' birthday, Thanksgiving, Christmas . . . Looking back now, I thought you were fine, but maybe you were just going through the motions, just doing whatever you could to cope, to get through those events. It wasn't until a couple of weeks after New Year's that you . . ." He trails off.

I nod. This makes sense to me. I'd have needed every bit of emotional strength I had to get through the children's birthday and the holidays without my parents. I would have put myself into whatever robotic state it took. Only when those days were over, when I was faced with a brand-new year and nothing on the horizon to look forward to, would I have allowed myself to confront my despair.

It was then, I realized, that my imagination would have taken over.

Next, I ask Lars, "Can you tell when I'm . . . when I have gone into my other world?"

"Usually I can tell," Lars says. "It often happens just before you drift off to sleep at night, or else early in the morning—I sense that you're awake, but you're not really conscious, not really present in the moment. Sometimes it happens during the daytime hours. Your eyes get sort of dreamy and lost . . . usually it's only for a few moments, and then you pop out of it and return to your normal self."

I laugh. "Those few moments here can mean *days* have passed, in my other life."

Lars doesn't respond to this. Instead, what he asks takes me completely by surprise. "What's it like there—in your other life?"

And so I tell him. I tell him about my apartment, my cozy home that I share only with Aslan. I explain about Greg Hansen, how when we started he could barely work out even simple sentences on a page. I speak of the progress Greg has made since then, and how much I enjoy working one-on-one with him. I mention how much fun I have writing books for Greg. Books about baseball, about Willie Mays and the San Francisco Giants.

Lars nods. "Well, you *are* an expert on that topic."

I give a hoot of laughter. But Lars's face is serious. "You're joking, right?" I ask him. "I know nothing about baseball, except what I've learned since I began writing for Greg."

"Katharyn." Lars is smiling good-naturedly. "You know *everything* about baseball. You became interested in baseball because I'm interested in it. And so are the children. We all followed the World Series last fall as if our entire future depended on it." He looks at me in astonishment. "You really don't remember that?"

I shrug. "I really don't remember that."

He shakes his head. "All right," he says. "Tell me more about your other life."

I talk about my parents' joyous homecoming, our long, relaxed dinners together. I smile fondly as I tell him about my conversation with my mother while she knit in the afternoon sunlight at my apartment.

And while I am telling it, I realize that—from the perspective of this world, at any rate—those moments are nothing short of a gift. They are an extraordinary gift that my mind has bequeathed me. With the help of my active imagination, I have been given the opportunity to spend a little time, just a little more time, with my parents, with Frieda—and even with Greg, learning through my experience with him who I want to be, what I want for myself.

I tell Lars about Sisters', which of course he knew about, but not in the way it is now. I tell him about Frieda's and my endless pots of coffee at the shop, our lunches at the sandwich place down the street, going out for drinks after we close up—and the conversations we've been having. I talk about the opportunity to close up Pearl Street and open in a shopping center—and my reluctance to do so, as well as Frieda's enthusiasm for the prospect. "Things are changing there, no doubt about it," I say. "But even so, it's . . . well, it's peaceful there." I shrug. "Yes, Frieda and I are at a crossroads. But it's an amicable one. I'm going to . . ." I feel foolish telling him this, because it doesn't fit Katharyn as well as it fits Kitty. "I'm thinking about looking for a job as a tutor or reading specialist," I say. "I'm finding that I love that kind of one-on-one work. That's the part I miss about teaching." I sigh, hearing the lilt of happiness and enthusiasm in my voice. "And I want to write books for children," I go on. "For children like Greg. And any other child . . ." I am thinking of Michael. "Any other child who struggles to learn."

"Do you now?" He smiles at this—and not because he's amused. He actually seems impressed. "Tutoring. And writing. These are things you'd really like to do?"

I shrug. "I don't know. Here, in this world, they don't seem possible, do they?"

"Why not?" He sits up straighter and takes my hand. "You're so bright, Katharyn. You handle things with such determination. At least, you did, until . . ." He presses his lips together. "I'm sorry. I shouldn't have said that."

"No, it's okay. You're right." I think about the sad triumvirate. "In this world, I've shut down. Things have worn me down. Michael, Frieda, losing my parents . . ."

"But it doesn't have to be that way," he says. "You can do anything you want to, love. I don't ever want you to feel tied down by our life here at home."

"Well." I glance at the newspaper again, then back at Lars. "I guess we'll just see."

We make love passionately that night. We are slow with each other, taking our time, touching each part, our hands moving as slowly as if we were uniting for the first time. I memorize the shape of his body, the warm feel of his skin next to mine. Laying my head against his chest, I inhale his clean, intoxicating scent. I press my hand against his heart, his beautiful and wonderful heart. I say a silent little prayer that it will keep ticking long enough for us to grow old together.

Afterward I nestle myself against him, pressing the length of my body against his. I don't ever want to let him go. "I don't know where I'll be when I wake up," I whisper to him. "When I go to sleep here, I feel like I ought to say good-bye to you, because it might be forever."

The snowy sky outside has made the room brighter than usual, and in the half-light I can see his dazzling blue eyes. "Isn't that true for everyone?" he asks. "Any one of us can be gone in a second." He looks up at the ceiling. "Don't think I don't consider that . . . all the time," he says. And then he repeats hoarsely, "All the time."

We go to sleep with our arms wrapped around each other.

Chapter 30

I'm standing in front of the shop. The morning is misty, almost foggy. I can barely make out the street in front of me, the few cars parked along it. I glance to my left, looking north on Pearl Street. Through the haze I can see the sandwich shop, the Vogue Theater, the drugstore. Everything is where it belongs. I twist my neck and look behind me, through the plate-glass window. I see my meticulously constructed display of fall colors and cozy-up-with-them books. Beyond these, Frieda is sitting at the checkout counter. She glances up, sensing my eyes on her, and gives me a smile and a small wave. I automatically smile back, feeling my heart skip a beat or two.

"I love you," I whisper, although of course she can't hear me through the glass. "I love you so much, sister. More than you'll ever know."

And then, looking at her, I feel suddenly, irrationally angry. Something she's done makes me furious. I feel betrayed, like I could never trust her again. Having no idea why I feel that way, I try to shrug the emotions away.

I'm not sure why I'm outside. Was I going somewhere? I don't think I was. It's cold out here, and I'm not wearing a coat or hat, nor holding my handbag. I wrap my arms around my ribs, tucking my hands under my sweater sleeves.

No traffic passes. The street is silent and still. Will Pearl Street always be as still as this? It makes me sad, thinking about Frieda and me leaving this place, about things changing. I know it has to happen; I know it's the right thing to do. The future, at least the near future, is not here. It's in the vast shopping centers and the sprawling ranch houses and the highways that go on forever.

Is that the future just for a time—or is it for always? Is that Denver's future; is it America's? I wish I could look in a crystal ball and see what the world will be like in fifty years. But I am not a fortune-teller.

I think about the world I share with Lars and the children. If I had a crystal ball, what would it tell of that world, in fifty years? What would become of my children? Mitch and Missy would, I am sure, discover their passions in life, whatever those passions may be. They would, I hope, marry and have families. They would live with integrity and commitment and love, the way that Lars and I would teach them to.

And Michael? I hadn't thought I could get any colder, standing out here, but considering a future for Michael makes me shiver. What would become of him, if that imaginary world were real?

I think about the woman who came into the shop with her autistic daughter. I wish I could talk to that mother again. If I could, I would be more gracious. I would smile kindly and welcome her to my store. I would then go about my business and not stare at her child.

Perhaps I would have been smarter about how I set up that silly, wobbly display of books. But if not, and if the child still knocked it down—well, then, as the mother made her hasty retreat, I would not ask rude questions. Instead, I would hand her a complimentary copy of *Ship of Fools*. And as I did so, I would look in that mother's eyes, and without words, I would try to let her know that I understood.

I turn and go inside. The bell over the door jingles as I enter. Frieda looks up at me, a wordless smile twitching around her lips. The phonograph is turning silently, softly, its stack of records completed. Frieda swivels on her stool, selects a new stack, and places the records on the phonograph's stem. The first disc drops onto the turntable; the needle moves into position. Patsy Cline's voice fills the bookstore.

If you got leavin' on your mind . . . Tell me now, get it over. . .

I shake my head. This song doesn't exist yet. In the other world, in the Italian restaurant we went to with his clients, Lars told me that Patsy Cline had just released it.

And that happened in February. Which is three months from now.

"Patsy Cline is going to die, you know," I tell Frieda, my voice surprisingly even. I feel like I am listening to myself from a space a few feet away.

"It will happen in just a few months' time," I go on. "She's going to die in a plane crash."

Frieda nods, as if I'm telling her something she already knows.

"But she'll release this song as a single first," I say, crossing the room.

Serenely—how can I be so calm?—I turn toward our stacks of best-seller fiction. My eyes go straight to the new Salinger anthology. Next to it, I see *The King's Persons* by Joanne Greenberg, the local author I'd made a mental note to learn more about, the day I browsed Frieda's big bookstore in the other world.

These books are not yet in print. They cannot be found in any stores. Yet here they are, in our little bookstore.

I run my hand over the Salinger; was this the book that Frieda placed my fingers on, just the other day, when she was trying to assure me that this world is real? I shake my head again, trying to clear my thoughts. Perhaps it was; it *seems* like it could have been.

I can't remember.

And then I think about the things that have happened in the last few weeks, things that seemed merely pleasant or convenient at the time. My peaceful, quiet mornings at home and here in the shop. Reading my mother's lovely, lyrical postcards. Stumbling across Lars's obituary so randomly, yet so easily. Running into Kevin—his misery proving that I had done the right thing in delivering him an ultimatum all those years ago. The odd, out-of-nowhere free drinks that Frieda and I received at the Stadium Inn the other night.

And finally, my parents—conveniently, pleasantly—getting on the right airplane. One that did not go down in the Pacific during a storm.

Don't leave me here, in a world . . . Filled with dreams that might have been . . . Hurt me now, get it over . . . I may learn to love again . . .

I look at Frieda. She stares knowingly at me. She seems to be waiting for me to speak.

"Sister," I say to her, and then I say no more.

Chapter 31

I awake with a gasp. Lars and I are still entwined, exactly as we were when I fell asleep in the green bedroom.

Lars opens his eyes. "Are you all right?"

I am shaking, and I take a deep breath to calm myself. Slowly, I say, "This . . . is . . . *it*." Rubbing my eyes, I look around. "This is the real world. Isn't it, Lars?"

"Katharyn." He pulls me close and whispers in my ear, "This is the real world."

I move my head so I can look into his eyes. "How can that be? How could that other world have felt so real, and not *be* real?"

He pulls back from me and tilts his head thoughtfully. "I don't know, love."

I think about all the times in the past few weeks when I went into the world where I'm Kitty. Often I believed I was sleeping in this world. I believed that I had to go to sleep here to get back home, to wake up where I thought I belonged.

But—with the exception of last night's episode, which felt like a dream and clearly *was* a dream—all of those other times, I was not sleeping. I know this now. I was right here, making up stories in my head, stories that helped me cope. I was here—and yet, I *wasn't* here. I must have been completely absent to those around me.

I swallow hard. "I'm sorry," I tell Lars. "I am so sorry."

He wraps his arms around me again. "It's okay. I understand. It's okay."

Tears form at the corners of my eyes. "I don't know if I can bear it," I say. "I don't know if I can be the person you think I am. I don't know if I can be here—truly *be* here, the way I ought to be, if this is real."

I squeeze my eyes shut, and in my head I can see myself as Kitty—but she is only a make-believe image, that person.

"You can," Lars tells me. "You can be here, and you will be here." He runs a hand through my hair, and I open my eyes to look at him. "I want you here," he says. "Everyone—we all want you here." He swallows hard. "We need you, Katharyn."

I look into his beautiful eyes. They *need* me, I think. They need me here.

"All right," I say slowly. "I'll try."

He smiles and kisses me deeply.

When we break apart, I turn my head. "Look outside," I say, pointing through the panes of the sliding glass door. The sky is strikingly blue and cloud-free; the sun is almost blinding in its brightness, reflecting off the snow on the lawn. "Such a fine new layer of snow on everything."

He stands up and walks to the doorway. "Beautiful," he agrees. "But Missy and Mitch will be disappointed. There's not enough snow to cancel school."

I am actually a bit disappointed myself. A day with all three children at home sounds quite pleasant.

I rise from the bed and swing my feet to the floor. As I do so, I notice a hardback book on my nightstand.

"Lars," I say, picking up the book and rotating it, so the cover is faceup. "Have I been reading this?"

He turns from the doorway and walks over to me. "You have," he confirms, leaning over my shoulder to peer at the book. "You said it was haunting your dreams."

I smile, tracing my fingers over the book's cover, the shadowed images, the flame-colored, wavy typeface rising in a ghoulish shape to spell out the book's title: *Something Wicked This Way Comes,* by Ray Bradbury.

"Indeed," I say to Lars. "It's haunting indeed."

There are minor fits from Mitch and Missy before school. Mitch is upset that a snow day wasn't called; he had planned, he explains, to spend the entire day setting up a toy train layout in the basement. "And now it's ruined!" he cries, his face flushed, his voice heightened with an uncharacteristically dramatic lilt. "My whole day—it's ruined!"

To my surprise, it's Michael who offers words of comfort. "It's okay, Mitch," he says gently. "The weekend starts in two days. You can make the layout then." He doesn't look at Mitch, but he sidles a bit closer to his brother. He continues speaking, his voice soft. "I'll help you."

Missy, for her part, is angry that she must wear boots to school. "They're ugly," she proclaims, her perky nose turned up disdainfully at her cherry-red fur-lined boots. "They're horrid boots, Mama. I need new ones."

I shake my head. "We just got these a few months ago," I say firmly. "They're perfectly fine. They're warm, they fit you, they'll keep your feet dry. Put them on."

Reluctantly, she pulls on one boot and then the other, glaring at me the entire time. I shrug, not giving in.

Lars, Mitch, and Missy leave the house at eight. Since kindergarten, when Mitch and Missy started attending the elementary school a few blocks away, Michael and I have walked them to school most mornings, and walked back in the afternoon to pick them up. It's been a few years since Mitch and Missy were in nursery school, when the separation disturbed Michael so much; he has matured enough by now that he expects and can handle these daily transitions. Nonetheless, on snowy days, Lars generally drives Mitch and Missy the few blocks to school. These are more of those household facts that I suddenly know, without any discussion of them.

After they are gone, I stand in the doorway between the dining room and the kitchen, holding the swinging door open with my shoulder and taking a look around. My eyes find Michael's slumped form; he is seated wordlessly on the living room couch, staring at the floor.

"Michael."

He does not look up.

"Michael," I repeat, crossing the room and standing in front of him. "It's time for your lessons."

This gets his attention. He does not make eye contact with me, but he does speak. "We have not done lessons in over three months, Mama."

"Well." I stride back into the dining room, to the small desk by the wall. It's dust-free; even if it's not been used recently, Alma undoubtedly keeps it as clean as everything else in the house. I reach inside and pull out an opened notebook. A scrabbled line of capital A's is penciled on the page. The line falters to the right, and the last letter is only partway done—just the first slanting line of the A, nothing more.

I stare at the notebook for a while. My thoughts turn to Greg

Hansen, to the stapled-together books I crafted for him in the other world. The awkward pictures I drew for him. The set of index cards tied together with a string.

"Michael." I set the notebook on the desk, walk back to the couch, and sit beside him. "You know I've asked you to learn the letter A. Can you tell me some words that begin with A?"

"Apple," he says dully, and then he closes his mouth.

"True." I nod. "But let's think about some more interesting *A* words. What about . . . wait a minute." I run upstairs; I know exactly what I am looking for and where to find it. I go directly to Missy's room and pull the *Picture Dictionary for Young Readers* off the bookshelf. Hurrying down the stairs, I turn to the front of the dictionary, to the *A* section.

"Here's a word," I say, putting the book down on the sofa between us. "*Above.* That means something that is on top of something else, like this . . ." I dash over to his desk, pick up a pencil and his notebook, and bring them back to the couch. Leaning over next to Michael, I draw an airplane flying over several tall buildings. Beside the drawing, I write *ABOVE* in capital letters. "You see, the airplane is *above* the city. *Above.*"

I wait, breathless. Michael studies what I'd written and drawn. "Above," he repeats softly.

"Yes," I go on. "Every word, each word has a meaning, and if you remember what it means and can picture it in your mind . . . and you can picture the letters that make up the word . . . why then, you'll be able to read that word every time you see it. Let's try another one." I turn the dictionary page slowly. "Here's one that I think you know," I say. "*Add.* Like adding numbers together." In the notebook, I write *1 + 1 = 2*, and under that I write *ADD.*

"Add," Michael echoes me. "*Add,* that word is *add.*"

"Yes. That's exactly right."

"What's the book you're looking through, Mama?" he asks. "Can I see it?"

"Of course." I lean back, allowing him to study the pages.

"Here's one I know," he says, pointing at *anchor*—with, handily, a drawing of an anchor right next to it. "That says *anchor*, doesn't it? Like a ship's anchor."

"Yes!" I cry. "Yes, it does, Michael. You've got it!" I can't help myself; I pull him—notebook, dictionary, and all—onto my lap and squeeze him with all my might.

He screams and pulls away from my grasp. "Too tight! Too much!" he yells, and runs up to his room.

Yikes—I ruined it, I think. Nice going, Katharyn.

And then I smile. I don't care. He has *learned*. He has learned something, and *I* am the one who taught him. I sigh and lean against the back of the sofa, hugging the dictionary to my chest, bathed in happiness.

After a while, I go up to the boys' room and coax Michael back downstairs. "I don't want to read anymore, Mama," he says, as I lead him gently to the desk in the dining room. "Reading tires me out."

"Okay." I can see there's no point in pushing it. I need to take this slowly. If I want it to happen at all, if I want Michael to learn to read, then I need to take it in baby steps.

"Let's do some math instead," I suggest. "Can you count?"

"What a funny question, Mama." He sits at the desk and begins to count aloud. He makes it to one hundred in less than three minutes. I interrupt to tell him he can stop.

"What about adding?" I ask. "Do you know two plus two?"

"Mama." He rolls his eyes. "I know two hundred and two *times* two!"

"Really?" I smile. "And what is that?"

He sighs, bored. "Four hundred and four."

"Okay," I say, turning away from his desk. "Let's work on money instead."

"Real money?" he asks eagerly.

The excitement in his tone makes me smile once more; he is so rarely enthusiastic about anything. "Sure," I reply. "Real money. Come with me."

We raid the coin jar in the kitchen, the one perched on the windowsill. Sitting at the kitchen table, we count every coin. I am astounded by his concentration, and how easily he grasps the denominations, adding the amounts in his head. "Thirty-three dollars and sixteen cents!" he says triumphantly when we're done.

"That's a lot of moolah."

"What's moolah, Mama?"

"Money."

He laughs, that wonderful laughter that reminds me of my mother's. What a gift, hearing that sound. "Moolah is a really funny word."

"You're right. It is." I stand up. "I'll go see if Alma is ready to make your lunch."

On the way down the hallway in search of Alma, I pass the photograph of the mountain scene, of Rabbit Ears Pass. And suddenly, finally, I understand its significance: Lars proposed to me at that exact spot.

We'd been dating steadily for about six months. Our courtship was like nothing I'd ever experienced; it was as if we couldn't get enough of each other, as if we had to make up for all the time we'd lost in trying to find each other. He'd call me several times a day at the shop; I'd take the calls in a breathless voice, like a schoolgirl. Frieda would roll her eyes at me, but she did turn away to give me privacy.

Lars and I spent nearly every evening together—dinner at his place or mine, movies, sometimes going out dancing.

"I never see you anymore, outside of work," Frieda complained—a bit peevishly, I remember thinking, as if Lars and I had planned our blossoming romance for no better reason than to upset Frieda. "I miss you, sister," she'd beseech me. "Make some time for me, would you?" I'd nod and tell her I was sorry; perhaps she and I could do something that week, some night after we closed. But then Lars would telephone or show up at Sisters', and I'd forget my promise to Frieda.

The day Lars proposed was a beautiful late-spring Sunday. We'd gone for a drive with no particular destination in mind. We drove into the mountains on Highway 40, meandering through Winter Park, Granby, Kremmling, gazing out the window at the vast mountain ranges and the tiny towns and the melting snow. At one point, after we'd been driving for several hours, I suggested that we ought to turn back. Lars simply shrugged. "What for?" he asked, and since I could give him no answer, we continued on.

At the summit of Rabbit Ears Pass he parked the car, and we walked to the top of a rise to admire the view. The late-afternoon sun was warm on my bare shoulders, but the breeze was cool. Lars took off his sweater and draped it around me. "Wait," he said, reaching around me into his pocket. "Can't hand over the sweater without handing over this first." He'd bent onto one knee and opened a small jewelry box, holding it in front of me. "Will you marry me, Katharyn?" he'd asked. "Please say yes."

I looked at the ring, and then into his blue, blue eyes. "How could I say no?" I replied. "Of course I'll marry you." I wrapped my arms around him. "Yes," I'd whispered. "Forever—yes."

Now, turning away from the photograph, I shake my head, smiling, and veer into our bedroom.

I find Alma in our bathroom, cleaning. I am suddenly guilt-ridden. I don't mind watching Alma iron or wash the dishes—I did such things willingly in my other life, my made-up life, and I didn't consider them taxing chores. But cleaning a bathroom? I can't recall anyone, except for my mother when I was a child, ever cleaning a bathroom for me. But Alma doesn't seem fazed; she is smiling and humming as she works. I am surprised that I recognize the tune: "De Colores." It is a song that I don't recall ever hearing in my other life, but one that I know for sure Alma has taught my children. It's all about colors, about everything colorful in the world.

De colores, de colores . . . Se visten los campos en la primavera.
De colores, de colores . . . Son los pajaritos que vienen de afuera.

And then I know all sorts of things about Alma that I haven't remembered until now. I know that she is forty-seven years old. I know she and Rico grew up together in a small town in Sonora, the northwest part of Mexico, and that they married young. I remember how Alma's eyes teared up, years ago, when she told me about their eldest children, a boy and a girl; as toddlers, the two were fatally trapped while staying with relatives whose house burned down one summer night. I know that although Alma and Rico grieved for this loss, they went on to have two more children. Not long afterward, Rico, with urging from his brothers, immigrated to Denver, where he joined those brothers working restaurant jobs. It took Rico four years to save enough money to send to Sonora for Alma and their daughters. The children were young when the family immigrated; they received most of their schooling here in the States. I know that Alma is fiercely proud of both girls—the elder, who is attending the University of Colorado-Denver with the intention of becoming a journalist, and the younger, who married right out of high school and recently gave Alma her first grandchild.

I think about the first time I saw Alma—the first time after I began going into the other world, the world where I was Kitty. I think about how, as Kitty, I did not really understand this system, this world in which darker-skinned people serve lighter-skinned people. I did not understand it because *Kitty* had not become accustomed to it gradually, over the course of many years, the way *Katharyn* did. As Kitty, I was thrust abruptly into this lifestyle, and—quite understandably—it jarred me.

But in truth, I have been Katharyn, not Kitty, for a long time now. So is the view of this world through Kitty's eyes—a new awareness that, even as Katharyn, I need not treat someone working for my family as somehow less than me—another gift? Is it like the gift of imagining myself quietly conversing with my mother? I believe it is.

The fact is, I owe everything to Alma. If not for her intervention, when would I have realized how Jenny was treating Michael? How much longer would it have taken me to grasp that? How much more cruelty would my child have had to endure, were it not for this woman who today is washing my bathroom floor?

"Alma," I say.

She stands and faces me.

"Thank you." I look around, feeling suddenly foolish for interrupting her work. Hastily I go on, "Thank you for everything you do. For taking care of my family, when you have your own to take care of, too."

She nods. "*Sí*, señora."

"How *is* your family?" As soon as I ask this, my cheeks redden. In this context, with work to do, Alma will surely find my chitchat silly and distracting.

But she smiles, visibly pleased to be asked. "*Bebé* is getting so big," she tells me. "He sits up now, all by himself."

I find myself genuinely delighted to hear about her grandson's development. "Oh, I love that stage," I say. "When babies learn to sit up, when you can put them on the floor on a blanket with a few toys, and they stay there happy as clams."

Alma nods. "*Sí*, I love that, too. And so does his *mamá*."

"Alma," I ask her, "when was the last time you had a raise?"

She looks thoughtful. "It is a year ago, maybe," she recalls. "Señor Andersson, he raise me from one dollar fifty an hour to one dollar seventy-five."

I'm shocked. "That's all we pay you? You ought to make more than that. As of today, we're doubling your wages."

She tilts her head. "You discuss this with Señor Andersson, señora? No?"

"No." I shake my head firmly. "But trust me—he won't mind."

After Michael and I have lunch, I ask Alma what her plans are for the afternoon. "*No mucho*," she says. "I think I go after the kitchen drawers. They need *organización*. And cleaning."

"How would you feel about watching Michael for a few hours?"

She eyes me suspiciously. "You sure, señora?"

"Alma." I put my hand on her arm. "If I have ever acted as if I didn't trust you . . . please believe me, it's not because of you." I can feel my eyes pleading with her. "It's because of me. It's my guilt, and . . . this is my life." I remove my fingers from her arm, but keep my gaze on her. "In the meantime, I think Michael would have a fine afternoon with you." I turn to glance at him, still seated at the table. "Wouldn't you, buddy?"

He does not look up. "Can I count the money again?"

I'd hoped he'd want to page through the dictionary some more, but counting money is better than nothing, I suppose.

Baby steps, Katharyn, I remind myself. Baby steps.

"Sure," I say to him. "Why not?"

He nods. "Well, then I think I'll have a fine afternoon with Alma."

And so it is that at exactly one fifteen on a snowy Thursday afternoon in early March 1963, I find myself opening the garage door of the big house on Springfield Street and sliding behind the wheel of my green station wagon.

Starting the car's engine and waiting for it to warm, I take a look at the bicycles, in a haphazard pile near the east wall of the garage. Michael's blue bike is among them, next to my old Schwinn. I study the two bikes, side by side, and remember the day I was so determined that Michael had to learn to ride a bike. Why did I think this was so important? I can no longer remember. Who cares if he learns to ride a bike now, at age six? Who cares if he ever learns? I shrug. He might never learn. Or someday he might decide—as he did this morning, when he voluntarily looked in the dictionary and found the word *anchor* all by himself—that he is ready to take it on.

Either way, it is not my decision to make. I am Michael's mother, but I cannot control who he is. My attempts to do so, I realize, only make both of our lives more difficult than they need to be.

I remember how excluded I felt on that day—just this past Sunday, it was—as I watched Lars comfort Michael. I am quite certain that Lars and I rarely quarrel—but when we do, it's nearly always about Michael. Does Lars consider it my fault that Michael is who he is? No, I don't think that's it. I think it's more that, while he does not believe I am responsible for Michael's condition, Lars can become irked with me for my impatience, my blunders. And I, in turn, become angry that Lars does not realize how irrational, how unfair, it is for him to be cross with me about that. After all, Lars is not the one who spends every day caring for our son.

I bite my lip. I cannot change the mistakes of the past. All I can do is move forward with whatever future my new reality holds.

I put the car in gear and back down the driveway. Leaving the neighborhood, I make my way north on University Boulevard, then get on the Valley Highway and head toward downtown.

I looked up her address in the telephone book before I left home. It was right there: Green's Books and News, Corporate Offices, with an address on Eighteenth Street, downtown.

Whether she will be at the office, whether I will be able to get in to see her—whether she will even be willing to see me—is a different matter entirely.

After finding a parking space a few blocks away, I walk to Frieda's block. As the salesgirl at the Green's in University Hills mentioned, there is a Green's bookstore across the street, in a rather modest, single-story row of storefronts. The other side of the street, where the corporate offices are, is another matter. Craning my neck to look up at the soaring office building, I wonder if Lars's firm designed it. No sooner have I begun to speculate about this than I'm struck with the knowledge that this was not Lars's project, that the work was done a couple of years ago by an out-of-state architectural firm. I have a distinct memory of Lars telling me about it—I recall his disappointment at not getting the job, which he bid on. I also remember that it was Lars who told me, after construction started, that he'd heard Green's Books and News had plans to lease office space here. The structure is clean and modern, constructed of concrete, with large plate-glass windows. There's a small plaza with a fountain out front; next to the fountain are several heavy concrete sculptures in geometric designs—a cube set on its tip, a pyramid with a sphere balanced atop it, like enormous children's blocks defying gravity.

The office building is fifteen stories tall; the Green's offices are on the eleventh floor. I glide up smoothly in the elevator, pressing my hand nervously against my hair, putting on fresh lipstick, straightening my stockings.

At the reception desk I ask for Frieda Green, and am informed coolly that she is in meetings for the rest of the day. "Truly, with no break?" I ask. "I'm . . . an old friend. I would love to see her, even for just a few minutes."

The receptionist regards me suspiciously. "Are you a writer?"

I smile inwardly at that. Indeed, I am not a writer. But I'd like to be.

"No," I tell the receptionist, shaking my head. "As I said, just . . . a friend."

"We get a lot of people off the street wanting to sell their books here. At our stores." Her look is disdainful. "But we do all our book buying through publishers and distributors. I want to make sure you understand, ma'am."

I tap my foot impatiently. "I'm perfectly aware of how books are purchased for bookstores." I lean forward and put my hands lightly on the receptionist's desk. "I'd just like to see my old friend."

She gives me a look of resignation. "And your name?"

I pause. "Andersson," I say softly. "Please, just tell her that Mrs. Andersson is here." I glance back toward the glass outer door, see the bank of elevators a few feet away. So invitingly polished, those elevators—so safe, like big metal wombs. I could walk out of here, press the button to summon one of them. I could abandon this preposterous plan before it goes any further.

"She'll know," I say bravely, turning toward the receptionist and squaring my shoulders. "She'll know."

I spend half an hour waiting in the reception area. I am beginning to wonder about picking up Mitch and Missy at school. I know now, in the way I abruptly know things that previously baffled me in this world, that fetching the children from school is my responsibility. I also know that school lets out at three o'clock, an hour that is quickly approaching. Will I come this far and have to leave, simply because I must go back to my duties?

But finally another secretary arrives and nods at me. We make our way past a typing pool to a corner office. FRIEDA GREEN, PRESIDENT, it says on the door.

"Miss Green," the secretary says, pressing a button on her desk. "I have Mrs. Andersson."

It seems an eternity, and then finally I hear Frieda's voice, crackly through the intercom. "Send her in."

Frieda is standing, facing outward toward the windows behind her desk. She turns when I enter.

In some ways she looks the same, exactly as she did when I last saw her—which was yesterday, after all. Her thick, dark hair is teased up slightly, to give it more lift, then flipped under becomingly. Her heavy brows still arch in a way that makes her look like she's concentrating even when she's relaxed, just as they always have. Her mouth is outlined precisely with the bright red lipstick she favors.

She is dressed more formally than she would be for our shop, of course. She wears a smart, crisp suit in beige wool, with a short jacket, a straight skirt, and a silky purple blouse under it. Large silver hoops in her ears and an abstract silver pin in her lapel give her outfit just the slightest edge—businesslike, but still creative. I find myself nodding slightly, looking at her. Her attire makes perfect sense. It's exactly how Frieda would play it, in this corporate life.

She looks me up and down. Compared to Frieda's chic ensemble, I realize that my getup—plain navy-blue dress, low heels, no jewelry save for the wedding set on my left hand—makes me look outmoded. But not fun, artsy, who-cares-what-anyone-thinks outmoded, the way that Kitty would dress. More conventional-housewife outmoded, the way Katharyn would.

Well, I think, I can't control everything in this world, but my wardrobe is one thing I can certainly transform. That restrained, sensible clothing collection in the big closet at home is long overdue for an overhaul. I resolve to do something about it this weekend.

"What brings you here?" Frieda asks finally, sweeping her hand toward the chair in front of her desk.

I sit nervously, perching my purse in my lap. "Frieda, I just . . ." I shake my head. "I don't even know how to explain it," I say softly. "You'd never believe it, and none of this seems real to me—not yet, anyway. So I don't even know why I'm here."

She sits across from me and puts her chin in her hands, a gesture she's always made when she's interested in what's in front of her. "None of this seems real," she repeats pensively. "What exactly does that mean?"

I sigh. "Tell me if I have this straight. In this world, I'm married to Lars Andersson, I have six-year-old triplets, and I live in a big house in Southern Hills. And you run half a dozen bookstores, and have God-knows-how-many employees, and you are expanding all over the region. And you've closed our little shop on Pearl Street. Do I have all that right?"

She regards me with disdain. "That sounds about right, Kitty."

"And nobody calls me Kitty anymore," I go on. "Lars calls me Katharyn, and so does everyone else I've met since I became a married woman. And the only people who really knew me and loved me in that other life, the life I had before, are you . . . and my parents . . ." I feel tears stinging my eyes, and I blink them back.

Frieda softens her gaze. "I'm sorry about your parents," she says. "I did hear."

"But you didn't come!" I burst out. "Their funeral. You didn't come."

She looks away, toward the window. "I sent flowers," she says, rather faintly.

"Flowers?" I am incredulous. "My parents were killed in an airplane crash, and your response is to send *flowers*?"

She hangs her head, just a tiny bit. "I didn't think you'd want me at the service."

"Why wouldn't I?" I fish in my purse and retrieve a hankie, wiping my nose. I am furious with myself for getting this emotional, but I can't help it. "You're my best friend, Frieda. Why wouldn't I want you at my parents' funeral?"

"Kitty." She stands up and reaches forward, across the desk, almost as if she plans to take my hand in hers. I hold my breath, waiting. But then Frieda's look changes, becomes hard again, and it seems as if some moment, some potential, has passed—before it had a chance to fully form itself.

She straightens her shoulders and rather hastily reseats herself. "You walked out on me," she says. "You were the one who left, Kitty." She looks out the window again. "Not me."

I shake my head. "Why would I do that?"

She eyes me skeptically. "You know perfectly well why." For emphasis, she taps her desk with her long, manicured nails. "At least, you know the reason you gave."

I am completely stumped. "I don't remember," I say softly. "I don't know the reason, Frieda . . . but whatever it was, I'm sure it was just a misunderstanding."

"A misunderstanding. Yep." She presses her lips together. "That's quite a way to put it, Kitty."

The intercom buzzes, and the secretary's voice comes through, saying something I don't quite catch. "All right," Frieda responds, leaning toward the intercom. "Put it through." She looks up at me. "Excuse me a moment while I take this call." I start to rise, and she waves her hand dismissively. "You can stay," she tells me. "It's just business." She eyes me pointedly, and I lower my gaze to my lap.

While she is speaking into the telephone, I force myself to try to remember. What am I doing here? What happened? What am I not remembering?

Trying to concentrate, I close my eyes.

Chapter 32

Kitty."

I open my eyes, but I cannot see anything. Wherever I am, it's light—very light. There is too much brightness, too much glare, to make sense of anything else.

"Kitty, can you hear me? Are you all right?"

I'm not all right, I'm not all right. I'm saying it, but Frieda is not hearing it. I cannot focus on her. I cannot make out her features. I feel her grip on my shoulder, but my mind cannot make my muscles move. I'm unable to reach up and clasp Frieda's hand with my own.

"Kitty, listen to me. You have to listen to me."

Vaguely, as if from far away, I hear myself say, "I'm listening, Freeds."

"We need to have this conversation," she tells me. "We need this." Her fingers, familiar and soothing, gently massage my shoulder. "Back there, back in the real world—you and I need to talk."

I think about the day, in our shop, when Frieda tried to convince me that my life with Lars and the children is false, and that my life as Kitty is the real one. I wonder that she could have been so convincing that day, yet today she is saying just the opposite.

But of course I invented Frieda that day in the shop, didn't I?

In the other world, I can invent a Frieda who is as credible as I like.

For that matter, I can give my imaginary Frieda any qualities I want. She can be as loving, as kind and warmhearted, as I choose.

In the made-up world, Frieda can be anyone I want her to be.

"Are you following me, Kitty?" Frieda's voice is urgent. "Do you understand?"

"Yes," I whisper. "I understand."

Chapter 33

Then I am back in her office. Frieda is still on the telephone; she has turned slightly away from me, the cord wrapped around her waist. Everything is in perfect focus. I can see little glints of sunlight on the plastic of the coiled wire. I can hear her murmur into the phone, an occasional harsh note as she raises her voice slightly at something the other party says. I can smell her sharp perfume-and-smoke scent.

And sitting there, looking at her back turned toward me, it comes to me. I remember it all.

It was about four years ago, the spring of 1959. Sisters' Bookshop was at a crossroads. Business was slow; we were behind on our rent and our loan payments. We needed to go out of business completely or move or do *something*. In my other life, my made-up life as Kitty, this was just before my small inheritance from my grandfather kept us afloat. But in this world, at the point I am remembering, Frieda and I did not yet know that money would be available soon.

Instead, Frieda had begun to talk—as she did in my other life for many years before we made a decision—about closing our store on Pearl Street and opening in a shopping center. But we didn't have the funds for a move like that.

One day she sat me down and put it to me straight. "You need to ask Lars for the money. It's the only way we're going to be able to finance a move." She lit a Salem and breathed smoke toward me. "He's got to be good for something, right?"

I smiled. "He's good for plenty," I said. "But I don't know if he wants to front our business." I shrugged. "He's always said this is my thing, not an Andersson thing."

Frieda rolled her eyes. "Hmm. I've always been led to believe that marriage is a partnership." Her eyes were dark, challenging me.

I remember that I shrugged again. A partnership? Yes, Lars and I were partners—when it came to the children and what church to attend and who to invite to a dinner party. But not when it came to business. His business was his, and mine was mine. It was something we'd established long ago, when we first became engaged. It was something we were in complete agreement about. "I don't know . . . " I stammered.

"Just suck it up and ask him, Kitty."

So I did. Surprisingly, he took it better than I thought he would. "I'm interested," he'd said, sipping his late-evening Scotch. "Especially if it's what you want . . . if it will make you happy."

If it was what I wanted? I had no idea what I wanted. I had no idea how to be happy. I had some vague feeling that if everyone *else* was happy—Frieda, Lars, the children—then I would be happy, too.

Frieda clearly was not pleased with the things the way they were. But if we changed things, if we did what she wanted—well, she would be happy then, wouldn't she? I could do that for her, I reasoned, by getting Lars to finance this big move of ours.

Lars seemed fine, Lars seemed happy. But he was—he *is*—like that. His optimism, his utter conviction that when he'd met me, he struck gold—those things seemed to keep him going, no matter what was happening. It was a trait I admired, but never quite managed to emulate.

And the children? Well. Young children are always happy, aren't they? My children were two and half then, no longer babies but not full-fledged kids yet, either. They seemed fine—most of the time, anyway. Mitch and Missy were talking, running, climbing. Looking at books, learning to use their imaginations.

Michael was . . . I admitted to myself that I wasn't sure how or what Michael was. I knew he wasn't like the other children. He spoke only a few words. He sat in a corner. He played alone, the same simple games over and over. Neat stacks of blocks or books, toy cars lined up in a row. He didn't look at anyone. He kept his head down.

But that was all right, wasn't it? That was normal for some kids. We'd had Jenny for over a year, and she was the expert, wasn't she? If something was wrong, why then, surely she would tell me.

Remembering this years later, knowing what I know now, I feel a hot flush of fury with myself. How did I fail to see it? How could I have turned a blind eye?

What kind of mother was I, anyway?

Nonetheless, in those days, happiness for all was my goal. So I'd nodded at Lars. "A new store, a new future. It's what I want," I told him.

"Well, then." He rose from the sofa. "We should all get together and talk—you, Frieda, and me. Let's have her over for dinner sometime soon. After the kids are in bed, we can talk business."

I'd smiled gratefully and put my arms around him. "Thank you," I whispered in his ear.

The next morning I woke early and dressed quickly, eager to get to the shop and tell Frieda what Lars had said. I remember getting ready to leave the house, an animated smile on my face as I impatiently searched for my keys and gathered a few books and some office supplies into my arms.

And then I'd felt a small, tentative tap on my shoulder. It was Alma.

"*Por favor*," she'd said softly, glancing furtively toward the stairway, toward the children's rooms, where Jenny was with the triplets. "*Por favor*, Señora Andersson, there is something I must tell you." She'd tightened her fists, pressing them against the sides of her body, against her clean, crisp uniform. "I can keep silent no longer. Señora, I must tell you about Jenny."

Now I stare at Frieda, sitting in her big office on the eleventh floor, the telephone pressed against her ear. "Yes, I agree," she says into the receiver. "Yes, but I think we need to talk further about that." She pauses, glancing at me. "Look, can I call you back in ten? I have someone in my office."

After she hangs up, I say quietly, "I remember now."

She laughs. "How very convenient," she says drily.

I bite my lip. "I'm sorry!" I cry. "I'm sorry this sounds so ridiculous to you." I feel a bitter taste in my mouth. "Though I also remember now why I have *no* reason to apologize to you."

"Oh, really?" She leans forward and presses both hands against the desktop. "You were the one who walked away. You were the one who left me in all that hot water."

"I had to walk away," I say to Frieda. "My child needed me. My family needed me."

She shakes her head and reaches for the pack of Salems on her desk. "You made it all sound worse than it was. The truth is, you *welcomed* an excuse to leave. You weren't happy. All you could think about was the time you were spending away from them. You said—" She pulls a cigarette from the pack and tightens her lips around it as she lights it. "You said the store was a waste of your time." She blows smoke in my direction. "Do you remember that, Kitty?"

Yes. I remember that, too. And I remember why I said it. Because Frieda was the one who'd found Jenny for me. Frieda was the one who'd convinced me that Jenny, with all her credentials, was the right person to watch the children.

I remember telling Frieda that it was her fault that Michael was the way he was. "If I'd been at home, he would have been just fine!" I shouted. "If I'd never hired Jenny—that awful woman that *you* found, Frieda—if I'd never done that, everything would be different now. But you—you convinced me to stay here at the shop, you found Jenny to watch my children, and I trusted you, I trusted you, Frieda. I trusted you to help me do the right thing. But it was all wrong. And now look at what's happened to him." I sat down on my stool behind the counter, flushed and trembling. Then I took a breath and looked up at Frieda.

"I want out," I said firmly. "I don't care what you do, but I want out. This isn't working for me—and let's be honest, it's not working for you, either. You figure this out, Frieda. It's your fault, not mine. So you get out of this mess, if you can. Go on and do all the big things you want to do with this business. I don't care."

"How can I do that?" she challenged me. "I have no money, Kitty."

I crossed my arms over my chest. "That," I told her, "is *not* my problem."

It *wasn't* my problem—I made sure of it. I got out, and I stayed out. I remember it now. The money I inherited, not long after Frieda and I quarreled—in this world, that money did not go toward saving Sisters' Bookshop. What did I do with it? I shrug, and then it comes to me. I used it to hire a lawyer to get me out of the Sisters' mess—that's where most of it went. And the remainder? I smile wryly. That nice sofa and the other fine furniture in the living room on Springfield Street—that's where the rest of my grandfather's money went, in this world.

Frieda had strode to Sisters' front windows and looked out on empty Pearl Street for a few seconds. Then she turned back to me. "What will you do with yourself?" she asked. But not nicely, not like she actually wanted to know. Her tone was mocking. "Mrs. Housewife, huh? Well, fine. It's what you always wanted, anyway."

"It is *not* what I always wanted. It's just what happened. It's just how things turned out." I stood up, wringing my hands. "It turned on a dime, Frieda. For God's sake, I almost didn't even *meet* him. The poor man could have died."

She snickered. "Yes. Quite a tale. You ought to call the newspapers. It would make a charming human-interest story."

"With what ending?" I asked softly. "How would it end?"

"Well." She turned away again, refusing to look at me. "I guess we're finding that out, aren't we?"

Now, seated across from me in her office, Frieda glares at me. "You left me with nothing," she says. "Next to nothing. A pile of bills. A few hundred books in our inventory. Some miscellaneous store equipment. And not a dime to move forward with."

I look down at my lap. "You could have asked your parents for help." I tentatively raise my eyes to meet hers.

"How could I do that?" She presses her lips together. "How could I ask them? How could I go to them, tail between my legs, and admit failure? I hadn't . . ." She looks out the plate-glass window, then back at me. "I hadn't made a success of the book-store. I hadn't done anything right, in their eyes. I hadn't . . ." She hesitates, and then adds, "I hadn't married. I hadn't found another . . . person . . . to share my life with."

I wait for her to go on. But she is silent, her eyes downcast. She taps her cigarette against the ashtray on her desk, and a few ashes float in the air for a moment before settling into the por-celain dish.

I think about Jim Brooks, the man Frieda told me about in the other world, the imaginary world. He sounds so right for where she is in her life—in that life. Well, of course, I think. Nat-urally, I would invent a happy ending for Frieda, in that happy-ending world.

In this world, the real world, things are different for her, both personally and professionally. I don't know where or how she got the funds to move forward with the business. I don't believe she would have gone to her parents, but Frieda is clever and re-sourceful enough to have come up with something. Perhaps she did find an investor, just as she did in my made-up world. None-theless, I doubt that the affable and smitten Jim Brooks—or any actual person who resembles him—has a place in the life Frieda has here.

And I realize, quite suddenly, why that is.

Frieda doesn't want Jim Brooks, or anyone like him. That sort of person was never the partner she longed for.

What Frieda wanted was a *true companion*. Just as my mother said. No—more than that. More than what my mother thinks Frieda and I have, in the imaginary world.

But I made a different choice. What did my choice do to her?

Not just to our business—that was one thing, a small thing, really.

The real question is, what did my choice do to her heart?

I shake my head. I can't believe I failed to see it until today.

"Freeds," I say softly. "Freeds. I'm so . . . I'm sorry."

She looks up. "Well," she says, putting her cigarette to her lips. She breathes in, then turns her head to the side and exhales. "Life takes its own peculiar twists and turns, does it not?"

I lean forward, the fingers of both hands clutching my handbag, rhythmically closing and opening the gold-toned clasp. "I hope you . . . maybe someday you can . . ." I trail off, because I don't know what to say.

Frieda watches me silently. "Perhaps you're right," she says finally. "Perhaps I can." Her eyes gaze into mine. "Maybe seeing you is what I needed. Maybe it will help me . . . go on from here."

I smile timidly. "I hope so, Freeds. I truly hope so."

She stands up, takes one last drag on her cigarette, and stubs it out. "I need to return that call," she says, her voice even. She comes around the desk and puts her hand lightly on my shoulder, then removes it immediately. "Please know, Kitty, that I really am very sorry about your parents." Our eyes meet—and hers, usually so dancing and light-filled, look dreary and dark.

I turn away, blinking.

Frieda takes a breath. I force myself to swivel my head, to look at her again. "And I'm sorry I didn't come to your parents' funeral," she goes on. "You were right. I should have been there."

I rise. My knees feel wobbly. "Thank you," I say. "It means a lot to me, hearing you say that."

She nods. "Well. Take care of yourself, and that husband, and the children."

"I will. You take care of yourself, too. Maybe . . ." I hesitate. "Maybe we can see each other again . . . sometime."

"Maybe." Her eyes turn again toward the window, then back to me. She wraps her arms around herself, tucking her hands under her sleeves. "My secretary will see you out. Good-bye, Kitty."

Frieda swallows hard, and I can tell that she not only wants but *needs* me to leave.

I nod at her one last time before crossing the carpet and walking out the door.

Chapter 34

Outside, the snow is melting on the sidewalk. Cars whiz past on Eighteenth Street; a bus rumbles to the curb, then pulls away without dispensing any passengers. The sun gleams in the west, and I shade my eyes as I step through the revolving door of Frieda's building.

And there, standing on the sidewalk in front of me, are my parents.

"Mother," I breathe. "Daddy."

They smile at me, and I want to go to them, hold them—but I know that my parents are not actually there. They are present only inside my head.

"I'm imagining you," I say. "I'm making this up. Right?"

"Kitty." My mother comes forward and puts her hand on my shoulder. I marvel at the way my mind has conjured her touch, exactly as if she were truly standing there with her fingers pressed to the fabric of my coat.

The imagination, it turns out, is a remarkably clever and hardworking creature.

"We just want to say good-bye, honey," my dad says. "That's all. Just good-bye." He steps next to my mother, inches from me. "And that we love you."

"I love you, too," I whisper. I'm vaguely aware of a man in

a dark topcoat and hat passing on my right, then turning back to look at me quizzically. To him, I must appear nothing more than a crazy lady on the sidewalk, a mildly insane person who is speaking to thin air.

"So I won't see you anymore?" I ask my parents. "I won't . . . I'm not going back there anymore?" I turn away, biting my lip. "Back to the other world, I mean. I'm not going back there again, am I?"

Even as I ask these questions, I already know the answers—because I am the one who is directing what my parents would say. If they were actually here speaking to me, that is.

"Kitty." My mother puts her fingers on my forehead. "Take it out of here," she says. "Put it here instead." I watch as she taps my heart.

"I understand," I say, nodding. "I'll miss you."

My father shakes his head. "You won't need to," he says. "You'll always have us—just in a different form. Not in the way you thought you would."

"You'll help me . . . watch over my babies . . . won't you?" I swallow hard. "I can't take care of my children . . . Michael . . . without you."

My mother laughs her beautiful laugh. "You can, Kitty. Don't doubt yourself. Don't doubt Lars. And especially"—her smile is generous—"don't doubt Michael."

I blink back tears, and then I close my eyes.

When I open them again, my parents have vanished.

Chapter 35

I sit in the station wagon outside Mitch and Missy's school, my gloved hands on the wheel. I am thinking about the other world, about being Kitty. I remember my mother's hand, how I could feel her touch. How I could hear her voice. I will always, I think, be able to hear my parents' voices in my head.

I glance at my watch. Two forty-five. Mitch and Missy will come out that door soon, the one to my right, the double set with the snowman drawings taped to the windows. They will emerge with satchels flying behind them, jackets unbuttoned, mittens loose on their strings. Their blond curls will shimmer in the afternoon sunlight as they skim across the sidewalk, coming toward me as I wait.

By ten minutes after three, I will have returned to the house on Springfield Street with Mitch and Missy in tow. Michael will still be counting coins. Michael has probably counted and re-counted coins all afternoon. Michael may very well do little else besides eat, sleep, and count coins for as many days as we allow him to.

Alma will give everyone a snack: milk, an apple, a cookie. I will make a fresh pot of coffee and sit with the children while they eat, while Mitch and Missy tell us about their days. While Michael rhythmically counts nickels, pennies, quarters.

Afterward, we will leave him to his counting, and Mitch and Missy will begin their homework. They will have reading to do; their reading has improved tremendously this year, and I know that if I took the time to listen to them read aloud more often, it would get even better. After each of them has read to me for fifteen minutes, I will have them work on handwriting. Alma will put a cut-up chicken in the oven and start washing and snapping green beans.

At four thirty, I will allow the children one hour of *The Mickey Mouse Club*. Michael will bring the coin jar with him to the living room and will sit on the floor counting coins, occasionally glancing at the television when the other two laugh at something one of the Mouseketeers has said or done. This activity will get us to five thirty, when Lars will walk in the door and dinner will be placed on the table.

Michael will spill his milk, because Michael always spills his milk. And I will clean it up, because I don't think it's fair to expect Alma to do that.

In the evening, we will attempt a family game of Parcheesi. Either Lars or I will have to be on Michael's team, because he won't be able to sit still long enough to move his pieces properly. He will wander away, back to the coins. He will be tired after his long day, which I know from experience means he is more likely to retreat into babyish habits that he ought long ago to have given up. I will have to keep a watchful eye on him, to make sure he doesn't put any coins in his mouth.

At seven fifteen, Missy will take a bath, and when she is done, the boys will be bathed. It will be Lars's night with Missy, so after her hair is brushed—a job he leaves to me—he will tuck her in and tell her a story.

I will supervise the boys as they don their matching pajamas and climb into their matching beds. Michael will ask if he can sleep with the coins, and I will tell him no. He will scream, and Lars will have to come in and comfort him. We will compromise by letting him have the empty coin jar in his bed all night, the coins dumped into a bowl that I take into our bedroom and place on a high shelf in the closet. That way, I know Michael won't be able to get to them without waking Lars or me up.

Once the children are settled in bed, Lars and I will come downstairs, and he'll fix us a drink. We will catch each other up on our days. I will tell him about going to see Frieda, and he will be surprised that I did it, but not surprised at the things she said. Lars will hold me and comfort me as I choke up.

I will *not* tell him all the details; Frieda's sentiments are not mine to share with anyone, even Lars.

After we finish our drinks, we will move on to separate tasks—Lars to his office to catch up on paperwork; I to the bedroom to tidy up, then perhaps back to the living room to read. I will seek excuses to walk down the hallway. I will stare at the photograph of my parents and me. I will go out of my way throughout the evening to pass by and glance at it once, twice, again and again. When Lars catches me at this, he will put his arms around me from the back and hold me tight, looking at the picture over my shoulder.

At ten o'clock in the evening, we will retire. We will climb quietly into bed, and we will make love affectionately, openly—but slowly, as always, to protect his heart. Afterward, I will rest beside him as he gently rubs my back.

And then I will sleep.

I know all of this. I am as sure of it as I've ever been of anything.

I am as sure of it as I am of everything in the world where I was Kitty.

The other world, I know now, has faded. I am here. I am where I belong.

I open the car door, blow warm air into my hands, and rub my cheeks. And then I walk up the sidewalk to the school, pausing a few feet from the doorway. I am waiting to embrace my children.

Acknowledgments

My thanks to Claire Wachtel, my amazing editor at Harper, for her sharp insight, enthusiasm, and great stories. Hannah Wood deftly and gracefully kept the process on track. Miranda Ottewell's keen eye caught the smallest details and made the manuscript all the better for it. Susanna Einstein is an incredible agent who loved this book from the first time she read it. For her professionalism and friendship, I am grateful. To the staff at Einstein Thompson Agency, thank you for your passion and dedication.

To Shana Kelly, who pointed me in the right direction, and in the process became not only a mentor but also a friend, I offer thanks. To everyone at Lighthouse Writers Workshop, thank you for providing inspiration, thought-provoking workshops and conferences, and an outstanding writers' community. Gary Schanbacher and Rose Fredrick contributed literary discourse, coffee, and handouts. Susan Wright, Mary Elliott, and Jocelyn Scheirer read early drafts and gave me both suggestions and cheerleading; I am fortunate to call them sister and virtual sisters. I am blessed to have Mary Hauser and Sandra Theunick in my life; to both of them, I am grateful. To my "friends who live in my computer"—thank you and M4L. The Book Club That Changed the World has done more than that—its members have changed my life, always for the better and always with my gratitude.

The staff of the Western History Department at the Denver Public Library provided maps, old newspapers and phone books, and friendly assistance. Phil Goodstein's volumes on the history of South Denver supplied considerable background and historical data. Joyce Meskis, owner of the Tattered Cover Bookstore, and Sonya Ellingboe, former owner of the Book House, provided marvelous details about working in and owning a small bookshop in the 1960s. Many clinical volumes about autism offered context on the condition, but Michael Blastland's heartfelt memoir *The Only Boy in the World: A Father Explores the Mysteries of Autism* helped me truly appreciate the challenges faced by parents of an autistic child. The First Universalist Church of Denver Women's Book Club shared their memories to help me visualize life as a young woman in the early 1960s; to them, I am grateful.

A note on historical accuracy: although many newspapers in the 1950s published "lonely hearts" advertisements in their classifieds sections, the *Denver Post* was not one of them. I hope readers will grant me poetic license in creating a fictional personals section in the 1954 *Denver Post*.

This book would not have come to fruition if not for the encouragement and devotion of four remarkable people. Thank you, Charlie, Dennis, and Jane, for being my inspiration and the loves of my life. And to Sammy, for absolutely everything; I am so, so glad we met.

About the Author

CYNTHIA SWANSON is a writer and a midcentury modern designer. She has published short fiction in *13th Moon*, *Kalliope*, *Sojourner*, and other periodicals; her story in *13th Moon* was a Pushcart Prize nominee. She lives in Denver, Colorado, with her husband and three children. *The Bookseller* is her first novel.

The Storm Child

Rita Bradshaw was born in Northamptonshire, where she still lives today. At the age of sixteen she met her husband – whom she considers her soulmate – and they have two daughters, a son and six grandchildren. Much to her delight, Rita's first novel was accepted for publication and she has gone on to write many more successful novels since, including the number one bestseller *Dancing in the Moonlight*.

As a committed Christian and passionate animal-lover her life is full, but she loves walking her dog, reading, eating out and visiting the cinema and theatre, as well as being involved in her church and animal welfare.

BY RITA BRADSHAW

'Cynthia Swanson's novel will make you think about the paths you could have taken – but even more so, what you can learn from them to make your reality richer'
Redbook Magazine

'The novel delivers on its fantasy scenario like a modern-day fairy tale . . . highly satisfying'
USA Today

'Swanson masterfully crafts both Kitty's and Katharyn's worlds, leaving open the question of which of them is real until the final pages. Swanson's evocative novel freshly considers the timeless question, *What if?*'
Publishers Weekly

'Dexterously traversing past and present, fact and fiction, Swanson's clever first novel ingeniously explores the inventive ways the human spirit copes with trauma'
Booklist

'This is a stunner of a debut novel, astonishingly tight and fast paced. The 1960s tone is elegant and even, and Kitty/Katharyn's journey is intriguing . . . This will especially resonate with fans of the movie *Sliding Doors* and the authors Anna Quindlen and Anita Shreve'
Library Journal, starred review

'Swanson's debut novel is slightly mysterious and thoroughly engrossing, one of those books that will stay with the reader long after it is complete'
Romantic Times

'This is the story of a woman coming to terms with who she is; both woman and novel are beautiful'
Shelf Awareness

'An accomplished first novel. It is interesting, intriguing, and ultimately satisfying'
New York Journal of Books